The Turn of The Tide

The Turn of the Tide

by

Philip K Allan

www.penmorepress.com

ISBN-13: 978-1-950586-01-1(Paperback)
ISBN :13: 978-1-950586-02-8(e-book)
BISAC Subject Headings:

FIC014000FICTION / Historical
FIC032000FICTION / War & Military
FIC047000FICTION / Sea Stories

Cover Illustration by Christine Horner

Address all correspondence to:
Penmore Press LLC
920 N Javelina Pl
Tucson, AZ 85748

Dedication

To my dear sister Tinou

Acknowledgements

Success as a writer requires the support of many people to help bring my vision to the page. These books start with a passion for the Age of Sail. Mine was first awakened when I discovered the works of C. S. Forester as a child. Later I graduated to the novels of Patrick O'Brian, and the research of Nick Rodger. That interest was given some academic rigor when I studied the 18th century navy under Patricia Crimmin as part of my history degree at London University.

Many years later I decided to leave my career in the motor industry to see if I could survive as a novelist.

I received the unconditional support and cheerful encouragement of my darling wife and two wonderful daughters. I first test my work to see if I have hit the mark with my family, especially my wife Jan, whose input is invaluable. I have also been helped again by my dear friend Peter Northen.

One of the unexpected pleasures of my new career is to have experienced the generous support and encouragement of my fellow writers. In theory we are all in competition for the same readers, but you would never know it. When I needed help, advice and support, I received it from David Donachie, Bernard Cornwell, Marc Liebman, Jeffrey K Walker, Helen Hollick, Ian Drury and in particular Alaric Bond, creator of the Fighting Sail series of books.

Finally my thanks go to the team at Penmore Press, Michael, Chris, Terri and Christine who work so hard to turn the world I have created into the book you hold in your hand.

CONTENTS

Prologue

It was a winter's night, and the moon hung above rags of drifting cloud. A cold breeze gusted out from the marshland, bringing with it a tang of brine and the promise of the sea. It whisked up dust from the road and swirled it around the two horsemen, peppering their faces and flapping at their cloaks. Both riders pulled their hats lower and crouched into their saddles. They came on, trotting down the road, their hooves loud on the grey river of cobbles. To one side of them was a low wall of turf and stone, over which could be seen a shingle beach. Beyond was an expanse of dark, choppy water.

The men passed a row of stone houses that straggled along the shore. Molten lines of firelight spilt out from around the shuttered windows and moonlight tangled in the skein of the fishing nets that dried on poles between the buildings. The smell of wood smoke and rotting seaweed drifted in the air, making the horses snort and toss their heads. At the edge of the settlement the cobbles came to an end and the road turned into a dirt track that led into the marshes. The horses became almost silent, and yet, the echo of their hooves continued to sound in the night. The lead rider pulled up his mount to listen.

'Merde!' he cursed. 'Gendarmes! We must fly, major. The enemy is upon us.' He spurred his horse forward down the track with his companion close behind. Mud and sand flew up as they dashed on, ever deeper into the marsh. The land ahead was flat, a mesh of pools and earth embankments. The path they followed turned one way and then another, with other routes splitting off to left or right, but the horsemen dashed on with barely any check in speed. As they rode, stretches of open water appeared beside the track, polished steel in the moonlight, and waterfowl clattered away from them with cries of alarm. After a quarter of an hour of hard riding, the path rose between two sand dunes, and they pulled in their mounts as they neared the top. The sound of the sea was loud now and masked the heavy blowing of the horses.

'Look, my friend,' exalted the lead rider. 'No one knows the Morbihan better than I, but then, my family have been Lords of the Marsh since the time of Louis the Good.' He pointed back the way they had come. The moon had broken through a gap in the clouds. In the gentle light they could see several groups of horseman dotted over the land, riding this way and that. None were nearer than a mile from them. They urged their mounts forward once more, up the last few yards to the top of the slope.

The roar of surf pounding on the shore greeted them as they reached the crest, and the wind snatched at their clothes. Beneath them a beach stretched away on either side, empty of life. Opposite them, beyond the waves, a dark ship with backed topsails on its twin masts rode on the moonlit sea.

'Your friends have come, major,' said the first rider. 'Let us hope they can pluck you from the shore before our pursuers arrive.'

'Aye, but how will you make good your escape, count?' replied his companion, in the soft lilt of the Scottish Highlands. 'They will surely have marked us up here, as readily as we saw them.' His fellow rider pointed along the beach to the north with an airy wave of his riding crop.

'While you depart by sea, I shall take the horses that way, and back inland by a small inlet I know. You need have no anxiety for me, *mon ami*. But I would urge you to summon your friends quickly.'

The two men rode down the face of the dune, their horses leaning back on their tails against the slope. Once on the flat they trotted towards the sea and halted just above the tide line of kelp. The Scotsman tossed his reins to his companion and jumped down. He pulled the saddle bag from his horse's back and dropped to his knees to unbuckle its leather cover. From inside he produced a small brass lantern, which he placed on the sand beside him, and a tinderbox. He drew his cloak into a billowing screen against the wind, and struck the flint repeatedly. After several flashes of cold white, the tinder caught. He crouched over the little spark and breathed it into life. In the warm glow there appeared a lean, heavily scarred face that would once have been handsome. One eye was alert and bright, the other lay behind a leather patch.

He lit the lantern, adjusted the wick, and then snapped closed its glass shutter. Then he pulled off his hat and rose to his feet, holding the broad circle of felt between the lantern and the ship out beyond the surf. He counted to himself aloud as he pulled the hat clear, and placed it back in the way. Four flashes, a pause, two flashes, a pause, then three flashes. He was half way through repeating the sequence when two red lights rose up one of the brig's masts. He blew out the lantern, returned everything to the saddle bag, and looked up at his companion.

'They will come for me directly, count,' he said. 'You have my thanks for all your assistance this past week.'

'While your thanks are welcome, Major Fraser, your country's support will be more so,' said the Frenchman. 'When will you have a reply for me?'

'Soon, once I have been able to report back to London,' said the Scot. 'I will send word via Jacque, in the usual cipher.'

'Very good. Farewell then, until we meet again.' The horseman leant down from his saddle to shake the

Scotsman's hand and then looked over his shoulder towards the sea. 'Here come your friends to take you home.' The major turned to see a wave breaking in a low, white wall. Black against the foam was the shape of a launch, pulling hard as it ran down the slope of water and slid to a halt in the shallows. In the moonlight he could see the figures of sailors as they jumped from the boat and started to turn her around amidst the last dying surge of water.

'I must go,' said the major. 'As must you; look!' In the gap between the dunes, three horsemen had appeared.

'Peasants mounted on mules!' scoffed his companion. He drew a long pistol from its saddle holster and pulled back the hammer with a sharp click. 'Go to your boat now! I will draw them away.' He spurred his horse across the beach, with the second beast trailing along beside him. The horsemen were still making their way down the slope of sand when he arrived at its foot. There was a flash in the night; a shot rang out and a gendarme tumbled from his saddle. The count then spurred away along the shore with the other two riders in pursuit.

'That fellow is not without courage,' said the major to himself, as he watched his guide disappear into the night. 'He must have acquired it in the years since we last met. Oh aye, Monsieur le Comte, you may not remember me, but I recall *you* very clearly.' Then he turned away and strode down the beach towards the boat.

CHAPTER I

HOME

The Reverend Tobias Shelley was a tall, spare man with a kind face that seemed to bear a permanent smile. But appearances can be deceptive. Within his heart burnt the hot fire of a zealot, for Shelley was one of the most active opponents of slavery in all of Devon. He was seated at a cloth-covered table at one end of a crowded Plymouth Methodist Hall. On the chair to his left was a small, smartly dressed man with a horsehair periwig. This gentleman sat angled back, with one thumb hooked into the pocket of his embroidered waistcoat, apparently asleep. Seated very upright on Shelley's other side was a solidly-built, handsome young man with dark, liquid eyes and curly black hair gathered with a ribbon at the nape of his neck. He was dressed in the short blue jacket and high-waisted trousers that marked him as a seaman.

'I am much obliged to you for coming tonight, Mr. Sedgwick,' said Shelley to the sailor. 'I know that your ship is not long returned from a considerable voyage, so I thank you for favouring us with your presence. It is splendid to have an actual Negro, and a former slave to boot, in our hall; is it not, Alderman Moore?' He nudged his companion back into consciousness.

'Six shillings and four pence!' spluttered the man, fixing an uncertain gaze on the clergyman. 'Oh, *more* you say? No, not for me, I pray. I have had a most excellent supper.

Capital drop of port wine, that.' Shelley was about to correct him, when he saw that Moore's eyes had fluttered closed once again and his chin was slipping back towards his chest. He returned his attention to his other guest.

'Generally, our members have to envisage the dire predicament of your race from second-hand accounts and the crudest of caricature. It is so much more satisfactory to have the true object of their concern here amongst us.' He indicated the large banner that hung on the wall behind them to illustrate his point. Sedgwick turned in his chair to look at it. In the centre was painted the image of a kneeling black slave, dressed only in a loincloth and holding up his manacled hands in supplication. Above the picture, in an arch of letters, was written *The Plymouth Committee for the Abolition of the Slave Trade*, while beneath it was the question *Am I not a man and a brother?* Another question altogether formed in Sedgwick's mind as he looked at the square of cloth. Is that really meant to be me, he thought, studying the strange figure with its enormous lips and tight, round balls of hair.

He returned his attention to the packed hall. The table where they were sitting was on a raised platform and looked out over a large rectangular room with whitewashed walls and plain wooden furniture. Two rings of candles hung from the ceiling above, shining down on the hats and bonnets of the crowd. Although it was a modest sized building with seating for no more than a hundred souls, every place was taken, and another twenty or so men were standing in a group at the back.

'What a prodigious turnout we have,' enthused Shelley. 'We seldom have above fifty to attend our regular meetings. Word of your presence here in Plymouth must have gone before you.'

'Aye,' muttered his guest. He gulped nervously. 'Ain't I the lucky one!'

'Think of all the new persons we can persuade to join the cause of Abolition!' continued Shelley. 'Most of our supporters are of the middling sort: tradesmen, shopkeepers, and the like. But look at those men stood at the back, close about the large gentleman in the black coat? I do not recall having seen any of them attend our meetings before. How splendid!' Sedgwick looked at the group of men. They were certainly rougher looking than the bulk of the congregation. Most of them were stood with their hands behind their backs, and one at least appeared to be holding a cudgel of some kind.

'Mind you,' continued Shelley, indicating a group of sailors in the front row, one of whom towered above those around him. 'I am not entirely sure about those three. If I am not mistaken, they have all partaken of ardent spirits in the recent past.'

'Ah... them lot? They're shipmates of mine, sir,' explained Sedgwick. 'We was all on the frigate *Titan* under Captain Clay. In the Indian Ocean, like.'

'Hmm, that sounds rather better,' conceded his host. 'I did read in the *Gazette* that the expedition was a triumph. You took several Frenchmen, did you not?'

'Aye, we done passing well. The big Jack in the middle is Sam Evans, the one with the blond pigtail and the earring is a Cornishman, name of Adam Trevan, and the dark haired fellow is Sean O'Malley.'

'O'Malley you say?' sniffed Shelley. 'Irish, and a papist to boot, I make no doubt. Let us hope he understands how to behave amongst civilised persons, as you will have doubtless had to learn yourself. Now, shall we get started? I will first address the meeting and then I shall introduce you and call on you to speak. Will that answer? Are you quite ready?'

'As ever I shall be,' muttered Sedgwick. He stared at the mass of faces, every one of whom seemed to be looking back at him.

*****

'Here we fecking go,' whispered O'Malley. He dug the point of his elbow into the rib cage of the huge Londoner sat next to him, and pointed towards the platform. 'Your man's about to speak, now that old fart of a priest has finally run dry.'

'Alright, Sean,' muttered Evans, rubbing his side. 'There ain't nothing wrong with me bleeding eyes. Shouldn't we greet Able with a proper huzzah or something?'

'Course we fecking should. Wake these sleepy arses up.'

'No, no,' said Trevan from his other side, his bright blue eyes full of anxiety. 'Bit of polite clapping be as far as your Methodists will go. Like this.' The Cornishman gently patted his hands together. O'Malley removed his forefingers from his mouth, allowing the lung full of air he had intended for a wolf-whistle to escape as a few gentle coughs. To a ripple of polite applause and the flutter of bonnets from the more respectable section of the hall, their friend got to his feet. Sedgwick's brow was beaded with pearls of sweat, and he toyed with the corner of his jacket, twisting the fabric between his fingers, while in his other hand he held a slim brown leather volume. When he spoke his voice was barely above a murmur, in spite of his large frame.

'Eh... I bid you... eh... all a good evening... eh... ladies and gentlemen...' he faltered.

'Speak up!' came a bellow from the back of the room. O'Malley looked around to see where the voice had come from. The man in the black coat, who stood near the door, had his arms akimbo and his hat set back on his head. He muttered a comment to the men behind him, and several of them tittered.

'Aye... very well. My name be Able Sedgwick,' continued the sailor on the stage, his voice settling into a louder bass, 'and I was taken from my village in Africa, like, when I was barely above a nipper, and brought across the sea to Barbados.'

'Able Sedgwick, you say?' queried the heckler. 'That don't sound very African to my ear. Are you sure of what you say, boy, or are you seeking to make game of us?'

'That name be what the navy gone and gave me,' explained Sedgwick. 'When I was a slave, I weren't permitted to keep my African name, nor in the navy neither. When I reached Barbados, I was bought by this right cruel bas... eh, this planter by the name of Haynes. He put me to work, first in his house as a flunky, and when I proved too wilful for him, he sent me to work...'

'But if we are unsure even as to your name, how are we to ascertain if the balance of what you say is true?' continued the man in the black coat. 'Hear him!' yelled one of the thugs that stood behind, amid a growl of approval. Several members of the congregation looked around and eyed the group warily.

'I'm after havin' a bad feeling about this, lads,' muttered O'Malley to his companions. 'That lot at the back are spoiling for trouble.'

'Aye, and the rest of this crowd will be as much use as Quakers on the Sabbath if it comes to a bleeding mill,' added Evans.

'Some order, please,' cried the Reverend Shelley, rising to his feet. 'At the very least, we owe our guest the courtesy of a hearing. The particulars as to Mr. Sedgwick's various changes of name are laid out with perfect candour in his published account of....'

'Ah yes,' interrupted the heckler. 'This *supposed* book of his. I have worked extensively amongst savages, and I can assure you that a blackamoor could no more write a book than my dog could. Yet we are to believe that this run slave has produced one?' His companions broke into peals of laughter at the thought.

'That just ain't true,' protested Sedgwick. 'For sure, I needed schooling with my letters an' all, and my mate Rosie helped with the setting down of my tale...'

'There, you see!' exclaimed a member of the group at the back. '*...helped with the setting down...* he admits it! Why I daresay the whole of his account is nothing but a tissue of abolitionist lies!'

'That's so,' agreed another voice. 'How can Negros be expected to know of Christian virtues like truth, as a civilised person might?'

'Tell me, boy,' resumed the man in the black coat. 'When you was taken, back in Africa, was your captors civilised men or savages?' The Reverend Shelley came to his guest's assistance.

'Mr. Sedgwick is quite open in his book. He was taken by a rival tribe that promptly sold him on...'

'There we have it!' announced the chief heckler, turning to the congregation. 'The truth at last! He was enslaved by his own kind. Because slavery is the natural state of your Negro! The damned Abolitionists don't tell you that, do they? Let me inform you of what else they don't tell you. Consider the consequences if the trade in slaves should cease.' He started to point to individuals seated in front of him. 'No sugar loaf in the pantry for your tea, madam. No tobacco for your pipe, sir. No treasure to fund the navy, to keep the wicked French on their side of the Channel. What loyal patriot would argue for such a thing in time of war, eh? I tell you, this whole gathering is an absolute disgrace!' There was a roar of approval from his supporters. A few members of the congregation rose to their feet to remonstrate with him, and some pushing and shoving broke out.

'Gentlemen,' pleaded Shelley. 'Do not be so uncivil! Remember, this is a place of worship!'

'It ain't going to end well,' predicted Evans, standing up,

too. 'They ain't about to let this here meeting carry on without a riot.'

'Aye, they does look proper murderous,' added Trevan. 'Look! They got clubs and the like, the villains.' A scuffle had broken out and from the back of the hall came the sound of furniture breaking. Several ladies screamed and one close to the sailors appeared to faint.

'You two keep a watch over Able,' said O'Malley. 'I'll be back in a moment.'

The Irishman dashed around behind the stage, where he had noticed a side door earlier. He slipped through it and out into the poorly lit street. A shadowy group of a dozen or so rough looking men waited outside the main entrance to the hall. As he looked, one threw a stone and there was a crash of breaking glass, followed by the sound of more screams from inside. Nearer at hand, several local urchins watched on with considerable interest.

'Over here, lad!' called the Irishman to one of them. 'Will you be after earning a Joey?' He held up a thruppenny bit in the square of light that flooded out from the window behind him, and the boy's eyes widen with delight.

'What you after, mister?' he asked. 'I can show you the best bawdy house this side of the Tamar. My sister works there.'

'Later, maybes,' said O'Malley. 'Do you know the inn they call the Crown, at all?' The boy nodded. 'Run like a hare, now. You'll find a good crowd of men from the frigate *Titan*. Tell them Sean has need of them, and lead them back here, sharp as you like. I'll give you another Joey if they arrive before my fecking head gets stove in.' He tossed the coin across, and the urchin plucked it from the air, before racing off down a cobbled street in the direction of the sea. O'Malley turned back towards the hall. From within came a loud crash, together with a number of angry shouts.

Inside, the meeting room had been transformed. The

banner above the stage had been torn down, much of the hall's furniture had been overturned and the wind that blew in through the broken windows had set the rings of candles swaying and guttering overhead. Most of the attendees had fled, including Alderman Moore, but the Reverend Tobias Shelley was still there. He stood amongst the ruins of his meeting, with a few of his bolder parishioners at his back. On one side of him was the solid figure of Sedgwick, patting a wooden chair leg in the palm of his hand, with Adam Trevan beside him. On his other side was Sam Evans, six foot six tall, with a herculean build to match. He was side-on to the mob, in a slight crouch, with his fists held up before him, the image of the prize fighter he had once been. The front of his shirt was dappled with spots of blood, although his face seemed unharmed. One of the attackers was trying to stem a bleeding nose, while another had blood trickling down from a cut over his eye. Shelley drew himself up to his full height, his lean face a mask of determination in the wavering light, as he confronted the man in the black coat like an avenging prophet from the Old Testament.

'You and your Philistine brood will leave this place directly!' he roared. 'And never return! Desecrators! Heathens! How dare you mete out such violence in the House of the Lord?'

'Now steady there, parson,' said the leader of the mob. 'It was your pugilist friend as landed the first blow. Tis just this blackamoor we're after. The rest are free to go.'

'He is my particular guest, invited here by the committee,' yelled the clergyman. 'Not one hair of his head shall you harm! Call your ruffians off, before the parish constables arrive.'

'You tell the bastard!' urged Evans from beside him.

'Come now, Mr. Shelley,' said the leader. 'You don't suppose we have staged such a riot without first taking the precaution of paying off the watch, do you? We outnumber you three to one, four to one with the men I have outside. Step aside, and let us come at the Negro.'

'Back! In the name of Our Saviour, you cutthroat!' shouted Shelley. He placed himself in front of Sedgwick, and held his arms wide. The man in the black coat shrugged, and turned to one of his associates.

'Bill, fetch Sam and the others.' He jerked a thumb in the direction of Evans. 'Tell him to bring the blunderbuss, to silence the bruiser. Let's get matters resolved before the garrison are called out.' After a pause, in which those around the Reverend Shelley all exchanged glances, Sedgwick started to push his way forward.

'I will go with them,' said the sailor. 'Fists'll not answer if they truly have a gun. We ain't going to prevail any.'

'Clever, ain't you, for an ape,' spat one of the mob.

'Holdfast there Able,' warned Evans, turning on his friend. 'Or I'll deck you myself. You ain't going nowhere with these turds.'

'Heed your man,' added O'Malley quietly. 'Helps in the offing, or I've burnt a fecking Joey for nought.'

'What can be keeping Bill?' asked the man in the black coat, turning towards the door. 'Ah, here they com...' His voice trailed off as a crowd of sailors poured into the back of the hall. Several stooped to break off chair legs, while others stripped off their jackets.

'Need a hand to deal with these whoresons, shipmates?' said a tattooed petty officer at the head of the new arrivals. 'Them ones outside scarpered as soon as they clapped eyes on us, but it shan't be so easy for this lot to push off.' The new arrivals spread out across the width of the hall, and began to advance, shoving aside the remaining furniture as they came.

*****

The Reverend Charles Costain stood in front of his altar in his best surplice and bit his lip, as a muffled curse, accompanied by a thump, came from behind the vestry door. Just like his fellow clergyman in Plymouth, he too was anxious about Able Sedgwick, although it was not any concern for the slave trade that was exercising him. He knew him as the amiable coxswain for Captain Alexander Clay RN, whose family lived in the village. He had always found the former slave to be a truthful and reliable man. It was only this that had prompted him to let the sailor conceal himself in his vestry, together with a further twenty seamen, all of whom were armed with cutlasses. The sound of a chair being overturned came from behind the door, prompting him to wonder if he had locked away his supply of altar wine sufficiently securely.

It was a shame that he was so concerned about his vestry, because he should have been enjoying this moment. For the first time in several years his church was filled to bursting. The modest living of Lower Staverton gave him few opportunities to see his benches this full. His regular congregation was generally stony ground. There were the dozen spinsters and widows who only came to share in the local tittle-tattle. Farmers who discussed grain prices at the back of the church during his sermons. As for the squire, he was a disgrace. He only came when the weather was too poor for hunting, and openly slumbered in his private pew.

But today the Lord had provided him with a splendid crowd. The small flint church of St. Dunstan was host to a wedding party of some quality. A fife, drum and fiddle had been engaged to accompany the hymns. Branches of yew and trails of ivy decorated the pew ends, while the light from tall shilling-candles glinted off the gold braid of the military uniforms that packed the space. The scarlet of marine officers contrasted with the dark blue of the navy, while the ladies wore dresses of every hue. In pride of place, on the bride's side of the aisle, were the Clay family. Mrs. Clay senior had forsaken the black dress she had worn since her husband's death, and instead wore dove grey. Beside her was her beautiful daughter-in-law, Mrs. Lydia Clay, in a dress of pale blue that perfectly matched her eyes. To one side of the altar was the groom, a handsome young man in his twenties with dark brown hair and eyes, in the full dress uniform of a naval commander. Beside him was an older version of the same man, a brother, in the much plainer coat of a lieutenant. Costain glanced down at the slip of paper in his service book, where he had written the groom's name in case he should forget it. John Richard Percival Sutton. You are a lucky man, he thought to himself, to be marrying the lovely Miss Elizabeth Clay.

At that moment his curate came into the back of the church and gave a nod.

'Pray be upstanding for the arrival of the bride,' announced the Reverend Costain, and with a scraping of feet and a murmur of conversation, the congregation rose in a wave of motion. The musicians set to, playing a jaunty version of *The Lass of Richmond Hill,* and through the open door came the bride, on the arm of her brother.

They did make a striking pair, thought the vicar. Alexander Clay was a tall, lean man with chestnut curls and sideburns. His face was still tanned after a year in the tropics, which served only to emphasise how pale his steel grey eyes were. His sister was much shorter, and fair, with a fashionably light complexion. She, too, looked towards him with the same grey eyes. The effect was disconcerting, as if a pair of wolves had entered his church in step. The brother was in the blue, white and gold full dress uniform of a naval captain, while the bride shimmered in pale green satin, embroidered with trailing silver flowers.

'My word!' he heard the groom mutter, as the pair advanced up the nave towards him. When they reached the altar, he gestured for the congregation to sit once more, and in a further pulse of coloured movement, they did so.

'Dearly beloved, we are gathered together here in the sight of God,' he began, the familiar words flowing on, while out of the corner of his eye he watched the happy couple. It was clear to him that Commander Sutton was entranced with his new bride to be, understandably so. The Reverent Costain was more familiar with Miss Clay in her Sunday best, always neat but unpretentious, compared with the magnificent dress she wore today. He noticed that Sutton was grinning at her, and had been rewarded by a blush of pleasure on her part. In a moment there will be some unseemly mirth, he concluded and he allowed a warning edge to enter his tone.

'And therefore is *not* to be taken in hand, unadvisedly, lightly, or wantonly, to satisfy men's carnal lusts and appetites, like brute beasts that have no understanding,' he paused for a heartbeat and his watery eye held that of the groom, 'but reverently, discreetly, advisedly, soberly, and in the fear of God,' he continued, in a softer tone.

Sutton returned his attention to his bride and squeezed the gloved hand that rested on his arm.

'Marriage is ordained for a remedy against sin, and to avoid *fornication,*' resumed Costain. He let the echo of the word roll around the small church, and favoured the groom with another stare.

But in Commander John Sutton, the vicar had met his match. I have passed through hell, to stand here next to Betsey, the young naval officer reflected to himself. I'll be damned if I will let some glum-faced parson spoil my day. He thought of the loss of his ship, his first command, beaten into a dismasted wreck and then driven ashore by its captors to prevent it from sinking. The French had not even considered saving the shattered little sloop. He could still recall the acrid smell and billowing smoke as the hungry flames licked over the hull and sent droplets of fire to race up the tar-soaked rigging. Then, there had been the tiny boat where he had been adrift for days at the mercy of the ocean. Beneath that burning tropical sun, he had felt certain he would die without ever seeing Betsey Clay again. His face grew grim with his memories, and a look of concern flickered into the eyes of his bride.

Much better, concluded the Reverend Costain. This is no moment for frivolity, and he continued to intone the words of the service.

'Therefore if any man can show just cause, why they may not lawfully be joined together, let him now speak, or else hereafter forever hold his peace.' He paused to let his words sink in. In the quiet, a muffled bang came from behind the vestry door. Heads turned and there was a gasp from some of the ladies, followed by a ripple of relief when no one stepped forward. Under the cover of the disturbance, he refreshed his memory from his slip of paper.

'John Richard Percival Sutton,' he continued. 'Wilt thou have this woman to thy wedded wife, to live together after God's ordinance in the holy estate of Matrimony? Wilt thou love her, comfort her, honour, and keep her, in sickness and in health; and, forsaking all others, keep thee only unto her, so long as ye both shall live?'

'I will,' answered Sutton. He took both of Betsey's gloved hands in his and allowed the image of the little boat to drift away and vanish.

*****

Commander and Mrs. Sutton emerged beneath the grey sky of a late winter afternoon, into the little churchyard, with its mossy headstones and dark yew trees, to find that it had been transformed. A double row of sailors in their best shore-going clothes now lined the path that led to the lichgate, and the waiting carriage beyond.

'Present arms!' bellowed Sedgwick. With a flash of steel, each pair of men drew out their cutlasses and held them up, the tips touching the blade opposite so they formed a glittering tunnel for the couple to walk through. There was a ripple of applause from the many villagers who had gathered to see Miss Clay on her wedding day. They were a fine body of seamen, with their white duck trousers, beribboned shirts, and matching tarpaulin hats. It was a shame that so many of them bore the black eyes and swollen lips of men who had recently been in a fight, but this was barely noticed by the newlyweds.

*****

The Suttons had departed on their bridal tour amid a flurry of good wishes. The majority of the guests had stayed a little longer, before they too had boarded their carriages and traps and driven away in various states of inebriation. That left the remaining members of the Clay family to settle down for a quiet supper in the small dining room of Rosehill Cottage. There were only four present around the polished walnut table. The normally cheerful presence of Betsey Clay had been replaced by the chill, aristocratic Lady Mary Ashton, Lydia's aunt and guardian. Mrs. Clay senior, who in truth was bursting to discuss the finer details of her daughter's wedding, felt foolish and tongue-tied at the thought of doing so in her presence. Alexander Clay and his wife did their best to keep the flow of polite conversation moving, but it was proving to be hard work.

As if to emphasise how quiet their gathering was, through the open window came the sound of the honour guard of sailors as they enjoyed their own supper. Clay had supplied them with plenty of food and rather less drink, but with the ingenuity of their kind, they had used these modest ingredients to continue the day's celebrations. They had installed themselves in the yard behind the house, found and lit two braziers and moved most of the tables and chairs from out of the servant's quarters. For entertainment they had persuaded the three musicians hired for the service to stay on for the night. Lady Ashton looked up and her frown deepened as a particularly penetrating peal of delight came in on the winter air.

'Is that not the sound of a girl's voice?' she asked. Clay paused to listen.

'I believe it is, Lady Ashton,' he said, looking towards the maid. 'Do you know what is afoot, Nancy?'

'Some of the more forward lasses has turned up from the village, sir,' she confirmed. 'When I was in the kitchen I saw the men teaching them some manner of dance.'

'Yes, the tune does have the sound of a hornpipe,' agreed Clay. 'And I suppose they have come by more drink.'

'I did see a few of them returning over the fields from Farmer Grey's place earlier, sir,' said Nancy. 'That big one from London was carrying a keg of cider on his shoulder like it weighed no more than a bolster.' Lydia noted the admiration in the maid's voice, and looked with concern towards her husband.

'I trust they will not become too dissipated, Alex?'

'There is no occasion for alarm, my dear,' said Clay. 'I asked Mr. Taylor to choose some of the steadier hands from the *Titan*. Sedgwick will see that matters do not get out of hand.'

'Sailors, wenches and drink,' sniffed Lady Ashton. 'What do you suppose could possibly go awry?'

'Would you care for a little more mutton pie, Aunt?' asked Lydia.

'No thank you, my dear,' she replied. 'The thought of all this vice so close at hand has rather taken away my appetite.'

'Didn't Betsey look happy, Mother,' said Clay. 'Yes, I will have another slice, thank you, Nancy.'

'Very much so,' said Mrs. Clay. Her eyes flicked across the table towards Lady Ashton. 'I thought her dress gave much consequence to her figure.'

'She looked handsome enough, I suppose,' conceded Lydia's aunt. 'For a provincial wedding. It would never have done for the marriage of an Ashton, mind. I had your dress cut in Paris, Lydia.'

'And then doubtless smuggled in, by Jove!' exclaimed Clay. 'It might be better if that was not generally known. It don't seem quite right for the wife of a King's officer.'

'Come now, Alexander,' said Lady Ashton. 'Everyone wears smuggled cloth. Why, all the superior dress shops in Piccadilly stock garments from Paris. You gentlemen may wish to have your little war, but I don't see why we ladies should be made to suffer.'

'Speaking of the war, what was the letter that the uniformed messenger brought earlier?' asked Mrs. Clay. 'Was it orders, Alexander?'

'Not as such, Mother,' he replied. 'It was a note from Lord Spencer, asking me to attend him at the Admiralty tomorrow. I daresay, I shall be ordered to sea promptly enough, mind. The dockyard has completed the *Titan*'s refit.'

'So soon, Alex?' asked Lydia. 'It seems only yesterday that you and John returned from the Indian Ocean.'

'Lord Spencer!' exclaimed Lady Ashton. 'Is it usual to be received by the First Lord himself?'

'It is a little curious, but then, I have been absent for over a year,' said her son-in-law. 'Perhaps he wishes to update me with all the choicer items of service gossip.' He smiled across the table to reassure his wife.

'It is a singular honour, of course, but I trust it does not mean he has some disagreeable task for you, Alex,' she said, too shrewd to believe such a lame explanation.

Lady Ashton seemed to be about to say something further, but then paused to listen as the noise from the yard grew appreciably in volume.

'Oh, for goodness sake, I do declare those wretched men are about to start singing!' Clay listened to the sound of the music as it drifted on the evening air.

'Two fiddles now,' he observed. 'O'Malley must have brought his instrument from the ship. I wonder which ballad they will perform?'

'How splendid!' enthused his mother. 'Are we to hear a sailor's song?' From out of the dark came the clear sound of a dozen strong male voices, all singing with enthusiasm.

As I was a walking down Ratcliffe Highway
A flash looking packet I chanced for to see
I hailed her in English, she answered me clear
I'm from the Blue Anchor bound for the Black Bear

'Oh, God, not *Ratcliffe Highway*,' muttered Clay, blanching in spite of his tan. 'Ah... Nancy, kindly close the window before Lady Ashton catches a chill.'

'Pray do not close it on my account, Alexander,' said his guest, smiling for the first time that evening. 'I am perfectly warm, and I confess the entertainment starts to grow on me.'

She had up her colours, her masthead was low
She was round in the counter and bluff in the bow
She was blowing along with the wind blowing free
She clewed up her courses and waited for me

I tipped up my flipper, I took her in tow
And yardarm to yardarm away we did go
She lowered her topsail, t'gansail and all
Her lily-white hand on my reef-tackle fall

'Lily-white hand?' queried Mrs. Clay Senior. 'Are they still singing about a ship, Alexander?'

'Ah..., not exactly, mother,' said her son. He looked, appealingly, across at his wife, but saw that her face had adopted the frozen look of someone trying hard not to laugh.

'I said, "My fair maiden, it's time to give o'er
For twixt wind and water you've run me ashore
My shot locker's empty, my powder's all spent
I can't fire a shot for it's choked round the vent"

Here's luck to the girl with the black curly locks
Here's luck to the girl who run Jack on the rocks
Here's luck to the doctor who eased all his pain
He's squared his mainyards, he's a-cruising again

The song ended with a roar of approval from the men in the yard, accompanied by female laughter. Inside, the conversation around the dinner table took a little longer to resume. Mrs. Clay Senior favoured her son with a puzzled look, while Lydia continued to stare determinedly towards the ceiling.

'I confess I did not understand the song at all, Alexander,' said his mother. 'It seemed to be about ships, but was received with a lascivious relish, as if it was some bawdy tavern ballad. I cannot comprehend why?'

'Do explain what the song was about, I pray,' pleaded Lady Ashton. Clay turned towards the maid.

'I believe you may close the window now, Nancy,' he said.

'Unless your men have a fresh song to entertain us with...,' added Lydia's aunt. Clay ignored her, and turned to his mother.

'It was a *double-entendre*, as the French would have it,' he explained. 'It was chiefly concerned with an encounter between a sailor and a lady of easy virtue.' Lady Ashton chuckled at this.

'It most certainly was,' she confirmed.

'I do not care to remain here and bear witness to such behaviour, Alexander,' sniffed Mrs. Clay. 'What your late father would have thought, I shudder to think. If you will excuse me, it has been a very emotional day, and I am quite fatigued.' Clay got to his feet and escorted his mother to the door, after which Lydia, too, rose from the table.

'I believe that I shall go and attend Master Francis, and then retire to bed,' she said. Her husband contemplated staying on with his aunt-in-law, and then decided it was beyond him.

'May I accompany you, my dear?' he said.

'Goodness, how you spoil that child!' exclaimed Lady Ashton. 'Do you not have a perfectly good wet nurse? Why keep a dog and bark yourself?'

*****

In the nursery, the pair of candles that flickered on the mantelpiece gave the room a soft yellow light. A young woman was slumbering by the glowing embers of the fire, but she woke up and rose to her feet when they entered, pulling her dress straight as she did so. She left with a curtsy and closed the door behind her. Lydia's hair was down now, and it cascaded in a wave about the sleeping child as she stooped over him in his crib. She kissed him gently on his forehead. As she stood upright again, Clay caught her around the waist and drew her close. Together they watched their son, his face calm in sleep. For a moment, the infant frowned and a single tiny clenched fist emerged from under the covers, as if he were about to wake. But then he let out a little sigh and returned to his dreams.

'Will you be ordered away soon,' asked Lydia, her eyes still on the baby. Clay kissed her on the crown of her head before he replied.

'I fear so, my dear. I can think of no other reason why I

would have been summoned to see the First Lord. It can only be the offer of some singular duty.'

'Offer?' she asked. 'Does that mean you can decline?'

'Not if I value my career,' he replied. 'These things are called "offers" as a courtesy. They are not expected to be refused.' Lydia nodded her head under his chin but inside she felt rival emotions churning. The deep, warm pleasure of watching her child sleep and the feeling of safety as she rested back against her husband seemed so at odds with the chill words he had said. Ordered away? The last time that had happened he had been gone for so many long months, leaving her to bring little Francis into the world alone. She waited for the tears that pricked at her eyes to pass, and then turned within his arms to face him.

'Come then, my love, if we only have a few evenings left together we should not dally here,' she purred. 'Let us hope that your "*locker is not empty*", nor "*your powder all spent*", Captain Clay.'

Chapter 2

Departure

'Captain Clay has arrived to see your lordship,' announced the clerk. 'Shall I pass the word for Major Fraser to join you?' Earl Spencer, First Lord of the Admiralty, looked up from his desk and contemplated the gilt carriage clock on the mantelpiece opposite him. A coal in the fire broke and shifted, releasing a tiny jet of yellow flame amidst the glow of orange.

'Not directly, no,' he decided. 'Have him shown in, but leave the major for the present, if you please, Higgins. There is a service matter that I wish to discuss with the captain.' The clerk bobbed his head in assent, and the door clicked closed. Spencer straightened his tailored coat, and then stared towards the fire for a moment, as he gathered his thoughts. He was a handsome man of medium height whose white powdered hair contrasted with the young face of a man just into his forties. His office door opened once more, and his visitor crossed the wide expanse of carpet towards his desk.

'Captain Clay, a pleasure to see you again, I am sure,' he said. 'And to welcome you home at last, from your latest exploits. Some madeira for the captain, if you please, Higgins.' He rose and gripped Clay's hand and then waved him towards a chair.

'I trust I find you well?' he asked.

'Indeed so, my lord,' said Clay. 'Thank you for your

enquiry.'

'Capital!' said Spencer, 'And though it is a little tardy, you have my felicitations on the birth of your son. Is the boy in good health?'

'Very much so, my lord,' smiled Clay. 'I understand from his nurse that he may cut a tooth before long.'

'Splendid news!' said his host. 'It is always gratifying to hear that the navy's next generation of young gentlemen are progressing well. On which subject, how was Commander Sutton's wedding to your sister?'

'I believe it was concluded to the satisfaction of all parties, my lord. The happy couple have now departed on their bridal tour.'

'I daresay he deserves some relief, after the unfortunate loss of his ship,' said Spencer. 'He had a vexing time with you in the Indian Ocean, did he not? Upon my word, there cannot have been a dull moment! His ship destroyed, himself captured, then his escape in a little boat. Is all well with him?'

'He was naturally concerned about the Court Marshal he was obliged to stand for the loss of the *Rush,* but since it acquitted him, he is restored to his old self once more, my lord.'

'Ah yes, his trial,' said Spencer. 'I understand that his commanding officer spoke very handsomely on his behalf, although Sir George wasn't actually present when the *Rush* was lost, I collect. Such a shame that Commander Windham could not have testified, but alas, he is no more. Shot with his own pistol, if I understand the reports correctly?' His dark eyes settled on his guest.

'So I understand, my lord.'

'Only understand, captain?' queried the First Lord. 'Surely these events must have been the talk of the squadron. Was no further light shed on matters?'

'Not in my hearing, my lord,' said Clay. 'I was not present

when the *Rush* was captured, nor when poor Windham perished. Sir George was the senior officer, of course. Was his account not satisfactory?'

'As far as it went,' snorted Spencer. 'But he was not present in person, either. What are the deuced chances of that? I send a squadron with two post captains to the far side of the Cape and provokingly, neither of them witnesses a thing.' The First Lord's eyes seem to grow in Clay's mind, until they were like those of an owl. Stick to the agreed account, he urged himself, as he felt his throat grow dry.

'A little more of the madeira, sir?' murmured a voice beside him, and Clay gratefully gulped down a mouthful.

'The enquiry into the loss of the *Rush* acquitted Commander Sutton, my lord,' continued Clay. 'And the French squadron we were sent to oppose was defeated. Is that not satisfactory enough for the board?'

'The outcome was quite acceptable, I make no doubt,' said Spencer, sipping at his own glass, 'in spite of the loss of the *Rush*. It is this whole business with Windham that is so troubling. I am not generally regarded as a fool, Clay. We both know that captains do not load or clean their own pistols, so let us speak no more of accidents.' Spencer tweaked the lace of his cuff, and then began to count off points on his figures.

'Sir George has reported the matter with the delicacy I would expect, but the facts still remain. Windham was melancholy for some reason, after the loss of the *Rush*. There is a suggestion of his taking to drink. Then, we have testimony of a marine guard that he was alone in his cabin, and a surgeon's report of a single fatal wound to his head. The direction in which all the evidence tends is obvious: he died by his own hand. What interests me is to understand what can have driven him to such an extreme. Might you be able to shed some light on that?'

'I know that Sir George investigated matters thoroughly,

my lord,' said his visitor.

'He inquired into the circumstances, I grant you,' said Spencer. 'But not into the reasons. Was there no note left, or did Windham not say anything to you?'

'I am sorry, my lord, but I regret not being in a position to oblige you with any further particulars. I truly have nothing to add to Sir George's report.' Clay composed his face into a calm mask. The First Sea Lord twisted the stem of his glass between his elegant fingers for a moment before he spoke again.

'Let us not trifle with one another. You know that your record in battle is decidedly superior to many captains on the list who have been preferred with knighthoods, while you have not. Of course, it is helpful to have a family with the best connections, and not to be the orphaned son of a country parson.'

'I am conscious that my position in life may have disadvantaged me, my lord,' said Clay. 'But I also have confidence that my ability will more than compensate for the inferiority of my situation.'

'Quite so,' said Spencer. 'Mind you, one never can tell when an opportunity for advancement will present itself. For instance, here we sit, you and I, alone, drinking a little of this very passable madeira. Are you quite sure you have no further observations to offer? I will naturally treat them in the strictest confidence.' Clay hesitated for a heartbeat before he replied.

'I have been quite as candid as I am able, my lord,' he said.

'I see why you have a reputation for pluck, captain,' said Spencer, putting down his glass. 'Let us hope your judgement is not found wanting, what?' He snatched up a hand bell that was on the corner of the desk, and rang it fiercely. 'It is a rare experience for me to have my condescension rejected. Now, to business.' He turned his attention to the door before Clay could reply. 'Will you kindly show in Major Fraser, Higgins.'

The major proved to be a solidly built Scottish officer, dressed in the scarlet uniform of the army. He wore his straight brown hair long, and had gathered it neatly with a ribbon at the nape of his neck. A sprinkle of silver over his temples and his scarred and battered face spoke of years on campaign. One eye was covered by a black leather patch, but his remaining eye regarded Clay with interest as they shook hands.

'Tell me, captain,' resumed Spencer, when both men were seated again. 'What do you know of the *Choannerie*?'

'The Royalist rebels in western France?' said Clay, trying to settle his thoughts after his grilling. 'As I recall, they caused a deal of trouble for the government in Paris, before their defeat a few years back.'

'They were certainly more active then,' agreed Spencer. 'But they still exist in a reduced way. We supply them with arms and support, and a few of the army's officers are in communication with them. Major Fraser is one of them, and knows them better than most.'

'Thank you kindly, my lord,' said the major, turning to Clay. 'During the Revolution in France the northwest portion stayed loyal to the crown. A few years ago, the *Choannerie* could muster as many as fifty thousand men, with the king's former army officers to command them. They forced Paris to despatch many times that number, just to maintain some grip. The fighting was hard, as only civil war can be, and many of their leaders have been killed in battle or gone to the guillotine. Now there are patrols of gendarmes on every road, but there are still numerous wee bands in the forests, capable of diverse acts of annoyance to their government.'

'Which is all to the good,' explained the First Lord, 'for we find ourselves in grave need of allies. While you have been away, captain, the war with France has not been proceeding well. We in the navy hold our own, but matters go very ill on land. The damned Russians have made peace. Most of our other allies are more trouble than they are worth, and the Austrian army gets a thrashing whenever they take to the field. What would be a godsend would be a sizable distraction, to draw French soldiers away from fighting elsewhere. An insurrection against the French government might be the very thing.'

'But if these Royalists are reduced to bands of brigands, how is that to be achieved?' asked Clay. 'It will surely require more than that to defeat the French.' Spencer looked across at Fraser.

'A new leader has emerged, sir,' said the Scot. 'Count Louis D'Arzon. He served briefly in the French Army before the Revolution, and has a considerable following in his ancestral lands. With arms and treasure, and the rigor of some military drill for his men, I believe something may be made of him.'

'This D'Arzon fellow is active in the Morbihan area of Brittany,' said Spencer. 'It is a ragged shore, much penetrated by the ocean. Forests and marshes, islands and peninsulas, somewhere that our command of the sea can be employed to bring these Royalists aid.'

'Was something similar not tried back in ninety five?' asked Clay. 'Commodore Warren landed an army of French émigrés on that coast. It all ended badly, if I collect.'

'Aye, I remember it well, sir,' said Fraser. 'The troops we put ashore were led by men chosen for their rank instead of their experience. What they lacked in knowledge of war, they made up for with stubborn arrogance and pride. Butcher Hoche and his soldiers made swift work of them. But I can assure you that Louis D'Arzon is quite a different stamp of man.'

'I should add that the Cabinet's view is that any prospect of a Royalist rising is most welcome,' added Spencer. 'A display of enthusiasm from within France for the restoration of their king is politically valuable. Seems hard to recall, after so many years of war, but that is what we are meant to be fighting for.'

'I understand that, my lord,' said Clay. 'But you must own that it is a considerable step from some brigands gathering in the forest to a serious armed uprising.'

'I agree,' said Spencer, 'which is why we shall proceed by degrees. Rome was not completed in a morning, as the scholars would have it. At present the plan is to offer modest encouragement to the Royalists. We have supplied them with much weaponry already, but we will provide more, together with Major Fraser and a number of drill sergeants, to see if something might be made of these *Choannerie*. If progress is to you gentlemen's satisfaction, some small scale actions could be attempted, perhaps using our command of the sea. And if that proceeds well, we might then consider a more ambitious enterprise. The Cabinet is minded to send some of our own troops, when you and Major Fraser deem that matters are sufficiently encouraging.'

'And what will my role be, my lord,' asked Clay.

'Notionally, you will be part of the Inshore Squadron of the Channel Fleet blockading that coast, but Lord St Vincent will be informed that the *Titan* is on detached service. That will give you a free hand to support the Royalists as you see fit. In the first instance, see that the materials we despatch arrive, and support this Count D'Arzon chap in whatever manner you and Major Fraser agree upon. When the rising shows some promise, report back to me, and we will consider something grander. As I say, the government is most anxious for this to be successful, but in the event of failure, your role may be to bring Major Fraser and any surviving Royalist leaders back to these shores.'

*****

The first hint of spring was in the air, and the West Country was starting to bud into life as the grip of winter slipped. A brush of emerald was evident on the hillsides that surrounded the natural harbour of Plymouth Sound and flocks of sheep grazed on Staddon Heights. The waters of the sound were green too. Sunlight danced off the little waves that broke against the black hulls of the warships moored close under Cremyll Point. There was a row of heavy ships of the line, with rounded hulls and lofty sides that pulled and snubbed at their cables. Closer in to Plymouth were several elegant frigates. They only had a single gun deck, but their long, sleek hulls and towering masts spoke of agility and speed. One ship in the centre of the line seemed to be almost ready for sea. She was low in the water, heavy with provisions, and her yards were crossed. On either side of her, boxes and bundles were being swayed up from the Victualling Board lighters that bracketed her hull. Beneath her bowsprit, her figurehead was the upper body of a muscular male whose painted eyes glared out at the world beneath a deep frown.

'I can't see where it's all to go, sir,' said the *Titan*'s boatswain, sporting a frown to match that of his ship's figurehead. He indicated the mounds of material still littering the deck, and ran his large fingers through his long grey hair. 'I have found place for them boxes of muskets in the hold, though the Lord only knows how. Poor Mr. Rudgewick has squeezed all them thousands of musket cartridges into the fore magazine, but he says it be jammed solid. Noah and arks ain't in it! It will be a sad pass if we has to fight the Frogs, for we'll never be able to come at the charges for the guns.'

'Now Mr. Hutchinson, you heard the captain as well as I did,' said George Taylor, the elderly first lieutenant of the *Titan*. 'We will be unloading all of this material in a matter of days. If it comes to fighting, I daresay the gunner will find a way to supply powder from the aft magazine.' He spoke confidently enough, but his eyes portrayed anxiety and he found himself running a hand through his own, rather shorter, grey hair.

'It's like I said, we has *somehow* managed to stow all the arms and powder, sir,' said Hutchinson, 'But now all these sacks has appeared. Cross belts, boots, cartridge boxes. It don't weigh nowt, but Christ, tis bulky!'

'Could we not bundle them into some old sails, and lash them down here?' said Taylor. 'When I was in the merchant service, we frequently carried cargo on deck.'

'Deck cargo!' exclaimed the boatswain, his grizzled face a mask of horror. 'On a man-o-war, sir? But how will the men be able to swab the planking?'

'I daresay cleaning might be left for a day or so,' said Taylor, aware of the blasphemy in what he was saying. 'I fear we shall just have to endure a little disruption, unless you have a better suggestion to offer?' Hutchinson puffed noisily, as he sought for some alternative, but with its full complement of two hundred and fifty men and six months of provisions aboard the frigate, he could not think of any unused space.

'No, can't say as I can, sir,' he conceded. 'The barky be stuffed tight as meat in a pie. I doubt if there will be room for the rats, presently.' He glanced over the first lieutenant's shoulder and stiffened to attention. Taylor turned around to see his captain approaching over the crowded deck, together with an army officer with an eye patch. Standing a respectful distance behind them were three soldiers in immaculate scarlet coats. Each stood ramrod stiff, and had a silver-topped cane thrust under his arm. The watery sun winked back from their glossy black boots.

'Good morning, Mr. Taylor,' said Clay. 'May I name Major Douglas Fraser to you?' The first lieutenant shook hands with the Scotsman.

'Delighted to make your acquaintance, major,' he said.

'Likewise, lieutenant,' said the soldier.

'Might I ask for the major to be accommodated in the wardroom for the next few days? He comes with an entourage of drill sergeants who will also need to be found births in the gunroom, together with their baggage.'

'I am sure that can be managed, sir,' said Taylor. The officers looked round as a sharp intake of breath was drawn into the cavernous chest of the boatswain.

'Do you have any observations to make, Mr. Hutchinson?' asked Clay.

'I... eh... no, not as such, sir, no,' he replied, his face a dangerous shade of purple. 'Shall I have these gentlemen's effects swung up on board, to join all these other items as we ain't yet found no space for?'

'If you please,' said his captain. The boatswain knuckled his forehead in salute and departed, shaking his head in disbelief.

'Mr. Russell!' called Taylor. A teenage midshipman with a pleasant face came over in response. Taylor indicated the three burly sergeants. 'I would be obliged if you could make yourself known to those soldiers there. Kindly conduct them down to the gunroom, and make them welcome. They will be joining you and the other junior officers for the next few days.'

'Aye aye, sir, said Russell, after a pause, as he, too, pondered how the extra men would be accommodated.

'Perhaps you would care to accompany me, Major Fraser,' said the lieutenant. 'I will show you to your quarters.'

'My thanks, but before I go, may I have a wee word with both you and Captain Clay?' The Scot dropped his voice and the two naval officers bent closer. 'Can I impress on you gentlemen the supreme importance that our destination, and the nature of our mission, should be kept a secret for as long as possible?'

*****

It was only much later that evening, when the sun had set, and the chill of winter had returned to Plymouth at twilight, that the final bundle was stowed away. The last of the canvas mounds that cluttered the centre line of the ship had been lashed down to the boatswain's satisfaction, and the rope tackles had been taken from the yardarms. It was a weary crew that went below to the warm, stuffy gloom of the lower deck. A row of orange lanterns had been lit and hung from the beams overhead, and the sides of the ship were lined with mess tables, around which the men ate their evening meal.

'Tis plain as the nose on yer face, we're bound for France on some manner of secret undertaking,' announced O'Malley, through a mouthful of food. The sailors sitting around the mess table looked up in interest.

'How'd you figure that out, Sean?' asked Evans, his large body occupying much of the bench opposite.

'Didn't I hear your man Duplain jabbering away in Frog to one of them new Lobsters in the fecking gunroom, at all?' said the Irishman, pointing aft with a ship's biscuit that chanced to be in his hand. 'Them two knows each other, both being fellow Jerseymen, like. They speak the French there from the cradle, so they do. But what do you make of this? Them other two speak Frog an' all. One had a French seamstress for a ma, and the other was raised in Paris as a nipper.'

'All three of them speak Frog,' marvelled the Londoner, chewing thoughtfully on a mouthful of salt beef. 'What are the odds of that?' The other sailors around the table exchanged glances.

'No, Sam, it ain't chance,' said Trevan. 'We ain't shipping Frog speaking Lobsters and arms for nought. I reckon we're about to serve them Frenchies back for all the trouble they caused, arming those wicked rebels in Ireland.'

'Steady, Adam,' interjected O'Malley. 'Wolfe Tone and his lads was Soldiers of Liberty, martyred by the fecking English. Rebels, indeed!'

'So are we just nipping across the Channel to drop off a load of bleeding muskets and them Lobsters?' asked Evans. 'That seems passing easy.' Sedgwick looked up from his square platter and shook his head.

'There's more to it than that,' he said. 'If it were that simple, why would they not just ship this stuff in a merchantman, and why are we carrying enough provender for months on station?'

'No smoke without a blaze, be it?' asked Trevan.

'You be right about us helping them Frog turncoats, lads,' said Hibbert, a bear of a man at the next table, with a pelt of black chest hair. 'That Mystical Jack was saying as much earlier.'

'Mystical Jack!' exclaimed O'Malley. 'Who the feck is Mystical Jack?' Hibbert pointed towards the far end of the deck. A thin, wiry man with long greasy hair sat holding court, with some sailors grouped around him.

'He ain't much to look at, is he?' said the sailor. 'John Beaver be his name. Just joined the barky as a landsman in the starboard watch. They say he be a proper marvel, with all manner of powers to know what be a coming, in the future, like.'

'Weren't he that feller as can predict the weather?' chimed in another sailor on Hibbert's table. 'Said last night how it would be cloudy today, with the wind in the west. He were spot on.'

'That's just gammon!' protested O'Malley. 'It's Plymouth in March! Course it'll be fecking cloudy!'

'So how'd he get these here powers, then?' asked Sedgwick.

'Seems he were up on the forecastle of the old *Naiad*, when she were fighting that Spanish frigate, back in the autumn,' explained Hibbert. 'One of her shot passed that close, he fell down stone dead, without so much as a mark upon him. The sawbones was all for stitching him into his hammock with a ball at his feet, when he ups and opens his eyes. An' ever since that day, he has had the Sight.'

'That do sound impressive, Sean,' said Evans.

'I know a few of the lads on the *Naiad*,' added Trevan. 'They didn't mention no Mystical Jack, mind, but they fought that Don ship right enough.'

'We shall know his worth presently, now he's nailed his colours to the mast,' pronounced Hibbert. 'Bold of him to come out and say as we be bound for France.'

'No it's not! Of course we be bound for fecking France!' said the exasperated Irishman. 'Haven't I been after telling you as much all evening?'

'I be of your way of thinking, Sean,' said Davis, an elderly seaman who was part of Hibbert's mess table. 'I seen his sort before. Weaselly little men as can't hold their own, other than by playing at having some power. Jacks has been falling for such things since I was a nipper.'

The conversation ran back and forward amongst the mess tables on the merits and supposed abilities of the new arrival, and whether he was a charlatan or not. After some time the discussion had become heated, without any firm conclusion in sight. Hibbert slammed down his knife and rose to his feet.

'Right, let's settle this once and for all,' he growled. He rounded on another new member of the crew, a solid looking man with a bald pate and bristling ginger sideburns. 'This here be Joe Vardy, just joined as a volunteer landsman, on account of needing to leave home a bit sharpish.' The new recruit smiled weakly as the attention centred on him.

'How do..., all,' he offered, in a voice a touch above a whisper.

'Have you told that John Beaver anything about you?' demanded the sailor, pointing towards the self-declared mystic with a tattooed arm.

'N-no,' he stuttered. 'I... ain't had o-occasion to tell... no one.'

'That be good,' smiled Hibbert. 'Just you come along with me.'

It was a large, jostling group of sailors that pushed their way down the lower deck to where the thin figure sat cross-legged on a mess table, speaking to those around him. The sturdy figure of Hibbert led the way, pulling the reluctant new recruit in his wake. O'Malley followed, his arms tightly folded.

'Now then, John Beaver, this here is Joe Vardy,' said Hibbert, hooking his thumbs into his belt as he towered over the supposed mystic. 'I wants you to tell me what calling he had, afore he came to sea.' Vardy found himself pushed forwards by willing hands, until he stood in the centre of a pool of light that fell from a nearby lantern.

'My Sight don't work like that,' protested Beaver. 'It be a gift, what comes to me or no. I can't just summon it, like whistling for a dog.'

'Now ain't that a fecking surprise, fellers,' said the voice of O'Malley from the back of the group. 'This here Jack is about as Mystical as my arse, if you asks me.' There was general laughter amongst the sailors. Beaver ignored the Irishman, and looked at Vardy. His dark eyes darted busily over him.

'If I was to use my Sight, 'tis also custom to offer silver for such matters,' he said. Hibbert dredged a coin from out of his jacket, and it flashed in the light as he tossed it across. Beaver plucked it from the air, and then spun and caught it a few times, his eyes not moving from Vardy. After a while he pocketed the coin.

'All right, I shall try,' he said. The sailors muttered their approval at this, and others came to crowd around. Beaver held the back of one hand to his forehead, which shaded his eyes, and he swayed back and forth on the mess table, as if entering a trance. He tried to suppress the rising panic he felt inside, and forced himself to relax. Come on, he urged himself, you have done this countless times before. He drew in a deep breath, and peered through half closed eyelids at Vardy. The volunteer shuffled his feet on the planking, awkward at being the centre of so much attention. He has big hands, thought Beaver to himself, and strong arms.

'I see you labouring hard,' he announced, in a faraway voice. The feet stopped moving. 'Yes, very hard,' said the diviner, encouraged. 'I see you working with your hands,' he offered. Through the mesh of eye lashes he saw Vardy start to turn away. 'But not just your hands,' he added. The sailor again stopped moving. 'Maybe... legs an' all?' he offered, and watched Vardy turn back towards him 'Aye, legs as well as hands,' he muttered, as he searched his mind for possible professions. He was still watching Vardy's bare feet, illuminated where the disc of lantern light fell on the deck. They are very brown, he thought. Not unusual in a sailor, who works barefoot, but Vardy was a recently joined landsman. Interesting, he mused, studying the feet more closely. Now, surely those nails were stained. He returned his attention to the man's large hands. His fingernails were stained brown, too.

'With legs, as well as hands,' he repeated. 'Not a nice trade, by any means.' Vardy remained rooted to the spot, and Beaver rocked his head back a little more as he ran his eyes up Vardy's clothes. He stopped at his belt. It was made from excellent quality leather, but had been crudely cut. And the knife that hung from it was unusually wide. Got you! he decided. He shut his eyes fully and removed his hand from his head so all could see they were closed. Then he relaxed back into the role of Mystic Jack, swaying and murmuring to himself.

'No, a very ill favoured trade, banished to the edge of town,' he said with confidence. 'I see a yard, with you at work, Joe Vardy. There be barrels full of all manner of vileness, all about you. I see you working down in a pit with a foul liquor in it. I can almost smell the piss and the turds, all mashed with... with leaves, oak leaves. And piles of hides, left to rot in the rain and the sun. I see you clear as clear, Joe Vardy, and I see that you was a tanner by trade!' He opened his eyes, and found he was staring into the open mouth of the new recruit.

'Is he right?' asked Hibbert, puncturing the silence. Vardy could only nod.

Chapter 3

The Glenan Isles

A few days later the *Titan*, replete with all her cargo, was passing the cliffs and reefs of Brittany on her way to the wild southern coast of that peninsula. A low grey sky hung over the ship, and ranks of green waves marched in from the open Atlantic to thunder against her bow. But the *Titan* was a weatherly ship, designed for these very conditions. Her reefed topsails drove her onwards into each fresh roller, sending plumes of spray across her forecastle. Her hull rolled and flexed under each fresh assault, while behind her counter a long, foaming streak of wake led back across the sea towards the coast of England, now far behind.

Aboard the ship, the crew were bubbling over with excitement. The start of a new voyage was always an exhilarating time, but this commission seemed particularly promising. No sooner had the shore of Devon vanished into the haze behind them, when they learnt the extraordinary news, unheard of on a warship, that they were to be excused from scrubbing the main deck before breakfast. Many aboard had decided that the frigate was sure to be bound for a period of dull blockade duty before the French naval base at Brest, in spite of the predictions of both Mystical Jack Beaver and Sean O'Malley. Yet, the following day the frigate passed the ships of the Inshore Squadron in the approaches to that port with no more than an exchange of flag signals, and the *Titan* continued on her way. Now she sailed alone, through the bracing wind and dashing waves, the black coast of Brittany off to one side, and some important, secretive mission ahead.

But the conditions were not to the taste of all of those on board. Up on the weather side gangway stood three tall figures, solemn as judges, as they stared towards the land. Their scarlet tunics were concealed behind greatcoats, but there was no mistaking the green tinge that coloured each man's face.

'Tell me, mate,' said Sergeant Bristow to a seaman with a blond pigtail who was coiling down a rope. 'Will this here motion grow any less troublesome?'

'Troublesome?' queried Trevan, as the frigate plunged into a particularly large wave, and a deluge of white smothered her forecastle. 'What this? Why it ain't blowing above a cap full of wind! Just you wait until the barky goes about to weather yonder cape. Then, it'll get proper lively.'

'Oh God,' muttered one of the other soldiers as he leant over the rail. He retched dryly, while his two companions looked on.

'I hope you lads ate your burgoo this morning,' added the Cornishman. 'An empty stomach will only makes matters worse.'

'I couldn't scoff a thing,' offered one.

'Mine has long since gone to the fishes,' said the sergeant at the rail. 'Ain't there nothing we can do? I would rather storm a breach than endure more of this.'

'There be but the one remedy that us sailors knows of, as is wholly certain to answer,' said Trevan.

'There is?' Sergeant Bristow grabbed the sailor by the arm. 'What the hell is it? Tell us, now.'

'It may not be that easy to do, mind,' warned the Cornishman.

'No matter,' said the sergeant by the rail. 'I will scamper up the mast, if I must.'

'Very well,' said Trevan, summoning them close. 'They do say that the seasickness goes clean away when you stand beneath a tree. Good day to you now, I must be attending to my other duties.'

Up on the quarterdeck, the frigate's second lieutenant, John Blake, was officer of the watch. He was a slim, pleasant looking young man in his mid-twenties, with sandy hair and blue eyes, who was examining the French coast through his telescope.

'Are you considering the view for one of your paintings, John?' sounded a New England accent next to him. He looked round to see the large figure of Jacob Armstrong, his periwig crammed down on his bald head against the tug of the wind. The frigate's sailing master pointed towards the north. 'The Inshore Squadron would have made a fine subject when we passed them earlier, with the cliffs and reefs behind them.'

'They would indeed,' said Blake. 'No, I was reflecting back to my time on this coast in the year ninety seven. The captain had just taken command then, and we spent many months trying our best to avoid perishing on all the reefs and rocks hereabouts.'

'Yep, it has an evil reputation, this coast,' agreed the American. 'Enough to turn a sailing master to drink. Yet, we shall be obliged to renew our acquaintance with it, this mission, I collect.'

'But to what end, Jacob?' asked Blake. 'I have tried to engage our guest on the subject, without reward.'

'Our mysterious Scotsman,' said Armstrong. 'I have met with clams that were more open.'

'I trust it is not I who presents any mystery?' asked Lieutenant Thomas Macpherson, the Scottish commander of the frigate's marines, who chanced to be walking by.

'No, it was your countryman of whom we were speaking, Tom,' explained Blake. 'How do you find him?'

'Major Fraser?' said the marine. 'He seems tolerable enough, for a man from Argyll. At least he has not spent his time puking over the rail like his men.'

'Do you not find him to be very close?' asked Blake. 'He has barely said a word about where he proceeds from, or what he is about.'

'As I understand it, he has spent much time dwelling on an enemy shore as an emissary to Royalist rebels,' explained Macpherson. 'Perhaps, if we were obliged to live in terror of being hanged for a spy, we might be mute ourselves. In any event, I shall be able to tell you first-hand what the experience is like. The captain has asked me to accompany the major when we land him in Brittany.'

'Bless my soul, but this ship is full of secrets!' exclaimed Armstrong. 'Will you be safe, Tom?'

'As safe as a man wearing a scarlet coat can be in France,' said the marine. 'Doubtless the enemy will do me harm if he is able, but that is also true if he should find me out here. But I own that I, too, am intrigued by the major. Since I am to spend so much time with him, I would dearly like to know more. I had asked around some army acquaintances of mine before we left, but found out nothing of his origins. He certainly does not seem to have served with any of the Scottish regiments.'

'Shall I get Britton to draw on a dozen of the wardroom's port wine to accompany supper tonight and see if we can loosen his tongue?' suggested Blake.

'*In vino veritas*, eh?' smiled Armstrong. 'I could play the part of a dull colonial, fresh out of the forest and full of questions.'

'If appearing dull is your object, you had best stow the Latin, Jacob,' observed the marine.

'Deck ho!' yelled the lookout from the top of the foremast. 'Sail in sight!'

'Probably another of our patrols,' said Blake. He pushed himself away from the rail and cupped a hand to the side of his mouth. 'Where away?' he yelled.

'A point off the starboard bow, sir,' came the reply. 'Might be a warship, from the cut of her topsails.'

'Mr. Butler,' said Blake to the midshipman of the watch. 'My compliments to the captain, and a ship is in sight, bearing east by south.'

'Aye aye, sir,' said the youth, running for the companion ladder.

'Good afternoon, gentlemen,' said Clay to the three officers as he came up on deck a little later. 'Do you suppose it to be one of ours, Mr. Blake?'

'Probably, sir,' answered the officer of the watch.

'Away, aloft with you, Mr. Russell,' ordered the captain. 'Take a glass and tell me what you make of this ship.'

'Aye aye, sir,' said the midshipman. He ran to the main mast shrouds and climbed them at speed.

'I think I can see the chase from here, sir,' reported Blake from the starboard side of the deck. 'A foretopsail, just lifting above the horizon. Looks to be very white canvas.'

'Clean sails, eh,' said Clay. 'Perhaps a French ship, then.' He joined the officer of the watch by the rail, and pointed his own telescope towards the sighting.

'Why so, Mr. Armstrong?' asked Macpherson quietly. 'Are the French more fastidious in the matter of their sails?'

'Ships cooped up in port by our blockade tend to have less weathered canvas than those obliged to keep to the sea in all seasons to guard them, Tom,' he explained.

'She looks to be a small frigate or a large sloop, sir,' yelled Russell, who had now reached the main royal yard. 'Rigged like a Frenchman, I would say.'

'Get those reefs shaken out of the topsails, if you please, Mr. Blake, and see if she will bear topgallants too,' ordered Clay.

'Aye aye, sir,' said the officer of the watch. He saluted his captain and hurried to the rail at the front of the quarterdeck. 'Call all hands to make sail, if you please, Mr. Hutchinson,' he bellowed.

From under Clay's feet came the squeal of boatswain's calls, accompanied by the roar of bare feet on oak as the watch below came up the ladderways. The top men flew up the shrouds in a mass and then spread out in lines along the yards, while more men ran to their places on deck. Clay pulled out his pocket watch and flipped open the case as the men worked aloft. Soon, the topsails grew as the reefs were shaken out and the wind distended them into great scoops of canvas. Higher up the masts, the smaller topgallant sails dropped down from their yards. As they, too, were sheeted home, the frigate steadily gained speed. The pitch of the deck tilted more and more steeply, until the foaming green sea seemed to be just beneath the lee rail. Clay reached out to grip the mizzen shroud beside him and felt the hum of the straining sails in his hand, overlaid by the faint vibration of the top men, as they descended the rigging towards him. A spider must know this feeling when he has netted a fly, he thought idly, before returning his attention to his watch.

'Perhaps not set as promptly as they should be in a king's ship, Mr. Blake,' observed Clay, snapping the timepiece closed and returning it to his pocket.

'That will be the dissipation of the men's time ashore, sir,' said the officer of the watch. 'Mr. Taylor has a few weeks of hard sail drill planned to sweat it out of them.'

'So he told me,' said Clay, before his attention was drawn elsewhere. 'Mr. Butler, will you kindly go forward and tell those damned lubberly soldiers that if they must spew in such a fashion, they are to do so to leeward.'

'Deck there!' yelled Russell from aloft. 'Chase has gone about!'

'An' making more sail, I should say, sir!' supplemented the lookout beside him. Clay returned his gaze to the strange sail on the horizon, and saw the silhouette of the other vessel narrow and then expand again.

'Doesn't care for the look of us, I make no doubt, sir,' said Blake. 'I will pledge my commission she's French.'

'No takers for that wager,' said Armstrong. He was balancing on the steep deck with one hand on the binnacle while holding on to his wig with the other. After a few moments he gave up the unequal struggle and in a neat manoeuvre, he plucked off the wig, stuffed it into his pocket and crammed his hat back down on his bald crown.

'Mr. Armstrong, now that you have adjusted you attire, could I trouble you to take a bearing on the chase,' said Clay. 'I fancy we have the beating of her, but I would like to have it confirmed.'

'Aye aye, sir, replied Armstrong, lifting his sextant out from its place by the wheel. He struggled up the pitched deck to join Clay and Blake, braced himself against the rail, and focused with care on the smaller ship.

'I am sure that we gain on her,' said Blake to Macpherson. 'We have much the heavier hull and spars, which, in these conditions, will favour us.' The Scotsman looked blank, so he continued. 'The same sea batters each ship, but will check the lighter hull of the Frenchman more than ours, Tom.'

'Very like,' agreed the marine.

'French colours, sir!' called Russell from the top of the mainmast.

'Definitely gaining, sir,' announced Armstrong. 'We are perhaps as much as a knot faster.'

'Only a knot?' queried Clay, looking up at the sky. 'Will it serve to get us up to her before dark?'

'Dusk is sometime after six bells tonight, sir,' said the American. 'It will be a darn close run thing.'

Mile after mile, hour after hour, the *Titan* raced on, slowly drawing closer to her opponent. The pyramid of white became a distinct little ship, with a stern of blue and gold. But, as the coast of Brittany rolled past, the sky became progressively darker.

'Deck ho!' called the lookout, a few hours later. 'Chase is changing course!' Clay, who had been talking with Taylor about his planned sail drill, pulled out his telescope once more and returned his attention to the French ship. The glittering stern lengthened into a sleek black hull with a broad, dull-red stripe running the length of its gun deck.

'Mark the number of gun ports, Mr. Russell,' yelled the captain towards the masthead. 'Mr. Taylor, follow them around, if you please.'

'Aye, aye sir,' said the lieutenant. Clay turned back to his sailing master. 'Where do you suppose they are heading, Mr. Armstrong? I have been expecting them to make a run for the coast, but their course seems wrong. They cannot be hoping to outpace us before dark, can they?'

'There is nothing on that heading, bar a scatter of islands, sir.'

'Islands?' queried Clay. 'What manner of islands? Is there a safe refuge for them?'

'I shouldn't have thought so, sir,' replied the master. 'The Glenan Isles, as they are set down in the sailing instructions. A few dozen of them, some barely above a rock, but others are large enough to sustain a few sheep. Doubtless a good place to fish for lobsters, to judge from the wicked number of reefs marked on the chart.'

'Hmm, with more that are not recorded, I have no doubt,' said his captain.

'Deck there!' yelled the midshipman. 'The chase is one of those corvettes the Frogs favour. I counted ten port lids a side.'

'Those twenty gun corvettes carry eight pounder cannon, sir,' said Taylor. 'No match for our eighteens.'

'Land ho!' called the lookout. 'Islands and reefs, dead ahead of the chase!'

'The surf is clear from here, sir,' said Taylor, pointing ahead.

Clay focused his telescope in that direction and saw multiple splashes of white being thrown up beyond the Frenchman, apparently in the middle of the sea. As the ships sped on, more detail began to resolve itself from out of the grey murk. Clay could see lines of rocks amongst the white foam, like broken teeth. Behind that was the first of the little islands. It appeared as a low cylinder of rock, black up to the tide line and then dirty brown above. Set on top of the island, like the crust on a pie, was a dome of grass. Clay returned his attention to the French ship. She was now much closer and her stern filled his view through the telescope. Several white faces stared back at him from beneath a billowing tricolour. He could see a run of five black windows set amongst the mass of gilding, and beneath that, a name was picked out in large gold letters that ran across the counter.

'She is called the *Moselle*,' he announced, closing his telescope. 'And since I can read that from here, she will be in range presently. Kindly have the bow chasers manned, Mr. Taylor, and let us see if we can wound her rigging or knock away a few spars.'

'Aye aye, sir,' said the lieutenant. He touched his hat and hastened away to issue the orders.

*****

'Gun's loaded,' announced Evans, as he pulled out the rammer with a flourish and stood to one side.

'Run her up, lads!' ordered O'Malley. The men strained at the tackles, and the carriage trundled forward until it thumped to rest in the port. They were at the very front of the forecastle, with the frigate's bowsprit thrusting skywards past them. Ahead was the corvette, just within range, and beyond her, the first of the islands. The forecastle was slick with water thrown across the deck from the *Titan*'s headlong chase, and the brass barrel of the nine pounder was covered in droplets. The Irish gun captain leant forward, cupped a hand around the flintlock firing mechanism to shade it from the light and yanked at the line. The wet flint snapped forward, without any trace of a spark.

'No fire here, sir,' he reported to the officer in command of the two guns. 'Whole thing is wetter than a mallard's arse.'

'Mine, too,' called Richards, the gun captain of the other bow chaser.

'Really?' said Midshipman Butler. 'But the whole ship has been newly fitted with these flintlocks.'

'Was it Frogs as was working in the dockyard, sir?' asked Trevan.

'Ain't they supposed to be more reliable?' asked the big Londoner.

'That's correct Evans,' said Butler, peering at the breech, and trying the lanyard himself. 'At least in the dry.'

'Tis a mighty shame that ships are obliged to take to the fecking water then,' muttered O'Malley to the others.

'Are you proposing to open fire today, Mr. Butler?' came the voice of Taylor, as he strode up from the quarterdeck.

'Sorry, sir, only, the lock of the gun is wet.'

'Which is why you will find the gunner has supplied you with a length of slow match in the tub over there!' roared the first lieutenant. 'Gun captains, go and fetch a linstock. Let us do this the old fashioned way.'

The Irishman returned with the lit linstock, whirled it a few times in the air until the end glowed red, and then returned to the bow chaser. He pushed his barbed spike down the touch hole until he felt the serge of the cartridge burst, then filled the touchhole up with fine powder from the horn he carried round his neck and held his arm aloft to show that the gun was ready to fire. The gun captain of the second bow chaser held his arm up, too.

'Are you at maximum elevation?' asked Butler.

'Aye aye, sir,' replied both gun captains.

'Ready to open fire, sir,' said the youngster.

'Carry on, if you please, Mr. Butler,' said the first lieutenant.

'Larboard side first,' said the midshipman, moving to stand upwind of the cannon. 'Open fire!'

'Stand clear,' yelled O'Malley, and then he paused for the corkscrew motion of the bow to complete its cycle. At the moment that the forecastle was level, he brought down the linstock. There was a brief hiss of flame and the gun shot back with a roar. The crew leaped forward to reload it, while O'Malley turned towards Butler.

'Short and to the left,' reported the midshipman. 'Starboard side, fire!'

As the crew completed the loading of the cannon, O'Malley felt for the swoop and twist of the deck beneath his feet, trying to gauge when the best moment might be to fire. The blue and gold stern was directly in front of him, twisting and pitching itself, the movement exaggerated by the masts of the corvette.

'Right fecking there,' he muttered to himself, as the bow started to climb up the next wall of water.

'Gun loaded,' said Evans, and the men at the tackles heaved the little nine pounder forward once more.

'Starboard your aim,' ordered O'Malley to the handspike man. He levered the carriage around a little. 'Another inch.' The gun moved a bit farther. 'Stand clear now lads!' He waited for the view of the gilded stern to disappear from the square of the port, replaced by an angry sea the colour of jade. Down plunged the bow of the frigate, corkscrewing to one side and then starting to rise again. He brought the linstock down, and the gun thundered back underneath his body. He looked back towards Russell as he scanned the Frenchman with his telescope.

'That was close,' said the midshipman. 'Ah, I have it, hole in the mizzen topsail. That is more like it, O'Malley.' He hastened to look back at the target as the other chaser fired.

On and on the ships raced, and the two bow chasers kept up their steady barrage, but even though the range was dropping all the time, hits were few. O'Malley realised that his second shot had been more by luck than judgement, and his next four balls were scattered across the sea. Although the ship's roll seemed to be predictable, the size of the waves varied, as did the tiny delay between his bringing down the spluttering linstock and the discharge of the cannon. Rocks and islands filled the horizon now, and the sky was growing ever darker. Clay and Armstrong came marching forward along the gangway to see what was happening.

'Now then, Mr. Butler, I need this Frenchman slowed directly,' said the captain. 'It will be night within the hour. I do not want the enemy to have the satisfaction of giving us the slip.'

'The men are doing their utmost, sir, but these are very trying conditions,' said the midshipman. 'The forecastle is a most unstable platform to fire from with this sea running. O'Malley here has hit her aloft twice, and Richards's gun has put a ball through her stern rail.'

'But nothing vital struck, I collect,' said Clay. 'How soon before she is amongst those islands, Mr. Armstrong?'

'She'll be level with the first of the reefs presently, sir,' replied the American. 'Indeed, if you direct your gaze towards her, I declare she is taking in sail.' A line of tiny figures had appeared along her yards, their bodies invisible in the gloom but their legs showed, black against the white canvas. Her topgallant sails narrowed as they were gathered in. A plume of smoke masked their view, and when it cleared, the *Moselle* was turning to one side. A few moments later she straightened her course, and then went about again. A line of surf now lay between the ships.

'What is she about, Mr. Armstrong?' asked Clay. 'Does she mean to dash through all these reefs and rocks?'

'I fear that is her intention, sir,' said Armstrong. 'With a local pilot aboard and a crew who know these waters, I make no doubt she can do so with perfect convenience.'

'Can I follow her?'

'Not if you value the ship, sir!' exclaimed the sailing master. 'I have no accurate chart. Even if I could mark the course she has followed, we are much larger. The *Moselle* will be able to make turns we could never accomplish, and will pass over rocks that would ground us, for certain.'

'Damnation!' exclaimed Clay, beating his fist on the rail in frustration. 'Is she going to scrape me off on these rocks like a whale ridding itself of a barnacle?'

Somewhere behind the heavy cloud the sun had set and it swiftly became dark. The next shot from the bow chaser produced a tongue of orange flame that lit up the front of the frigate. The hull of the *Moselle* was melting into the dark sea, leaving her topsails floating ghostly white through the air. Another gush of flame and when the smoke cleared, the *Moselle* had vanished, as if sunk by that one shot.

'I have her, sir,' said Armstrong. He pointed forward. 'She has turned behind that island. See, you can mark her mastheads, standing proud of the land.'

'The men have no mark to aim at now, sir,' said Butler, a little unnecessarily.

'And we must change course, sir,' added the American, indicating the first of the reefs ahead. The boom of wave against rock sounded close. Clay stared out into the twilight. The sea had grown dark as slate, and the surf flashed white in the gloom as it spat and boiled about the reef.

'Oh, God damn and blast it!' he exclaimed.

Chapter 4

Morbihan

Later that night, the wardroom was aglow with light. The rhythm of the frigate was much easier now that she was no longer dashing in pursuit of an enemy. Three oil lanterns swung gently from the low deck beams and candles guttered in their stands along the length of the table. Together, they made the cabin hot and close for the officers seated there. The wardroom was a stuffy, airless place at the best of times, tucked away at the stern of the frigate beneath the captain's suite of cabins. The only source of fresh air or natural light was through the two ports at the back of the room, but they were never opened when the ship was at sea. As a result, the atmosphere was pungent and close with competing odours: bilge water from the hold beneath, poorly washed linen from the officer's cabins that opened off the wardroom, the sharp smell of pickled cabbage and salt beef from the meal they had just consumed. Lying over all the others was the feral odour of the lower deck, like the breath of a huge beast whose lair was close by. Just beyond the cabin's door, the hundred-odd ill-washed men of the watch who were off duty lay in a carpet of hammocks that swung to and fro as one.

Supper was over now for the officers in the wardroom, although the cheese was still on the table, together with a ragged line of empty bottles. The ring of faces grouped about the table shone with perspiration. Those of Macpherson and Fraser clashed with the scarlet of their tunics.

'And so she proceeded to slither away through the rocks like an eel, gentlemen,' said Armstrong, as he completed his account of the *Moselle's* escape, for the benefit of those who had not witnessed it first-hand. 'We were obliged to make a lengthy circumnavigation about the rim of the archipelago, giving all its numerous reefs prudent sea room. By the time we reached the far side, the Frogs had quite vanished into the night.' A collective sigh of disappointment filled the cabin.

'Forgive my ignorance of matters nautical, but is it common for a foe to evade you in such a fashion?' asked Major Fraser, while Lieutenant Blake refilled his glass, unobserved.

'By no means, major,' said Taylor, from the head of the table. 'No ship would have run such risks, even if familiar with these waters, unless they were compelled to do so. We were hard upon her stern, and sure to overhaul her, were it not for the intervention of those infernal islands.' The soldier stroked at his sideburns as he considered this.

'Does this mean that intelligence of our presence here will shortly be reported to the enemy?'

'Doubtless it will, but what will they have to recount?' said Taylor. 'That they encountered a British frigate on patrol, and gave it the slip. It will hardly trouble the authorities long.'

'Perhaps not,' said Fraser, sipping at his wine.

'One of the hands had predicted the whole matter, I am told,' said Blake. 'John Beaver, a new seaman in my division. Some of the crew are rather taken with him, naming him Mystical Jack.'

'And when did he make his prediction?' snorted Armstrong. 'When we were in open water and certain to catch the *Moselle*, or after the chase had turned towards the islands? A shrewd guess can answer very well to make a man seem a prophet, in my experience. Doubly so amongst sailors, who seem ready to believe every charlatan and mountebank they encounter. Let me refill your glass, major.'

'I would not be so hasty to dismiss such predictions out of hand,' warned Taylor, wagging a finger in the sailing master's direction. 'I have heard tell of no end of strange things at sea, over the years. Even dismissing your grosser accounts of sirens and mermaids, there is still much that might trouble our philosophers.'

'I will gladly concede there to be no end of moonshine to be found in the discourse of sailors, sir,' said Armstrong, 'and that the gullibility of the mariner is a well recorded fact.'

'Perhaps so, Jacob,' said the first lieutenant. 'If you are so minded, would you care for an example, observed from my own experience, that you will struggle to explain?'

'Gladly, sir,' said the American. 'Let us hear the particulars.'

'Some years ago I served as a master's mate in the West Indies, where you will doubtless know there are plenty of schooners that trade between the islands,' said the first lieutenant. 'Whilst there, I observed that most of those vessels will not leave port without a small pig on board.'

'Carried to supply the crew with fresh meat, I don't doubt?' asked Richard Corbett, the *Titan*'s surgeon. He was a small man in his late thirties with thin, sandy hair and small round spectacles.

'Not at all, doctor,' said Taylor. 'They are carried in case the schooner should find itself lost at sea. If that happens, they toss the animal into the waves, and mark the direction the pig swims, certain that it will head towards land. They follow that direction until they raise the nearest island, and I have it on the best authority that it never fails. There, gentlemen, how will you explain that?' The first lieutenant sat back and folded his arms.

'Might it be something to do with your swine's prodigious sense of smell?' offered Major Fraser. 'They may use it to detect land that is invisible to their human owners, perhaps over the horizon? In France they employ such creatures to find a most delicious gall, named a truffle, which grows close about the roots of oak trees.'

'Pah! It has nothing to do with smell!' exclaimed Corbett. 'It is a simple matter of hazard. Your pig may swim in any direction he chooses, and doubtless the schooner will blindly follow. If the animal proceeds in a false direction, then that vessel will never be heard of again, so no report of the creature's failure is ever made. But those that chance upon the right course are saved, and the grateful crew tell all who will listen how it was accomplished by the pig! And so the tale grows in the telling, until all are convinced by such nonsense. Navigating pigs! I ask you, sir!' There was a rumble of approval around the table from all except Taylor.

'I collect, from your observations with regard to truffles, that you must be passing familiar with life among the French, major?' said Blake, filling the Scotsman's glass once more.

'Aye, that is correct,' said Fraser. Macpherson, Blake and Armstrong exchanged glances.

'You must have some considerable facility with the language, to be able to pass readily amongst the natives, sir?' asked the marine. Fraser turned his single good eye upon his fellow Scot.

'I flatter myself that I do, but it is not such a strange thing,' he replied. 'I lived in France for as long as I ever did in Scotland.'

'Is it there that you were wounded, major?' asked the sailing master, from Fraser's other side. He touched the fingers of his hand to his own eye.

'That is so, Mr. Armstrong,' said the soldier. 'I was wounded in the service of the king.'

'There can be no nobler wound then one gained in such a way. A glass of wine with you, sir,' said Blake, raising his own.

'Aye, perhaps so,' said Fraser. 'Although you may wish to reconsider your toast when I tell you in which king's service I fought, Mr. Blake.'

'Surely it was in our noble sovereign's cause?' asked the young lieutenant.

'It was not,' replied the major. 'I served in the *Garde Ecossaise*, as part of the household troops of his Most Christian Majesty Louis, the sixteenth of that name. Now, do you still wish to drink that dram of port wine with me?'

'I... eh,' said Blake looking around for help. Macpherson came to his aid.

'As king's officers, we are more in the habit of pledging damnation to the French in our toasts,' he said. 'But there can be no objection to drinking to the Royal House whose restoration we seek.' He drained his own wine, the others all followed suit and then held their glasses towards the wardroom steward to be refilled. After some hesitation, their guest did the same.

'So were there many of your countrymen in the service of the Bourbons?' asked Blake.

'Not above a few hundred,' said Fraser. 'Frenchmen were the most numerous of the Royal Guard, of course, but ourselves and the Swiss made up the chief part of the foreign troops. There is a long tradition in France of the king surrounding himself with guards recruited abroad.'

'Like the Caesars with their distrust of Roman soldiers, what?' said Faulkner, the *Titan*'s aristocratic purser. 'Wicked old Caligula's German bodyguard is about the only thing my Latin tutor succeeded in thrashing into me.'

'Aye, very like,' said the soldier, 'and for much the same reasons. The French Guards were never as wholly trusted as the Scots and Swiss. And rightly so, as matters transpired.'

'Do tell more,' urged Armstrong, as he topped up the glasses again. 'Were you in France during the revolution?'

'I was, indeed,' said the major, his voice quiet. 'A time of most uncivil strife, such that I pray God I never see the like again.'

'Were you present when the revolutionaries came for the king?' asked Faulkner.

'When the mob attacked the Tuileries Palace?' said Fraser. 'Oh aye, I was there, right enough.' His face grew stern at the recollection, and he stared past his listeners, towards the bulkhead beyond them. The wardroom became silent.

'That was the tenth day of August, 1792, by the old calendar,' he continued. 'It was a torrid, hot day and a smoke of dust hung over Paris. The night before had been full of evil rumours and distant shouts. Then, at dawn, we heard the noise of their approach, echoing down the empty streets. The roar of their voices was as a distant ocean. You can barely imagine the size of the mob, a multitude of bile and hatred. Their leaders had whipped them up into a mindless fury. I can see them now, numberless red bonnets, waving all manner of weapons. Some had muskets or sabres, others pikes and axes. There were even peasants with scythes, while those that boasted no formal arms tore up cobblestones to hurl.'

'But you were formally trained, disciplined troops, were you not, sir?' asked Macpherson. 'Defending a building. Could you not resist the onslaught?'

'At first we did,' agreed Fraser, 'with volleys of musket fire, but as our munitions ran low, the mob became bolder. We could still have resisted. The Swiss and ourselves were content to risk all to protect the Royal Family. Regrettably, the French guards were less resolute. Some amongst them bargained for their lives with the mob, and the revolutionaries were let through. Then the defenders melted away like snow. At the end, we and the Swiss were attacked on all sides, and it quickly became a massacre.'

'How did you survive, sir?' asked Macpherson.

'I barely did, in truth. I was left for dead by the mob, beneath a pile of the slaughtered. I would have certainly perished, but for a few kindly souls who found me later. I lost my eye, together with sundry other wounds you cannot see. They serve to remind me each hour of that sad day.' A sigh went around the wardroom as the major ended his tale. Macpherson turned in his chair and waved forward the wardroom steward.

'Another glass of wine for the major, if you please, Britton,' he ordered.

'You are most kind, Macpherson, but perhaps I have had… '

'Nonsense man!' urged his fellow Scot. 'You and I are to go ashore tomorrow. Heaven knows when we shall be able to avail ourselves of such excellent port wine again.'

'That should not have been said so openly,' cautioned Fraser.

'What?' queried the marine. 'We are amongst friends here. Every man in this company has fought the French with distinction, most of us more than once.'

'Oh, very well,' relented Fraser. He held out his glass. 'It is capital port, although the French are not without wine themselves, and our host has a fine cellar.'

'So you are to meet with a man of substance, I take it?' asked Blake. 'Is he some manner of nobleman?'

'He is a count, but pardon me if I do not name him here,' said the major. 'I mean no disrespect, but there are too many in Paris who would dearly like to have his particulars.'

'And you are to go ashore too, I collect, Tom,' said Armstrong. 'We shall miss your company in the wardroom.'

'It cannot be helped, Jacob,' said Macpherson. 'The captain has asked me to accompany the major and his men, and report back on progress ashore.'

'Progress with the training of troops?' asked Blake. Fraser looked uncomfortable.

'Perhaps,' he offered.

'Come now, sir,' said Armstrong. 'I long ago learnt that secrets are impossible to maintain on the king's ships. There are too many souls crammed into too tiny a space. Drill sergeants with a command of French? A magazine crammed with cartridges? One does not need the doctor's philosophical training or the assistance of this Mystical Jack to make a tally of those facts.'

'It will come as a blessed relief to bid adieu to all the stores we have been required to carry,' said Taylor. 'But I find myself as inquisitive as Mr. Armstrong, here. What is it you plan to do with all those stands of muskets and other warlike stores?' Fraser's good eye travelled around the ring of expectant faces.

'Why, gentlemen, I hope to pay back the revolutionaries who are now in power in Paris. I hope to raise such a Royalist rising, that the Morbihan will be aflame from end to end before this year is out.'

*****

Ezekiel Davis was one of the oldest members of the crew. In his prime, he had been an able seaman to match the best sailors aboard. He had never been a big man but had always been lean and fit, with a wiry strength in his limbs. After four decades at sea, his days as a nimble top man were past. His long mane of dark hair had first thinned and then vanished from the top of his head, while the thick, black pigtail that had once run down his back had shrivelled to a length of grey cord. But he was still a valued member of the crew. There were few knots and splices he hadn't mastered, and the boatswain made good use of him to bring along the more talented amongst the *Titan*'s new recruits.

Davis was seated on the forecastle, with a horseshoe of cross-legged sailors grouped around him. Each man had a short length of rope that lay across his lap. Davis waited for his last pupil to take his place and then began his lesson.

'Now shipmates, today I be learning you how to long splice,' he began. 'I dare say, you can all bend a brace of ropes together with a regular splice, and a proper strong join that will be. That will answer well enough for standing rigging, but such a thickened rope will never do to reeve through a block. Oh, dear me, no! The bugger would be a jamming every time we hauled upon him. For that we needs a long splice.' The old seaman's limbs may have lost much of their strength, but there was little wrong with the dexterity of his blue-veined fingers. He teased apart the strands at both ends of the rope, until he seemed to have made a pair of tiny cat o' nine tails, one in each hand. Then he rapidly wove the strands back together, picking first one from the rope end in his left hand and then from the right, twisting them into place.

'Left over right, then right follows left, and around she goes,' he muttered, almost in a mantra. 'Not too firm, mind, but none too slack neither.' He tugged the final pair of strands tight, pulled out his sheath knife to shave away the loose ends, and the rope was now a circle, with only a slight thickening to indicate the join. Davis held it up for inspection by the sailors.

'Bleeding hell!' exclaimed one. 'Folk would pay a farthing to see such a trick at our fair back home.'

'It ain't as lithe as an undamaged rope, mind,' explained Davis, pulling at the splice to demonstrate its strength, 'but it'll serve well enough in a tight spot. Now, you boys try. First you needs to unpick the rope back for a good two hand-widths at each end.'

Davis knelt forward on the deck and closed to a range where his failing eyes could see what the men were doing. He worked his way around the group, slapping a shoulder in encouragement here, guiding uncertain fingers there, and pausing to demonstrate again for the slower men. He was a good teacher, and by the time that six bells rang out from the belfry behind him, five of the seamen had completed at least one long splice. Only one of the group still struggled with the task, tugging at his rope with increasing frustration.

'You lads clear off,' said Davis. 'I will spend a little more time with Jack, here.' The others departed, and he settled down beside his last pupil. 'No, no, that will never do!' he admonished. 'You be pulling altogether too fierce.'

'That's because the stupid, thing won't hold fast, damn your eyes!' yelled the sailor, his face red with anger. He threw the rope down on the deck. 'I am done with this!'

'Come now, lad,' said Davis. 'It be a hard skill to win, I'll own. Why it took me no end of times to get it straight. You just needs a bit of patience, like. Now, attend while I shows you again.'

'You deaf, as well as a fool?' spat the man. 'I said I am done with this!'

'Now then, John Beaver, there be no call to come on so strong,' said Davis, getting to his feet. 'I only be trying to help you. If you don't want to learn rope work, it ain't no skin off my nose. It be a shame to kiss farewell to the best part of a bob a month, mind.'

'Shilling a month?' queried Beaver, rising to his feet too. 'What you on about now?'

'Why, that's what you gets for being rated ordinary,' said Davis, as he gathered up the pieces of rope. 'Mr. Hutchinson wouldn't have sent you to sit with me if he wasn't minded to see you raised. No matter, I will tell him how you be content to stay a landsman, and that shall be an end of it.' Beaver looked around the forecastle, and drew the older man close.

'Don't be hasty now, Ezekiel,' he said. His face was still mottled with rage, but he did his best to mould his features into a smile. 'How would it be if you just told him I can do it?'

'Oh, I ain't sure as how I could do that, Jack. That wouldn't be right at all.'

'Not even if I was to slip you a bob or two?'

'Certainly not, Jack Beaver,' said Davis. 'There be only one occasion I would say such a thing, and that were if it be true. Now, I don't mind sitting with'ee some more. Shall we try again?' He held out one of the loops. Beaver's face grew crimson again, and he knocked the rope aside.

'Have a care, old man,' he hissed. 'I have the Sight, you know. They don't call me Mystical Jack for naught. I can see your death, even as you stand here now.'

'What... d-death?' stuttered Davis. 'What you talking about?'

'There be a sickness in you, Ezekiel Davis. I can see it, just a waiting to burst out of thee, like a maggot from an apple. You've been touched by the scarlet pox, mark my words, now.' The older man stepped back, and the rope he held fell from his grasp.

'I... I ain't afraid of you, J-John Beaver,' he stuttered.

'No?' queried Beaver, following him close. 'You bloody well should be. See how you're sweating? That ain't normal on a chill day like this. I reckon that be the first sign.'

*****

Sergeant Bristow was feeling much better as he stood on the edge of the large forest clearing, doing what he had been born to do. He had now spent several weeks with good, honest soil beneath his polished boots. The miseries of the sea sickness that had tormented him as the *Titan* buffeted along in pursuit of the *Moselle* had vanished. From deeper in the forest he could hear the echo of shouted orders and the tramp of booted feet, as other recruits were put through their training. He looked up, searching for inspiration, as he translated the tirade he wanted to deliver from oath-laden English into its French equivalent. As he gazed upwards, he noticed that he was, indeed, standing under a tree.

His gaze returned to the line of Royalist rebels in front of him, and his face settled into an angry scowl. They were the strangest dressed soldiers that he'd ever had to work with. Most wore peasant smocks in various shades of unbleached linen, while others had jackets and britches of different colours. The recruit in front of him wore the shabby black coat of a clerk. On one side of him stood a green clad forester, while farther down the line he could see a portly man, dressed in what once had been a pale blue footman's coat of some magnificence. The only uniformity amongst them was the new boots on their feet, the British army cross belts draped over their chests, and the Brown Bess musket each man held, the barrel still shiny with grease from its packing case. His grip tightened on the silver headed cane that was tucked against his considerable chest. He began to pace along the ragged line of men.

'Does you all *want* to be bleeding slaughtered?' he asked. As he advanced, he sensed that the men behind him were all turning their heads to follow his progress, like cows in a field. 'Eyes front there!' he yelled, spinning round, and he was gratified to see the heads snap back into line.

'When the enemy is upon you,' he continued, 'and the gun smoke is thick as fog, and them big bastards from Paris is charging with bayonets like sabres, looking to cut you all into... into...' He sought for the French word for minced meat and, failing to find it, said "pate" instead. The man dressed as a forester began to chuckle. Sergeant Bristow rounded on him and delivered the rest of his tirade directly into his face, from a range of six inches.

'You will doubtless be shitting yourselves. You will have forgotten your bleeding name, or that your mother was a whore.' He paused for effect. 'But when I have finished with you lovelies, you will still recall how to load and fire your bleeding muskets, even with your eyes closed.' Then he softened his tone. 'Was something I said amusing to you, Pichon?'

'No, sergeant,' replied the man in green.

'Well, run twice around the clearing for me anyway, with your musket held above your head,' he ordered, hauling the man out of his place and sending him on his way with a kick.

'The rest of you will prime and load again,' he continued. 'Motion one! Poise your muskets!' All along the line, heavy weapons swung down off shoulders and were held jutting out, close to the waist. Sergeant Bristow surveyed his recruits.

'Better!' he announced. 'Motion two! Cock your muskets!'

*****

The first spring sunshine of the year had vanished with the arrival of the storm. Training had finished early, as sheets of cold rain had blown in from the Atlantic to turn the forest into a dark, forbidding place of dripping trees and dank leaf mould. Now the newest recruits to the Royalist cause were huddled in the long rows of shelters that covered what once must have been magnificent gardens surrounding the chateau. Lieutenant Thomas Macpherson watched from the window as a few smoky fires struggled into life in the twilight, and men emerged to try and cook their evening meal.

No such problems with our fire, he thought, as he turned from the rain-spattered glass, and contemplated the chateau's great hall. A blaze crackled in the cavernous stone fireplace that dominated one side of the room. Most of the Royalist officers stood close to the flames, drying themselves in the heat. Their flickering shadows ran across the hanging tapestries, the dark oil paintings and rows of weapons that dominated the other walls.

'How do you find my house, lieutenant?' called a voice in heavily accented English. Macpherson turned towards the speaker, a handsome man in his thirties with a head of dark curls and a pair of dominating brown eyes, set either side of his prominent nose. He was standing close by with Major Fraser.

'It reminds me very much of a laird's castle, up in the Highlands, Monsieur le Comte,' he replied.

'Ah, that will be the rain,' said Count Louis D'Arzon. 'But perhaps Brittany is more than a little like your Scotland. I have never been there, but I understand you also have our bagpipes, and are a proud, independent people.'

'Aye, that is true enough, although home is altogether wilder,' said the marine. 'I also must confess to my surprise that your castle is so well appointed.' He indicated the hangings and portraits. 'Was all this not destroyed in the Revolution?'

'That may have been the fate of those bloated aristocrats living along the Loire Valley, but here in the Morbihan, my father was loved by his tenants,' said his host. 'The family of D'Arzon have ruled these lands with wisdom and justice for generations.'

'The Revolution largely arrived in Brittany from outside,' explained Fraser.

'Democrats and Jacobins, with all their absurd talk of liberty and equality – as if men of different ranks could occupy the same station in life!' exclaimed the count. 'What nonsense! It quickly turned bad, of course. First we had The Terror, with a guillotine busy in every town square. Then we had Butcher Hoche with his gendarmes.'

'That is right, Monsieur le Comte,' growled one of the young men who stood by the fireplace. There was a rumble of approval from the other figures gathered around him.

'My uncle was the abbot at St. Aubin, and they threw him in prison,' said another. 'What sort of animals make war on priests?'

'They killed my mother because she served the late queen as a lady-in-waiting,' offered a man with a shock of auburn hair.

'You see, gentlemen?' said D'Arzon. 'I have no shortage of officers to lead our rising against Paris. Even now that the worst excesses of the Revolution have gone, there is still much for the people to resent. All these officials from Paris, interfering here, poking their noses in there. They force the people to abandon the old ways, with their meters and kilograms and their new taxes. And now, this endless war against the world, with the army taking our sons away, to go and fight God only knows where.'

A servant came into the hall at that moment, walked across the stone floor, and whispered in the count's ear.

'Gentlemen, please take your places for dinner,' said D'Arzon, indicating the oak table that dominated the room. The officers sat along the table's sides, with the count at the head and the two Scottish officers on either side of him. A row of serving staff came into the hall and began to place steaming dishes on the table.

'I hope you enjoy the wine,' said their host. 'It is the last of the eighty seven. Your good health, gentlemen.' The officers drained their glasses, and the count waved forward one of his servants.

'It is very passable, sir,' said Macpherson, holding his glass out for more.

'I am pleased you like it,' said D'Arzon. 'Some veal stew here, Pierre, for the major.'

'My sergeants tell me that training of the recruits is progressing tolerably well, count,' said Fraser. 'Perhaps in another week, we might be in a position to accomplish something, in a small way.'

'By all means,' said D'Arzon. He swirled the wine around his glass, sending points of firelight running over the front of his coat. 'What did you have in mind?'

'An easy victory would be desirable, to blood them, as it were,' said Fraser.

'Nothing too demanding, I would suggest, sir,' cautioned Macpherson, from his other side. 'From what I have observed, a battle in the open would be beyond them at present.'

'Perhaps an ambush,' suggested Fraser. 'Made on an isolated detachment of government troops?'

'That would be ideal, if such a thing could be contrived,' said the marine.

'Yes, perhaps that could be done,' mused the count. 'In fact, I may know just how it might be achieved.'

The prospect of some action at last served to animate the officers grouped around the table. Soon ideas and plans were being bandied backwards and forwards, and the conversation inevitably slid into French. At first, Major Fraser and the count tried their best to translate what was being said for Macpherson, but, as the evening wore on, they did so less and less. Some of the conversation was in Breton; the rest, in French, was spoken rapidly and was beyond the marine's limited knowledge. He began to feel isolated and lonely, missing the closely knit group of officers on the *Titan*. He looked around the huge hall as the torrent of speech rolled over him. The cold stone walls were too distant, the ceiling above him too lofty. He began to long for the oak cocoon of the frigate's wardroom, close and cramped as it was. The others seemed to have forgotten he was even present. The count was having a voluble discussion with someone farther down the table and gesticulated forcefully with his hands to emphasise his points. The marine glanced across at Fraser, and pulled himself straighter in his chair.

The firelight was flickering across his lean face,

emphasising the puckered scars. The patch he wore was blank and dark, but his good eye was fixed on D'Arzon. Macpherson could not remember ever having seen such a look of hatred before.

Chapter 5

Forest

A few days later, the officers of the French Republic's 71st Infantry Regiment were enjoying lunch in their mess. It was a clean, well-ordered room with a scrubbed wooden floor and plain but comfortable furniture. The walls were bare and devoid of decoration. On closer examination, squares of less faded paint could be detected, where once had hung the paintings that celebrated the regiment's various triumphs under the Bourbons. These had been wisely removed during the Revolution, and now languished in the back of a hayloft. Only the line of officer's coats that hung from pegs near the door provided any decoration, while through the room's two large windows a parade ground could be seen. Pleasant conversation flowed about the table in the middle of the room, punctuated by the clink of cutlery on plate.

'Excellent rabbit, Gilles,' enthused Colonel Chesneau, a darkly handsome officer who sat at the head of the table. He tore a piece of bread from the heel of a loaf and slid it around the rim of his plate. 'Just the right amount of mustard in the sauce, and the mushrooms were perfection.'

'Thank you, sir,' replied the mess steward, beaming with pleasure. 'Cook and I gathered them in the forest this morning. Shall I bring some of the goats' cheese, now?' His question was ill-timed, as the colonel had just crammed the piece of bread into his mouth, but one of the other officers at the table gave his assent, and Gilles disappeared back towards the kitchen.

'I sometimes doubt the wisdom of allowing a Breton to feed us mushrooms, sir,' said one of the other officers.

'You fear that we may suffer the fate of Claudius, eh?' laughed Chesneau, as he wiped his mouth on his napkin. 'I know that we are greatly resented here, but Old Gilles is reliable enough. His love of food would never permit him to use it as a weapon.' He waved forward one of the orderlies to refill his glass, and then drank thirstily of the cool cider.

'How was your patrol this morning, Captain Martin?' he said to another officer.

'It passed without incident, sir,' replied the man, a young, thin-faced soldier. 'Yet I do confess to feeling some unease. There is a strange atmosphere in the town. Men were congregating in the street to watch us pass, muttering to one another. I cannot quite put my finger on the reason why.'

'I agree, Guillaume,' said another officer. 'It was the same yesterday, as if they all know something. These damned peasants are even more surly than usual.'

'The Bretons are sulking, is that it?' scoffed the colonel. 'It is hardly worthy of a dispatch to headquarters. They have always hated outsiders. Let them resent us all they like, so long as they fear us. While that is the case, they will cause us little trouble, my friends.'

'I have never come across such a people!' exclaimed another officer, who had recently joined the regiment. 'Most are dirt poor, and yet they bear themselves like kings.'

'Yes, that is your Breton,' said Chesneau. 'Always so superior. They did very well under the Bourbons, but now we are on hand to help drag them into the modern world. This is 1800, after all. A new century lies before us, which will undoubtedly be the French century.'

'Bravo, sir!' exclaimed Captain Martin, while the others banged the flat of their hands on the table. As if others wanted to signal their agreement, too, the steady beat of a drum started outside the window. The colonel turned in his chair, and looked over the parade ground. A column of new conscripts were marching across it, the men's steps regulated by the drummer-boy who led them on and the shouts of the sergeant who marched beside them. A further commotion made him look past the recruits to the main gate, where the tricolour of the republic fluttered above the stone arch. Two horsemen had just arrived in a cloud of dust. One was leaning out of his saddle as he spoke to the sentry. The man stood at attention, and then motioned to his colleague, who ran to the guardroom. He returned a little later with a corporal, who was buttoning up his tunic as he came.

'Is that not a gendarme's uniform?' asked Chesneau, to the room in general. He pointed towards the riders, and Captain Martin stood up to follow his gaze.

'Yes, sir,' he confirmed. 'A junior officer, I should say. It looks to be urgent.'

Gilles had only just brought in the cheese when the door burst open, and in marched the corporal of the guard, accompanied by a dark-haired man in high, travel stained riding boots. Spurs chinked against the floor with each footfall as he crossed to the table. Colonel Chesneau looked over the new arrival, taking in his blue coat with its red facings and his buff yellow britches.

'An outrage has been committed, sir,' said the man, coming to attention. His face was red with fury. 'Not an hour's march from this very barracks!'

'My dear lieutenant, please calm yourself,' urged Chesneau. 'Come and join us, I pray. Gilles, a glass of cider for the officer, and perhaps some of the rabbit?'

'There is no time for food, sir!' exclaimed the gendarme. 'My patrol was ambushed in the woods. Three of my men were killed in the fusillade. God knows how my sergeant and I were able to escape.'

'That does sound grave, young man,' said the colonel. 'Sit

down here, drink some of this excellent cider, and tell me what has happened.' The gendarme obediently choked down a little of the drink, before he continued.

'I was leading a patrol towards St. Laurent le Bois, sir,' he explained. 'We had word of bandits operating in the woods near there, and my captain wanted me to investigate. We took the main road through the forest and had just crossed a little bridge when we came upon a tree that had been felled, blocking the way. I ordered two of my men to dismount and investigate. No sooner had they done so than a storm of fire came from all around us. Those two were slain before my patrol could even pull out their carbines, and I lost a further trooper as we withdrew. I tell you, it was dreadful.'

'Truly an outrage, lieutenant,' agreed Chesneau, stroking at his moustache for a moment. 'And you say this took place close to here?'

'Three, perhaps four miles away,' said the gendarme. The colonel looked at his officers.

'I don't know the exact spot the gentleman is referring to, sir,' said Captain Martin. 'But the forest is thick on the St. Laurent road, and it frequently runs between embankments. A good place for an ambush.'

'And the ambushers may still be there!' exclaimed the young officer. 'Make haste, sir, I implore you!' The colonel leant forward and patted the back of the gendarme's hand.

'We will naturally see your men avenged, but first I need you to think for me. Can you recall how many shots were fired?'

'Twenty, I should say, sir,' he replied, after a pause, 'or perhaps as many as thirty. It was hard to mark them in all the confusion.'

'I understand,' replied the colonel. 'This gentleman here is Captain Martin. I am going to send him out with two of my infantry companies. Captain Martin, this is Lieutenant...?'

'Deschamps, sir. Lieutenant Michel Deschamps.'

'Very good, Deschamps. Now, do you suppose that you can lead my soldiers back to the spot where you were attacked?'

'Of course, sir,' said the gendarme.

'Excellent,' smiled Chesneau. He leant back in his chair to address his officers. 'I think we now know why the locals have been acting so strangely. A sharp lesson is what is required. If these brigands have invested the effort to fell a tree and have enjoyed some success this morning, it is to be hoped that they will maintain their positions, to see what other mischief they can create. Captain Martin, I suggest your men leave the road, some distance before the place where the lieutenant and his men were attacked, and circle through the forest. See if you cannot ambush the ambushers. Bring back alive as many of the traitors as you can. The guillotine in the town square has lain idle for too long, eh?'

*****

While Colonel Chesneau was completing his plans, the two British officers were approaching a cottage in the forest. They had found the building, just where Count D'Arzon had said it would be, in a little clearing by the stream. It did not look to have been abandoned for more than a few years. The vegetable plot outside the door was rank with weeds and the picket fence that had once protected it from the creatures of the forest had been broken, in places, by foraging wild boar, but the building itself was still sound. Thomas Macpherson used his shoulder to force open the protesting door, and then stood back to allow Major Fraser to enter. Chill air from the long unheated interior flowed out like the breath of a tomb, and the officers pulled their coats close as they walked in across the dusty floor. The marine pushed the shutters open to allow in a little watery daylight and then surveyed the bare interior. There was a blackened grate with some leaves and twigs from a fallen jackdaws nest in it, a wooden table, thick with dust, a bench against the wall and two stools. Fraser tested one of the stools, and finding it sound, he wiped the seat with the sleeve of his coat before sitting down.

'I have had to endure much worse billets than this in my time,' he said. 'Doubtless this one will serve our purposes well enough.'

'Aye, sir,' agreed Macpherson, sitting on the bench. 'I hope the count doesn't take too long over his dispositions, and we are not obliged to stay here over long. My, but it is chill! I can feel this cold in my very marrow.' Fraser reached deep into his coat pocket, and pulled out a battered flask of tarnished silver, which he placed on the table.

'I fear a fire is out of the question, with the enemy at hand,' he said. 'The chimney is certain to be blocked, in any case, but perhaps a wee dram will serve to repel the cold?' Macpherson sat upright.

'That would be a grand thing indeed, sir,' he said. 'Is that brandy you have in your flask?'

'I fear not,' said the major, pulling the cork free with a pop. 'It is calvados, an ardent spirit they make hereabouts from apples. Regrettably, our accommodation appears to be deficient in the matter of glasses, but if you are content to drink turn-and-turn-about, it may answer.' He pushed the flask across the table towards the marine. Macpherson took a careful swig and felt a glow of heat flow down his throat.

'That is very welcome, sir,' he said as he returned the flask to its owner. 'It is not the whisky of home, but it will serve.' Fraser took a long pull himself and then pushed it back across the table.

'This flask has a few tales to tell, I will warrant, sir,' said the marine, after he had drunk again from it. He held it up to examine the metal. The grey surface had several large dents and a long, straight scar across one side, as if it had been struck by a sword. The low afternoon sun chanced to emerge at that moment and shone through the cottage window. 'Why, I do declare there is something written here in French, together with a name. "*C.H.R. Fraser*". But surely, your given name is Douglas?'

'So it is,' said his companion. He took back the flask and drank in his turn. 'Charles was my older brother.'

'"Was", sir?'

'Aye, God rest his soul,' said Fraser. 'Much loved and sorely missed. He was my superior in the *Garde Écossaise*, before this damned Revolution. Do you have any brothers yourself?'

'I have but the one, along with three sisters, all alive and prospering, sir,' said Macpherson, touching a hand on the battered wooden table. 'William is my older brother, so it is he who will inherit from my father, obliging me to make shift for myself. The law or the kirk was not for me, so I decided to try my hand as a redcoat. I have always had a fondness for the sea, which is why I joined the Royal Marines. On which note, what do you think of our Count D'Arzon's ability in the soldiering line?' Fraser passed back the calvados before he answered.

'I know very little of his soldiering, or his general character, for that matter,' he replied. 'We shall learn more today, I hope, but he does seem to have no shortage of dash.'

'You astonish me, major,' said Macpherson. 'I had thought that you were well acquainted with him?'

'By no means,' said Fraser. 'My connection dates only from earlier this year, when first I met with him.'

'But do you at least hold his dispositions for today to be promising?' asked the marine.

'I don't doubt that they are sound enough. So long as the French act as he supposes, all should finish well. Sergeant Bristow has assured me that the recruits he has trained have enough pluck to fight in the forest. How they will do when obliged to come out into the open, where they may face artillery and horse, will be another matter entirely.'

'Then let us build them up to such exertions by degrees, sir,' said the marine. 'Expose them to a succession of battles, each one a little harsher than the last. Is that not the way to proceed?' Fraser turned his single eye on to his companion.

'Sounds easy, don't it?' he said. 'Slowly train up a force of rebels, beating and tempering them like steel in the heat of many little battles. If only our enemy would give us such leisure, what a fine Royalist army we should built! Regrettably, being revolutionaries themselves, there is little Paris hates more than revolt. I fear the skirmish that D'Arzon has planned for today may bring down their wrath on us, long before we shall be prepared to receive it.'

'Come, sir, that seems a very gloomy prognosis,' said Macpherson.

'If you had seen as many uprisings snuffed out as I have done these last few years, you might think the same, lieutenant.'

'So what is all this for, sir? What are we doing, seated here in this damned croft, when we could be taking our ease elsewhere?' Fraser shrugged.

'We all have our reasons. D'Arzon, for his part, fights for a king he has never met, and probably will not care for when he does. As for you and me, Tom, we assist him in his enterprise at the bidding of our own masters.' He picked up the calvados, and drank heavily.

'But surely, that will not answer, sir!' exclaimed Macpherson. 'If you were so doubtful about the Royalist's prospect of success, why did you recommend our aiding him to the government?'

'The Cabinet know full well how slender are D'Arzon's chances of prevailing, my friend,' said Fraser. 'What have they truly put at hazard? You, me, three sergeants, some arms and a single frigate! A modest price for all the trouble we may cause the French in this god-forsaken corner of their country. As for my part, I have my reasons, Macpherson.'

The marine waited for more, but Fraser simply hunched deeper into his coat and stared towards the empty fireplace. After a while, he returned the flask to his lips. Macpherson was about to push him further when he heard the sound of distant gunshots. The men exchanged glances, and Fraser pushed the stopper back in the flask.

'And so it commences,' he said, almost to himself. 'Let us go, Macpherson, and see what resistance the count's *Choannerie* are capable of offering.'

*****

The afternoon had begun well for the detachment of the 71st Infantry Regiment commanded by Captain Martin. To the roar of drums and the bawling of corporals, the men selected for the mission had formed up on the parade ground while Captain Martin received a last few instructions from Colonel Chesneau. Then he and the young lieutenant of gendarmes mounted their horses and led the long column of soldiers as it snaked through the gate. Once out of their colonel's hearing, the men began to sing a marching song of the regiment's own invention. The tune was old, but the words quite new. The theme of the song was the similarity between bedding Breton women and various acts of bestiality, each one less plausible than the last.

'Your men seem in good spirits, sir,' said Lieutenant Deschamps, raising his voice over the jingle of the horses' harnesses and the steady thump of the drum behind them.

'Naturally,' said Martin. 'Garrison duty is often very dull, you know. When you expected to spend the afternoon polishing your buttons or sweeping the parade ground, the prospect of some action can be diverting.'

'If it is adventure they seek, they should join the gendarmes, sir,' said the young officer. 'My men are kept constantly busy, investigating here, bringing in suspects for questioning there.' The army captain looked across at the lieutenant of police, noticing for the first time the hardness of his expression.

'Perhaps your line of work is not to everyone's taste,' he offered.

'Sedition must be rooted out, sir,' replied Deschamps. 'The Revolution must be protected from reactionaries, wherever they may exist.' He looked Martin up and down, and the army officer felt a prickle on the nape of his neck. He turned his attention ahead, where the road bent around one last cottage before it disappeared into the woods.

'How far into the forest were you, when attacked?' he asked.

'Perhaps a kilometre from that building there,' said the gendarme. Martin turned in his saddle and called behind him.

'Still the drum and have the men stop singing,' he yelled. The order was passed back down the column, and the men marched on, accompanied only by the gentle clop of the two officers' horses and the steady tramp of feet. At the edge of the forest, Martin sent a reliable corporal with two of his soldiers ahead to scout the road, and after a pause to let them disappear from sight, the advance resumed. With a last brief glance behind him, Martin plunged under the first of the dark forest trees.

After a quarter of an hour they came to a stone bridge, built over a brook that splashed and chattered down the hillside towards them.

'This is it, sir!' the gendarme officer exclaimed. He pointed down the road, to where it curved around the side of the forested slope and entered a cutting. 'They attacked us a little way down there, just beyond that bend.' Martin held up his right hand, palm flat as if about to take an oath, and the column came to a halt.

'Let us await the return of Corporal Mercier,' said the infantry officer. He let his grip slackened on his reins and his horse began to crop the lush grass of the verge. The gendarme's mount tried to do the same, but Deschamps pulled its head back up. Behind him he could hear the gentle clink of equipment, and the occasional cough as his men stood at ease. Overhead the sound of woodland birds resumed their chatter amongst the trees. A little later the group of pickets came back down the road towards them.

'There's a dirty great tree down, sir, just around that bend,' reported Corporal Mercier. 'Proper blocking the road, it is. We also found some dead bodies -- men and horses. Apart from a deal of crows, it's all quiet.'

'Thank you, Mercier, you and your men may resume your places,' replied Captain Martin. He drew in his reins, and wheeled his horse around on the spot.

'The 71st will form line, across this slope!' he ordered. The men obediently fell in, and soon the soldiers were arranged in a dense, triple-row. The corporals and sergeants fussed over the dressing, while Martin led the gendarme to a position behind his men.

'The 71st will advance!' barked Martin, once the formation was straight, and they left the road and plunged into the trees.

After his soldiers had advanced a few hundred yards, Captain Martin began to feel the first niggle of doubt about the wisdom of this action. The operation had seemed so straightforward when Colonel Chesneau had described the plan, back in the officers' mess, he recalled: leave the road, circle around behind the enemy's fallen tree, and then, what had his phrase been? "Ambush the ambushers" -- that was it. But when they left the road, they had entered another world.

The ground was carpeted with a heavy pelt of leaf mould and dotted with the decaying remains of fallen trees. Progress ground to a snail's pace for the soldiers in their unwieldy line. Martin considered allowing the men to march in a looser formation, but quickly rejected the thought. They might become separated and scattered in such dense forest. The land rose up from the little stream but then became broken, with slopes seeming to run in different directions. Amongst the closely packed trees, the soldiers could see no more than a few dozen yards ahead and began to lose their sense of direction.

Captain Martin had just turned his horse around yet another tree, ducking to fit beneath a low branch that dripped with moisture, when the first shot rank out. He looked up and caught sight of a ball of grey smoke amongst the trees, farther into the forest.

'That's curious,' he remarked to Deschamps, as the gendarme pulled up his horse next to him. 'I was about to order the men to wheel to the left and descend on the men that attacked you. But that shot came from ahead.' More firing echoed through the trees, accompanied by smoke, and a gash of yellow appeared on the trunk besides them. Martin swung his body from one side to the other in his saddle, but try as he might, he could see nothing of their attackers, other than the gun smoke as it drifted away. In front of him, his soldiers continued to advance forward, in a line that was becoming increasingly ragged. Another puff of grey blossomed between the trees ahead, and this time one of his men collapsed with a cry of pain.

'Damn!' muttered Martin to himself, then louder. 'Keep advancing lads! Lieutenants! Send forward skirmishers to keep those sharpshooters back.' The line continued to struggle through the trees toward the enemy, while a scatter of soldiers ran forward to screen the main party.

For the next hour, the line ground on deeper and deeper into the forest, led on by the echo of the occasional shot or a glimpse of gun smoke amongst the trees. Martin rode past a groaning soldier who sat propped up against a tree with a bloody rag tied around his arm. He had been made comfortable, with a canteen of water in his lap and his pack by his side. The next soldier he passed was less fortunate, motionless and face down in the leaf mould. The line of soldiers was badly broken now, as some men pressed forward, eager to find their tormentors, while others hung back.

'The 71st will halt!' he roared. 'Sergeants! Reorder the line!' While his troops were pushed back into well-aligned ranks, he turned towards the gendarme. 'How far do you suppose these bloody woods extend, lieutenant?'

'I am not sure, sir,' replied Deschamps. 'My men seldom visit them. Generally we only patrol the road. We do seem to find ourselves chasing shadows.'

'Shadows that fire back!' exclaimed the infantryman. 'I have had several men killed or wounded now, and still no sight of these Royalist rebels of yours.' Another shot rang out from ahead, as if to reinforce his point. One of his officers marched over and saluted.

'Line is correctly dressed now, sir,' he said.

'And how are the men taking all of this?' asked Martin. The young infantryman rubbed his chin before he replied.

'The older men are steady enough, but some of the new recruits are becoming nervous, sir. Might we try a volley? See if we can kill some of the bastards? If they could pass by some enemy bodies, I am sure that would help.'

'At what target?' replied Martin. 'Do you suppose these bandits wait after they have fired to admire their work or run like hares? Come on, let's get the line moving again. The enemy cannot run forever, and eventually these damned woods must come to an end.'

Captain Martin's prediction proved accurate. After a while, the trees did begin to thin and the land became more level. Green shoots of bracken and fern sprouted amongst the trunks, and the French soldiers found their advance easier. The odd patch of grey sky was visible through breaks in the canopy of trees. Now that they could see farther in front of them, the galling fire had petered out altogether. Martin called back his skirmishers, and the infantry line swept forward with renewed purpose. Ahead of them, he could see an end to the trees and what looked like a meadow in the middle of the forest. He leant down until his body lay on his horse's neck and peered in front. On the far side of the clearing, just where the wood began again, was a solid line of men in a wide variety of clothes. The only common feature he could see to connect them was that each man wore the same white cross belt and held a musket by his side. What little spring sunshine there was winked back at him from the line of bayonets fitted to every weapon.

'71st will halt!' he yelled, and his soldiers came to a stop, just inside the fringe of the wood. Martin urged his horse forward, until it stood close behind the line of his men, and pulled out his small spy glass. He ran it along the enemy troops opposite him. Smocks, civilian coats and a variety of hats passed through the circle of his view.

'They appear to be little more than a rabble,' he said, 'although there are a great deal more than thirty of them, Lieutenant Deschamps.' He paused to examine a large man opposite him in a bright blue coat.

'What on earth is that man wearing?' he asked, passing the little telescope across to the gendarme and pointing with a gloved hand.

'I should say it was a footman's uniform, sir,' he replied. 'And I think I can see a pair of scarlet tunics beyond him, farther back in the trees. Do you suppose the English are behind this rising?'

'More than likely,' said Martin. 'And much good it shall do them. These traitors will not detain us long. A couple of volleys and a push of steel will sort out the bastards.' He drew his sword out with a grating rasp, and Deschamps did the same. Then Martin stood tall in his stirrups, and raised his voice. '71st, twenty paces forward! Advance!' Like a smoothly-running machine, the line of French soldiers marched out into the open and came to a halt. There was a little shuffle as the dressing was corrected, and then the troops stood motionless. The two officers urged their horses forward.

'Strange,' said Martin, to himself. He had expected to see nervousness in the enemy ranks at the sight of his soldiers coming boldly on. Instead, the Royalist line continued to stand firm, almost as still as his own men. In his stomach he felt the first knot of anxiety begin to form.

'They do seem steady,' muttered Deschamps, echoing his thoughts. 'Should we not retreat and fetch the rest of your regiment?' Martin glanced across at the young gendarme, and noted the sweat beading on his forehead.

'I take it they are not the usual run of insubordinate peasants that you are familiar with, lieutenant, to be dragged off for a beating in the cells?' he asked. 'If they choose to remain in position they merely present us with the opportunity to kill them all the swifter.' The young gendarme said nothing, but glanced over his shoulder towards the tree line. Martin returned his attention to his men.

'Present arms!' he yelled. All along the line, muskets were swung up to shoulders, and their aim settled on the line opposite.

'Aim low lads,' supplemented the bass of a sergeant from away to Martin's left. There was a sharp cry on the far side of the clearing, and the shape of the enemy line seemed to slide and change before his eyes, as each man turned side on. A hedge of muskets now pointed back towards him. He noticed two of his soldiers exchanging puzzled glances.

'Eyes in front there', growled Corporal Mercier, leaning forwards to tap the two offenders on the shoulder.

'Open fire!' yelled Martin. Moments before his men fired

their volley, the far side of the clearing lit up with a ribbon of yellow flame, and an instant later the whole space filled with billowing gun smoke. 'Independent fire,' shouted Martin, and he heard his officers take up the call.

The meadow in the forest was transformed into an inferno of fire and noise. Muskets banged and crashed, their stabbing flames flashing in the smoke. Along the short portion of the line that he could see, a few of his soldiers were already down. He watched as a figure near him crawled away through the undergrowth, whimpering with pain.

'They fire tolerably, for brigands,' he said, forcing himself to be calm in front of the men. Deschamps said nothing, his eyes wide and staring. In front of them, a soldier held a trembling cartridge up to his mouth, bit the bullet off, but then poured much of the gunpowder past the muzzle of his musket and over his hand.

'Take your time, lad,' urged Corporal Mercier. 'Spit out that ball, and fetch a new cartridge.' Then the corporal's hat flew off and he fell straight backwards like a felled tree. Martin shook his attention away from the men in front of him and tried to concentrate on the battle. Flashes of orange flame rolled up and down the ranks of his men, the noise of the concussions deafening. My lads are firing well, he concluded. Then he turned his attention to the enemy line, eighty yards away in the smoke. Here, he could see short bars of massed flame in the gloom, crashing out towards him.

'Platoon firing,' he explained. He leant towards Deschamps, to be heard over the sound of the musket fire. 'They are not trained sufficiently for independent fire, but they show an impressive level of discipline, none the less.' When there was no reply, he looked round at the gendarme. His face was white and he was staring at the body of Corporal Mercier, which lay just in front of him. His horse pawed at the ground, nostrils flaring at the smell of blood.

'Sir, sir,' shouted a voice. The figure of a soldier bounded out of the smoke. 'The Royalists, sir! Hundreds of the bastards, on our right flank. Sarge has wheeled the end of the line back, but I am not sure it will answer!'

'More firing has started away on the left, sir!' bawled an officer.

'God damn and blast all this smoke,' exclaimed Martin, twisting one way and then the other in the saddle. 'Cease firing there! I can't see a bloody thing!'

In the quiet that followed, he heard the bark of orders from the smoke ahead, followed by the steady tramp of approaching feet. A soldier off to his left backed out of his place in the ranks, but was pushed forward again by one of the sergeants placed at intervals behind the line. While the NCO was distracted, another soldier took his opportunity to break and run. A lieutenant standing farther back drew out his pistol, swivelled around and paused, in the silhouette of a duellist. There was a gush of smoke, the crack of a shot, and the fleeing soldier tumbled forward. The officer thrust his pistol into his sash, and returned his attention to the battle. Then, from off to one side, more soldiers ran out of the smoke towards Martin.

'The enemy are coming!' gasped one of them, who had lost his musket. Faces in the line ahead of Martin looked back towards him.

'Steady there, lads!' he called out, his voice strained. He pointed with his sword, and the silver blade trembled a little. 'There is your enemy! Give him a volley, now!' Ahead of him a solid block of Royalists were appearing out of the thinning smoke. The 71st levelled their muskets, and all fired as one. Clouds of smoke filled the clearing once more, and there were screams and cries from ahead. And then the enemy fired a volley of their own.

Martin heard a double smack of impacting bullets, and his horse snorted with pain, staggered to one side, and collapsed, pinning him to the ground. His sword was thrown from his grasp as he crashed down, and he felt a shooting pain in his arm. More soldiers were fleeing past him now, throwing aside their muskets, and tearing at their packs. He looked up in despair at Lieutenant Deschamps.

'Help me then!' he yelled as he struggled to get free of his horse. The gendarme stared at him for a moment, his mouth working soundlessly, and then he pulled his mount around and galloped away into the trees. 'Deschamps! Come back!' Martin screamed.

In front of him, the solid line of his men was disintegrating like a dam breached by a river, as more and more soldiers turned and fled. There was still the occasional knot of resistance, where a few brave souls huddled around a bawling officer or sergeant, but most of the line had broken into a mass of fleeing figures as the exultant Royalists charged from out of the smoke. He tried again to heave himself free of the dead horse, but the enormous weight of the animal held his leg firm to the ground. A large figure loomed over him. It was the Royalist that he had seen earlier. He stood so close that Martin could see that his blue footman's coat was stained and filthy, the braid that covered the front, torn away in patches. But there was little wrong with the musket he held poised above his head like a spear, the long silver bayonet angled down towards the stricken officer. Captain Martin stared up into a face contorted with fury.

'For the King!' spat the man, and he brought his musket plunging down.

Chapter 6

Moselle

Out at sea the *Titan* was also drilling her crew for war. The frigate lay in the lee of the Glenan Isles, her main topsail backed and balancing with the canvas on her foremast. This held her across the wind, her rigging humming with tension, ready to get underway at a moment's notice. But for now she kept her position, rising and falling to the remains of the green Atlantic rollers, as they crashed and fretted their way through the mass of little islands. A welcome breeze blew in through her open gun ports and across her main deck, where her crew were going through the endless practice of gun drill. At a barked order, they hauled their big, stubborn eighteen-pounders out through her sides. The men were stripped to the waist, their knotted arms inked with tattoos. The thunderous rattle of gun carriage wheels on planking ended with a collective thump as the cannons came up against the ship's side.

On her quarterdeck, the same breeze snatched at the board that John Blake held on his knees. The young second lieutenant was seated on the slide of one of the carronades as he worked away at a sketch. He was so engrossed in his drawing, adding strokes of charcoal to the picture and then softening them with the pad of his finger, that he started when a loud sniff sounded, close to his ear. He looked around to find Richard Corbett peering over his shoulder.

'Your pardon, John,' he said. 'I trust I did not startle you?'

'You did a little, in truth, but no harm has been done to my composition.'

'It makes an agreeable subject, does it not?' said the surgeon. He waved towards the mass of islands. 'The tumult of the ocean as it beats upon the reefs, the barbarous cliffs beyond them and our longboat, sailing boldly in amongst those hazards. What do you suppose Mr Armstrong is doing out there?'

'He takes the opportunity to chart these islands a little better,' said the young lieutenant. 'The captain was vexed by the ease with which the *Moselle* avoided us, and Armstrong hopes we shall be better prepared, should she try such a base trick again.' The men watched the ship's longboat as she moved steadily forward. The blond haired Trevan was easy to pick out, standing in the bow with one foot on the gunwale, whirling the lead around in circles and then casting it out in front. The bulky figure of Armstrong had the tiller, while next to him was a hunched form, trying to control the sheaf of papers he was writing on. They flashed white as the wind grabbed at them, and an angry bellow from the American sailing master sounded across the water.

'Is that young Mr. Russell he has with him?' asked Corbett.

'Indeed so,' confirmed Blake. 'Armstrong despairs of the other midshipmen, but holds that Russell may yet make a tolerable navigator. Mind, if he allows a morning's worth of soundings to escape his grasp, he will earn himself a tryst with the Gunner's Daughter.'

'I am not sure I have the pleasure of following you?' queried the surgeon. 'Surely if Mr. Rudgewick has a daughter, she will not be on board?' Blake chuckled at this.

'Your pardon, Richard,' he said. 'I forget you missed the pleasures of serving as a boy. Kissing the Gunner's Daughter is when an errant youngster receives correction, by being placed across the breech of a gun and thrashed with the boatswain's cane.'

'Ah, another of those quaint seamen's terms, designed to confuse rather than illuminate,' said Corbett, with another sniff. 'I do wish you mariners would speak plain. Why, only this morning I had Ezekiel Davis present to me, telling me he was suffering from a malady he called "Scarlet Pox". He kept speaking of maggots in apples, and sundry similar nonsense. It took a deal of questioning to find that he meant simple Gaol Fever by it.'

'Good heavens!' exclaimed Blake. 'Is that not highly contagious?'

'It might be, if indeed, he was suffering from it,' said Corbett. 'Fortunately he has little fever, no skin blemishes nor any of the stupor or delirium associated with the condition. I took an ounce of his blood to calm him, and sent him back to work.'

'How curious,' mused the lieutenant. 'I would have thought Davis to be one of the steadier men. He is the last person to try his hand as a malingerer. Besides, if he wanted to be excused duty at his age, why not claim something more plausible, such as a bad back?'

'He gave his reasons plain enough,' said the surgeon. 'One of the people has convinced him that he will presently die of the condition. The poor fellow has been unable to eat a thing these past few days. I am most uncertain I was able to persuade him that he was well.'

'Do you know who it was that told him he was sick?'

'He would not say,' said Corbett.

'I think I might be able to name the man, nonetheless,' said Blake. 'I wonder if Mystical Jack has now taken to doctoring? I shall have to keep an eye on that one.'

'Deck there!' yelled the lookout. 'Sail ho!' Blake and Corbett looked around as Lieutenant Preston, who was officer of the watch, strode to the rail at the front of the quarterdeck.

'Where away?' he yelled towards the figure high on the fore royal yard.

'Off the stern quarter, sir,' came the reply. 'Could be that there *Moss Hell*, ag'in?'

'Mr. Butler,' called Preston to the midshipman of the watch. 'Give my compliments to the captain, and tell him a sail is in sight, due east of us.'

'Aye, aye, sir,' said the youngster, running for the companion ladder. Preston cupped his hands into a cone about his mouth, and yelled towards the forecastle.

'Mr. Hutchinson, kindly have the longboat recalled, if you please.' The boatswain waved his hat in acknowledgment and sounded the ship's bell in an urgent clamour. The officer of the watch turned his attention to the main deck beneath his feet. 'Mr. Taylor, sir, you might wish to curtail gun drill. A sail is in sight, which may be hostile.'

'Very well, Mr. Preston,' drifted up the disembodied voice of the first lieutenant. 'I shall secure the guns and come directly.'

'You pardon Richard, but I must go below and stow my sketch,' said Blake, as he hurried away. 'If there is to be some action, I would not want it to be trodden upon.'

'No indeed,' said Corbett, looking around him at the transformation that the hail from the masthead had caused. Out to sea, the longboat swooped back towards them, battering her way through the rollers and leaving a line of creamy wake behind her. Beneath his feet, he could hear the rumble of cannons being housed and the bang as port lids were slammed shut. The first of the gun crews ran up onto the gangways, pulling on their shirts as they came. Blake reached the ladderway to go below, and then stiffened to attention when the head of Clay appeared at this feet. It was soon joined by the rest of the captain, bounding up and striding across the deck towards the wheel.

'Where is this sail, Mr. Preston?' he demanded. He

snapped his fingers in the direction of Midshipman Butler, who stood near the wheel. The youngster hunted through the various items of equipment stowed around the binnacle, hoping for inspiration. Old Amos, the veteran quartermaster, took pity on him. He cleared his throat and then looked significantly at Clay's telescope. Butler retrieved it from its place, and held it out to his captain.

'Beating up from the east, sir,' replied the officer of the watch. 'The lookout believes it may be the *Moselle*. It's Pickford, who is normally to be relied on.'

'I do hope so,' said Clay, striding towards the stern of the frigate. 'Is Mr. Armstrong returned?'

'I recalled him as soon as the sighting was reported, sir. Mr. Hutchinson is preparing to sway the longboat on board now.'

'Very good,' said his captain, scanning the horizon. 'Now where is this damned corvette?'

Clay ignored the sound of shouted orders as the dripping boat was swung up from the sea beside the frigate and settled into place on the skid beams. Instead, he stared towards the east. The grey sky paled until it was almost white at the horizon. Almost, but not entirely. Clay's telescope paused, and then backtracked a little. Just proud of the green bar of sea, a tiny oblong stood out. He thought of the startling white canvas the *Moselle* had carried and snapped shut the telescope.

'Is that longboat secured yet, Mr. Hutchinson?' he yelled.

'Just lashing her into place now, sir,' came the boatswain's reply. 'A moment more, if you please.'

'Now Mr. Preston, the second we are able, I want the ship put about, and let us get the topgallants on her. I will not have that damned Frenchman making sport of me again.'

'Aye aye, sir, topgallants it is.' The officer hurried away, to be replaced by the large form of the sailing master, who mopped at his face with a handkerchief the size of a modest flag.

'Ah, Mr. Armstrong,' said Clay. 'Was your survey a success?'

'Tolerably so, sir,' replied the American. 'I have this side of the larger island marked down, together with some of the reefs and the inner passage, but I am most uncertain if Mr. Russell has wholly preserved the soundings we took. We shipped a deal of water on our return run.' As if to emphasize the point he pulled his sodden periwig from his bald head, and wrung it out like a mop. A stream of discoloured water cascaded into the scuppers.

'Most unfortunate,' said Clay, forcing his expression to grow solemn, so as not to laugh. 'But I believe we have the elusive *Moselle* to leeward of us, and on this occasion we are between her and the islands.' He handed the sailing master his telescope and pointed, just as Preston issued a volley of orders. The huge main topsail was slowly hauled around by the united weight of half the watch; its canvas flapped and volleyed in the wind and the frigate began to move through the water once more.

'Headsails!' roared Preston. 'Ready to go about!' The wheel went over, and the *Titan* swung ponderously around. Clay continued to point towards the distant speck of white, pivoting on the spot as the ship turned, until the bow faced towards the distant enemy.

'Sheet home there!' yelled Preston. 'Set topgallants, if you please, Mr. Hutchinson.' Boatswain's pipes squealed and twittered from beneath their feet.

'All hands! All hands to make sail!'

'Do you have her, Mr. Armstrong?' asked Clay. He moved away from the mizzen shrouds to allow the rush of top men to flow past him and bolt up the mast.

'I do, sir,' replied the American. 'Just now coming up over the horizon. If she holds to her course we shall close with her rapidly.'

'Pray God she does, Jacob,' said Clay. He looked aloft at the lines of top men doubled over the yards and pulling to release the topgallant sails. The wind tugged at them, making their clothes balloon about them.

As each successive square of canvas was set, the *Titan* seemed to bound forward. Soon she was outpacing the waves, rising to the crest of each, then seeming to hang for a moment before swooping down to crash into the next with a flurry of spray. Faster and faster the frigate went, and the little white square grew steadily into a column of marble.

*****

'No you don't, little barky!' exclaimed O'Malley, leaning against the forecastle rail as if to reach out and haul the *Moselle* closer. 'You're not after giving us the slip this time.' He was one of a row of forecastle hands, all lined up at the front of the *Titan*. Beneath them the sharp bow of the frigate sliced into another slope of green water, throwing sheets of foaming spray to either side and bathing the figurehead in dripping foam.

'You reckon we'll catch the bleeder, then?' asked Evans. 'She still seems a way off to me.'

'With our Pipe clapping on in such a fashion?' queried the Irishman. 'Why that Flighty Hollander himself wouldn't escape us.'

'It be called the Flying Dutchman, and you shouldn't go a-naming a ship of such ill omen, Sean O'Malley,' said Trevan from his other side. 'For them as has voyaged below the Cape, she ain't no cause for mirth.' A number of pigtailed heads nodded in agreement at this along the sweep of the rail.

'Deck ho!' yelled Pickford from the masthead above them. 'That chase be a changing her course!' The line of crewmen all stared up towards the little figure perched a hundred and fifty feet above them, and then, as one, looked back towards the French ship. The single mast with its spotless sails had now spread into three separate poles as the *Moselle* headed north.

'No doubt about it,' said Trevan. 'She be heading for the coast.'

'How far away does that bleeding lie?' asked Evans, but before anyone could answer, there was a roar from behind him.

'What's all this?' yelled Josh Black, the herculean captain of the foretop. 'Look at you, all in a row like tits on a sow! Man the headsail sheets there, you lubbers. Ain't it obvious we be about to change course?' No sooner had he finished speaking than a series of orders came from astern, and the *Titan* hauled herself around, until she was pointing ahead of the *Moselle*, on a course designed to intercept the Frenchman.

With the wind on her quarter, the frigate was broad reaching, which was her best point of sail. Instead of her sails masking one another, they barely overlapped, presenting a wall of canvas two hundred feet wide to the keen westerly wind. Her hull heeled over until a band of bright copper flashed in the waves to windward, while bottle green water rose up to her lee rail. This was exhilarating sailing for the men up on the forecastle, now all soaked to the skin as they clung to the weather rail. As their courses converged, the hull of the *Moselle* appeared beneath the columns of sail, heeling over, in her turn, as she, too, battled along. But ahead of them was a line of black, like the stroke of a pencil along the horizon. The coast of France was in sight.

Closer and closer the ships drew, with more detail becoming visible on the corvette all the time. The rich hues of her new tricolour snapped and streamed in the wind. The sunlight flashed on the *Moselle*'s copper, as gusts of wind pushed her far over. But detail of the coastline, too, were emerging from the haze as the ships flew towards it. The blank streak of land nuanced into cliffs and coves. It became lined in white, where surf, silent at this distance, beat on remote beaches and against rocky shores. A scatter of little islands appeared away to the west, and ahead a broad river estuary opened up. Fields of green and brown rolled away from the shore towards the skyline. On the west bank of the inlet, the men could now see the tongue of a breakwater, with the grey stone buildings of a little town tumbling down the slope behind it.

'A tanner says she be heading for that there port,' said Trevan. 'Why, it looks a little like St. Mawes, back home, only with a sight less fortifications.' The two ships had slowed now, as they left the open waters of the Atlantic and entered the more sheltered bay. The *Moselle* was almost straight ahead, sliding towards the little port and still comfortably beyond long gun shot.

'She'll get there fecking first, an' all,' said O'Malley. 'Mother of God, I truly thought we had her this time!'

'So we would have, if you hadn't gone rattling on about that ghost ship!' protested the Cornishman. 'Christ, I could have used some prize money to send home to my Molly.'

'Too bleeding right!' added Evans. 'My purse has been at low water ever since our last night in Plymouth.'

'It weren't Sean as jinxed the chase, Adam,' said one of the other forecastle hands. 'Earlier, that Jack Beaver was telling all as would listen how we was never going to catch her.'

'I am going to deck that fecker,' exclaimed O'Malley. He pointed to the French corvette, as she turned around the end of the breakwater and gathered in her sail. 'How are we to catch a prize at all, with that Jonas aboard? Don't you go saying as how it was anything I said, Adam Trevan. It was all that mystical fecker's doing!'

A cloud of smoke gushed from the cliff top above the little

port, and the water ahead of the *Titan* boiled, as a salvo of shot tore into the sea. The boom that echoed off the water was ominously low in pitch -- large calibre pieces were firing. The frigate came up into the wind, frustrated again, and began to beat her way out to sea. Meanwhile, back in the little fortified port, the last of the *Moselle*'s sails vanished as she swung at her moorings in the turning tide.

*****

A week later, the *Titan* lay just beyond the line of surf that beat against a lonely beach. Her launch had collected a pair of scarlet coated officers from the sand, who now sat at their ease in her great cabin. They were enjoying some of her captain's madeira at his cherry wood table. A large chart was spread before them, while around its edge sat a circle of officers.

'So you hold these Royalists are now capable of offering some resistance, Tom?' asked Clay.

'Aye, in the right circumstances, sir,' said Macpherson. 'It was a tolerably well-conceived ambush and the government soldiers were heavily outnumbered, but credit where it is due. I witnessed two companies of French line infantry sent tumbling by the dash of the count's men.'

'Do you concur with that view, Major Fraser?' asked the captain. 'You know these *Choannerie* best of all.'

'I do agree in part, sir,' said Fraser. 'There is no stimulant for a rising better than a victory. The men we have under arms are now quite persuaded that they can march on Paris, while D'Arzon has more recruits flooding in than we can comfortably train. But I would urge a little caution. We have defeated a detachment of a single regiment. I agree that it was well done, but we have inflicted but a minor wound. And our enemy is now forewarned. I very much doubt that he will place himself in such a false position again.'

'Does the count want for resources?' asked Taylor, who sat alongside his captain. 'What with all these new recruits presenting themselves?'

'A steady flow of arms and gold comes in from London, in the usual manner,' said Fraser. The others waited for the army officer to say more but, instead, he looked past them towards the bulkhead. After a pause, Clay cleared his throat.

'Perhaps it is best if such matters are not openly discussed,' he said. 'Can I enquire if the count and you have any further military endeavours in mind?'

'Several, but none that are ready to proceed at present,' said Fraser. 'Until more soldiers are properly trained, we must limit the scope of our ambitions.'

'Good, because, to that end, I believe I have a proposal for you,' said Clay. 'Would the count's forces be capable of attacking a small town, protected by two batteries that face the sea? Such an attack would be supported by this ship, together with Lieutenant Macpherson and his marines.'

'That might be done, if the defenders were not too numerous, sir,' said the army officer, stroking his sideburns. 'Which settlement did you have in mind?' Clay twisted the chart around until it was the right way up for his guest, and ran a finger along the coast.

'Do you see this broad inlet here, where the estuaries of these two rivers meet the sea, major? On the western side here is Port Manec'h, if that is the right way of saying it. There is a French national ship moored there, the *Moselle*, which I very much wish to bring out. Regrettably, she is quite safe from my attention, thanks to the two batteries sited up on the cliff behind the town. In the normal course of things I might have attempted something with my own marines, but towns tend to have garrisons of soldiers.' Fraser studied the map with care for a moment.

'I daresay, D'Arzon's men could capture this wee place of yours easily enough, sir,' he said. 'A thorough recognisance would need to be carried out, but I would not anticipate a settlement of that size having above a company of soldiers in it. Add to that the gunners in your batteries, some customs officials and a detachment of gendarmes. Let us say, four hundred adversaries at most. With surprise, and if the place is not fortified, it could be seized.' The naval officers sat back from the table and smiled at one another.

'That is splendid, major,' enthused Clay. 'And when might our Royalist friends be in a position to conduct such an attack?'

'Not presently,' said Fraser calmly.

'Not presently!' repeated Clay, flushing red. 'Whatever do you mean by that? You just said it could be done, by Jove!' Fraser held up a hand.

'Your pardon, sir, but let me explain. Taking this place is one matter, coming at it quite another.' He returned his attention to the chart. 'These broad estuaries of yours lie between D'Arzon's base in the Morbihan and this Port Manec'h. His men would need to go far inland to seek a bridge, and such a march in the open will attract the attention of the enemy. They would be brought to battle long before they arrived. And even if they could somehow slip past unobserved to descend on this place, what would happen after the attack? They would be trapped in the port with the sea at their back when the French sent in a relief force.'

'What if I can guarantee that your Royalists arrive at Port Manec'h unmolested, and then are returned from whence they came before any such relief force could arrive?' said Clay, his face impassive.

'That might answer, sir,' said the Scotsman, his face suspicious. 'How would such a thing be done?'

'Why, by sea, of course!' exclaimed Clay. 'I am forever amazed how the army fails to appreciate the true worth of our mastery of the ocean. We find a suitable beach in the

Moriban to bring them off, much as we collected you gentlemen this afternoon. Then we ship them in this vessel to Port Manec'h, and land them in secret, close by. Once the place is carried, and the *Moselle* captured, we take them off again and return them home.'

'Aye, 'tis a bold plan, but it might serve,' said Fraser. 'When would you want to make such a descent?' Clay looked across at Armstrong, who had his almanac to hand.

'I would recommend twelve days hence, sir,' reported the sailing master. 'That is when tide and moon will serve the best.'

'That should answer for D'Arzon to carry out any reconnaissance,' said Clay. 'Shall we proceed to the details? Mr. Armstrong, your hand is the clearest. Would you kindly take notes of the points as they are resolved? Now, how large a force of the count's soldiers will be required?'

*****

On the lower deck below the great cabin, the hands were eating their evening meal. Little of the spring sunshine from outside had permeated down through the gratings from the world above, but the space was lit with warm, yellow lamplight. The crew were in good spirits, and there was a lively buzz between the mess tables. The casks of salt beef, selected by the purser for tonight, chanced to be from a more recent batch of animals, with a good flavour. If this was not enough, the return of Lieutenant Macpherson, together with the mysterious one-eyed major, was considered by most a sure sign that an adventure was at hand.

'So how long you reckon they've been a rattling along, back in Pipe's quarters like?' asked Trevan, as he tapped a ship's biscuit on the top of the mess table. Weevils dropped past his fingers to writhe amongst the crumbs, and he idly crushed them with his palm.

'A couple of hours or more, to be sure,' said O'Malley, his mouth full of beef. 'It was afore the first dog watch when they went in. Harte was saying how they had charts spread everywhere, and pages of notes an' all sorts. The Yank was after writing it all down. He means business, that Pipe, you mark my fecking words!'

'Too bleeding right, Sean,' added Evans. 'He wants to lay hands on that there *Moss Hell*, like a miser coverts a guinea. I never saw a bloke so hot as when the bugger gave him the slip again. Hello, Able!' The coxswain came up to them, took his normal place at the mess table, and drew his square wooden platter towards him. He took a long draft on his beer and then turned to his friends.

'Sorry about that, lads,' he said, wiping his mouth on his sleeve. 'I've been helping Harte sort the Grunters out with their scoff.'

'They be finished with all of their plotting, have they?' asked Trevan.

'Aye, on to vittles and grog now,' confirmed Sedgwick. 'The way they was cracking on, they'll be pissed as bishops soon. It were all, "*Death to the French*" here, "*a glass of wine with you*" there.' Evans peered into his mug of small beer and sighed.

'All right for some,' he muttered. 'What they all so bleeding pleased about, then?'

'Some sort of plan to use these turncoats to come at that Frog ship,' said the coxswain. 'Not for a few days yet, from what Harte could gather.'

'I ain't sure about it,' said Evans. 'Us fighting alongside a bunch of Frogs? It don't seem natural, somehow, whether they be on our side or no.'

'That be your food over there, Ezekiel,' came the bass voice of Hibbert from the mess table behind them, loud and urgent. 'Over there, abaft the mast.' The friends looked around to find Davis, standing alone and uncertain. One of the sailors seated with Hibbert had moved a stool away so there was nowhere for the old seaman to sit.

'But, I don't understand, messmates?' queried the veteran sailor. 'I always eat here.'

'Aye, that were before,' continued Hibbert. 'We ain't robbed you any. You'll find full measure, only it be placed over there.' He pointed to an unoccupied table with a lone mug and a plate of food on it.

'Come on lads,' said O'Malley. 'Why you doing this to a fecking shipmate?'

'You stay out of this, Sean,' said another sailor, a former slave by the name of Perkins. 'I ain't catching the Scarlet Pox for no one.'

'But the sawbones says I ain't got no sickness!' exclaimed Davis.

'So why did he take a cup of your blood when you saw him last week, then?' asked Hibbert. 'Don't make no sense, less you be ailing, I am thinking. And you've been talking these last few days of not feeling right.' His messmates all nodded at this.

'But Mr. Corbett said that were only 'cause I been a-worrying upon it, like,' protested the older man.

'An' so is we a-worrying about it an' all, now. That Mystical Jack explained it to us. I am sorry for your sickness, mate, an' that's gospel. But there ain't no cause to go and spread it to your mates, now? Away with you!' Without waiting for an answer, Hibbert turned his substantial back on Davis, and resumed his meal.

'Mystical Jack, damn his eyes!' exclaimed O'Malley, his face colouring. 'The devil take the fecker! I ain't putting up with his hocus-pocus, no more.' He lay down his spoon with a bang. 'He's gone too far, pickin' on poor Davis an' all! He'll be eating his damn words when I'm finished with him.'

'Holdfast a moment, Sean,' said Sedgwick, but his comment was addressed to the Irishman's back as he strode across the lower deck.

'Right, you little fecker,' he spat, as he arrived at the end of Beaver's mess table. 'What's all this shite you've been after spreading about Davis?' The scrape of spoon on plate stopped and the buzz of conversation faded amongst the sailors grouped at this end of the deck. O'Malley became aware of other sounds as they emerged from beneath the usual roar of noise that accompanied meal times: the wash of the sea as it rushed past the hull, the gutter of the lamp that swung close to his head and the thump of footfalls on the deck above him. He could almost hear the working of Mystical Jack's jaw as he continued chewing until his mouth was quite empty. Only then did he turn his dark eyes on the Irishman. He raised a bony hand, and pushed a few strands of his thin hair back behind his ear.

'You know it be a terrible burden, O'Malley,' he said. 'This here Sight of mine. I don't ask it to show me stuff, but when the visions come, it don't seem right to hold them in my heart. I am sorry for poor Davis, truly I am, but there you have it.' He spread his hands wide. 'That man will sicken and die, and there ain't a thing you or I can do about it, other than warn them as might be brought low by the same pox as ails him.'

'Is that so,' said the Irishman. He gritted his teeth and started to push forward, but he felt himself constrained by a hand on his arm. From around him came the sound of mess stools and benches scraping on the planking.

'Leave it, Sean,' hissed Sedgwick. O'Malley turned to shake off his friend, and realised that all about them, sailors had now stood up from their places, and were scowling at him. One who had been seated on the far side of Beaver's table rolled up the sleeves of his shirt. Others were moving towards them from nearby tables.

'He's right, mate,' growled Evans, in his other ear. 'You knows I don't shrink from a mill, but this ain't a fight we can win.'

'There ain't no cause for any trouble, now, is there, Sean?' said Beaver. 'We all be shipmates here, after all.'

'No, no trouble, Jack,' agreed Sedgwick, as he turned the unresisting O'Malley away.

'Good, then perchance I can get back to my vittles?' asked Beaver. He picked up his spoon once more. 'This beef is proper good. Be a shame not to eat it while it be hot.'

When they got back to their mess table, Davis was still stood at a loss, his arms loose by his sides.

'Ignore them feckers,' urged O'Malley. 'You go and get your food, and come and join us, Ezekiel. We ain't troubled by none of that dross Beaver's been talking. You're not sickening any.' Trevan cleared his throat at this, but said nothing further.

'It be alright, Sean,' said Davis, glancing across at the Cornishman. 'Shan't be the first time I've eaten alone.' The veteran sailor crossed to the far end of the lower deck, took his place at the empty mess table and began to toy with his dinner.

Chapter 7

Night

After a warm spring day, with enough heat to hint of the summer to follow, it was evening on the Brittany Coast. The pearl water was cut by the wakes of returning fishing boats, their brick-red sails dark in the last light of the day. One by one, they turned around the end of the breakwater that protected the little harbour of Port Manec'h, and passed under the stern of the *Moselle* as they headed towards the shingle beach and home. The light faded from the sky and the tricolours that fluttered over the two batteries set high on the cliffs above the little town were hauled down, to the mournful beat of drums. Night stole across the land, its progress marked by the little yellow lights that appeared, clustered in the port or scattered along the coast wherever a croft or cottage was standing.

A few hours later, a keen observer out at sea might have noticed those lights first vanish and then reappear, as some large object passed between himself and the coast. If his attention had been piqued, and he looked more closely, he would have seen a faint line of silver on the dark water. It was the wake of a ship that carried no navigation lights as she stole along the coast and then turned in towards the land.

'We shall be off the beach presently, sir,' reported Armstrong, one of the shadowy figures grouped around the glow of the binnacle. 'Another cable's length and then we should round up into the wind.'

'Thank you,' replied Clay. 'Kindly have the top men lay aloft, Mr. Taylor, and prepare to anchor.'

'Aye aye, sir,' replied a different figure in the night, and a series of hoarse instructions were passed along the gangways. Clay felt, rather than saw, the men as they raced aloft, hearing the patter of their bare feet like rain upon the deck and feeling the thrum from the shrouds as they climbed the masts. The main deck seemed to stir like a field of wheat when a night breeze passes across it, as the packed mass of Royalist soldiers stood up and stared into the rigging. The inevitable murmur of conversation broke out before it was hushed by the officers and sergeants sprinkled amongst the men.

'Am I to understand we have arrived, Captain Clay?' asked a voice at his elbow. The perfume of expensive cologne told him who was speaking, even before his mind registered the heavy French accent.

'Yes count,' he replied. 'Do you observe the line of surf over there? It marks the start of a long tongue of sand that extends inland. Lieutenant Macpherson and his marines will go first and secure the beach. There is a fisherman's cottage that needs to be taken, to prevent any alarm being raised. Once he signals to us that he has it in his possession, we can start to land your men. From there it is but a short step along the cliffs.'

'Get the sail off her,' called the voice of Taylor. 'Anchor away!'

'Remarkable, is it not!' exclaimed the Frenchman. 'Even on my swiftest horse, I could hardly have completed such a journey by land in less than two days. Why, my men have not been more than eight hours in your boat.'

'The route is certainly more direct by *ship*,' corrected Clay. A figure in a cloak came over and saluted. 'Are you ready to leave us, Tom?'

'Aye, sir,' replied the Scot. 'I'll be on my way now.' Clay felt for the marine officer's hand and shook it. 'Good luck.'

'Thank you, sir. I shall signal in a wee while if all is quiet. If not, I daresay you will see the discharge of our muskets from here.'

'Go with God, Monsieur Macpherson,' said D'Arzon.

'We shall see you presently ashore,' added Fraser, from farther away in the night.

A bump sounded from over the side as the marines took their places in the frigate's boats.

'Mind yer fat arse,' complained someone, before being hissed into silence. A little later Clay heard Sedgwick as he ordered the bow oarsman to shove them off. He looked over the side, and saw two patches of greater darkness in the night, both heading for the shore. A little white appeared and vanished as the lines of oars swung and dipped in the starlight, and then they were gone. Clay looked towards the land, a few hundred yards away. The gleam of sand showed faintly, just where a notch in the cliffs led inland. Behind was sky, mainly cloud covered, but with stars that shone through the occasional gap. The minutes ticked by as he stared at the beach, one of a line of officers grouped along the rail.

'Come on,' urged the voice of Fraser. 'What can be keeping them?'

Then Clay saw it. A flash of light farther back that appeared and disappeared three times. An audible sigh sounded across the quarterdeck.

'Will you start to load the Royalist soldiers into the remaining cutter, please Mr. Taylor,' ordered Clay, 'The other two boats will be back presently.' Then he turned towards D'Arzon and Fraser. 'I imagine you gentlemen would wish to be in the lead boat.'

'Indeed we do, sir,' agreed Fraser.

'*Bon chance*, captain,' said the count. 'We shall rely on you to collect us from the quayside tomorrow.'

'I shall be there for certain, and here is my hand upon it,' said Clay. 'Besides, you forget that I have business of my own in that port. I shall wait for your signal, when it is safe for us to approach.' He felt D'Arzon's hand tremble with anticipation, even through his calf skin glove.

*****

It was the middle of the night now, and the frigate had covered the few miles back down the coast. She waited in the estuary mouth, her backed topsails silvery squares in the night. A sliver of moon like the pairing of a nail hung in the sky. The tide was rising, pulling them gently towards the land. The night seemed dark and calm, with only a few points of light to show where Port Manec'h lay.

'Can it be so very far from that beach to here, sir?' muttered Taylor beside him. 'Why, it is barely two miles. Unless they are quite indifferent at marching, they must surely have arrived by now?'

Clay had just completed much the same calculation in his mind, but he answered with practiced calm. 'I dare say, marshalling their troops in the dark will have taken some time, and the lane that runs from the beach to the cliff top may be circuitous. I am sure they will attack presently.'

'If it is not soon, we may need to beat back out to sea, sir,' said Armstrong, from beside the wheel. 'This tide will bring us within range of those batteries soon.' Clay focussed his night glass on the port, yet again. He found the glimmer of surf where the harbour's breakwater lay and traced his way up through the sleeping town to the first battery, a block of darkness against the night sky. Still nothing, he thought, and then he stiffened. A tiny flash of orange came and went so quickly that he wondered if he had seen it at all. The faint report of a shot sounded, and he looked around at Taylor.

'Musket, sir,' confirmed the first lieutenant. 'Perhaps it is a sentry, availing himself of the swiftest means to raise the alarm.'

'Or a Royalist with his gun at full cock, stumbling in the dark, sir,' added Armstrong. Clay returned his attention to the shore. A last moment of inaction, and then the cliff top erupted with a mass of twinkling lights, grouped all around both batteries. Lines of fire lit up the night as attackers and defenders exchanged volleys, and the steady pop and bang of musket fire sounded clear across the water. From down in the port, a bell clanged in alarm and more lights appeared on the hillside. Clay refocused his telescope on the fighting. The two lines of fire seemed to merge on the first battery, and several much larger tongues of flame stabbed out, followed by the boom of heavy artillery. Clay tried to envisage what was happening high above him: waves of attackers swarming up the parapet and the defenders desperately beating them back, guns on full depression, firing blind to sweep the ground before them. The firing died away, around both batteries, almost as quickly as it had begun, while the bell continued to toll, down by the port.

'What do you suppose has happened, sir?' asked Taylor. 'Are the batteries taken, or have our allies suffered a bloody repulse?'

'God knows,' said Clay, searching the cliff top.

'The tide is still making, sir,' warned the sailing master. 'I need to know if I am to con her towards the harbour or beat back out to sea.'

'A moment longer, I pray,' said the captain. They were deep in the throat of the estuary now. On either side, dark headlands loomed up above the ship. Port Manec'h was ablaze with light, while overlaying it was the web of the *Moselle*'s masts and rigging. Suddenly a twisting strand of gold rose up from the top of the cliff and burst in fiery vermillion.

'A red Bengal!' exclaimed Taylor. 'That was the signal if

they held both batteries, was it not sir?'

'That's correct,' said Clay. 'You may take us in now, Mr. Armstrong.'

'Aye aye, sir,' replied the American, his relief evident. Clay strode to the front of the quarterdeck, and looked down onto the main deck beneath him. Battle lanterns lit the twin rows of cannon, each with their gun crews seated around them, waiting. A ripple of faces looked towards him as he appeared, and men rose to their feet, nudging their companions awake as they did so.

'Mr. Blake!' he called.

'Sir?' replied the lieutenant. He appeared from under the quarterdeck, and looked back towards him.

'Have the larboard side guns run out, if you please.'

*****

'Up ports, larboard side!' yelled Blake from his place by the mainmast. He looked along the line of big cannon, as the lids swung open, and a chain of black squares appeared in the side of the ship. But not a complete chain, he thought. 'Number three gun! Why is your port still closed? I want the name of the person who is not attending to their duty, Mr. Jamieson.' The last port lid hastily banged open.

'Run out, larboard side!' ordered Blake, and with a squeal of gun trucks on oak, the battery was hauled across the deck until the gun carriages thumped into place against the side. Beneath his feet he sensed the slight shift in the angle of the deck with the transfer of weight. He turned to face the petty officer in charge of the first division of guns.

'It were Davis what was tardy in opening the port lid, sir,' Jamieson reported. 'He says he ain't feeling too good at present.'

'Truly? Unwell, just as we are about to go into action?' queried the officer. 'How convenient! What, pray, is wrong with him?'

'Don't know, sir, but he ain't generally shy. Shall I send him down to see the surgeon?'

'No, not now,' said Blake. 'Mr. Corbett will have enough to deal with presently, as shall we. Besides, I believe I may know the cause of his malady.'

'Aye aye, sir,' said Jamieson. The petty officer returned to his guns while Blake stared towards the stern of the battery, contemplating the place where Beaver stood, holding the fall tackle of the last of the cannon.

O'Malley, whose gun was closest to the officer, had been crouched down behind the breech during the conversation. Like the others, he was stripped to the waist, in spite of the cool of the spring evening, with his ears protected by his neck cloth bandana. He had pulled it from over one ear so as to be able to listen clearly. Now he beckoned his crew nearer.

'Fecking hear that?' he hissed. The others all removed their own bandanas.

'Say what?' said Evans loudly.

'Davis has been taken poorly, but the Grunters are on to who's behind it. That mystical fecker's going to catch it soon, mark my words.'

'Sure he will, Sean,' said Trevan, exchanging glances with the others. 'But ain't we after bigger fish this night? Can you see that Frog ship yet, Sam?'

'Nah,' said Evans, as he thrust his head out of the gun port. 'Still black as a Newgate privy, bar a little moonlight on the water.'

'That'll change, with this tide a running,' offered Trevan. He pointed towards the foremast, which was swinging across the stars. 'She'll hove into view presently.' The Londoner's bare feet scrunched on the sand scattered across the planking as he shifted position, while the frigate continued to turn across the tide. The wide estuary passed before his eyes, and the entrance to the little port appeared in the square.

'Ah, here we go lads,' he announced. 'I can see the port, plain as plain. Why, every house in the place must be lit up. There's a proper mill going on near the top of the hill, with muskets firing and all sorts going off.'

'Never mind what them Frog turncoats is about,' complained O'Malley. 'What of the fecking *Moss Hell*?'

'She's there, right enough, and coming out, I reckon,' said Evans. 'No end of her jacks scarpering aloft. Funny how plain they are to see. It were proper dark earlier.' When there was no response, he stood back upright and looked at his fellow gun crew. All of them were staring at the shore, their faces lit by yellow light. He turned to follow their gaze.

The frigate was close in now, with the steeply sloped village of Port Manec'h before them, rising up from the little port towards the cliff-top batteries. A prickle of musket fire, now close to the centre of the settlement, marked the Royalists' progress. Above them the hillside looked like a volcano, with ribbons of fire advancing down the slope.

'Christ, that's burning thatch!' exclaimed O'Malley. 'The feckers must be torching the place as they come on.'

'What kind of devils be we in league with?' asked Trevan.

'Stand by your guns, larboard side!' roared Blake, and the crew all crouched down next to their cannon.

'This new-fangled lock better fecking work tonight,' muttered O'Malley, as he wrapped the lanyard that fired the gun around his fist. Then he held up his other hand to show that the gun was ready. All along the side of the ship, similar arms were raised. The frigate sailed on towards the burning port.

*****

'The *Moselle* is coming out, sir,' reported Taylor, pointing towards the French corvette. Her topsails had been sheeted home now, squares of bulging canvas, half in shadow and half lit by fire. Over the bang of muskets from the heart of the town came the steady beat of a drum as the enemy manned her guns and prepared for battle.

'That's sporting of her,' said Clay, 'coming out to face us. Foolish too, mind.'

'I fancy she doesn't care to be caught in that harbour like a rat in its hole when the terrier is at hand,' said Armstrong.

'Doesn't that make us a dog?' queried Lieutenant Preston. 'Or a rat-catcher, perhaps? I had never thought of a king's ship in such low terms.'

'A rat hole that is ablaze, moreover,' said Clay. 'Why do those damned Royalists feel obliged to set fire to the place, for God sake?' He shook his head for a moment and then turned towards Taylor. 'I imagine she will try and slip by us towards the open sea. Heave to, over there, if you please, blocking any such passage.'

The frigate moved smoothly across the estuary towards Port Manec'h. Columns of little sparks could be seen, spiralling up into the air above the blazing town. The hull of the French corvette was masked behind the stone breakwater, but her masts and sails were visible as the ship slid towards open water. The *Titan* came to a halt, just outside the harbour entrance and waited for her opponent. Waves slapped against the big frigate's hull, counterpointing the bang and crackle of flames. The masts of the *Moselle* came ever closer, each spar and rope backlit by fire. Her bowsprit cleared the breakwater, and Clay saw her figurehead for the first time, in the flickering light. It was a young woman painted in white, who held out a bright sickle with one extended arm. Then the hull slid into view, a chequered line of open gun ports, each one a square, lit orange by lamplight from within. She was close enough for him to see the black mouth of every cannon, all trained on the *Titan*.

'Open fire when her stern is visible, Mr. Blake,' ordered Clay.

'Aye aye, sir,' came the echo of a reply from the deck beneath him.

'Be ready to get the ship underway the moment we fire, Mr. Taylor. I want to stay between her and the open sea.'

'Aye aye, sir,' replied the first lieutenant. The hull of the French ship sailed on, as gun after gun appeared.

'Five, six, seven,' counted Preston by the rail. A large boom sounded from the top of the headland, causing him to stop his count. 'What was that?'

'Lieutenant Macpherson destroying the first of the guns up in the batteries, I hope,' said Clay. 'There is the tenth of their broadside, and here comes the stern.'

'Open fire, larboard side,' yelled Blake, just as the *Moselle* fired, too. The entrancing scene of beauty with two ships lit by firelight on the water, all gold and black, vanished in smoke and thunder. The *Titan* rolled away from her opponent as all of her cannon thundered back inboard together, to fetch up against their breechings. From below Clay's feet came the crash of at least one French ball striking home.

'Head sheets!' yelled Taylor towards the forecastle. 'Man the braces!' and then more softly to the helmsman. 'Put her before the wind.' Within a few moments, the frigate transformed from an inert floating battery to a live ship, once more. Over the sound of the gun crews reloading came the whisper of wind through the rigging and the gurgle of a bow wave forming. The *Moselle*'s momentum had taken her ahead of the *Titan*, but having chased her twice in the last few months, Clay knew he had the swifter ship. There would be no escape for the little corvette this time, he resolved. The *Titan* emerged from the bank of smoke her broadside had created and into clear air again. The French ship was ahead of them, perhaps two cable lengths off the port bow, on the same course but safe from the main gun batteries, ranged along the sides of the frigate. She was heading straight across the estuary, towards the headland on the other side. At first, the wakes of both ships were molten gold in the light of the burning town, but this gradually faded as they left Port Manec'h behind.

'Be ready for when she turns for the open sea,' ordered Clay. 'Head her off, so she is caught between our guns and the shore ahead.'

'Aye aye, sir,' replied Taylor.

'That'll learn them feckers,' agreed O'Leary, shamelessly listening to his betters from his place beside one of the quarterdeck carronades. His captain and first lieutenant both looked around at him. 'Beggin' yer honours' pardon, sir,' he added a little sheepishly.

'Deck ho!' yelled the lookout. 'The *Moss Hell* be a changing course!' Both officers returned their attention to the battle, much to the Irishman's relief.

'Ready about, Mr. Taylor,' said Clay. He focused his night glass on the Frenchman's sails, waiting for the moment that she began to turn. 'Upon my soul! What are they about now?'

'What is it, sir?' asked the first lieutenant. 'Do I make the turn?'

'She is turning the other damned way!' exclaimed Clay. 'Heading into the estuary! What can she be about this time?'

'Surely we have her trapped then, sir,' said Armstrong as they watched the *Moselle* complete her manoeuvre until she was side on to the onrushing frigate. She erupted in a mass of flame and smoke as she fired off a defiant broadside. Columns of water sprung up around them and a shot rushed over their heads with a sound like ripping canvas.

'Unless she has some plan to escape us once more,' said Clay. 'By Jove, their captain has already shown himself to be very cunning, and he knows these waters much better than we do. Follow her around, if you please.'

'Aye aye, sir,' replied Taylor.

'Man the starboard guns, Mr. Blake, and give her a

broadside as we turn.' There was a rush of feet as some of the portside crews crossed the deck to help man the other battery of cannons. Fire rippled down the side of the ship from bow to stern as each gun bore in succession. Before the smoke of the quarterdeck carronades obscured his view, Clay saw tall splashes rising up, silver in the night, all around the French corvette, and then she was, once more, too far forward for the main guns to bear, as she made off up the eastern arm of the estuary.

'Her manoeuvre has gained a good two cables distance, sir,' estimated Armstrong.

'She does not escape me again, damn her eyes!' declared Clay. He rounded on his officers. 'Mr. Taylor, I will have the topgallants on her, if you please. Mr. Preston, away to the forecastle, and get the bow chasers in action. Throw some shot in amongst her rigging.'

'Aye aye, sir,' replied both officers together, before turning away in separate directions. Preston ran for the gangway, while Taylor reached for the speaking trumpet.

'Now, Mr. Armstrong, what do you know of this estuary we are entering?' asked Clay.

'It is that of the River Belon, and runs a good few miles inland, due east from here, sir,' replied the American. 'Vexingly, there is little more than that set down in the sailing instructions. The chart shows it to be an empty stretch of water, touching no settlements of any note.'

'Then I suggest we follow close upon the heels of the *Moselle* and assume that where she can float, so can we.'

'Aye aye, sir,' replied the American. He eyed the dark banks of the estuary as they closed in on either side, filling the air with the smell of wet mud and kelp. The two bow chaser cannons crashed out from the front of the ship, lighting up the night with tongues of flame as they fired towards the silver glimmer of sail a few hundred yards ahead of the *Titan*. The last glow on the water from Port Manec'h disappeared behind them as the ships worked their way inland.

'I believe I shall go and see how Mr. Preston is faring,' said Clay.

*****

'I am quite certain we are hitting her, sir,' reported Preston as Clay joined him on the windward side of the bow chasers. From there, they had an uninterrupted view of the ghostly ship just ahead of them. He handed his night glass across to his captain. 'If you direct your gaze towards her mizzen topsail, you will see it has several holes in it now.'

'It does indeed, Mr. Preston, but this water is flat and still. I would be amazed if nine pounder chase guns missed one shot in ten at this range, even in the dark. Holes in canvas will not serve – I need that damned ship halted!'

'Aye aye, sir,' replied Preston. 'I am confident that we shall be wounding her rigging something cruel.' Clay snorted at this and turned towards the gun crews.

'Come now, my lads,' he urged. 'Can you bear to see our prize slip from our grasp once more? I'll pay a guinea per man for the crew that first brings down a mast.' The men at the cannons growled in appreciation at this, but Clay could see they were already working as swiftly as they were able.

'Stand clear!' yelled the captain of the nearest piece. In the confined waters of the estuary there was no up-roll to wait for, and he jerked back on the lanyard. The flint snapped down, there was a crimson sparkle in the dark and a moment later the gun fired. The *Titan*'s figurehead briefly flashed into Clay's vision, before all was dark once more.

'No splash, Richards,' said Preston from his place by the rail. 'Another hit, then.'

'Any damage?' demanded Clay, but Preston's reply was drowned by the second bow chaser as it roared out. A feather of silver lifted up to one side of the *Moselle*'s stern.

'Shoot straight, damn your eyes!' roared Clay.

'Aye aye, sir,' muttered the other gun captain. A new figure appeared in the dark beside Clay, and touched his hat.

'What is it, Mr. Butler?' asked the captain.

'Mr. Armstrong's compliments, sir, and he says he is most uncertain as to the depth of the water. He submits we should reduce sail, and set a hand to work with the lead.'

'Yes to the leadsman, but I will be damned if we will reduce sail.'

'Aye aye, sir,' replied the midshipman, and then vanished back into the dark. Clay paced back and forth behind the two guns while the crews reloaded. Then he joined Preston as they were run up again. The first bow chaser roared out, and he stared towards the corvette's sails, willing the shape to change.

'Another hit, sir, but nothing vital,' reported Preston, with the night glass to his eye. There was a splash in the water just off the bow, and for a moment Clay thought the ship had been fired on.

'By the mark, four!' yelled out the leadsman from his position on the fore chains just behind them. He hauled up the dripping line, ready to make the next cast. Clay and Preston exchanged a look of surprise.

'That is damned shallow,' muttered Clay.

'If I was able to walk on the seabed, I could pass beneath the keel, but I fancy you would strike your head, sir,' observed the lieutenant.

'Eloquently put, Mr. Preston,' replied Clay. He turned back towards the quarterdeck and yelled into the dark. 'Have the topgallants taken off her, Mr. Taylor, if you please.'

'Aye aye, sir,' came drifting back. Shortly after, there was a squeal of boatswains' pipes as the top men were summoned.

'And a half, four!' offered the leadsman.

'Barely enough water to float the barky, lads,' said Clay, clapping his hands together. 'I need that Frenchman halted directly.' The second bow chaser roared out once more, and Clay leant forward on the rail staring into the night.

'It has struck home,' said the lieutenant, peering through the night glass. 'Now, is she starting to turn?' Clay watched as the silver column of sail seemed to spread into two, like the fanning out of a hand of playing cards. For a moment the second set of sails hung behind the first. A crackle of breaking shrouds sounded, and the *Moselle*'s main mast toppled down into the water beside her.

'By God, that's better!' exclaimed Clay, as he pounded the back of the gun captain. 'See you and your crew apply to my clerk for your reward, Rogers.' Both gun crews were cheering and banging fists together, and the sound spread down onto the main deck.

'By the mark, five!' added the leadsman in the chains.

'We even have a little more water, sir,' said the lieutenant, his smile a glimmer in the night. Clay thumped his arm.

'Well done, Mr. Preston! Secure the chasers, and join me on the quarterdeck when that is done.

*****

Down on the main deck, Sean O'Malley rubbed his hands together with glee, his face ghoulish in the light of the battle lantern that swung under the break of the quarterdeck.

'Take yer places, ladies,' he ordered. 'The fecking dance is about to commence.' The grinning crew all crouched down around the squat bulk of the cannon, and looked out through the open square of their gun port. A black shore with dark, rippling water drifted by. From somewhere close at hand came the thud of axes and the sound of shouted orders.

'That's Frog they be a talkin' in,' said Trevan from his place beside the gun. 'No idea what they're after saying, mind.'

'What you reckon the Frog is for '*we're up to our arses in a world of shit*?' asked Evans, to general laughter.

'Silence there!' ordered Blake. 'Stand by, larboard side!'

'And a half, four!' yelled the leadsman.

'Close enough, Mr. Taylor,' came the sound of Clay's voice. 'Back topsails, if you please. Mr. Blake you may open fire as your guns bear.'

'Aye aye, sir,' replied the lieutenant, seemingly from just behind O'Malley. The Irishman checked that all was as it should be and raised his left arm once more.

The deck beneath their feet heeled a little and then began to turn. The backed topsails volleyed and flapped for a moment before settling back against the masts, and the black square of the gun port filled first with the elaborate stern of the *Moselle* and then with the line of her hull. She was a bare hundred yards away, rocking gently in the breeze. The sails on her foremast were still swollen with the wind, but behind, all was devastation. The stump of her main mast rose a few feet proud of the rail before it ended in a crown of splintered wood, splayed like an old paintbrush. A mound of broken spars and torn rope trailed over her side, and her mizzen topmast had been dragged down in ruins. In the soft light, her deck teemed like a disturbed ants' nest; axe blades and knives flashed silver as her crew struggled to cut their ship free of the wreckage.

'Too late for all of that, messieurs,' gloated Evans. He dipped the sponge end of his rammer into the bucket of water beside him.

'Open fire, larboards, and keep at it,' yelled Blake.

'Stand clear!' warned O'Malley. He glanced down the barrel and then jerked the lanyard. The lock snapped down amid a gush of smoke, and a heartbeat later, the gun shot back inboard. The moment the carriage stopped, the Londoner was thrusting the dripping sponge down the barrel.

'Clean!' he yelled, as he pulled it free. Trevan took the serge bag of powder from out of its leather case, and thrust it into the barrel, his arm vanishing into the wide mouth. He then tossed the empty container to the eleven year old boy standing behind him, who caught it in his skinny white arms.

'Fetch us another, nipper,' yelled the Cornishman, and the powder monkey dashed off towards the ladderway. Ball followed charge and wad followed ball, each stage driven home by Evans, using the dry end of his rammer.

'Loaded!' yelled the Londoner, and the crew threw their weight against the gun tackles. With a rumble, the eighteen pounder shot back out again, and O'Malley leant forward to prime the vent.

'Stand clear!' he yelled, glanced down the barrel and jerked the lanyard once more.

*****

Clay stood by the quarterdeck rail and watched the remorseless destruction of the dismasted French ship. Beneath him, bursts of orange fire erupted up and down the side of the *Titan*, each blast illuminating their stricken opponent. Through the smoke, he could see the impact of the heavy balls. A spray of splinters flew up from the *Moselle*'s side, caught in an instant of light before darkness returned. A line of figures tumbled down like corn before a scythe as a shot from the carronade beside him found the crowd of sailors that worked to clear away the downed mast. The corvette would always have struggled in the unequal fight against a frigate more than twice her size. Now that half of her guns were masked by wreckage, she was doomed. For weeks Clay had longed for this moment, ever since the corvette's blue and gold stern had vanished into the twilight amongst the reefs and rocks of the Glenan Isles. But now victory was at hand, he found himself saddened by the scene before him. The beautiful pyramids of snow-white sails that she had spread aloft now lay in a dripping fan around the little ship. Two of her small cannons stabbed out with defiant flames of their own, and he heard a crash from somewhere beneath his feet.

'She will not long endure this, sir,' exulted his first lieutenant. 'The hands are firing as briskly as ever. Has she struck her colours yet?'

'She has not, Mr. Taylor,' said Clay quietly. 'I do hope her captain will feel obliged to do so soon, if only to spare his people from this unequal contest.'

'The carpenter says her shot are barely penetrating our sides, even at this range, while she starts to resemble a German flute,' continued Taylor.

'They have hulls like egg shells, those twenty gun corvettes,' added Preston. 'Good for raids on our commerce, but not built to toe the scratch in a proper fight.'

'Come on, strike, damn you,' muttered Clay, as the remorseless pounding went on. Smoke wreathed the two ships, lit from within by cones of orange fire. It clung to the chill water and obscured the hull and lower masts of the *Moselle*. Only a desultory fire was being returned from the French ship, the occasional flash in the gloom, and then that, too, stopped. A few moments later, the clang of her ship's bell sounded, peeling continuously.

'Cease firing, if you please, Mr. Taylor,' said Clay. 'And get the longboat in the water on our disengaged side.'

'Aye aye, sir,' replied the first lieutenant. He pulled out the whistle that hung around his neck and it flashed in the moonlight as he brought it to his lips to blow a shrill blast.

'Cease fire!' bellowed Blake from the main deck. There was a last blast of orange light from the forecastle carronade, and the frigate became quiet. The *Moselle*'s bell stopped too. All that could be heard was the lap of the few small waves that had penetrated this far up the estuary and the low moan of the Frenchman's many wounded.

'Has she struck?' asked Clay. Preston and Taylor looked towards the enemy ship, the first lieutenant even waving his hand in front of him, as if this might thin the gun smoke. Slowly the image of the corvette appeared as the wind bore away the grey fog. She was low in the water, her sides pockmarked with jagged holes. A section of her rail was missing, the broken wood white against the black of the night. From the remains of her mizzen mast no flag flew.

'Aye, she has, sir,' said Taylor. The other officers just looked at the devastated little ship.

'To work, gentlemen, before the tide should turn and leave us upon a mud bank beside our prize,' said Clay. 'Mr. Preston, take possession of the *Moselle*, if you please. I shall send across the carpenter and Mr. Hutchinson to assist you with repairs presently. We had better take you in tow for now, until you are able to set up some manner of jury mast.'

'Aye aye, sir,' replied the young lieutenant, touching his hat.

'Oh, and pass the word for Mr. Corbett. He had best accompany you. I doubt if he has many wounded amongst our people, while the French surgeon will be sadly burdened.'

*****

It was only when the pale light of dawn spread from the east that the *Titan* returned to Port Manec'h, pulling her battered prize along in her wake. Mist lay close to the pale sea, blending with a few trails of wood smoke as they approached the harbour. Thin twists spiralled up from the blackened shells of the village's houses. The quayside was packed with tired but jubilant *Choannerie* who rose to their feet to cheer the approaching frigate. Assorted hats were raised up on the ends of muskets, and waved like banners, while off to one side stood Macpherson at the head of a solid block of scarlet. Clay smiled at the sight of the Scotsman, imagining the look of distain on his face at the ill-disciplined antics of his allies. His smile vanished when he saw the port's residents. They dotted the hillside like crows, picking their way through what remained of their dwellings, or stood in forlorn groups and stared at the approaching ships. The frigate picked up the mooring once occupied by the *Moselle*, and then launched all her boats to bring off the soldiers.

'Welcome aboard, count,' said Clay as the young Frenchman came through the entry port, followed by Major Fraser and several Royalist officers. The normally immaculate D'Arzon was pale with weariness and his face was streaked with soot, but his wide smile had lost none of its charm. He ignored the captain's extended hand, and instead enfolded him in a bear hug. For a moment Clay thought he was about to be kissed on both cheeks, in front of his grinning crew, but the difference in the two men's height came to his rescue, and he managed to wriggle free.

'What a triumph, *mon ami!*' the count declared, indicating the smoking ruins with a sweep of his arm. 'We captured both of your batteries, as you can see, and then took the town with fire and sword! Your Monsieur Macpherson has destroyed all of the guns, as you wanted, and I see you have your prize. Magnificent, is it not?'

'Most satisfactory,' said Clay. 'But perhaps I might suggest we depart as quickly as convenient? Doubtless, word will have reached the authorities of the events of last night. It would be best if we were out at sea when they arrive.'

'Very prudent, Captain Clay,' said D'Arzon, tapping him on the chest. He turned to one of his subordinates and gave him some instructions in French.

'If you can, order your men to come on board the *Titan* once more,' said Clay, 'together with any wounded. I thought that it would be best if your prisoners join the French sailors we captured in the *Moselle.* I can then send them all back to England with that ship.'

'No need to concern yourself with prisoners, captain, for we took none,' smiled D'Arzon. 'Once my men are all on board, would it be possible to impose on you for some breakfast? I confess I am quite famished, after such a very busy night.'

Chapter 8

Morning

The great cabin of the *Titan* was full of noise and bustle later that morning. The eighteen pounders, which were normally concealed beneath draped covers, had been run out to create more space. All the furniture that was not required had been moved into the captain's sleeping quarters. Clay's dining table had been extended to its maximum and his desk had been swept clear and then connected to one end. Extra chairs had been brought up from the wardroom to accommodate the many officers who had been invited to breakfast. A mixture of Royal Navy and *Choannerie* lined both sides of the table, all of whom were busy discussing the night's events in a combination of French, English and guttural Breton. Clay sat at the head of the table, and contemplated the best his private pantry had to offer, as it was spread before them. His cabin stores had been running low before today, and from the enthusiasm with which his hungry guests were working their way through the food, would soon be gone completely. D'Arzon, who was seated on his right hand, was consuming the last of his host's smoked herring, while Fraser sat opposite him, enjoying the final few slices of a Wiltshire ham. The count leant towards his host, and pointed a fork laden with fish towards the gilt-framed portrait on the bulkhead.

'Tell me, captain, who is that magnificent lady?' he asked.

'That is the women I have the honour to call my wife, sir.'

'Indeed? It is a remarkably fine piece of work,' said the count. 'The painter was French, of course?'

'By no means,' replied Clay, the slightest twinkle apparent, deep within his grey eyes. 'Would you care to be presented to him?'

'Is it possible that he is here?' exclaimed the Frenchman.

'Count Louis D'Arzon, allow me to name the second lieutenant of the *Titan*, John Blake.' The young artist flushed red beneath his sandy hair, and lowered his eyes to the table.

'I had no idea that such talent existed within your service,' replied D'Arzon. 'Naturally one has heard of your naval explorers, Cook, Byron, Wallis, Vancouver and so forth, but not of any committed to the higher arts.'

'Most naval officers are of the regular sort, for sure, but there are a few more talented coves amongst our ranks,' said Clay. 'Lieutenant Preston, over there, for example, once served with an officer who had presented papers to the Royal Society. He was an authority on all manner of sea creatures; upon which subject, how do you find your herring, sir?'

'Delicious, thank you,' said D'Arzon. He rang his knife against one of Clay's best glasses and the table fell silent. 'Can I ask you all to drink to the health of the captain, with our thanks for his splendid hospitality?' The toast was noisily consumed in a variety of beverages -- small beer and coffee amongst the *Titans*, their host's finest claret for the Bretons. The count held his empty glass out towards the steward to be refilled and then turned back towards Clay.

'When I saw your ship vanish into the night yesterday, I did wonder if you had forgotten your promise to recover my men, captain,' he said.

'I am sorry to have alarmed you,' said Clay. 'But we had to follow where the *Moselle* led, and she seemed determined to lose us in the shallows of the estuary. Fortunately we caught her before her project could succeed. It was a pity, for it meant I was not able to witness more than the commencement of your assault.'

'We captured the two batteries with reasonable ease,' explained D'Arzon. 'It was clear they had given little thought to an approach from the landward side. Were it not for an alert sentry, we might have taken them quite unawares. I left them in the hands of your Lieutenant Macpherson, to destroy the guns and so forth, while my men proceeded into the town.'

'I see,' said Clay. He raised his voice to attract the marine officer's attention. 'Did you succeed in rendering the guns unserviceable, Tom?'

'Aye, my men struck a trunnion off from each,' explained the Scot. 'The French will be obliged to bring up fresh cannon before they can hope to protect this part of the coast again.'

'I am not sure that I follow you, Mr. Macpherson,' said the surgeon, from farther down the table. 'What is it that you did? I have heard talk of guns being spiked, but never of these truncheons of yours?'

'*Trunnions*, Mr. Corbett,' said the marine. 'They are the round projections cast onto the sides of a gun barrel that secure it to its carriage.' He reached behind him to slap the relevant part of the nearest eighteen pounder. 'If the enemy affords you the leisure to blow them off, it is the surest way to render a cannon beyond all repair. Spiking is a mere inconvenience. An armourer with a drill can remove it from a touch hole swiftly enough.'

'And how was this notable feat achieved, pray?' asked the surgeon.

'Oh, as for that, one loads a cannon with a full charge and ball and places the muzzle an inch behind the trunnion of its neighbour,' explained Macpherson. 'Light a short fuse in the touch hole, and withdraw in haste. We proceeded in this manner along the line of guns, disabling each with its neighbour. It produced a most satisfactory result, save one is always left with an undamaged gun, but in this case we had the convenience of a sea-cliff to roll it off.'

'That was handsomely done, Tom,' said Clay. He turned his attention back to his principal guest. 'So while my marines were busy on top of the cliff, how were matters proceeding lower down in the town?' The count was about to reply, when Fraser came into the conversation from Clay's other side.

'The garrison were prepared for us, sir, having been alerted by our attack on the batteries, but the superiority of our numbers proved decisive.' Clay waited for Fraser to say more, but the major returned to his meal.

'There is one aspect of the attack that I would want to understand better,' continued the captain. 'Why did you gentlemen feel obliged to set fire to the town?' The sound of breakfast around the table seemed to fade a little.

'That was not our intention, sir,' said Fraser.

'In which case, why did it occur?' persisted Clay.

'Some of my men had become enraged,' explained D'Arzon. 'A blast of canister from one of the guns of the battery caught their fellows in the open, earlier in the night. And with so many of the buildings being roofed with thatch, naturally the conflagration spread.'

'That seems a pity, count,' said Clay. 'I always imagined risings to be founded on the support of the people. It is a shame that such an excellent night's work may now be portrayed by Paris as an act of barbarism.'

'Come now, Captain Clay,' said D'Arzon, patting his host's arm. 'You are not familiar with the pronouncements of our papers. The Government will accuse us of such things, whether we are guilty of them or not. At least the rumour of what happened here may ensure that the next town we attack will yield all the swifter. One must break some eggs to make a cake, you know.'

*****

Later that morning, Clay stood at the quarterdeck rail, with his hands gripped behind his back and glared down onto the main deck of his ship. Most days, it was a place of strict order. The wide expanse of planking would have been scrubbed to an even shade of off-white. Down each side would be the twin rows of evenly spaced guns with their dull red carriages and glossy black barrels, ready for action. Every one of the ropes that led aloft would be neatly coiled and hung in its place, ready for any manoeuvre.

Instead, what he saw resembled a camp of fugitives. The guns had all been run out to create more space, but they were in no fit state to be used if an enemy should appear. Lines of musket were propped up against their barrels and discarded knapsacks were piled in drifts against their carriages. The end of a brass candlestick protruded from one bag just beneath him, and a dead chicken was strapped to the back on another. Even if the cannon could have been cleared of all encumbrances, there was no room for the gun crews to work their pieces. Every inch of deck seemed to be covered by prostrate and sleeping Royalist soldiers, unshaven, dirty and dressed in ragged clothing. They lay in a variety of positions, some curled on their sides like foetuses, while others sprawled out with limbs that lay across their neighbours. Beneath him, a large man in the remains of what must once have been a footman's coat lay on his back, his head resting on the thigh of another man, who slept prone on his stomach. To Clay's ear came a strange mixture of sounds. The normal shipboard creak of rigging and wash of sea was overlaid by a symphony of snores.

'How long until we will be in a position to land our passengers, Mr. Taylor?' asked Clay, turning away from the rail.

'Not before seven bells, sir,' replied the first lieutenant.

'Hmm, at least I shall not be obliged to offer our guests luncheon, then,' grunted the captain. 'Where have are all the count's officers disappeared too?'

'I have provided some hammocks for their convenience at the aft end of the lower deck, sir. Some of the hands had to acquaint them with how to get in and out of them, but most are now comfortably settled. How does the count fare?'

'Have no fears about his nibs!' exclaimed Clay. 'I loaned that rogue the cot in my sleeping quarters, and with a pipe of my best claret shipped on board, he is sleeping sounder than his men. By rights, I should be busy completing my report of last night to send off to London with the *Moselle*, but with him snoring only a bulkhead away, I found I could not order my thoughts. I had hoped to find some peace on deck.'

The mention of their prize made both men look sternwards, to where the corvette followed in their wake. In the light of day the damage she had taken looked stark. A spare main yard from the *Titan* had been set up and rigged to serve as a stubby mast, and she had been able to let slip the rope with which she had been towed out of the estuary. Many of her shot holes had yet to be patched, and the steady thump of hammers could be heard. A thin pulse of water shot out from her side to show where her prize crew still had to work the pumps to keep her afloat.

'She will fetch a pretty penny when Mr. Preston brings her into Plymouth, sir,' remarked Macpherson as he came over to join the other two officers. 'Even I can see she'll be a bonny wee ship, once all is set to rights once more.'

'Indeed she will,' said Taylor, rubbing his hands at the prospect. There was a flash of reflected light from near the wheel as the sandglass was swung over and the midshipman of the watch raised a hand towards the forecastle. A moment later three clear bell strokes sounded from the front of the ship, echoed by irritable muttering from the main deck. Taylor touched his hand to the brim of his hat. 'Would you gentlemen excuse me, but I have an engagement with the sailmaker. He has a problem with damp in his storeroom, which he is anxious to discuss.'

Clay watched his first lieutenant stride off towards the companion way and then returned his attention to the mass of soldiers on the main deck.

'So these *Choannerie* made a tolerable fist of it last night, I collect, Tom,' he said.

'Aye, sir,' replied the Scotsman. 'They will never pass for guardsman, but what they lack in discipline, they certainly make up for in ferocity.'

'Indeed!' snorted Clay. 'They attack a small garrison in overwhelming numbers, and yet I am to believe that none of the enemy offered to surrender? Only a poltroon kills a man after he has yielded.'

'Perhaps the defenders sought no quarter, because they knew none would be offered, sir,' said Macpherson. 'Civil wars always have a less savoury character than conflict between civilised nations.'

'Is that what you witnessed?' asked his captain.

'In truth, I saw little, sir. I held my men back from the fray, as I needed them to serve as reliable pickets on the cliff top to warn of any approach of the enemy from inland. Also, I did not wholly trust these Royalists with the task of destroying the guns. I witnessed little of the fighting in the town until matters were concluded. Major Fraser and the count will know more.'

'Ah yes, the count,' said Clay. 'If he is troubled by a guilty conscience, he hides it well. He seems perfectly content with how matters proceeded last night, while Fraser barely said a word, between slices of my finest ham.'

'I am sure the major knows more than he lets on, sir,' said the marine. 'Perhaps an excess of discretion is only to be expected of a man who operates, for the most part, in enemy country, where he might be taken at any moment.' Clay idly rolled a ring bolt on the deck under the sole of his shoe as he considered this.

'I dare say you're right, Tom,' he said eventually. 'I just wish we had allies who were easier to respect. War fought in a regular fashion is an unpleasant enough business. There should be no call for the destruction and slaughter that occurred last night. How disciplined do you find these *Choannerie* to be?'

'Their soldiering is certainly tolerably drilled, sir,' said Tom. 'The sergeants we provided have now been joined by some former members of the old Royal Guard. There is quite a military camp in the forests around D'Arzon's chateau.'

'How extensive is it?' asked Clay.

'Oh, I should say it spreads over a dozen acres, with perhaps three thousand under arms at present, sir,' said Macpherson. 'But more join all the time.'

'God bless my soul!' exclaimed Clay. 'As many as that? It's a wonder that the authorities have not had word of all this activity. I daresay it is very remote?'

'Tolerably so, sir,' mused the Scot. 'But now you mention it, it is curious that it remains undetected. I wonder why?'

'Do you think it strange, Tom,' asked Clay, 'suspiciously so?'

'I had not truly considered it before, sir. It has grown so, slowly, by degrees.'

'I need you to consider it now, then Tom,' said his captain. 'Intelligence of last night's success will encourage London. The time is coming when I shall be asked if our nation should commit fully to the count's uprising or not. How am I to answer?'

'I am but a humble marine, sir. Such matters are above my rank.'

'I make no doubt that Fraser is the First Lord's eyes in D'Arzon's camp,' said Clay. 'I need you to be mine. When you return ashore, see what you can discover.'

*****

Lieutenant John Blake was writing at the desk in his cabin. It was a tiny space in which to live, barely seven foot square, tucked down close to the waterline of the frigate. Through its curved outer wall came the constant sound of the sea as it rushed past, inches away from where he sat. With no natural light, the only illumination came from the horn lantern that swung from a low beam above his head, sending triangles of orange back and forth across the walls. The light played over the furniture that crowded the little box. Fully half of the space was occupied by his cot, which hung suspended over his sea chest, and a jumble of easels, paint boxes and several half-completed canvases. Fixed to the opposite bulkhead was the tiny desk at which he sat and a washstand, a little larger than a soup plate ashore. Fortunately, Blake was not a big man, so when the expected knock came at his door, he was able to move his chair back against the ship's side, to permit at least one visitor to enter.

'Come in,' he said, laying down his pen. A marine ducked through the door, and stood with his head folded beneath the low ceiling. He managed an awkward salute.

'Got this 'ere sailor at the wardroom door, sir,' said the soldier. He jerked a thumb over his shoulder. 'Name of Beaver. Says as how you sent for him.'

'Thank you, private,' said Blake. 'Would you kindly show him in?'

'Aye aye, sir,' said the marine, backing out carefully. A few moments later he was replaced by the small, wiry form of John Beaver. He stood legs apart with his hands behind his back, his eyes fixed on a point a little above thc officer's head.

'You sent word for me, sir,' he said.

'I did, indeed,' said the lieutenant, looking over the

seaman. 'I hear that the men name you Mystical Jack, and say that you can predict the future, Beaver?'

'Aye, sir,' he replied, with a smile. 'There be some as hold that I can.'

'What do you suppose I am going to say now?' asked Blake. Beaver's eyes flickered towards the officer's, and he ran a hand through his thin hair.

'I don't rightly know, sir. The Sight don't work like that.'

'Ah, I thought it might not,' said the officer. 'So tell me how it does work, then.'

'Most ways it just be a sensation, like,' Beaver explained, his chest swelling a little. 'Folk ask me stuff, 'bout the weather or where we be headed, and if I knows, I gives them an answer. But then there be other times when I gets a sort of picture of what will be. In my head like, when I be dozing in my hammock. Stuff as ain't happened yet.' His proud smile was met by stony indifference.

'And is it truly a gift, or are you not just a man who is shrewd at conjecture? One who knows when to offer an opinion and when to hold his council?'

'I am not sure what you mean...'

'You're a landsman, are you not?' interrupted Blake.

'Aye, sir,' replied Beaver.

'A newly arrived landsman,' repeated the officer. 'In the hierarchy of the *Titan*, your rank is barely superior to that of one of the boys, and certainly inferior to most of your shipmates. As you were on your previous frigate, the *Naiad*, and like to remain so, from what Mr. Hutchinson tells me of your seamanship.'

'I does my part, sir.'

'You look to be too weak a man to let your fists speak for you in a fight,' continued Blake. 'For a person of your undoubted intelligence, this must all be very vexing for you, Beaver. Which is, doubtless, what is behind all this Sight nonsense?'

'It ain't nonsense, sir,' protested the seaman.

'Really? Then how do you explain that Davis, who has been an excellent servant to this ship for many years, was taken ill before the start of the action last night? Have you told him that he suffers from some form of malady?'

'It were only what the Sight showed me, sir.'

'Yet thanks to your so-called "Sight", a once valued member of the crew is now unwell, and shunned by his shipmates,' said Blake. 'Mr. Corbett, who is a trained Naval Surgeon, has examined Davis, and finds him to be in perfect health. Do you presume to know more of such matters than he does?'

'No, sir, but it ain't like that at all,' said Beaver. 'I can't help what comes to me.'

'Of course you damned well can!' shouted Blake. 'You can hold your tongue, rather than spreading such wicked lies!'

'It ain't lies, sir!' exclaimed the sailor.

'You will not contradict me!' said Blake, his face red with fury. 'I do not know what grip you have upon your fellow sailors, but it will not work with me. I can have you flogged, or worse!' Beaver's mouth worked for a moment, but he said nothing.

'Is it true that you told your shipmates that this ship would fail to catch the *Moselle,* on two separate occasions?'

'It weren't like...' Beaver noticed the frown on Blake's face sharpen. 'I ain't gainsaying you, sir, but it weren't like that at all.' Blake ignored him, and picked up a document from the desk instead.

'I had occasion to peruse the Articles of War earlier,' he said. 'They are particularly stern on the offence of discouraging your fellows in the face of the enemy. Death is the punishment.' He returned his attention to Beaver. 'I may seem young, with milk behind my ears to you, but I have served aboard this ship since I was a boy. In that time, I have seen no end of rabble-rousers come and go. They are often small or bitter men, who pretend much to gain some standing amongst their fellows. The last of them tried to raise the crew to mutiny. He failed, like all the rest, and concluded his worthless life at the end of a rope, dangling from a yardarm over Plymouth Sound.'

Blake rose from his chair. In the tiny cabin, his face was a matter of inches from that of the sailor's. He could smell the man's foul breath, and his lank, un-washed hair.

'Now hear me good and clear, Beaver,' he said, his voice thick with rage. 'I shall be watching you, from now on. I will have no more of your uncivil nonsense. Is that clear?' He stared deep into Beaver's brown eyes, searching for fear, but found only defiance. After a pause, the sailor spoke.

'Aye aye, sir. May I go now?'

*****

Louis D'Arzon knew that he was below ground. The temperature was much cooler down here in the cellar, the air pungent with the musk of damp stone. The walls of the passageway were stained with patches of mould, black in the light of the lantern that swung in his left fist as he hurried along.

It seemed to him that he had been striding along the corridor for hours now. Every so often he would pass an opening, first on one side and then on the other. Some were blocked by sturdy oak doors, studded with rusting iron; others were yawning voids of darkness, where the light of the lantern flickered across stone flags or onto the curve of wine barrels. The sound of his footfalls echoed back at him from out of these chambers, but still he hurried on. He knew that whatever it was he was searching for lay ahead, in the blackness, beyond the last reach of the light.

From somewhere above his head he could hear a low rumble that grew and shrank like waves beating on a shore, although he was certain it was not the sea. He had been listening to it for some time now. Then it was joined by a new, more staccato sound. He could hear a banging that came from much nearer. He hurried on, the sword scabbard by his side rattling against the stone of the wall and the hilt bouncing against his thigh. Louder and sharper the noise grew, until he could recognise it at last. It was the sound of an urgent beating upon something solid.

'Wait a moment,' he called into the dark, but the noise simply redoubled in fury. He left the endless corridor at last, as it opened into a chamber with a dirt floor and a low, vaulted ceiling. On the far side of the room was a door. It was starting and rattling against its bolts with the impact of the blows delivered to it from the far side. Dust and flakes of rust showered down, but the thick, reinforced oak stood firm. Off to one side was a spiral staircase that disappeared upwards. D'Arzon hurried towards the door, but then stopped and returned toward the steps. Had he detected a second light, shining down from higher up the stairwell? He drew his sword with a rasp, and advanced towards the bottom step. The whisper of retreating footfalls seemed to echo down the curve of stone.

'Is there anyone there?' he demanded. His voice echoed off the curves of the vaulting and, in response the hammering, stopped at the door.

'Aristo? Is that you?' demanded a muffled growl from behind the woodwork. 'Open this door, in the name of the People!' D'Arzon listened for a moment longer, and then placed his lamp on the floor, and hastened towards the voice. He grabbed hold of the first bolt, and began to force it back.

'I support the will of the Commune!' he shouted through the wood. The fastening shot back and he began to work on the next one.

'Quickly now!' urged the voice. 'Before those pigs make their escape!' The banging at the door started again and grew louder and louder, now with his name mixed in with the thuds.

'Count D'Arzon, sir, Count D'Arzon!' He opened his eyes, and the studded iron melted away, leaving just the oak planking swaying gently to and fro, a few feet from his face. The distant sound was the sea, after all, overlaid by the rap of knuckles on wood. He sat up in the cot and looked around the tiny sleeping cabin.

'What...what is it?' he called towards the door.

'It's Yates, sir,' said the voice. 'I am Captain Clay's servant. May I come in?' D'Arzon, shook the sleep from his mind and yawned.

'Please do,' he replied, and the youngster entered with a pewter can of steaming water.

'The captain sends his compliments, and we shall be able to land you and your men back home within the hour. I have some water here, hot from the galley, and one of the captain's razors, what he is happy to lend you.'

'Please pass my thanks on to your master,' said D'Arzon, running a hand over the black stubble that clung like a shadow to his lower face. He pushed himself up from the cot, which brought his head crashing against the low beam that transected the cabin ceiling. 'Merde!' he cursed, sitting back down again. He swore partly because of the pain and partly because the blow had driven the last of his dream away, just when he felt sure that he was about to remember something very important.

Chapter 9

Plans

Earl Spencer's office at the Admiralty was much as Clay remembered it from his previous visit. The fire of sea coal in the grate had gone, replaced by a fan of cut flowers in a silver urn now that summer was here, but everything else seemed the same. The marble mantelpiece still held its gilt framed carriage clock. His shoes still made no sound on the thick pile of the carpet as he advanced towards the desk, with Fraser beside him. The coat that the First Lord of the Admiralty wore was every bit as well tailored as he remembered from his last visit. Beneath his powdered hair, the same dark, thoughtful eyes regarded his two visitors.

'Good day to you both,' he said. 'I trust I find you in passable health?'

'Perfectly so, for my part, my lord,' said Clay. Major Fraser smiled in agreement.

'You have made good time, gentlemen,' said the First Lord, glancing towards the clock. 'The Plymouth road must be running fast after all this fine weather. Have you been offered some refreshment?'

'Your clerk was kind enough to provide us with claret and cold beef while we were waiting, my lord,' said Clay.

'Capital! Then, if you have no objections, we can get directly down to business. That will be all, Higgins.'

'Yes, my lord,' came from over Clay's shoulder, followed by the sound of a door closing.

'Be seated, gentlemen, I pray,' said their host. He parted

the tails of his own coat and settled behind his desk. 'I have your various reports here, and the tale they have to tell is encouraging. Your attack on this unpronounceable little port and the capture of the *Moselle* have been very well received. They even feature in this morning's *Gazette*.' He passed across a newspaper, which was folded open, and tapped the relevant article. Clay looked at his name in print and recognised the words as having come from his report. It was not the first time that his activities had been in the papers, but he still felt a tremor of pleasure. He passed it on to Fraser.

'I am relieved to see that at least my name, along with that of the count, has been omitted, my lord,' he said, returning the journal and adjusting his eye patch. 'That would have been most imprudent.'

'Indeed so,' said Spencer. 'I have no doubt that the London papers arrive in Paris almost as swiftly as they do here at the Admiralty. But let us speak of your campaign. How do matters proceed?'

'Satisfactorily, my lord,' said Fraser. 'There are now several thousand *Choannerie* under arms, with more in training. Barely a day passes without a raid on one government post or another, somewhere in the Morbihan.'

'What of their chief? Is he as active and able as we hoped?'

'Count D'Arzon has impressed me very much,' confirmed Fraser. 'He shows great merit as a leader of the uprising.'

'And for my part, our sources tell us that Paris is becoming increasingly concerned over the insurrection,' said Spencer. 'Your success has resulted in greater resistance to the government across much of the western part of France; rioting in the Vendee and tax collectors assaulted in Normandy, all of which is quite splendid. What is your view, captain?'

'The major is naturally much closer to the Royalist rebels

than I am, my lord,' said Clay. 'But for my part I would concur with much of what has been said.'

'Only much? Why not all, pray?' queried the First Lord. Clay felt the penetrating gaze he remembered so vividly from his last visit settle on him.

'If you press me, I confess that I do find the brutality with which operations are conducted troubling, my lord,' he said. 'Take the attack on Port Manec'h mentioned in the gazette. What is not reported in this account is that no prisoners were taken by the *Choannerie*, and that the place was torched, for no good reason that I have observed.'

'I see,' said Spencer. 'It is my understanding that risings are often bloody affairs, on both sides. Looked at our own troubles in Ireland? What is your view, major?'

'I agree with you, my lord,' said the Scotsman. 'By its very nature such revolt is sure to be brutal, conducted without the usual constraints of civilised warfare. The *Choannerie* know that only the guillotine awaits them if they should fail, under which circumstances we should excuse them for a lack of delicacy in their actions.'

'Well put, sir,' agreed the First Lord. 'Let us not be excessively righteous, Clay. The French have been this island's foe for many centuries, now. Surely, it is not our part to be overly concerned if Frenchman now choose to slay one another. Don't it save us the task, what?'

'Quite so, my lord,' said Fraser, before turning towards Clay. 'With respect, sir, you were away chasing your wee prize when Port Manec'h fell. I was present the whole time, and I saw little to occasion concern.'

'Was there anything else that troubles you, captain?' asked Spencer, his eyes straying towards the mantelpiece.

'I make no doubt that we shall soon move on to discuss an expanded operation, but before that is committed to, I would want to know a little more about the character of this Count D'Arzon,' said Clay. 'We are placing a great reliance upon him.'

'Very well,' sighed the First Lord. 'Was there a particular concern you had?'

'There is, my lord,' said Clay. 'I am puzzled as to how he is able to train so many soldiers in the woods upon his land without arousing the suspicions of the authorities.'

'Major Fraser?' asked the First Lord. 'What is your view? You know him the best of us all.'

'I would not go as far as to say that, my lord, but I believe I can offer some reassurance to the captain. The count's relationship with the authorities is excellent, on account of a particular service he is known to have rendered, during the time of the Revolution. It is why he was permitted to retain his father's lands, and I understand that this places him above suspicion. The exact particulars of that service are not known to me, but the result is undoubtedly fortuitous for us.'

'That all appears satisfactory,' said their host. 'Would you not agree, captain? By all means, be suspicious of a Frenchman, Clay. By Jove, I know that I would be! It is a perfectly natural state of affairs in a king's officer, but pray do not let it cloud your judgement. Be questioning, by all means, but do not permit the ultimate prize to be missed by an excess of caution.'

'And what is the ultimate prize to be, my lord?' asked Fraser, leaning forward in his chair. Spencer leaned back in his, as if in response.

'I discussed the Royalist rising in Cabinet yesterday,' said Spencer. 'Naturally, everyone is very pleased with your efforts, but they are also mindful of the overall situation. You should understand that the war with France is not popular at home. It has been going on too long, with no damned prospect of victory. Matters are deuced tricky, at present, and an embarrassing debacle could easily bring down the government.'

'I understand the predicament, my lord,' said Fraser. 'But

I should also say that the rising is now at a delicate point. Large enough to prompt a reaction from Paris, yet not so well set as to be able to resist a determined attack. The Royalist cause will surely fail without material assistance beyond the simple provision of muskets and funds.'

'All of which was discussed when we first met, my lord,' added Clay. 'Progress by degrees, I believed you termed it.' Spencer held up his hands to quieten them both.

'I made those very points most forcibly, and I did gain a certain degree of commitment,' he said. 'To that end, a force of regulars will be assembled at Plymouth, under General Maitland.' He pulled a bound notebook towards him and leafed through a few pages. 'Let me see, now,' he continued, running his finger down a page. 'Here we are: five regiments of foot, including the Gordon Highlanders, a battery of artillery and sundry other supporting troops. The Channel Fleet to supply a squadron of the line, under Sir Edward Pellew. He will naturally take overall command, captain. You know Sir Edward, of course?'

'I do indeed, my lord,' said Clay. 'I was part of his Inshore Squadron back in ninety-seven, when he had command of the *Indefatigable*. That sounds more satisfactory. Might I ask when I will be superseded by him?' Spencer closed the notebook, and formed his hands into a steeple.

'Ah, now we come to the rub,' he said. 'That all rather depends on you, gentlemen. The Cabinet won't approve the deployment of those forces unless there is an absolute prospect of success.'

'But no act of war can be accompanied by such an assurance!' protested Clay. 'By its very nature, even the best laid schemes will be accompanied by some element of hazard.'

'Might I ask what that means in practical terms, my lord?' asked Fraser.

'Another victory for the Royalists,' said Spencer.

'Something that will convince my colleagues that, this time, we have allies in the field we can rely upon. The destruction of a little fishing village like this Manec'h place is all very well, but it don't cut it. Accomplish a feat of note, and Sir Edward's and General Maitland's forces will be despatched.'

'Did you have an object in mind, my lord?' asked Clay.

'Let us see, I daresay a decisive victory in the field is unlikely,' mused Spencer, 'what with Count D'Arzon's deficiency in horse and artillery and so forth. Might something not be attempted against a settlement -- a proper town this time, defended by ramparts and walls and the like?'

'But surely that would require a formal siege, my lord,' protested Clay. 'Heavy guns and trenches, together with sappers and engineers. How are men to take such a place, armed with nothing larger than a musket?'

'Oh, they could take it by surprise, for example. And as for guns, you have plenty on board the *Titan*,' offered the First Lord. 'Were you not involved in such a siege in the Caribbean, a few years back?'

'I was, my lord,' said Clay. 'And it was sufficient to inform me of the formidable nature of such an undertaking. It was only a minor fort with a small garrison, and we benefitted from the support of engineers and regular troops. We also had the leisure to be able to advance the siege without the fear of the French descending on us.'

'This is all very vexing, captain,' said Spencer, his face colouring. 'From your record, I had assumed you to be a fighting commander of some pluck and initiative. No doubt, the task is passing difficult, but then, what endeavour is straightforward in time of war, what?'

'My lord, I must protest!' exclaimed Clay, 'I was merely trying to...'

'How about you, major?' interrupted the First Lord as he turned to the Scotsman. 'Are you also in despair of achieving anything worthwhile?'

'By no means, my lord,' said Fraser. 'Captain Clay is correct; a formal siege will surely be beyond the resources of the *Choannerie*. Treachery, on the other hand, comes readily to them, and may be made to answer our purposes just as well. Allow me to give the matter some thought, and see what I may be able to propose.'

*****

The parlour at Rosehill Cottage was a modest sized room with lemon walls and contrasting sage-green hangings and furniture, but it did enjoy the most pleasant aspect the house had to offer. Its bay window was framed by a clambering dog rose and looked down, across a garden packed with flowers, toward an old, red brick wall with an arched gateway. Through it could be glimpsed the gnarled trees of an orchard. Above its fireplace, a portrait of the late Reverend Nathaniel Clay, dressed all in black, save for a white neck cloth, glared down into the room with the same pale grey eyes with which his son looked back at him.

'How old was father in this portrait, Mother?' he asked. Mrs. Clay senior craned her head round to peer up from her wing backed chair.

'I dare say he was much the age that you are now, Alexander,' she said. 'It was painted when we first moved into the parsonage, here in Lower Staverton.'

'I have always thought his to be a handsome face,' said Lydia Clay. 'But what a frown, and what gravity in his countenance! It is as if he were about to deliver a particularly thunderous sermon.'

'That is so true!' laughed Betsey Sutton, placing her hand on that of her sister-in-law. 'As a child I was rather fearful of this room, on account of his disapproving stare.'

'Pshh! There is no occasion for such talk, Elizabeth,'

sniffed her mother. 'Your father had a most kindly disposition when the occasion merited, which this artist has been very ill in displaying. Why, I daresay your brother can adopt a savage look when required, to face down the ne'er-do-wells upon his ship.'

Clay demonstrated such a look, out of sight of his mother, and was rewarded with guffaws of laughter from his sister, wife and brother-in-law.

'Oh, it is good to see you again, Alex,' said John Sutton. 'How long before you must return to the *Titan*?'

'I am afraid this will be but a fleeting visit, brother,' replied Clay, his eyes on Lydia. 'I will be obliged to take the Plymouth coach in the morning.'

'And how do matters progress?' asked his friend.

'In truth, it is hard to say,' said Clay. 'Tolerably at present. We have taken a fine little prize, but as for the rest, I am at one remove from events. It is chiefly Tom Macpherson and Major Fraser who engage with the Royalist rebels.'

'Ah, yes, the mysterious Major Fraser,' teased Lydia. She held a cupped hand across one eye. 'My husband can relate so little of his character or history that I begin to wonder if he exists at all.'

'Very unsatisfactory, I am sure,' laughed Clay. 'In my defence, he does take discretion to a level I had never thought to exist. I dare say that such behaviour is a virtue in his line of work. But what of you, John? Are you in danger of returning to the service of your king, or have the delights of my sister's society quite driven the war from your mind?'

'All in good time,' said Sutton. 'We thought to first find ourselves a settled home, but as we are just now engaged to take on Colonel Forster's place, I shall be writing presently to the Admiralty, requesting a ship.'

'Bob Forster's house?' queried Clay. 'Here in the village? But, how splendid! We shall be neighbours.'

'Isn't it wonderful?' said his wife. 'When you are both at

sea, I shall have my closest friend on hand and your mother, the comfort of her daughter, and young Francis can be spoilt by his Aunt Betsey. What could be better contrived than that?'

'Mind, that place is rather a grand establishment,' said Clay. 'I don't wish to be impertinent, but will your half pay stretch so far?'

'You forget my novels, Alex,' said his sister. 'They continue to prove as popular as ever. *The Bramptons of Linstead Hall* is already in its third edition. On the subject of which, how does my fellow scribe Sedgwick fare?'

'He is in good health, but he has abandoned his writing for now, and is quite resolved to never speak in public again,' said Clay.

'Oh, but he must!' insisted Betsey. 'We are so close to a ban of that wicked trade in Negros. He has such a natural honesty and dignity in his discourse. It is men like him that can most influence common persons.'

'After events in Plymouth, it is the excesses of the common people he fears,' said her brother. 'If it were not for the intervention of some of his shipmates, matters might have ended ill for him, last winter.'

'I hold it very proper that he should know his place,' chimed in Mrs. Clay senior, from her own place beside the fire grate. 'Blackamoors addressing honest folk, in public! I never heard of the like! Small wonder the gathering was accompanied by violence.'

'Mother!' exclaimed Betsey, rolling her eyes upwards. 'And what should the poor man's place be then? Back as a field slave in Barbados?'

'For my part, I would like, above all things, for him to remain as my coxswain,' said Clay, 'where he can use his influence to do good amongst my people.'

'Do you have problems on your lower deck again, Alex?' asked Sutton. 'Not more mutinous Irishman or another murderer on the loose?'

'Merely a charlatan by the name of Mystical Jack, who claims to be able to see the future,' said his friend. 'You know how credulous sailors can be, and this man has my crew in his thrall.'

'Perhaps he *can* see the future, Alex,' said Betsey. '*There are more things in heaven and Earth, Horatio, than are dreamt of in your philosophy.*'

'Perhaps he can,' said Clay. 'In which case it is surprising he has not found more profitable employment jobbing shares, or setting up as a bookmaker. The fact that he passes his time as a lowly landsman aboard my ship tells me all I need to know, sister dear. No, I can rely on Sedgwick to find the measure of him, mark my words.'

*****

The following day, back in Plymouth, a small group of the *Titan*'s crew had pushed deep into the warren of streets and cobbled alleyways that lined the shore on the far side of Sutton Pool. They had left the stone quayside behind them, with its bustle of people and piled up goods, and now entered a quieter, more pungent world. The upper stories of the houses crowded together over their heads, leaving only a thin strip of the evening sky visible. Water and worse trickled along the drain that ran down the centre of the narrow lane. Grimy, bare-foot children and misty-eyed old men regarded them from the doorways that opened into the street on either side. A stray dog with a trailing leg limped from out of their path.

'Next turn on the right, to be sure,' said O'Malley as he led the group. Trevan paused to scrape some filth from the sole of one of his best shoes, while Sedgwick and Evans pressed on after the Irishman. An urchin called across to him from the door opposite.

'Who be that Turk with you, mister?' he asked, pointing at Sedgwick's broad back.

'He ain't no Turk, nipper,' replied the Cornishman. 'That be the rightful King of Africa. But mind you take care of him. Back home in his savage court he has no occasion to drink, so ardent spirits do bring out all his animal ferocity. Just you make sure you ain't about when we pass back this way. He be partial to sup on little boys, when the mood be upon him.' The youngster stared wide-eyed at Trevan, looking for a trace of humour in his impassive face. Finding none, he retreated back into his hovel and pulled the door closed behind him. Only then did the sailor allow a chuckle to escape, as he hurried after his friends.

He found them around the corner, contemplating a tavern that fronted onto the lane. It was made of poorly painted wattle, divided up by an occasional oak beam split with age. The whole structure bowed out over the street, but showed no immediate sign of collapse. A few small windows had been cut into the wall, none with any glass in them, while from inside came the sound of oath-edged conversation. Above the door was a wooden panel, painted with crude letters and a whitewashed crescent.

'The Moon,' read the King of Africa, out loud, for the benefit of his illiterate friends. 'This be the place, right enough. He wrinkled his nose a little at the acid-smell of burning tallow that wafted out like incense through the nearest window.

'Like I said, it ain't what you'd call fecking grand, at all,' explained the Irishman. 'But it'll serve for us, well enough.'

'And we can drink in this place all night, for a bender?' queried Evans, looking at the tavern and sniffing loudly.

'On my honour,' replied the Irishman. The other sailors exchanged glances.

'I got plenty of chink from all them books I sold, you know,' said Sedgwick. 'I don't mind paying for us up at the

Crown.'

'We can't be going up there!' exclaimed Trevan. 'You forgotten the riot at the Methodist Hall already? Pipe may have seen us right, but half the tipstaffs in Plymouth know our faces and all will have heard of Big Sam here. Somewhere quiet, where no traps will dare to come, that be what we need.'

'He's right, mate,' said Evans, ducking low to enter under the lintel. 'Here'll suit us fine.' The others followed him in, each patting the coxswain on the arm till Sedgwick found himself alone in the lane. He glanced around and saw a small grubby face peering at him from around the corner. He smiled at the little boy, who let out a squeal of alarm and vanished. With a sigh, he followed his friends inside.

If the outside of the tavern had been crude, the interior could have been that of a cowshed. The floor was beaten earth and the low ceiling was made of bare planking supported by smoke-blackened beams. There were several wooden tables, each flanked by a pair of benches. The most comfortable looking one was occupied by some local fishermen, to judge from the scatter of fish scales that winked from their clothes in the dim light. Another two tables had other sailors taking their ease. There was no bar in the place, but in one corner a trap door led down into a cellar. Up the steps came a small, thin man in a dirty leather apron who carried an earthenware jug of ale.

'A good evening to you,' said O'Malley, adopting his most polished voice. 'Me and my shipmates will be favouring your establishment this evening, an' partaking of your finest fecking ales.' He held out a sixpenny bit, and the others followed suit. The landlord collected the thin silver coins and flexed them between his fingers, before he pocketed them.

'By rights, the big feller should pay double,' he grumbled, eyeing the huge Londoner, but he waved them to a table and returned shortly after with earthenware tankards and another jug of beer.

'There's a bleeding first for you!' exclaimed Evans, after he had swallowed his first mouthful. 'I never thought to find a weaker piss than the beer what the Navy Board give us, but tonight I declare I may have done so.'

'How do you know this inn, Sean?' asked Sedgwick.

'Your man Conway said as how the ale was fine, the miserable fecker.'

'You took the word of a bleeding Lobster?' said Evans, aghast. 'An' Ryan Conway, to boot! He's the dullest marine of the lot.'

'We've been an' paid now,' said Trevan through clenched teeth, as he lit his clay pipe from the tallow reed on the table. 'If the brew's a mite weak, we shall just need to drink twice as much.'

'So how long you reckon we're after staying here in Plymouth, Able?' asked Evans. 'Will it just be until the barky is fixed? Cause that ain't going to be long. That *Moss Hell* barely scratched our paint.'

'Not sure, Sam,' said Sedgwick. 'Pipe left for London last night, in a perishing hurry with that Major Fraser. I took them across to the Hard. Mind, from the size of their cases, I don't reckon they'll be long gone.'

'Aye, but what'll it fecking mean for us when they return?' asked O'Malley. 'More arsing around with them turncoats, to be sure. I don't trust that Scottish fecker, with his single peeper. Too close to them Frogs, if you asks me. What do you reckon, Adam?'

But Trevan's attention had drifted away from his friend's conversation. Instead he looked towards a pair of sailors who had just come in through the door.

'Hoy! Jude Ward!' he called out, rising from the table. One of them, a tall, dark-haired man with a thick pigtail, looked around and his face split into a grin.

'Adam, you Cornish bastard!' he exclaimed, and the two

men embraced.

'This here is an old shipmate of mine, lads,' said Trevan to the others. 'We was on the same whaler, afore the war like, and got pressed off her together in The Soundings. You got sent to that old tub, the *Bellerophon*, wasn't it? You still be on her?'

'No, mate,' said the sailor. 'I left the *Billy Ruffian* when I got my step. They made me a boatswain's mate, if you'll credit it. Now I terrify the jacks on board the *Naiad,* a-blowing on my call, and shouting "out or down" when the buggers won't shift from their hammocks.'

'Was that the fecking *Naiad*, you just said,' queried O'Malley.

'Aye, what of it?'

'You ever hear tell of a sailor calling himself Mystical Jack?' asked O'Malley.

'Mystical Jack, you say?' repeated Ward. He scratched at one of his bushy sideburns as he pondered.

'Runt of a man with lanky hair, claims to have got some manner of second Sight,' added Trevan.

'Oh, you mean John Beaver!' exclaimed the boatswain's mate. He hooked his thumbs into his belt. 'Aye, I know all about that little turd, right enough. He used that weird Sight to proper big himself up. He had quite a grip on the lower deck, at one time. Even made some chink off the dafter hands. Course it was all so much gammon. No more than crafty guesses. Once he got rumbled, it wasn't safe for him on board no more. He had made fools of too many of the lads. Then he volunteered sharpish for some other bleeding ship, God help them.'

'God help them indeed,' muttered O'Malley.

'He's only been and turned up on our barky,' explained Trevan. 'Calls himself Mystical Jack now, and says how he got his sight after he was missed by a Don cannon ball. Dropped him down in a faint, and when he came round he had this Sight of his.' Trevan's friend threw back his head and roared with laughter.

'He be a proper villain, that one,' he said at last. 'Why I remembers that very shot! We was after a Don frigate, and she turned and let fly at us with her starboard guns. They shot high, as usual, but one ball passed close over the bow. It missed him right enough, and it made him swoon, but he came to a moment later, ducked down behind the foremast and squealed like an autumn hog as had just spotted the knife! Captain Rose gave him a dozen at the grating for cowardice, and told him he were lucky not to be hanged for his want of pluck.' Most of the sailors joined in Ward's laughter, except for O'Malley, who banged his tankard down on the table and rose to his feet.

'I knew that fecker was a fraud!' he exclaimed. 'Mystical Jack, my arse. Wait until I tell the others. He'll be a squealing like a pig again.'

'Holdfast there Sean, I ain't sure as that will answer,' said Sedgwick. 'Think as what happened last time you wanted to mill with him. That Beaver still has such a grip on the men, there'll be plenty as won't heed what you say. Besides, the whole ship knows you hate the bugger. You pitching up, half-cut on grog, with a tale from a jack you met in some tavern won't sway them any. No offence, Jude,' he added, for the benefit of Trevan's friend.

'Aye, you listen to Able,' urged Evans. 'I'll be first in line to knock the bugger down, but for now most of the lads will take his part, an' them ain't odds as I fancy.' Trevan turned to his friend.

'So tell us then, Jude. How comes things went astray for him, back on the old *Naiad*?'

'Why, like I said, he got altogether too cocky,' explained Ward. 'He was awry in a couple of his predictions. So them as he had made to look an arse wanted to deck him, while the ones he had touched for money asked for their chink back.

When he couldn't pay, things got hot for him. After that, he scarpered.'

'We could wait for that I suppose,' said Evans. 'He's sure to make a shambles of it sometime.'

'That bugger! Nar, he'll have gone and learnt his fecking lesson,' said O'Malley. He gloomily swilled his beer around in the hope of producing a head. 'He's too deep to make the same mistake twice.'

'Unless it were something he was truly certain of,' said Sedgwick. 'Then he would pipe up quick enough.'

'But if it ain't true, how are we going to make him hold it be right?' queried Evans. The coxswain clapped his hands together, and leant forward, his eyes alight.

'I've got an idea!' he exclaimed. 'Adam, you still pals with that surgeon's mate what looked after you last commission?'

'Henderson? Aye, we be close enough.'

'And you and Harte are tight as kin, ain't you Sean?' continued Sedgwick.

'Fecking right, but what has Pipe's steward got to do with anything?' asked the Irishman.

'Ain't he the biggest gossip on the barky, after you that is, Sean?' said the coxswain. 'I can get the captain's clerk to show me how a purser's indent looks, and to see that Beaver gets sent ashore with it.'

'Easy there!' exclaimed Evans. 'You're going way too swift for them as ain't as sharp as you -- me, most of all. What exactly is it you're planning?' The coxswain pulled the others close. Ward bent down so he could eavesdrop on their conversation.

'Listen up, lads, and I'll tell you how we shall catch friend Beaver out,' he said.

Chapter 10

Summer

Major Fraser returned to Plymouth some weeks later and in his absence, full summer had come to the Devon coast. For most of his journey west he had been uncomfortably warm inside the crowded coach, and it came as a relief when the outskirts of the port began to crowd in on either side. The horses swung under a broad arch of stone and, with a final lurch, they came to a halt. The Scotsman pulled his coat straight and emerged from the stuffy interior, cramped and stiff, into the bustling yard of the George Inn. Grooms led horses to or from the stable block. Bundles and bags were handed down from the roof of the carriage. Passengers were being met with enthusiasm all around him. The warm air had tempted many of the inn's customers outside to enjoy their drinks and pipes in the sunshine, and he found his uniform and eye patch attracting attention. He ignored the looks and instead breathed in the warm scented air. The smell of the sea came to him, laced with gorse blossom, wafting down from Rame Head. So lovely was the weather, and so stiff his legs from the journey, that he chose to walk the quarter mile or so from the inn to the Hard, from where he planned to get out to the frigate. A little later he found himself strolling down Bath Street behind a familiar looking sailor with a large, athletic frame. Under his arm he carried a sack.

'You there! Would you be Captain Clay's coxswain?' he

called. The man turned around, and touched his hat to the Scottish officer.

'That I would, sir,' he said. 'Sedgwick be the name. I just been an' collected the *Titan*'s mail from the port admiral's office, like.' He patted the sack. 'Was you looking to return to the barky, sir?'

'I was, indeed,' the soldier replied. 'I had planned to contract the services of one of the boatmen down by the shore.'

'Oh, you doesn't want to do that, sir,' replied the coxswain. He pointed to Fraser's scarlet tunic. 'One look at your regimentals, and the fare would have tripled. They do love to fleece a Lobster something cruel, being ex-navy for the most part. Highwaymen ain't in it! You had best come along with me.' He picked up the major's bag with his spare hand and led the way down the cobbled street, and out onto the quayside. The wide waters of Plymouth Sound opened up in front of them, blue beneath the warm sun. It was busy with small boats, moving this way and that. Flat lighters, laden with stores, worked their way down from the dockyard. Battered fishing boats with stained brown sails were streaming towards the open sea. Out in the Sound a line of yellow and black warships swung at anchor, each astride its wavering reflection. There were several ships of the line, massive and squat, while farther off was the long, low hull of the *Titan,* beneath her towering masts.

'Lovely sight, ain't she, sir,' said the coxswain. 'She weren't handled too rough by that *Moss Hell*. The dockyard has put her back to rights.'

Fraser paused to admire the view, while Sedgwick turned to one side, and marched to the top of a stone ramp that led down to the water. At the bottom was the *Titan*'s barge. Sedgwick let out a piercing whistle, and the crew of the boat looked around.

'Hoy, Rodgers!' he called. 'Come and clap onto the

major's dunnage.' One of the men padded up the ramp, and picked up Fraser's travelling case.

'This be all you're bringing aboard, sir, or is there more to come?' he asked, sampling the weight of the leather bag.

'No, just that valise,' said the major, his attention returning from the moored ships.

'Are you sure, sir?' queried the sailor. 'Beggin' yer pardon, like, only that don't seem much for such a long passage.'

'Now don't you go answering the major back, Tom Rodgers,' warned the coxswain. 'Just you run along and stow that there bag in the stern sheets.'

'Aye aye, Cox,' muttered Rodgers. He swung Fraser's luggage up onto his shoulder and returned to the boat.

'I am not sure that I follow, Sedgwick,' queried Fraser. 'What long journey is that seaman referring to?'

'Oh, I shouldn't worry about him, sir,' said Sedgwick, with a shrug of his shoulders. 'I daresay he's got his self in a muddle. Shall we get you across to the *Titan*?'

'If you please,' said Fraser. He followed the coxswain down the ramp with an impassive face, but his single eye rested on Sedgwick's back. I wonder why that sailor thinks we are going somewhere distant, he pondered, and why is that Negro lying to me about it?

*****

The wardroom of the *Titan* was a light and airy place, now that the ship was at anchor in sheltered waters. The stern chase-ports, always securely bolted while the frigate was at sea, had been flung open. Two squares of sunlight rested on the planking of the deck, while reflected light from the water danced across the low ceiling. A warm breeze ruffled the open shirts of the officers who took their ease around the table. Amongst them, for once, was the ship's lieutenant of marines, stroking his dark sideburns as he waited for Charles Faulkner to make the next move in their backgammon game. Macpherson was comfortably the wardroom's best player, but the purser occasionally threatened to defeat him, perhaps one game in ten. Across the table from them was Lieutenant Blake, who was adding colour to a sketch of the frigate he had made earlier from the top of Tor Point. Next to Blake sat Edward Preston, scribbling notes onto the margin of a large sheet of paper that did its best to flutter away with each flurry of wind. Two further piles of paper were held in place by a pair of uncocked pistols that served as unusual, but effective paper weights.

'What on earth are you about, Edward?' asked Macpherson. 'I didn't have you marked as a scribe.'

'I am putting my affairs in order, if you must know, Tom,' said the young Yorkshireman, looking up from his work.

'What has brought this on?' asked the marine. 'Do you fear your time is up? Have you been obliged to call out a fellow officer in an affair of honour? In which case, I am a little hurt you did not ask me to be your second.' He picked up one of the pistols and held it upright in front of his face, as if about to turn and fire at an opponent. Preston just managed to slam his hand down on the released pile of papers before a gust of air plucked them away.

'Every officer should make proper provision for his demise, especially if his ship will shortly be ordered to the West Indies in the season of rain,' he said, removing his hand as Macpherson placed the pistol back. 'Yellow jack, ague, swamp sickness. At least in a duel, a man has an even chance of survival.'

'But, my dear Edward, where have you come by such a strange notion?' exclaimed Blake, glancing up from his picture. 'We are about to return to the coast of Brittany.'

'Are you certain?' said Preston, his face still doubtful. 'The lower deck are convinced that we are to sail for

Jamaica.'

'Then they are quite out in their reckoning,' said Macpherson. 'The captain confirmed as much to me this morning. He said that once Major Fraser returns, we shall depart, and that he wishes me to march with the Royalists once more.'

'If it was only the idle gossip of the men, I might take no notice, but I have had it confirmed by my own observations,' said Preston.

'What, pray, have you seen, Edward?' asked the marine.

'Why, only yesterday, for example,' continued the young lieutenant. 'I was at the entry port, waiting for the return of the cutter to take me ashore. When it arrived, it contained Mr. Corbett's assistant coming aboard with several crates of Jesuit Bark. You will own, that is an odd physic for us to be carrying if we are not bound for the tropics?' Faulkner paused with one of his counters in mid-air.

'Upon my word, but that is a strange coincidence,' he said.

'Do you have something to add to this wee conundrum, Charles?' asked Macpherson.

'Perhaps I may,' said the purser. 'The dockyard delivered the last of the gunner's stores this morning, together with new slops for the crew. I explained that there must have been some mistake, as I ordered no clothes. The clerk was most insistent that they had received an indent from me two days ago, and even showed me the document. The writing and signature bore no relation to my own, although the ship was set down as the *Titan*. I sent them back and thought no more about it, but now I wonder if someone may be making game of us.'

'Why so, Charles?' asked Blake.

'Because the slops were white duck trousers with a quantity of straw hats and the like,' explained the purser. 'Now, isn't that just the order one would expect a ship to place, if it was truly bound for the West Indies?'

The officers were mulling all this over when the wardroom door opened, and in came the surgeon.

'Oh, but it is so much more agreeable in here with those ports open,' he said, blinking like a mole behind his glasses.

'Mr. Corbett!' exclaimed Macpherson. 'The very man we need to help us solve our mystery! Pray, pull up a chair.'

'A mystery, you say,' replied Corbett. 'I will endeavour to help you, if I can. What are the particulars?'

'We were speculating as to why you received such a large delivery of Jesuit Bark yesterday.'

'That is simply answered. I receive nothing of the kind.'

'What! But I saw the cases!' exclaimed Preston. 'Three of them, which bore the clearest of labels. Your assistant, Henderson, brought them on board, together with of one of the hands.'

'I fear you are mistaken, Edward. I did send Henderson ashore to collect supplies, but only some crates of new dressings, to replace that which I used to treat the wounded on board the *Moselle*. I supervised their stowage just now, and none bore such a label.'

'But this is madness! I am quite certain of what I saw,' said an exasperated Preston.

'May I ask a question, Edward?' said Blake. 'Who was the hand who helped Henderson to bring them on board yesterday?'

'Oh, I forget...is it of any import?' said the lieutenant. 'No, I remember now. It was that indifferent looking landsman in your division. The one with the thin hair.'

'John Beaver?'

'Indeed, the very same,' confirmed Preston. 'Is that of any significance?'

'Perhaps it is,' said Blake, looking towards the ceiling and smiling. 'Yes, perhaps it is.'

*****

The sunshine was just as welcome on the deck above the wardroom, where Clay and his first lieutenant sat on either side of his desk. The two men were coming toward the end of their daily meeting, at which they went through the minutiae of the wooden world that was the *Titan*. A square of warmth lay upon the dark blue coat of the frigate's captain, as he sat at his desk. It soaked through, into his body, easing the ache of an old wound. Clay raised and stretched his left arm in front of him with a contented sigh before returning it to rest on the desk.

'Does your shoulder still trouble you, sir?' asked Taylor.

'Aye, it does, George,' said Clay. 'I am not certain whether the Spanish musket ball or Mr. Linfield's extraction of it did more harm, but it is still a hindrance to me, even after all these months. The sun does help matters, and for that I am grateful.'

'A musket ball can be a most unwelcome visitor,' said Taylor. 'Not that I have had that misfortune.' He patted a hand down on the wooden surface of the desk.

'Now, we seem to have covered most points,' resumed the captain, returning to his notes. 'Dockyard repairs all finished; new bower anchor fitted – the *Moselle* wounded us there, at least -- provisions largely complete, with only some of the boatswain's stores and our fresh water to come. When Major Fraser joins us presently, we shall be in a condition to set sail with the next tide.'

'Aye aye, sir,' said Taylor. 'May I move on to the subject of discipline? I am afraid I have some malefactors that require your attention.'

'Indeed?' said Clay, still busy with his list. 'What is the nature of their offence?'

'A breach of Article Fifteen, sir.' Clay looked up from his notes in surprise and stared across his cluttered desk.

'Deserters, George?' he queried. 'That is unusual. We have not had anyone run, this past twelve month. Who was it?'

'Some of the steadier hands, sir,' replied Taylor. 'Hibbert, able seaman in the larboard watch seems to have been the leader. The other two were messmates of his, Perkins, and Vardy, who is new to the ship. It was most ill-conceived. They got no farther than Efford before they fell in with one of the patrols. The master at arms has them outside.'

'Very well. Bring them in and let us see what is behind all this,' said Clay.

The three deserters shuffled into the cabin, accompanied by a marine and the master at arms. All were large, solid built men, who stood bare-headed in a line and stared toward the sunlit windows with defiance in their eyes. Clay adopted an expression similar to that of the late Reverend Nathaniel Clay, in his portrait, and waited until the silence became uncomfortable.

'Mr. Taylor informs me that you are guilty of trying to desert,' he began. 'This is all very troubling.' His eyes flicked along the line, looking for weakness, and settled on Vardy, who was twisting his hat between his hands.

'What have you to say for yourself, Vardy?' he said. 'Your officers had told me that you were settling into your new life tolerably well. Yet now, I learn you have forgotten your duty to your king, and have disgraced yourself and this ship.' Vardy muttered something unintelligible and looked down at the deck.

'Do you recall the Articles of War that were read to you when you volunteered?' continued Clay. Vardy shrugged his shoulders, his eyes still fixed on the deck.

'You will answer the captain with "Aye aye, sir"!' snapped Taylor.

'Aye aye, sir,' muttered the former tanner.

'Then you will doubtless recall that the punishment for

desertion is death, or such lesser sentence as the circumstances of the offense shall deserve – is that not correct, Mr. Chilton?'

'Quite correct, sir,' said the master-at-arms. Vardy looked up, terror flickering across his face.

'So what has occasioned you to take such a risk?' asked Clay, continuing to stare at the volunteer. Hibbert glanced across at Vardy and then took a half pace forward.

'Permission to speak, sir,' he said, in his rumbling bass.

'Are you the leader of this little rebellion then, Hibbert?' asked Clay, switching his grey eyes onto him. 'I had supposed that you had served long enough to know better than to be involved with such nonsense. But pray, go ahead and say your piece.'

'We ain't going to the Caribee, sir,' said the sailor firmly.

'Keep a civil tongue in your head, Hibbert,' warned Taylor. 'You know better than to address the captain in that fashion.'

'Sorry, sir, I don't mean no disrespect, but I just can't go back there! Not in the rainy season. I been there three times before, and the Yellow Jack near done for me last time. I got a wife now, and two little nippers. I can't see them thrown on the Parish, sir. And as for Perkins, here, he's a run slave, with none of the connections of your coxswain. It would be same as murder to make him set foot back in Jamaica.'

'What on earth are you talking about, man!' exclaimed Clay. 'We are not bound for the West Indies!' Perkins and Vardy's mouths opened wide.

'Are you sure, sir?' asked Hibbert. 'Perhaps word ain't come to you yet.'

'Hibbert, you will not contradict the captain!' roared Taylor, but Clay held up a hand.

'Mr. Taylor is quite correct, it is certainly not your place to question what instructions I have been given, but I will confirm that we are most certainly not bound for those waters. What on earth led you to suppose that we were?'

'We was told by a shipmate, what knows about these things, sir,' said Hibbert. 'He were proper certain.'

'Oh, for goodness sake!' exclaimed Clay. 'Have you been listening to that wretched Beaver fellow?' The sailors looked uncomfortably at one another. 'Well, he is either guilty of a cruel deceit, or has sought to make fools of you. I suggest you look to your officers for such information in the future, rather than taking heed of idle gossip.'

'Aye aye, sir,' muttered the three men.

'As for your attempt to desert, I am afraid that it cannot be overlooked,' continued Clay, his eyes steel. 'Perkins, Hibbert, you both need to be reminded of your obligations to this ship, and as for you, Vardy, you have to be made to understand the seriousness of the commitment you entered into when you joined the service. You shall all be punished shortly. Take them away, if you please Mr. Chilton.'

*****

Back in Brittany, later that night, Count Louis D'Arzon was preparing for bed. His was a large room, full of heavy gilded furniture and dominated by a four-posted bed. Two mullioned windows overlooked the grounds of his chateau. Crisscrossing the dark gardens were rows of glowing orange points from the dying embers of his men's cooking fires. His valet released the heavy drapes and cut out the night.

'Leave me now,' ordered the count. The valet stepped back from the window and bowed low, then wished his master a goodnight, retreated to the door and closed it behind him. The nobleman looked around the large room to confirm that he was quite alone and then reached inside his nightshirt for the key that hung around his neck. He picked up one of the candles from his dressing table and stood before the richly decorated wall beside his wardrobe. The panel in front of him was painted with a hunting scene, so packed with dense detail that the tiny hole cut in the wood was lost amongst the tumbling hounds and cornered stag. There was a dry click from inside the panel when he turned the key, and a concealed door sprung a half-inch ajar. D'Arzon pulled it open with his fingers and stepped through, into the dark chamber beyond.

The light of his candle flashed and glittered back at him from something on the far wall. Using the flame, he lit more and more candles, until the tiny space was ablaze with light. He stood in a little stone cubicle with cold flagstones beneath his bare feet and a crude vault overhead. Resting against the wall was a travelling altar, no more than four feet wide and perhaps a foot deep. The back was a beautifully decorated screen. In the centre was the Virgin Mary, swathed in blue and sitting on piled clouds, whilst holding a plump baby Jesus in her arms. Rays of gold leaf spread out from both of their heads, while various bearded saints looked on with approval from the margins. On the altar were two framed portraits and a plain wooden box. From one picture, the round face and hooded eyes of Louis XVI looked out, while from the other, the dark gaze of Marie-Antoinette appraised him, from beneath hair piled high with feathers.

The count bowed low, although it was unclear whether to the figure of Christ or to the two dead monarchs. Then he pulled his nightshirt over his head and dropped it to the floor. Naked, he knelt on the stone flags, his head low, his eyes shut. Tears began to spill from them, flowing down his cheeks to drip into the dark hair of his chest.

'Forgive me my sins,' he wept. 'Forgive me my weakness.' After a moment or two of reflection, he reached forward and opened the box. He picked up the small scourge that lay inside and, with his eyes fixed on those of the dead king, he began to whip at his back and shoulders.

CHAPTER II

PUNISHMENT

The *Titan* left her moorings in the cool dark, when the ebbing tide was at its strongest, carrying her down the Sound and out to sea, past the Eddystone rocks. The lights of Plymouth narrowed to points and then vanished, one by one, as they were drawn back into the black coast. At dawn she was heading south by west into the Channel, under easy sail. When the rind of sun appeared over the horizon, it first gilded the mastheads before travelling down the rigging, until it warmed the face of the officer of the watch. Edward Preston closed his eyes against the light and continued to see the sun as a glow of peach through his eyelids as he stood by the rail. For once, a gentle easterly was blowing in the Channel, replacing the usual Atlantic rollers with a calm sea that creamed and broke along the frigate's sides. Preston turned from the rail with a sigh of pleasure, opened his eyes and found that his friend, Lieutenant Blake was also watching the sunrise.

'You are up early, John,' he said. 'Besides, it is Mr. Armstrong, and not you, who is due to replace me.'

'I couldn't get back to sleep after we weighed anchor,' explained Blake, 'so I resolved to come up on deck.'

'You have witnessed a noble sunrise,' said Preston. 'It would make for a fine picture, if you wished to paint it.'

'A fine day for an ill affair,' said his friend. He turned his back on the rising sun and slumped against the rail.

'I am not sure I follow you, John?' said the officer of the watch.

'I refer to those three unfortunates who are to be flogged this morning.'

'Ah,' said Preston. 'I take no pleasure in these matters, but surely offenders must be punished, if only for the benefit of those tempted to follow their example. As I understand it, there is no question as to their guilt.'

'Except that they were cruelly deceived,' said Blake. 'They only ran because someone thought to trick Beaver into imparting that we were bound for the West Indies.'

'Who was responsible for the mischief, then?' asked Preston.

'That I cannot say, but I do at least understand how it was done,' said Blake. 'A series of suggestive acts, arranged for his benefit, and that foolish man swallowed it all.'

'He was not the only one deceived,' said Preston. 'My affairs have never been so well regulated. But how intriguing! Pray tell, how was the deceit accomplished?'

'Oh, with preposterous ease!' snorted his friend. 'A forged indent for tropical clothes, with Beaver the hand sent to deliver it, some labels changed on cases of physic for the surgeon and a few injudicious rumours spread by the captain's servants. It does make one wonder what other deceits the men are planning for the confusion of their betters.' Preston laughed aloud at this.

'So why are you so melancholy, John,' he asked. 'I would have thought you would be excessively pleased. Mystical Jack proved a fraud. Why, only last week you were in despair as to how you were to break his grip on the hands. Rejoice! The lower deck, in its own mysterious way, has solved your problem for you.'

'You misunderstand me, Edward,' said his friend. 'None will be happier than me at Beaver's fall, except perhaps old Davis. It is the flogging of three innocents that troubles me.'

'They are hardly innocents,' protested Preston. 'They ran and were caught, and so are obliged to be punished. Where is the problem?'

'You hold I should not intervene on their behalf, then?' said Blake. 'In private with the captain, or when I am asked to speak for them?'

'No John, you should not,' said Preston. 'What possible good will it achieve? The captain is no Tartar. I am sure he will be as lenient as he is able, but he certainly cannot fail to punish desertion, however eloquent your protest.'

'But, it feels wrong to do nothing!'

'Nevertheless, that is my council,' said Preston. 'Now, here comes Jacob to take my place. I suggest you leave well alone, and concentrate instead on more pressing matters -- such as whether you will have a mutton chop or salt bacon with your egg this morning. Because I am quite famished, and intend to break my fast in some style.'

Four hours later, the *Titan* was out of sight of land. She sailed under topsails alone, across a wide blue sea. Her decks had been scrubbed clean and flogged dry again in the warm breeze. Her crew had stowed their hammocks away and been fed. Now a cloud of foreboding hung over the frigate, as all waited for what was to follow. The sudden squeal of the boatswain's pipes, as they echoed through the ship, came almost as a relief.

'All hands! All hands, to witness punishment!'

Up the ladders poured the seamen, spreading out across the main deck and taking their places in each division. Behind them came their less agile shipmates, the idlers who made up the rest of their community afloat: the coopers and cooks, the gunners and armourers, the sailmakers and stewards. Meanwhile, on the quarterdeck, the frigate's marines clumped to their places, before being shuffled into a perfect line by their sergeant.

The crew of the *Titan* were gathered in a hollow box

around an up-ended grating. Beside it stood Powell, the ship's fierce-looking boatswain's mate, fingering the cat-o'-nine-tails through the fabric of the red cloth bag that held it. Second only to Evans in size, he had been struck by a cutlass to the head, earlier in the war. The puckered scar lay across one eye, turning his face into the stuff of nightmares. By his side was a bucket of seawater. When all was quiet, Clay stepped out from under the quarterdeck in full dress uniform. The sunlight that filtered down through the sails and rigging of the frigate winked and sparkled off the gold braid of his uniform. At his throat was his Nile medal, while by his side hung a finely crafted sword, its pommel shaped like the head of a lion. Behind him came Taylor.

'You may bring up the prisoners, if you please, Mr. Taylor,' said Clay.

'Aye aye, sir,' said the first lieutenant. The three deserters were brought forward and arranged in a line before him. Hibbert and Perkins looked impassive but Vardy seemed to be on the verge of tears.

'Off hats,' roared Taylor, and with a rustle of movement, the crew became bareheaded.

'What are the charges, Mr. Chilton?' asked the captain. The master-at-arms pulled out the punishment book and read from it, in a toneless bellow.

'They have offended against Article Fifteen, sir, what states "*Every person in or belonging to the fleet, who shall desert or entice others so to do, shall suffer death, or such other punishment as the circumstances of the offense shall deserve.*" He snapped his book closed, and touched his hat to Clay.

'What have you to say in answer to that?' he asked. 'Hibbert?'

'Nothing, sir,' replied the sailor, staring past his captain.

'Perkins? You have always been a reliable hand.'

'Nothing, sir,' said the former slave. Clay moved on to

Vardy.

'What about you, Vardy? Do you wish to speak?' The ex-tanner looked as if he was going to say something. His mouth worked, and he stared across at the others. They continued to look ahead.

'No, sir,' he whispered. 'N...nothing, sir.'

'Very well,' said the captain. 'Does anyone wish to speak on these men's behalf?' Blake stepped forward from his place.

'I do, sir,' he said.

'Yes, Mr. Blake,' said Clay. 'What is it you wish to say?' The lieutenant glanced briefly toward Preston, as he collected his thoughts.

'Hibbert and Perkins have good records, sir. Both have proved to be diligent members of my division, who have done their duty well this commission. Vardy is new to the sea and to our customs, but has proved obedient and willing. All three men fought with courage against the *Moselle*, and have given me no occasion to reprimand them, prior to this offence.'

'Thank you, Mr. Blake.' Clay turned back towards the men. 'Desertion is a wicked act. It is doubly so at a time when your country is at war. However, on account of the handsome way that Mr. Blake has spoken up for you, I am prepared to be lenient in this case. You shall each receive a dozen lashes. Boatswain's mate, do your duty.'

The punishment was witnessed in silence by the crew, with each stroke delivered with a whistling crack. The first few blows left vivid red wheals, but these then split, until the men's skin ran with blood. Between each prisoner, Powell rinsed the cat in his bucket, running his fingers between the tails to remove the fragments of skin and gore. Perkins, the run slave, had a back already criss-crossed with scars from his time on a plantation, while Hibbert's had a few marks from a flogging, many years earlier. Both men took their punishment in silence. Vardy, who was last and had watched his messmates' backs in mounting horror, had to be dragged forward, weeping and protesting. There was a grumble of disapproval amongst the men, silenced by the petty officers. Once he was tied to the grating, however, he became quiet. The crew all watched his smooth back, fascinated as to how he would react. But for all his noise earlier, he too, took his flogging with only the occasional gasp of pain. When he was cut down, he glared across to where John Beaver stood, a look of hatred in his eyes.

*****

A few days later, the great cabin of the *Titan* was full of soft light. The glow from the brass lanterns above melded with the candles that burnt on the table. All this light sparkled off the silver and glassware that was strewn across the surface and winked on the gilt buttons and braid of the officers who took their ease around it.

'I am not over fond of made dishes, but that was a capital steak pie, sir,' said Taylor, picking at a few crumbs that lay near his plate. 'The savour of fresh meat is so superior to our usual fare of salt beef.'

'Not to mention true pastry, rather than some concoction derived from crushed biscuit,' added Blake. He patted contentedly at the front of his tunic.

'I fear our fresh provender will not long endure, gentlemen,' warned their captain. 'We shall be partaking of ship's fare soon enough.'

'It is soft tack that I generally miss the most,' said Armstrong. To demonstrate he popped the last of some Plymouth bread into his mouth.

'Of course you gentlemen will have no such problems,' said Clay, waving a glass of wine towards Fraser and Macpherson. 'Living off the fat of the land in D'Arzon's chateau, once we land you on that beach tonight.'

'The count does look after us very tolerably, sir,' conceded Fraser. He indicated the sun that had begun to shine in through the window lights at the rear of the cabin. 'Have we now made our turn eastwards towards the shore?'

'Bravo, Douglas,' smiled Clay. 'We shall make a mariner of you yet. We are now standing towards the Morbihan. We are sailing easy. No occasion to arrive before it is quite dark.'

'And wholly the wrong way for the West Indies, if there are still any doubters on board,' added Taylor, to general laughter.

'Precisely so,' said Clay. 'If we have completed our meal, let us drink the health of the king, and then Harte can draw the cloth. Once that is done, we can attend to more important matters before we are sundered. Mr. Blake, you must be the youngest.' The officer rose to his feet, and raised his glass.

'Gentlemen, the King!' he said. As Macpherson drank his wine, his eye was attracted by a curious movement of Fraser's arm. The soldier picked up his glass, passed it out across the top of a water tumbler that stood beside it, and then took it to his lips. That was odd, thought Macpherson, and yet also familiar. Now, where have I seen someone do that before?

'Good, let us attend to business,' said Clay, waving Harte forward to refill the glasses. 'As you know, Major Fraser and I were recently at the Admiralty. I then left London to return to the ship, while he remained to engage with his superiors. Major, perhaps you would favour us with an account of their principal conclusions?'

'The government is pleased with our efforts so far and are minded to supply more definitive support. A force of regulars under General Maitland is to be assembled at Plymouth, together with transport, and they will be assisted by some vessels from the Channel Fleet under Sir Edward Pellew.'

'Intrepid Ted himself, sir,' whistled Blake. 'Matters are becoming serious!'

'But surely, Sir Edward will supersede you, sir?' asked Taylor.

'He shall indeed, and General Maitland will likewise supplant Major Fraser on land,' said Clay. 'We have played our parts, and now it is time for our superiors to come and take the credit. But none of this will happen until the rising is truly set. Previous interventions on this coast have been attended by embarrassing failure, and the government will countenance no repetition. So we shall be required to orchestrate a further, superior type of Royalist victory with only our resources to rely upon. Fortunately, Major Fraser has a proposal that he has agreed upon with London. Perhaps it would be best if we were to look at the chart, at this point. Harte, would you bring it over, if you please?'

When the map had been unrolled and the candelabras brought closer, Fraser leant forward and indicated a place.

'May I draw your attention toward this finger of land... here,' he said, pointing to a long, thin peninsula that extended out from the mainland for, perhaps, seven or eight miles. It was thicker toward its seaward end, perhaps a mile wide, but then abruptly narrowed to a spit of land only a few hundred yards across. A small, fortified port was marked at the seaward end of the peninsula. Macpherson leant forward to read the name of the settlement.

'Quiberon?' he asked. 'That name sounds familiar, but why, I cannot say.' Taylor looked at him in surprise.

'It is familiar, Tom, because it is in these waters that Lord Hawke won his splendid victory back in fifty-nine. Have you truly never heard tell of the Battle of Quiberon Bay? He fought the French in a gale so fierce that two of the enemy's ships sank like stones, the moment they were obliged to open their lower gun ports. Why, *Hearts of Oak* was wrote to commemorate the triumph. If you would know more, old

Ezekiel Davis was one of the ship's boys aboard the *Swiftsure* that day.'

'Apart from honouring the site of an old battle, is there a more firm objective that we hope to achieve?' asked the marine.

'The capture of the port of Quiberon itself,' explained Fraser. 'It is a reasonably substantial town, with good facilities. Troops and supplies can be conveniently landed, so it is ideal for General Maitland. Once captured, it should be tolerably easy to hold. Quiberon has well laid-out fortifications against an enemy approaching by land, and any attacker passing along this narrow part of the peninsula can be assailed by gunfire from the sea.'

'It is also set all about with treacherous reefs and shallows,' muttered Armstrong. 'That, at least, is plain from the chart.'

'If it has such formidable merits to resist an attack, sir,' said Macpherson, 'how do you propose that we shall take it in the first place?'

'By negotiation,' said the soldier. 'I had some contact with the authorities in the town earlier this year. The governor is an acquaintance of D'Arzon's and at one stage, I had hoped he might join with us. I have tolerable confidence that, with the right inducement, a capitulation can be arranged.'

'Inducement?' queried Taylor, looking up from the map.

'Life as an official of the New France is not always comfortable,' explained Fraser. 'The government has informers in each community and a guillotine in every town square. Much may be achieved with a bag of guineas and a free passage to the French speaking portion of His Majesty's Canadian possessions.' Fraser looked around the table and noted the distaste in most of the faces.

'Can a man's honour truly be purchased for so low a price?' queried Macpherson.

'Troubling as it may seem, I find, in my line of work, that it very often can,' said Fraser, 'Although it would be more correct to say men's honours. We must also have the officer who commands the military garrison at Quiberon in our pocket. Fortunately, nepotism is endemic in this part of France, and he is the younger brother of the governor.

'It seems too straightforward, sir,' said the marine. He leant back from the table. 'Will they yield so readily, or are we being drawn into a trap?'

'*Too straightforward!*' exclaimed Fraser, his face colouring. 'I trust you did not intend such a disrespectful tone, Lieutenant Macpherson? You have not been privy to the delicate negotiations that I have undertaken, at considerable personal risk, I might add. Only ignorance of the facts can excuse your want of deference towards a superior.'

'Come now, gentlemen, let us not quarrel,' said Clay. 'Harte, some more wine. We are all friends here. I know that no disrespect was intended, major. Tom is only motivated by his zeal for the success of our enterprise. Isn't that correct?'

'Aye, sir,' said Macpherson. 'My limited experience of soldiering has made me distrustful of simple solutions.'

'Good,' said Clay. 'We need not trouble you for the particulars of how your part will be done, major, and well done, I make no doubt. Perhaps we could move on to how matters will proceed, once the governor is made amenable?'

'He is not wholly of our way of thinking yet, sir,' said Fraser, mollified a little. 'He will certainly not commit before he has met with D'Arzon and received various assurances from him directly. Then, for a surrender of Quiberon to occur, there needs to be an appreciable show of force, to permit him and his brother to capitulate with honour.'

'What might constitute such a display?' asked Taylor.

'The appearance of four thousand *Choannerie* before the gates and the *Titan* in the offing to blockade the port,' said the soldier. 'That would have the desired outcome.'

'But how will so many Royalists arrive before the gates of the town?' exclaimed Taylor. 'Four thousand is far more than the *Titan* can carry.'

'On this occasion, they will come by foot,' said Clay.

'With some preparation, the count should be able to descend on Quiberon by marching onto the peninsula from the mainland,' explained Fraser. Macpherson had been studying the map, and pointed to a place half way along the peninsula.'

'And what of this wee fortification here, built just where the peninsula is at its narrowest?' he asked. '*Fort de Penthievre*, it is set down. Surely their guns must block any approach, or will your bag of guineas serve to buy them off, too?'

'No, that place will first need to be taken,' said Fraser.

'That is to be our part in this enterprise, gentlemen,' said Clay. 'We have time to form our plans, and we shall start presently by learning a little more about this place. To summarise the enterprise, Major Fraser completes his negotiations with the authorities in Quiberon, we remove this fortress from the Royalist's path, and they march on the town and occupy it until General Maitland arrives.'

'What could possibly go wrong?' muttered Macpherson, beneath his breath. He looked around at the faces of the gathered officers, seeing eagerness and concern in equal measure. Only Fraser's expression, in his single eye, was inscrutable.

*****

John Beaver had just started his meal when he became aware that the lower deck around him had fallen silent. The other men sitting at his table gathered up their things and began to rise, one after another, muttering their excuses and departing with their food. Soon there was only his square plate, together with a spoon, knife and mug of beer that remained on the scrubbed wood. His scattering messmates briefly masked the rest of the deck from him, concealing the large figure who was looming up through the crowd. The bench on the opposite side of the mess table groaned in protest as Hibbert lowered his bear-like frame onto it. He placed both of his arms on the table and stared at Beaver. Perkins and Vardy moved around the end of the table. Each sat on a stool, one on either side of him, and both uncomfortably close. Beaver's eyes darted around the deck, seeking help, but wherever he looked, he saw only the backs of sailors, all turned away from him. The buzz of quiet conversation had resumed, as if nothing out of the ordinary was happening. His stomach seemed to knot and contract as he realised that all the petty officers who shared the lower deck with the men had vanished from sight. He gulped once and then resumed tapping a ship's biscuit on the surface of the table. Hibbert reached across, enveloped his hand, biscuit and all, in one huge fist. He tightened his grip, crushing inwards, whilst he watched as the mystic squealed with pain. When he released Beaver, after giving his fingers a final mangle, a little avalanche of crumbs and crushed weevils pattered down.

'What you done that for?' protested Beaver, wringing his hand. 'You've gone and bust it!' Hibbert ignored the outburst.

'Looks a bit dismal here,' he remarked to his two companions. He indicated the empty table, with its single place setting. 'Seems to me like no jack wants to scoff with him no more.'

'Bit like how poor Davis has had to eat his vittles these last few weeks,' added Perkins. 'On account of someone telling us he were ailing with the Scarlet Pox. Strange that, coz he seems much improved, now that he is messing back with us.'

'Neighbourly as it is of you lads to visit…' began Beaver.

'You ever been flogged, Mystical Jack? interrupted Hibbert, staring directly at him for the first time.

'Aye, back on my last ship,' he replied.

'That's right,' agreed the big sailor. 'O'Malley told us about it. They flogged you for shirking. Squealing and hiding when the enemy was close, weren't it?'

'I can explain…'

'So you'll recall that it hurts like buggery, being flogged?' asked Hibbert, cutting across him again.

'It weren't my fault you boys went and ran,' said the mystic. 'I never told you to go and do that.'

'You looked over the side recently, Mystical Jack?' resumed Hibbert.

'I… I may have done, shipmate,' replied Beaver.

'And does it look like the fucking Caribbean to you?'

'No, not at present,' conceded the mystic. 'But we may yet be ordered there. Perhaps I were a bit out in my reckoning.'

'That ain't what Pipe said, when we was taken before him,' hissed Perkins, his mouth close to Beaver's ear. 'He told us straight, the barky ain't going there. And he should know, being the captain an' all.'

'That's right, said Vardy from his other side. 'He said it plain as plain, just before he told us what fools we been, attending to the likes of you, and how we was to be punished. That's coz this whole thing has always been so much gammon. Now I has to kip on my belly, what with the cuts on my back.'

'You know, the Sight can be awful confusing, sometimes,' said Beaver. He would have gone on, but Hibbert held up his hand.

'You *still* rattling on about them visions of yours? See, we all got flogged on account of this Sight of yours. In fact, I've a good mind to put out your eyes, and see what manner of Sight you got then.' For such a big man, his left arm was swift as a cobra. It flashed across the table and seized the back of Beaver's head by his lank hair. He pulled out his knife with his other hand and drew the mystic's face towards the blade, turning his head this way and that as if inspecting a large fruit he intended to peel.

'But it weren't my fault!' babbled Mystical Jack, his eyes wide with terror. 'Them bastards tricked me, good and proper! It's that idiot Henderson what's to blame. He went an' swopped the labels on them boxes! And that fool of a clerk, with his bleeding requisition. It's them you should be after, not...what? Why you looking at me like that?' Hibbert stood up, still with a firm grip on Mystical Jack's hair. He seemed to fill the space beneath the low beams.

'Did you hear that lads!' he roared, his face mottled with rage. He turned to address the rest of the lower deck. 'Reading Henderson's labels! Peeking at the clerk's ledger! Now, I am asking myself how comes someone with magic sight should have to be taking heed of labels on a box?'

In the quiet that followed, Beaver's mouth worked as he struggled for an explanation. Hibbert's face became almost sad.

'You gone awful quiet, for a mystical bloke,' he said. 'But I reckon that's coz, for the first time this commission, John Beaver, it be the truth as is coming out of your mouth. Shame it be a touch bleeding late for that.'

Without warning, Hibbert slammed Mystical Jack's head down onto the solid wooden plate in front of him. Food splattered across the surface, laced with blood. As Beaver's head came up again, Perkins smashed his fist into it, knocking the mystic backwards off his stool. The three sailors gathered around the stricken figure, kicking and punching. Beaver cried for help, but no one on the lower deck even looked around.

Chapter 12

Fort de Penthievre

No sooner had high summer arrived on the coast of Brittany than the weather turned, once more. The wind became blustery, grey clouds veiled the sky and the Atlantic returned to a sullen shade of green. Cutting through the choppy water came the long hull of the *Titan*, under reefed topsails as she closed with the western side of the Quiberon peninsula. A streak of land lay across the horizon ahead of the ship. It was formed from a chain of grass-covered dunes at the landward end, rising abruptly into brown, rocky cliffs. The *Titan* was passing through a number of small islands, columns of stone surrounded by clouds of birds. The air above the ship seemed alive with the noise of them as they slid across the wind, some heading out to sea, others returning to their nests of urgent chicks, amongst the rocks. Clay shut his telescope and turned from the rail, to face the two gangly youths who stood on the deck behind him.

In some ways, they were a well-matched pair. Both were fresh-faced seventeen year olds and were dressed in matching dark blue coats with the white colour patches that identified them as midshipmen. Both boys' faces bore faint shading beside their ears, easily mistaken for dirt, to mark where they were trying to cultivate the sideburns that every adult member of the crew possessed.

'Now gentlemen, kindly direct your gaze ahead. Do you mark where the coast changes from a low spit of sand to the higher part?' asked Clay.

'Aye aye, sir,' chorused the pair.

'There you shall find this Fort de Penthievre, on top of those cliffs. With my glass, I fancy I can see a wall of stone and, perhaps, some roofs and a flagstaff beyond, but I daresay more will be revealed as we approach, and much more from the masthead. We shall stand on and do our best to provoke them to fire upon us. I want you to observe all that you may. Note how many guns are in action and how quickly served they are. How many are positioned facing the sea, and how many cover the landward approach, what walls, ditches and the like the fort enjoys, and anything else of import. Also, mark down suitable beaches where we might land, to come at them. Do you have any questions?'

'No, sir,' they replied, still as one.

'Mr. Butler, do you have your glass?' he asked the largest of the pair, who produced a telescope from his coat pocket. 'Very good, and Mr. Russell, you have a notebook upon you, I trust? Very well, aloft with you both.' The two scampered to the main chains, and set off up the shrouds at a speed that would not have disgraced one of the frigate's topmen.

'Shall I have the ship cleared for action, sir,' asked the first lieutenant.

'Turn up the watch and man the guns, by all means,' said the captain. 'And we had better have the galley fire put out, if you please, Mr. Taylor. There is no need to inconvenience ourselves further than that. I only wish to observe this place. I do not countenance any full engagement.'

'Aye aye, sir,' replied the first lieutenant, hurrying away to issue the orders. Clay crossed to where the sailing master stood by the wheel.

'What do you think of these waters, Mr. Armstrong?' he asked.

'Very ill, sir,' said the American. He pointed to a reef a bare hundred yards off the port side. 'We are obliged to pass within a biscuit toss of hazards that would rip the keel from the hull, if we but gave them the chance.' Clay regarded the line of rocky teeth, black and slick with seaweed that stood proud of the white water around them. A cormorant rested on top of one, with its wings spread to dry, and stared back at the passing frigate.

'And could you navigate your way back here in the dark?' asked Clay.

'If the tide had ebbed, and I had the advantage of some moonlight, sir.'

'Moonlight I cannot promise,' said his captain. 'Perhaps a little starlight, but any assault on this fort will need the cover of darkness.'

'Steer southeast by east now, quartermaster,' ordered Armstrong, as the frigate continued to thread her way in towards the land.

'Southeast by east, aye sir,' replied Old Amos. He spun the wheel over, his eye on the binnacle in front of him.

'I daresay, I may be able to, sir,' resumed Armstrong. 'But do we really mean to assault that fort? It looks mighty formidable atop its headland.'

'Not today, for sure,' said his captain. 'I only wish to learn more, but Major Fraser's project to seize Quiberon requires us to take this place.' Now that they were closer in, both men could see that the rock face rose straight up from the sea before it turned into a solid wall of grey stone. Above the battlements, a large tricolour rose, the colours bright against the silver sky. The sailing master scowled at the shore and shook his head.

'Deck there!' came a voice from high above them.

'What have you to report, Mr. Russell?' yelled Clay.

'I believe the fort may be about to open fire, sir. They have hoisted colours, and I can see gunners manning their pieces.'

'Maybe,' said Clay, as he focussed on the approaching

shore. He could see embrasures in the wall now, and a suggestion of movement behind them. As he watched, a cloud of smoke billowed up and, a heartbeat later, a chain of splashes rose from the surface of the sea, coming straight toward him. Water from the final spout splattered down onto the quarterdeck beside him. A flat boom echoed across the sea.

'They are firing, sir!' yelled Butler, from aloft.

'You don't bleeding say,' muttered the gun captain of the quarterdeck carronade, brushing water from his arms. 'What *would* we do without them Snotties?'

'Mr. Armstrong, bring the ship about, such that we sail parallel with the coast,' ordered Clay.

'Aye aye, sir,' replied the sailing master. His captain strode forward until he could look down onto the main deck. 'Mr. Blake, do you suppose you can reach those guns on the shore? I wish to throw a few balls into this fort and get them to show their hand.' Blake stooped to peer through the gun port nearest to him. As he did so the fort disappeared behind a much wider blanket of smoke, and the water between the ship and the coast erupted in splashes. A crash sounded from forward.

'Still a half cable short, by rights, sir,' he said. 'They must be a good six to eight fathoms above the surface of the sea. Something might be achieved if we fire on the up roll.'

'Make it so, Mr. Blake. Engage the battery when you are able.'

'Aye aye, sir,' replied the lieutenant. He touched his hat and then turned back to his gun crews. 'Starboardside! Out quoins! Wait for my word to fire.'

As a wave passed under the *Titan*, her hull rolled, first towards the shore and then away from it. Just as her guns pointed towards the sky, Blake gave the order to fire. The coast vanished behind a wall of smoke, and the recoil of the guns heeled the ship still further over. Crews rushed to reload as the frigate emerged from her own smoke, just in time to receive another hit from the shore, this time accompanied by a shriek of pain from forward.

'They make good practice at this range, sir,' commented Taylor. 'Large calibre guns, too, I should say. At least twenty-four pounders.'

'Indeed,' said Clay. He turned his attention to the two figures up on the masthead.

'Make haste with your observations, gentlemen!' he yelled. 'I do not propose to let the Frogs knock us wholly to pieces.' The midshipmen's response was masked as the *Titan* fired again, with only the word "nearly" coming across before the roar of a fresh broadside.

'I think I heard the gentlemen say they required a little more time, sir,' said Taylor, still watching the fort. 'I can't see that we have hit them at all.'

'Eighteen pounders will barely scratch those walls from here,' said Clay. 'I only wish to unsteady the aim of their gunners. Put the ship about for another pass, Mr. Armstrong, but try and edge out of range, if you are able.'

The frigate moved on until she was free from the reefs around her and into open water once more. She tacked around and came back. Each time she fired, the blast of sound sent a fresh cloud of seabirds up from the little islands all around her. The fort kept up her bombardment, but failed to hit the *Titan* again. Smoke drifted across the sea, torn into clumps by the breeze. A column of water lifted from just behind the frigate, prompting Clay to look back toward the masthead, where the two midshipmen now stood on the royal yard, each reaching for one of the backstays. They leapt clear at the same moment and came swooping down at a speed that suggested a race. Russell's feet touched deck a moment before Butler's, and both youngsters came running over, wringing their hands.

'It's a wonder you have any skin left on your palms, Mr.

Russell,' said Taylor, glaring at the youngsters. 'I trust the wager will be worth the pain.'

'Ah good! You have completed your observations?' asked Clay.

'Yes sir,' said the midshipmen, in harmony once more.

'Back out to sea, if you please, Mr. Armstrong,' ordered the captain, 'before we are struck again.'

'Aye aye, sir,' replied the American.

'Mr. Taylor, kindly have the guns secured,' said Clay, before he turned back toward the midshipmen. 'Now gentlemen, what have you discovered?'

Russell handed over his open notebook, the cream pages fluttering in the breeze. On it he had drawn a crude sketch. The fort was an oblong shape with its longer side parallel with the coast. At each short end was a small, triangular shaped bastion with a further large triangle of wall on the landward side. In the centre of the landward side, the midshipman had marked a gate, with a question mark next to it.

'I have to assume the entrance is there, sir,' explained the midshipman. 'It wasn't plain from the masthead, but there is a track leading to it from the main road along the peninsula.'

'And what is your opinion of this place?' asked Clay.

'Very strong, I should say, sir,' said Russell. 'I counted eight guns on the side that faces out to sea and six more covering the beach. Guns on the landward side too. Walls all the way around, with a deep ditch on all save the seaward side. No need there, what with cliffs rising straight up from the water.'

'Hmm,' pondered Clay. 'That does sound formidable. Could you see any beaches for us to land on?'

'I only marked the long one that you can see from here, but that will be swept by the guns on that side of the fort, sir,' replied Butler, pointing to a place on the sketch. 'They could make it very hot for anyone coming ashore.'

'There is a small cove a little farther up the coast, about there, sir,' added Russell, his finger tapping a cross on the sketch. 'No more than a creek, in truth. I doubt if anything above a single boat could enter it.'

'Were you able to see how deep these ditches are? Or how high the walls?' asked Taylor, who had come across to join the group.

'Not really, sir,' said Russell. 'We were too far out, and what with all the smoke and firing and the like; even from the masthead it was hard to make out more than the general structure.'

'Then we must take a closer look, gentlemen,' said Clay. 'Could one of our launches find this cove of yours in the dark, Mr. Russell?'

'I should imagine so, if they had the benefit of a good boat compass, sir,' said the midshipman. 'I took a bearing on the entrance from that tall island over there. Just a touch off east by south.'

Clay looked towards the column of rock. The side that faced towards the frigate was stained white with guano.

'At least the easement of all these birds hereabout should serve to make your island visible in the black of night,' he observed.

'It is a shame that we do not have Mr. Macpherson with us, sir,' said Taylor, 'He is the man most skilled with such reconnaissance.'

'I shall make certain that he is returned to us in good time for an actual assault on this fort,' said the captain. 'In the meantime, we shall have to shift for ourselves, George.'

'Aye aye, sir,' said the first lieutenant. 'I do wonder how he fares amongst our Royalist friends.'

*****

Before the Royalists departed on their march towards Quiberon, Major Fraser had insisted on one more attack.

'A diversion, to draw attention away from our true objective,' he had described it, as he sat with Macpherson and the count in their host's great hall. 'Somewhere inland, to put our opponents off the scent.' D'Arzon's eyes had lit up at the prospect.

'I know the very place, mes amis,' he said. 'Remote, not too stoutly defended, and in quite the wrong direction. I can lead a raid on it tomorrow. Would you care to accompany me, lieutenant? It is some distance from here, but I can lend you one of my horses.'

Lieutenant Thomas Macpherson was not a confident rider, but D'Arzon had shown enough tact not to comment on the young marine officer's nervousness as they stood together in the stable yard the following day. Instead, he had simply indicated an old, placid looking mare to his groom. Mounted on this animal, Macpherson had been able to accompany the band of *Choannerie* on their long sweep through the forest. So he had been there, in the grey dawn, to witness their attack on the isolated gendarme post, accomplished with their now customary savagery. The sentries had been quickly overwhelmed, the gate forced, and after some desultory fighting, the slaughter had begun. He had tried to intervene, but D'Arzon had held him back.

'Let them play,' he had urged, his teeth bright in the first light of the sun. 'They have many long years of hurt to avenge. Do you imagine these gendarmes would show us more kindness, if the positions were reversed?' So he had sat on his restless horse as the young troopers were dragged from the barracks in their shirt tails to kneel in the mud. He had listened to their pleas for mercy, each one received with jeers before it was cut short by the crack of a musket.

At least the horse had served to get him away from the band of Royalists. He had used the excuse of a report to complete on that morning's attack to hurry back to the chateau. This had allowed him to ride ahead, rather than jolt alongside D'Arzon, listening to the men's triumphant chatter. Further and further he rode, until the sound of the marching *Choannerie* had faded into the distance, leaving him alone to brood. What sort of allies were these, he asked himself, able to mete out such savagery on their own countrymen?

So engrossed was he in his thoughts that it was only the first rumble of the approaching storm that brought him back to the here and now. The track he followed had worn a cutting into the hillside, through centuries of use. As he wound his way up to the top of the gentle rise, he saw a clearing ahead of him, bright in the gloom of the forest. He urged his elderly mount on, until he was in the centre of the opening. The sun was warm on his scarlet tunic, but away to the west he could see the gathering cloud. Distant cliffs billowed up above the trees. A thread of silver flickered amongst the grey, and seconds later he heard another deep growl of thunder.

Macpherson swung down from the horse and stretched his legs, grateful to be out of the saddle. He looked around him and recognised the big clearing as the one where he had witnessed the rising's first triumph. It was now empty of all the corpses and abandoned equipment. What the Royalists had not taken must have been cleared up by the French, he concluded. His horse stretched her neck down and began to crop at the summer grass, while the marine reached up to the back of his saddle. He unbuckled his rolled-up boat cloak, and pulled it over his shoulders. Then he placed his boot back into the stirrup, and after a few uncertain hops beside the circling mare, he managed to haul himself back up onto the horse. Once he was mounted, he spread his cloak around him, as he had seen Fraser and D'Arzon do, creating a cone of shelter.

It did not take him long to realise that a naval garment designed to offer protection to a man crouched in an open boat was much too short to provide the same for someone astride a horse. Major Fraser and the count had cloaks that stretched from their animal's rumps to lie over their necks, covering the rider and much of the horse like a huge candle snuffer. He looked down at his legs, protruding from beneath the hem on both sides, and at the scarlet arm that held the reins. The thunder sounded again, much closer. I am in for a soaking, concluded the Scot, as he urged his horse forward.

But just as the first heavy drops began to patter on the leaves above, a solution occurred to him. Around the next bend in the trail was a second, smaller path that led off to one side, with a little stream running beside it. Surely, this is the turn to that abandoned cottage where Fraser and I shared some excellent local apple brandy, he thought. He pulled his horse's head around, and with memories of the dwelling's sound stone roof and comfortable bench, he dug his heels into the mare's flanks to force her into a lumbering trot.

The grass had grown much higher and the trees were all in full leaf, but the cottage, with its dilapidated garden, was much as he remembered it, standing in the middle of its clearing. What had not been there before, however, were two strange horses, tethered to the broken fence. He hastily turned his beast back on herself.

'This is a fine pass,' he muttered. 'All alone in enemy country! Why didn't I stay with D'Arzon?' He was about to dig his heels into the mare's sides again, but something made him hesitate. The rain had thickened to a steady downpour. He could hear it thundering on the canopy of leaves overhead, and drips began to patter all around him. It became darker as heavy clouds blotted out the light. He pulled his horse to a halt and then turned her off the path, making her push onwards into the undergrowth.

When he was sure he could not be seen from the track, he dismounted and tied his horse to a tree. Then he drew out a pistol from its holster, and shielding it from the rain under his cloak, he set off through the wood in the direction of the cottage. He was sure that he had seen something out of place, and as he walked, he tried to recall what it might be. He was approaching the edge of the clearing now, and his pace slowed. He kept his sodden cloak close about him, concealing the bright scarlet of his tunic. An old oak, gnarled and massive, was the last tree on the forest edge. He crouched behind it, removed his hat and inched his head around the side of the trunk.

The two horses by the fence held their heads low in the downpour, ears back and flanks slick with water. The nearest one was a large chestnut mount with equipment that had a military look. The saddle cloth was dark blue, trimmed in white, and appeared to be of excellent quality. No wonder it looked familiar! He had seen a similar one that very morning, being pulled out of the tack room at the gendarme post, as the Royalists had ransacked it. An officer of gendarmes then, Macpherson decided, and a senior one at that. He turned his attention to the second horse. This was a darker animal, its equipment plain and civilian in appearance. He shifted his position a little to gain a better look, and a branch snapped beneath his boot. Both horses looked towards the sound, their ears pricked forward, and Macpherson knew why he had returned. There was no mistaking the thin snake of white that ran down the second horse's nose, nor the single white sock on one leg. The rain was forgotten as he realised he was looking at the mount that Major Fraser always rode.

*****

The night had been chosen with care. The moon had set

early, and the clouds overhead masked all but a handful of stars. The tide was still making, pushing the *Titan*'s launch in towards the shore, but an hour from now it would turn, ready to draw the boat back out to sea. The launch had a mast stepped, and the gentle breeze that blew from the southwest drove her hissing through the black water. Their line of approach was similar to that which they had followed a few days earlier aboard the frigate, but now the land ahead looked altogether more menacing. They were much closer to the surface of the sea, and in consequence, everything had grown in size. The tall islands around them loomed up like wading giants. The cliffs ahead, with their crown of fortifications, seemed much higher than before. The fort was a square of deeper black against the dark sky. They ran along the line of a reef, the spray flashing in the night, and then a column of rock glimmered white in the dark beside them.

'That will be the isle covered in bird shite, sir,' reported Sedgwick.

'Bring us into the wind, if you please,' came the voice of Lieutenant Preston, from just beside his shoulder. 'We had best get the sail off her, before we are seen from the shore.'

'Aye aye, sir,' said the coxswain. 'Man the sheets! Ready about!' He pushed the tiller round, and the launch came up into the wind, its main sail flapping. 'Look lively there! Trevan, drop the main sail! O'Malley, Rodgers! Unstep the mast, and lay it along the centre line. Rest of you, out oars!'

The launch crew were all experienced men, and even in the dark, aboard a rocking boat, they could rapidly transform their craft from one driven by the wind to one powered by oars.

'Belay there!' came the bass voice of Evans from forward.

'Watch yer fecking arse!' hissed a waspish O'Malley, followed by a more mild, 'mast secured, an' all, Cox.'

'Give way,' ordered Sedgwick. 'What course sir?'

Preston held the boat compass up to his nose, but the tiny

glimmer of light was too little to read by. He felt down around his feet, until he came across the warm brass of the shuttered lantern, and eased it open a little. A line of gold appeared, up-lighting him as he bent over the compass. He glanced towards the shore, back at the compass again, and then closed the lantern once more.

'Do you mark the red-looking star, just above the horizon, a touch off the larboard bow? That is east by south.'

'Aye aye, sir,' said Sedgwick. 'Red star it be.'

In the black night it was hard to perceive that the boat was moving at all. Only the crew swinging backwards and forwards on the benches and the faint jar of the stern against Sedgwick's back recorded each pull of the oars. Preston was counting the strokes softly beside him, using them to measure their progress. Once he reached three hundred, Sedgwick noticed how much closer the shore had grown. He could now hear the sound of waves as they crumpled on the beach, away to his left. Ahead, the dark bulk of the fort on its cliff loomed high above them. An orange light was shining from somewhere on the walls. Probably a watch keeper's lantern or a lit window, he told himself, pushing aside the feeling that it was a burning eye, staring back at him. The gentle sway of the waves started to build into rollers as they approached the coast. An oarsman on the starboard side missed his stroke with a clatter, drawing a crescent of white foam on the inky surface.

'Pull clean!' growled Sedgwick, before he turned his head towards Preston. 'I can't see this little cove of Mr. Butler's, sir. An' we be getting proper close now.'

'He was quite certain of the line,' said the lieutenant. 'Keep on the same bearing, and I am sure we shall see it presently.'

Closer and closer they came. A splash of white appeared ahead of them, accompanied with the sound of crashing water.

'I need to port my helm a little, sir,' warned the coxswain. 'Else we'll get ourselves sucked onto yonder reef.' Now there was breaking water all around them, and still the land ahead presented an unbroken wall across their path. The sound of waves surging against the base of the cliff boomed back at them and the air was full of spray. Sedgwick sensed the stroke of the men starting to falter as they looked around. 'Eyes in the bleeding boat, unless you wants a dunking!' he ordered, still scanning the way ahead. A pulse of swell passed under the boat, lifting them up, and he saw the line of breaking surf, white in the starlight, as it found the base of the cliff.

'Where's this damned cove, sir?' he yelled.

'There!' said Preston, pointing off to the right. Sedgwick stared hard in that direction and saw it, too. There was a gap in the waves, and a darker patch appeared against the black of the cliff, like the mouth of a cave.

'Now lads!' urged Sedgwick. 'Put your backs into it! Pull hard!' The launch surged forward through the water, corkscrewing as they cut across the swell. Another chain of rocks appeared alongside, and one of the men clattered the blade of his oar against it. Sedgwick held his breath as the boat seemed to race towards disaster, and then the angle changed a little and he could see the calmer waters of the cove ahead. With a long exhalation, he steered them through and into it. Now there were cliffs all around them, while off to one side, grey in the starlight, was a little stretch of sand and shingle, a bare dozen yards wide. Sedgwick pulled the tiller round and headed towards it.

'Easy there!' he hissed, and with a sliding crunch, the launch came to a halt.

'Over the side,' whispered Preston. 'Pull us up the beach.' The men slid the heavy boat forward until it rested at a steeper angle and then stood around it, shapes in the dark, more to be guessed at by the sound of their breathing and the gentle clink of their equipment. They were cut off from much of the sound of the ocean now. Cliffs of rock surrounded them on the tiny stretch of shore, with only a patch of stars overhead to supply any light. Preston issued his instructions into the dark.

'O'Malley, Trevan, Rodgers, go and investigate towards the fort. There will be a way up from the back of the beach,' he breathed. 'See what you can find, but do so quietly now, and avoid any contact with the French.'

'Aye aye, sir,' muttered the sailors, and the scrunch of their feet on the shingle faded into the dark.

'Evans and Hibbert,' he said to the two largest shadows, 'come with me. If anyone approaches, they are to be silenced with cold steel. Sedgwick, take command here, and get the launch turned about, ready to depart.'

A little later, Preston returned with his two huge minders.

'Is all ready?' he asked.

'Aye aye, sir,' answered the coxswain. 'Boat's held in the shallows by Abbott, and the others are manning their oars. The mast and sail are nice an' handy. We can get them up quick as quick if we needs to make haste, like.'

'Very good,' said the officer, 'and well done in conning us in here.'

'Thank you, sir,' replied Sedgwick. He drummed his fingers against the launch gunwale for a moment. 'Permission to speak, sir,' he asked.

'Go ahead,' said Preston. Sedgwick moved away from the others, drawing the officer with him.

'I ain't shy or nothing, but can the captain truly be meaning to land men here, sir?' he muttered. 'I was hard pressed just to bring the launch in. If we was burdened with a load of Lobsters, I couldn't answer for what might happen. An' I don't mean no disrespect to Mr. Butler and Mr. Russell, but I ain't certain they could take the cutter and the longboat past all them rocks in the dark with much hope of success.'

'As for what the captain is or is not considering, I am not privy to that,' said the lieutenant. 'Tonight is by way of a test. But I agree with you, this beach doesn't seem to be suitable for our needs. Rest assured that I will pass on your concerns.'

'Thank you, sir,' said Sedgwick, and then he touched the officer's sleeve. 'Someone's coming.' Preston listened and he, too, heard the faint sliding of stones.

'Who is there?' he challenged.

'O'Malley, sir,' came the reply, and the shape of the Irishman appeared from out of the gloom.

'What have you to report?' asked Preston.

'No path to speak of, sir, but Trevan an' I was after climbing up anyways, and we got that lump Rodgers to the top with a deal of hauling. The fort is just over the rise, away yonder. Only the one sentry outside the walls on this side but he don't seem too alert. Rodgers and Trevan are watching him. There are plenty more on the walls, mind. You can hear them clear enough, prattling away like.'

'Did you get as far as the ditch?' asked Preston.

'That I did, sir,' said O'Malley. 'Christ, but that fecker's deep, pardoning my language, yer honour. Three fathoms, if it's an inch, and a good four wide, an' all. The wall is higher yet, and drops straight to the bottom of the ditch. Overlooked by guns and soldiers galore and seeming to go around the whole fort, bar the side facing the cliffs.'

'I had best come and see for myself. Wait for us here, Sedgwick.'

It was sometime later that the crunch of feet against stones sounded on the beach once more. The tide had turned now, and the sea looked a little easier in the starlight beyond the entrance to the cove.

'Who goes there?' growled Sedgwick, his hand on the hilt of his cutlass.

'*Titan*!' replied the voice of Preston. Behind him, the others appeared out of the darkness, and the officer waved them forwards into the boat.

'Push off and take us back to the ship, if you please,' he ordered, as he settled himself in the stern sheets next to Sedgwick. 'It will be a disappointment for the captain, but I can see no prospect of us taking this fort without the necessity of a formal siege.'

Chapter 13

Undercurrents

'Might I have a word, Mr. Sedgwick, sir,' said a voice, laced with humility. The coxswain turned in surprise at the tug on his shirt sleeve. Jack Beaver stepped out from the space between the captain's pantry and the aft hatchway, where he had been waiting. Even in the gloomy half-light between decks, his face was a dreadful sight. His skin was black with bruising and one eye was closed. A cut on his forehead ran into his lank hair.

'No call for the 'mister,'' said Sedgwick. 'I ain't no grunter. Able will do fine.'

'Sorry, Able, I weren't thinking straight,' said the sailor. His swollen lips parted a little as he tried to smile.

'You lost yourself a tooth?' asked the coxswain, pointing.

'Aye, and another is wavering.' He pulled back his cheek with a finger to show the damage.

'Sorry to hear that,' said Sedgwick, surprised to realise that it was true. 'But it don't do to vex the likes of Hibbert and Perkins, unless you're proper handy with your fists.'

The former mystic shrugged. 'Aye, ain't that the truth,' he said. He looked directly at the coxswain with his open eye. 'So was it you what set me up?' he asked.

'I ain't got a clue what you're on about,' said Sedgwick, his face granite.

'I wouldn't mind if it were you,' continued Beaver. 'In truth, it would be easier to take. You're a proper deep one, see. It would finish me to think I'd been humbled by that arse O'Malley.'

'Seems to me as you was sure to get caught sometime,' said Sedgwick, 'carrying on as you were, with all that nonsense. You're plenty smart enough, mind. The way you figured Vardy were a tanner was a proper eye-opener, unless you knew already.'

'No, that were all me,' conceded the former mystic.

'Right, so if you're deep enough to have done that, what I can't fathom is why you need to go tricking folk, instead of doing some good with that head of yours.'

'I ain't like the rest of you!' protested Beaver. 'I hate going aloft. I got no beef for hauling lines on deck, I ain't got the pluck for a fight and I couldn't long splice if my life were to rest on the knot.'

'Then what did you volunteer to go to bleeding sea for?' exclaimed Sedgwick. 'It's not like you was pressed!'

'Cause of what this place has got!' said Beaver. 'Look at you! You're a run slave, a Negro, yet you got mates on board as would take a musket ball for you. I saw them bail you out when that church hall got wrecked, back in Plymouth. I've seen you with the others -- Adam Trevan, that lump Evans and even O'Malley. I never had no one as cared about me like that. How do you get them to do it?'

'By just being me! It ain't no bleeding trick!' said the coxswain. 'There's a heap less mystery to it than you seen to think. You just need to be straight with folk, watch out for them, an' they'll do the same back.'

'I've made a proper bleeding mess of it, ain't I?'

'Look, it ain't for me to go telling you what to do, but perhaps it's not as bleak as you figure,' said Sedgwick. 'I know you've had a thrashing an' all, but on the lower deck that settles matters. Stop tricking folk, for a start, stow the mystical bit and be plain Jack. In time, it will answer.' He went to bump a fist with Beaver's, but saw the man flinch, so he turned it into a handshake. Slowly, almost reluctantly, the landsman took his hand.

'Now, I got to shift,' said Sedgwick. He started up the ladderway towards the main deck.

'Able,' Beaver called after him. The coxswain stopped and looked back. 'It ain't as often as I been making out, but it is true, you know. I can see the future, sometimes.'

'If that be so, I would keep it to yourself, if I was you,' he replied.

*****

The *Titan* was sailing along the coast of the Morbihan once more, under easy sail. On her port quarter the blue Atlantic washed onto a long stretch of yellow sand, backed first by dunes and then farther inland with rolling, forested hills, made hazy by the distance. This being a Sunday, many of the crew were up on the forecastle, sitting in companionable groups. The rigging of the foremast was alive with lines of drying clothes, while many of their owners had taken the opportunity of fine weather to wash their hair. It now billowed free around them, giving those with the fullest pigtails the look of Macbeth's witches. The buzz of their chatter was laced with the sound of a fiddle, as O'Malley played a hornpipe for some of the younger top men to dance to.

Meanwhile, in the stern cabin of the frigate, the atmosphere was altogether more tense. Clay sat at his table with Major Fraser opposite him. On his right hand sat Preston, and on the other side was Taylor.

'Perhaps I have not made myself quite clear, sir,' said Fraser, tapping the chart spread out before them to emphasise his point. 'In which case, you have my apologies, but let me be plain now. The attack upon Quiberon must go ahead. The count is even now gathering the *Choannerie* together for their descent. Such a concentration of men cannot long escape the notice of the authorities.'

'As you have already explained,' said Clay, folding his arms.

'For my part, I have run considerable risks in my discussions,' continued the Scot, as if Clay had not spoken. 'I have brought the governor to a point where it only requires the direct meeting I discussed before, with D'Arzon and myself, to finalise the particulars of his capitulation. All I need from you is the assurance that Fort de Penthievre will be taken, so the way will be clear for the Royalists to advance up the peninsula. Am I now to understand that you can no longer deliver your part?'

'It is not for want of industry on our side, major,' said Clay.

'I do not question your activity, sir, but I am not persuaded that Earl Spencer will see matters in such a sanguine light,' said Fraser. 'A few shots exchanged, a brief reconnaissance in the dark, and the task declared impossible?'

'Don't be so damned impertinent, Major Fraser!' said Clay, his face flushing. 'You forget yourself, along with the difference in our rank.'

'My apologies, sir,' said the soldier, without a trace of remorse apparent on his face. 'It was presumptive of me to address you in such a fashion. I had been led to understand that the Navy regard themselves as models of pluck and ingenuity. Perhaps I was guilty of permitting my disappointment to show. But I stand by the substance of my observation. Why is it that this place may not be taken?'

'Oh, I make no doubt that it can be taken,' said Clay, still regarding Fraser icily. 'A regular siege would reduce the place in a matter of weeks. By which time half the French Army hereabouts will have arrived to interrupt us.'

'Which was why the place must be seized by a coup de

main,' said the soldier.

'Lieutenant Preston here landed on that shore to observe the fort from close quarters three nights ago,' said Clay. 'Kindly share your observations with us, Edward.'

'As the captain says, I cannot see how it can be taken by surprise,' said Preston. He pushed Midshipmen Russell's drawing of the fort in front of the Scotsman, which he had now made a few additions to. 'Firstly, the only practical place to land troops is this wide beach here, just to the north, but that is covered by the enemy's guns and is certain to be patrolled regularly. Once ashore, the attackers would need to climb atop the cliffs, without alerting the enemy. Then, the fort itself is surrounded on three sides by a wide ditch, which I estimate at just over three fathoms deep.' Fraser glanced at Clay.

'Almost twenty feet,' he supplemented.

'The wall that overlooks the ditch is even more substantial, has plentiful sentries and is swept by cannon,' added Preston.

'We counted eight heavy guns in the battery that faces the sea,' added Clay. 'Six more cover the beach, with others on the remaining two sides. Even with minimal crews of gunners, we can hardly expect a place with so much ordnance to have a garrison of less than three hundred men. What do we muster at present, Mr. Taylor?'

'Our entire crew number two hundred and forty, sir,' replied Taylor. 'But that includes the sick, ship's boys, idlers and so forth.'

'Yet, with the element of surprise, I would still hazard an attack,' said Clay. 'What I cannot see is how that surprise is to be achieved.'

'Mr. Preston managed to get ashore undetected, sir,' said the Scotsman. 'How was that done?'

'Via a tiny cove cut into the cliffs,' said Preston. 'I had a very small party. The approach to that inlet is much too hazardous for a boat, laden with troops and crew, to negotiate.'

'I am sure you understand these naval matters better than I,' said Fraser. 'Very well. Why not approach from the far side of the peninsula?'

'This ship carried out a survey of that coast the night before last,' said Clay. 'It is shoal water, even at high tide. The boats would ground long before we reached the shore.'

'You say the fort has a ditch on three sides,' continued Fraser. 'What of an attack mounted against the fourth side?'

'My dear sir!' exclaimed Preston. 'That is the side that faces the sea! It is guarded by cliffs, with a considerable swell beneath them. Assuming our boats are not beaten into firewood on the rocks, how do you propose that anyone -- even sailors -- are to climb directly from the sea and up a cliff face?'

'Mind, I will own that it would certainly surprise the French!' said Taylor. He and Preston laughed at this, but Clay bent forward over the little diagram. Then he consulted the chart, his finger running over the soundings marked on it. On the back of his neck, he felt the familiar prickle as the germ of an idea started to form.

'How much swell was there, the night you were beneath those cliffs, Edward?' he asked.

'Plenty, sir,' replied Preston. 'Far too much for our boats to survive, close in. Had we not had the comfort of the little bay, matters might have ended very ill.'

'And yet, as I recall, there was only a modest wind,' said Clay.

'That's correct, sir,' replied Taylor.

'Large waves, yet little wind,' mused Clay. 'So the sea must be shallow, to cut up so lively, even at the top of the tide?'

'I presume so, sir,' said Preston. 'May I ask what you are considering?'

'I was thinking that you approached when the tide was high, naturally, so as to have sufficient water to navigate your way into the cove,' explained the captain. 'But what might happen if you arrived at low tide? There would be far fewer waves and perhaps a beach of some sort, or at least a rocky shore, exposed when the sea recedes. Perhaps an assault up the cliffs could be launched from such a place?'

Taylor opened and closed his mouth at the audacity of what was being proposed, but Preston's face lit up.

'Perhaps it might,' he exclaimed. 'I could return at night and confirm if it exists, sir.' Fraser looked around the group of naval officers and cleared his throat.

'I confess to have not fully grasped the finer maritime details of your discourse, gentlemen, but am I to understand that you now believe that something might be attempted against the fort?' Clay held up a cautionary hand.

'We have some ground to cover first, major,' he said. 'Mr. Preston needs to discover if such a shelf or beach does, indeed, exist at low tide, under the walls of the fort. But if it does, and if the enemy are neglecting to patrol there when it appears, and if a low enough tide is approaching on a moonless night, then perhaps something could be tried.'

'Mr. Preston seems impatient to proceed with the reconnaissance, at least, so perhaps that can be done promptly, sir?' suggested Fraser.

'Let us say that it can,' said Clay, 'and that a satisfactory foreshore exists.'

'Indeed,' said the major. 'As for the night of your assault, with the requisite tides and so forth, we have not yet determined the time of our attack more generally, sir. The other parts of the plan could be adjusted to suit.'

'A week hence might work, sir,' offered Taylor, looking up from Clay's almanac. 'There is a particularly low tide at five bells in the first watch, and no moon until three hours later.'

'A week,' mused Fraser. 'Earlier than I had thought, but

that is often desirable in such matters, where secrecy is all. Very well, sir, the night before your attack, I will arrange for D'Arzon and myself to meet with the Governor of Quiberon, by your leave. I shall need you to bring us to the meeting place and supply a boat to land us there. It is a quiet spot, close to the end of the peninsula. An isolated cove, with a little fisherman's croft. With the final arrangements made for Quiberon to declare for the king and with the fort in our hands, the Royalists will be able to march on the place.' Clay considered matters for a moment.

'I shall need Lieutenant Macpherson to be returned to me, to lead my marines in the assault,' he said. 'And all is still contingent on Mr. Preston's confirmation that a beach exists at low tide. But if it is there, and it will serve, then I agree, we can proceed. Let us make it so.'

*****

Lieutenant Macpherson enjoyed his early morning strolls around the grounds of Chateaux D'Arzon. He was always up before dawn, walking briskly in the grey light, before most of the soldiers camped there were awake. He found that the tranquillity gave him the opportunity to order his thoughts for the day ahead. But today, he took his time to savour the place, knowing that in all probability he would never come here again. He gazed up at the cones of dark slate that crowned the towers at each corner of the main house and paused to admire the mist that trailed over the mirrored surface of the ornamental pond that lay beyond the kitchen garden. He listened to the forest birds as they greeted the approach of morning, in the woodland clumped thickly all about the property. He rested for a moment with his back to a tree and allowed the first rays of the sun to warm him. Then he arrived at the formal gardens, where the Royalist soldiers had, until recently, been camped.

They had all marched away now, deep into the forest and on towards the sea, ready for their descent on the Quiberon peninsula. The new bell tents provided by the British government had gone, leaving wide yellow discs where the grass had been starved of light, but the lines of little makeshift shelters remained. Nearer to the house, the elaborated pattern of a parterre could still be guessed at, although the tracery of box hedges had been crushed into the turf or torn up for kindling. Ranks of blackened cooking pits stretched away from him, each one at the centre of a ring of detritus. A discarded boot lay nearby, its sole curling free like a tongue. There were pieces of firewood, a broken pot, and close at hand, the remains of a rabbit, its pelt the subject of an angry tug of war between two stray dogs.

He saw the littered ground before him, but in his mind, other images swirled. That dark night, full of smoke and flame from burning thatch, with Count D'Arzon, sword in hand, urging his cheering Royalists to slaughter all before them. Then the other, softer firelight in the hall as it played on Fraser's face, twisted and bitter with hatred. He saw the long lines of *Choannerie* as they marched through the forest, singing in their strange, guttural Breton. Thoughts of the forest brought back to mind that little cottage in the rain, with two horses tied to the fence. The Royalists, the *Titan*, Major Fraser and Count D'Arzon. Memories and fragments swirled in his mind. Over all was the knowledge that something felt wrong, if only he could reach out and lay his hand on it.

He was pulled back into the present by something large and red, moving towards him. He looked up and saw the erect figure of Sergeant Bristow, picking his way across the rubbish-strewn lawn. He thought of walking on, unwilling to have his thoughts disturbed, but as he began to turn away, the tall soldier raised a hand in greeting. Macpherson waited for him to draw near, and soon the drill sergeant was in front of him, stamping to a halt and saluting.

'Good morning, sergeant,' said Macpherson, returning the salute. 'Kindly stand at your ease. You are up early.'

'Yes, sir,' agreed Bristow. 'I was just having myself a last look around, before we goes.'

'As was I,' said the Scot. He was tempted to dismiss Bristow, but his train of thought was quite broken now. 'Since we seem to be the only ones awake at this hour, would you care to accompany me?'

'Why yes, sir,' beamed the sergeant. 'Thank you very much.' Macpherson suppressed a pang of guilt at his earlier resolution to ignore the Englishman, and the two men walked on.

'May I inquire as to what time we shall be departing today, sir?' said Bristow, after a pause.

'We shall return to the coast this very morning,' explained the Scot. 'The arrangement is for the *Titan* to be off the beach at dusk, so there are a few hours before we need go. Are you and your fellow sergeants ready to leave?'

'We've been ready this last month or more, sir,' said the soldier. 'Not that being here ain't been diverting in its way, but if I never see another Breton for the rest of my life, it'll not be too soon. No, it's back to the Buffs for me, and the sooner it comes, the better I shall be pleased.'

'The three of you can be very satisfied with what you have achieved,' said Macpherson.

'Most obliging of you to say so, sir,' said Bristow. 'The Frog sergeants did their bit an' all, mind, but it is pleasing to have played our part. Some of them farmers may even pass for soldiers, where fighting is concerned, even if their camp discipline ain't quite up to King's Regulations.' He indicated the piles of rubbish. 'Like the blooming common after Southwark Fair, ain't it?'

'Aye, it certainly does present a melancholy aspect,' said the marine officer. 'These grounds would have been quite lovely in their day.'

'I did suggest a bit of a tidy up, sir, but the men are convinced they'll not be needing this place no more,' said Bristow. 'Billeted in feather beds by the grateful town's folk of Quiberon is what they're reckoning, if you will credit it.'

'You sound like you doubt that will be the case?' The sergeant brushed a little dust from his sleeve before replying.

'In my time I've been quartered in no end of places, and never yet found one as didn't resent the intrusion, sir,' he said. 'Why will this place be different, assuming they lets them in at all?'

'Major Fraser is very confident that they will,' offered Macpherson.

'You will know more about that than me, sir,' said Bristow. 'But if I had a nice house an' a brace of daughters, I ain't certain I should be welcoming in several thousand soldiers as had pitched up outside. Keep a ditch and wall between me and them, I would, whether the governor said they was sound or no, begging your pardon. Anyway, here I am rattling on and spoiling your walk. We shall be ready to depart when you give the word, sir.' Bristow saluted once more, and started to turn away.

'One moment, sergeant,' said Macpherson.

'Sir?' queried Bristow

'Was there a particular duty that you have to perform now?'

'Nothing urgent, sir.'

'Then perhaps you would walk with me a little longer,' said the marine. 'You seemed to have some decided views about Major Fraser's project. I would be interested to hear them.'

'It ain't my place to offer opinions on my betters, sir,' said Bristow, as he fell in beside him again. 'I spoke out of turn.'

'It is done now,' said Macpherson. 'You are a soldier of much experience. I would be interested in learning what troubles you about this proposed move to Quiberon?'

'If you press me, sir, I will share my thoughts gladly,' said the sergeant. 'Not that I am shy at all. I ain't taking no part in this 'ere attack, so no one can say as I am. But I have never been partial to campaigns what seem too good to be true. Coz more often than not, they disappoint. For instance, is this town really going to throw themselves over to the Royalists? Especially after what happened to that Port Manec'h?'

'As I said, Major Fraser is quite firm in his view that they will.'

'Which is all to the good,' said Bristow. 'But should he be wrong, and this place don't yield, wouldn't the Royalists all be trapped, hard against the sea, at the end of this peninsula?'

'They would be in a false position, I make no doubt,' said Macpherson. 'But as I understand the plan, they only advance on Quiberon once the town's fall is certain. The major and Count D'Arzon will finalise matters with the town's authorities before the Royalists commit themselves irreversibly.'

'An' if this Frog governor should play him false, sir?' asked the sergeant.

'Then things could go very ill,' conceded the marine. 'But the count seems content with the arrangement, and he has some knowledge of the governor.'

'Aye, and that is a comfort,' conceded Bristow. 'The count does know the folk hereabouts better than the likes of us, and him and Major Fraser are old comrades.' Macpherson nodded, deep in thought again, and they walked on a little farther. Then he slowed as something jarred in his mind.

'What was it that you just said?' he asked.

'Eh, that the count knows folk round here, sir?' offered Bristow.

'Yes, but then you said more,' persisted Macpherson. 'Did you not call the major and the count old comrades?'

'Sorry if I said a thing as I shouldn't, sir,' said Bristow.

'Nothing of the kind,' said the marine. 'I was just surprised by you calling them so. Do you mean they have become well acquainted over these last few months?'

'In truth I meant earlier than that,' explained the sergeant.

'Earlier?' queried Macpherson. 'How so? I asked the major about this very point, before the first Royalist attack. He told me he had never met him before last winter.'

'I dare say, that must be me getting the wrong end of stuff,' said Bristow. 'Some of the Frogs served with the count when he was in the old Royal Guard, before the Revolution. Sergeant Lagadec, for one. What with the major having done the same, I thought that their paths would have crossed, but I must be wrong.'

'D'Arzon served in the Royal Guard!' exclaimed Macpherson. 'I knew he had done some soldiering, but he has kept that quiet. Are you quite certain?'

'As certain as I can be, sir,' said the sergeant. 'Leastways, according to what I've been told. He were only a youngster back then, mind.'

'But...but if the count served the old king, why is he not an émigré, or dead? How is he still at large, permitted to keep his estates?'

'According to Lagadec, he helped out during the Revolution, sir,' said the sergeant. 'Some service to do with getting his men to lay down their weapons. His valet told me how the count burns with shame for what he did, muttering prayers on his knees long into the night, with candles and all manner of Popery.'

'Does he?' said Macpherson. 'He is certainly very committed to the Royalist cause now.'

'Aye, he's proper driven in battle, and no mistake, sir,' agreed Bristow. 'Why, zealots ain't in it! I should say he's a man with a few wrongs as he wants sorted.'

'Yes, that may be so,' the marine mused. 'Being driven to put matters right may explain much.' But in the marine officer's mind, it was not the eager young count he saw, but the face of Major Fraser, and the single-eyed look of hatred he had witnessed in the firelight, all those months before.

*****

Later that day, Lieutenant Macpherson was brought off from his deserted beach, and was soon back amongst his fellow officers in the wardroom of the *Titan*. All were pleased to see him, and the bottles of Calvados he had brought fuelled the conversation long into the summer night. Only when he had caught up with all the news and gossip from the close little world of the ship did he retreat to his cot. There he lay and pondered what he had heard, adding it to what he already knew. Edward Preston had found the shelf of rock beneath the cliffs at Fort de Penthievre, just as Clay had predicted, so the frigate's attack was to go ahead. His cabin seemed tiny compared with his room in the chateau. He lay there, unable to sleep, with his eyes fixed on the oak planking just above his head, as close as the inner lid of a coffin. Major Fraser and Count D'Arzon, *Choannerie* and *Gendarmes*, Quiberon and the fort, treachery and betrayal -- all the threads were running towards the same narrow peninsula on the coast of the Morbihan.

The three drill sergeants were less than pleased with their return to the stuffy dark of the frigate's crowded gunroom. Almost the moment they had stepped aboard the ship, their seasickness had returned, causing them to stumble clumsily, as they moved about the tiny space. Once Bristow had crashed his head against the low deck beams for a second time, he too, retreated for the night. There he lay and groaned with every rock of his hammock. He kept his eyes tightly closed in an attempt to shut out the world of swinging motion all around him as the *Titan* moved to the gentle rhythm of the sea.

Farther forward, the watch below were asleep on the lower deck. A little of the night breeze flowed down the ladderways and gratings from the world above. It stirred and mixed with the warm fug of stale air, alive with the snores and mutters of the crew. At his place close to the foremast, John Beaver opened his eyes and woke with a start. He let out a long shivering cry, as if a finger of icy air had found him in his hammock. The seamen all around were jerked into life.

'What the bleeding hell was that?' demanded one.

'Beaver! Was that you a hollerin' like an unpaid whore?' said another.

'What's all this alarm about?' demanded Jamieson. As one of the ship's petty officers, he hung his hammock in the more spacious area by the ship's side.

'Visions!' said the sailor. 'Dreadful visions!'

'Ain't you learnt your lesson yet, Beaver?' asked Jamieson. 'No one gives a damn about them no more. You just stow yer noise, or I'll have you scrubbing out the heads until Michaelmas next.' He rolled over onto his other side, banged his pillow flat and settled back to sleep.

'What manner of visions?' whispered the man on Beaver's other side. 'What you gone and seen this time?'

'I seen a rocky shore, with cannons a roaring, and a ship on fire,' he moaned. 'And I seen gore, plenty of gore!'

'Ah, well our Pipe be a proper fighting captain,' mumbled the sailor as he slipped back towards sleep. 'We dish out a fair measure of such stuff, but don't you go a-worrying. The old *Titan* always comes through.'

'No,' whispered Beaver. 'You ain't getting it. It were us as was being stuffed.'

Chapter 14

Ebb and Flow

Clay looked up from his breakfast in response to the knock at the door, his spoon poised over a boiled egg. It was one of four laid by the ship's hens that morning, and he was particularly looking forward to it. The cabin was bright with sunshine reflected off the sea, and bands of light flickered like waves across the ceiling with each surge and roll of the ship.

'Come in!' he called, placing his spoon back down next to his plate and rising to welcome his visitor. 'Lieutenant Macpherson, as I live and breathe! My apologies for not being able to greet you sooner, but I am excessively pleased at your return. Do come and join me. Have you broken your fast yet this morning?'

'Good morning, sir,' said the marine. 'I have eaten in the wardroom, I thank you, but I will gladly take a dish of coffee.'

'Harte! Another cup for Mr. Macpherson, if you please,' said the captain towards his steward. 'Are you quite sure you would not like to sample an egg, Tom? They are fresh this morning. No? Then perhaps you will not object to me having mine whilst it is yet warm?'

'By all means, sir,' said the marine as he stirred sugar into his coffee.

'You are settled back into the ship, I hope?' asked Clay, through a mouthful of food.

'Aye, as if I were never gone, sir,' said Macpherson. 'I

propose to drill my men this morning, to prepare them for the attack on this wee fort. We were discussing it in the wardroom last night. Out from boats, into shallows, directly up a cliff, and finally, over a wall I shall find at the top. Oh, and all to be carried out in the dark, making no sound, if I understand my part correctly. Have I missed anything?' Clay laughed aloud at his description.

'Sounds a troubling prospect, don't it?' he said. 'Mr. Preston will doubtless have given you the particulars, but it is perhaps not as daunting as you imagine. He took a good look over the ground the other night. The cliff is steep, but no more so than our mizzen shrouds, and he found plenty of gullies worn into them. He climbed to the top himself, with some of the launch crew. There is nothing that should trouble our younger top men in the ascent.'

'What of those unfamiliar with going aloft, like my men, sir?' asked the Scot.

'Mr. Hutchinson has fashioned a quantity of rope ladders for them, and anyone else burdened with a musket,' explained his captain. 'Mr. Preston also found the beach we shall land on to be unguarded, so the French clearly fear no assault from that quarter, which is a comfort.'

'Perhaps with good reason, sir,' muttered the marine.

'It is not like you to be disheartened, Tom,' said Clay. He pushed aside his food, and drew his own coffee towards him. 'If you are ill at ease at the prospect of this attack, pray speak your mind openly. I hope we have served together long enough for you to know I am no Tartar.'

'Your pardon sir,' said Macpherson. 'I will naturally play my part in storming the fort, and the arrangements made so far seem excellent.'

'I wanted you back on board as a condition of making this attack,' said Clay. 'I, too, had grave reservations at first, but I now believe we have a tolerable prospect of success. Without the fort in our hands, the rest of Major Fraser's plans will not answer. When I last met with him, he was very insistent that the attack should go ahead.'

'Aye, he does seem very keen for his scheme to proceed, in spite of its many flaws,' said the marine. 'Do you not find yourself wondering why that might be, sir?'

'Is it not because of his zeal for our cause?'

'To judge from the talk in the wardroom last night, this attack on Fort Penthievre has quite occupied every man on board these last few weeks,' said Macpherson.

'I suppose we have been preoccupied with the assault,' said Clay. 'But surely, that is to be welcomed, for the outcome will be most uncertain if we are ill prepared.'

'And what if that level of engagement was the major's true purpose, sir?' asked the Scot.

'I am not sure I follow you, Tom.'

'Have you ever witnessed a conjurer at a country fair, sir?' said Macpherson. 'How he draws the attention of his audience to the extravagant flourishes of one hand, while the trick is performed in a quiet way with the other?'

'I understand the principle,' said Clay. 'How does it pertain in this case?'

'Spying, deceit, bluff, treachery - this is the currency of Major Fraser's world, sir,' said Macpherson. 'I have observed him closely these last few months. He is as masterly in his way as any conjurer. So, when he is so insistent that we attack this fort, whatever objections are raised, I find myself wondering what it may be that he wishes to blind us to?'

'And do you have an answer to your question, Tom?' asked his captain. The young marine sighed long and deep.

'Regrettably not, sir. But I do find there to be something troubling about Major Fraser.'

'Oddly, so does my wife, who has never met the man,' smiled Clay. 'But for me to act, I need something beyond mere suggestion. What more have you observed?'

'Have you noted the manner in which he drinks the

health of the king?' asked Macpherson. 'He lifts his wine over his water glass before drinking. I first marked him doing it in this very cabin, and thought that it looked familiar. As a boy, I recall that when my grandfather was required to drink the Loyal Toast, he did so in that same manner, thus.' Macpherson passed his coffee cup over Clay's, and up to his lips. 'It is an old Jacobite ruse. Toasting the king, over the water. Not King George then, but the Stewart pretender.'

'Did he, by Jove?' said Clay. 'In truth, that is odd for an officer of the crown. But is it particularly concerning? I daresay his Jacobite sympathies will have been behind his decision to serve the King of France before the Revolution, which he has spoken of, freely. There must be many Highland families with a past that will not bear close scrutiny in this regard, not least your own, I collect. And not just in Scotland. Why, as a boy, I remember Old Squire Paterson arguing with my father that the king was a German rogue, with no more right to the throne than a milkmaid had for her stool.'

'There are still other reasons for caution, sir,' said Macpherson. 'You bid me keep my eyes open, and I trust I have done so.'

'What else do you have to report?' asked Clay.

'The major is guilty of telling me several falsehoods, sir. For example, when we took shelter together, before the Royalist's first engagement in the spring, I had occasion to ask him how well he knew the count. He told me quite decisively that he had never met with him before the start of this year; yet I now find that to be untrue. I have intelligence from Sergeant Bristow that they both served together in the old Royal Guard.'

'Does Bristow's intelligence come directly from Major Fraser?' asked Clay.

'No, it comes from members of the *Choannerie* who are former guardsmen,' said the marine.

'I see. And do D'Arzon and the major recognise each other?'

'I do not believe that the count does, but I have seen the way Fraser looks at D'Arzon in unguarded moments, sir,' said the Scot. 'There is revulsion in his gaze.'

'Hmm,' said Clay, tugging at one of his sideburns. 'Might they have been enemies back then, perhaps over some affair of honour? Maybe they choose to ignore their past connection in the interest of the present cause. I have known officers who found themselves obliged to serve together, who have done as much.'

'That could be possible, sir,' conceded Macpherson. 'But I have not detected any hostility on D'Arzon's part. And there is more. I recently chanced to stumble over a private meeting that was taking place in the forest between the major and a senior gendarme officer.'

'If the major were here now, he might point to his role in intelligence, as requiring such contact,' offered Clay. 'He has been very open about his negotiations with the civil authorities in Quiberon. Might this meeting have been part of that?'

'Perhaps, but my heart tells me otherwise, sir,' said the Scotsman. 'As you say, he has been candid about his other discussions, so why not be frank about this encounter? I have thought much about all of this. I know I have no absolute proof to offer you, but this reckless attack on Quiberon at the instigation of Major Fraser, combined with all the rest, makes me fear the worst. You are the senior officer, and can halt this attack if you choose.'

'I can,' said Clay, his face grave. 'And I can also envisage how such an intervention will be seen in London. The moment they receive word that Quiberon has fallen, they have a brigade of infantry and a squadron from the Channel Fleet ready to descend on this coast. How do you suppose they will greet the news that I have decided not to proceed, without a shot being fired?'

'But I know this whole project is conceived with some other object, sir!' urged Macpherson. 'There is something else afoot here, I know it!'

'Yet you cannot tell me what that other objective is?' said Clay.

'No, sir, I regret I cannot.'

'Tell me Tom, have you confronted the major over all of this?'

'I have not had occasion to, sir,' replied the marine. 'It was only yesterday that I learnt that he had deceived me about his previous association with the count. Would you like me to do so?'

'I am not certain that it will answer,' said Clay. 'Major Fraser can be a wily cove. Eels ain't in it! I raised your previous concerns with Lord Spencer, as to how the count's activities seemed to have escaped the attention of the authorities, but he had a very ready explanation to hand.'

'Then we do nothing, sir?'

'Nothing hasty, certainly,' said Clay. 'Let me reflect on what you have told me. Major Fraser will be on board later. We shall collect him and the count this evening to take them to their rendezvous with the governor of Quiberon. I shall consider what you have said with care, and contemplate what action to take. In the meantime, kindly continue with your preparations for our attack on the fort tomorrow.' Macpherson drained the last of his coffee and rose from the table.

'Aye aye, sir,' he replied. 'And thank you for hearing me out.'

*****

'Another four feet lower, if you please, Mr. Hutchinson,' ordered Lieutenant Preston from his place close to the forecastle.

'Aye, aye, sir,' replied the boatswain, who stood in the centre of the deck. He turned his back on Preston, giving the officer a fine view of his long grey pigtail, thick as a backstay at his bull neck and tapering to a more modest halliard as it drew level with his belt. He raised both arms as if about to conduct an orchestra, and the men tailing back on the lifts braced themselves.

'Let go both, handsomely now!' he roared. Above his head, the *Titan*'s main yard, a full eighty feet across, rumbled slowly down toward the deck. The trucks that held it in place squealed like a litter of piglets as they turned against the mast. 'Avast lee side, another foot weather side!' he ordered, his right hand clenched in a fist, his left still gesturing for more. The tilted yard became flat again. 'Easy all!' He ran his gaze along the huge spar to check that it was square and then turned towards the lieutenant.

'Will that serve, sir?' he asked, moderating his voice to a steady bellow. The yard looked oddly out of place, only part way up the mast. Preston stared at it and then half-closed his eyes. He pulled from his memory the wall of the fort as it had looked two nights ago, when he had scaled the sea cliff and stood at its base. He could almost see the dark mass against the stars and the silhouette of the big cannons that had rested in each embrasure. He recalled the sound of sudden laughter in the night, cut off by the slam of a door, and the constant clink and rattle of a block and halliard as the wind knocked it against the fort's flagstaff. He opened his eyes fully. The spar was just where the top of the wall had been.

'That will do very well, thank you Mr. Hutchinson,' he replied.

'Aye aye, sir,' said the boatswain. He turned back to his men with a touch of his hat. 'Belay all! Make fast them lifts! Powell, get a temporary sling rove.' Preston turned to the men gathered around him.

'Right, Mr. Butler, Mr. Russell, where are your grappling-hook men?' Each midshipman called out four names, and a group of sailors stepped forward. 'Excellent,' enthused the lieutenant. 'Do you all have your ropes?' The eight men held out coiled lines for him to inspect. 'Now, are they securely muffled?' He examined the cloth strips that had been wound around each hook's three iron claws.

'Hmm, I daresay, they will make little noise against the stone, but new, white canvas will show up in the dark,' he said. 'See that they are all made dirty with soot from the galley chimney before the attack, gentlemen.'

'Aye aye, sir,' chorused the two youngsters.

'Very good,' said Preston. 'From now on, you are to assume we have reached the base of the fort's wall.' The lieutenant waved towards the main yard. 'Mr. Russell, let me see your men launch their attack.'

'Aye aye, sir,' replied the midshipman. 'Grappling-hook men, forward!' he yelled.

'Stop!' roared Preston, followed by a more moderate. 'Do you propose to bawl your commands in that fashion when we attack in earnest, Mr. Russell?'

'Eh...I suppose not, sir.'

'Then kindly proceed as if it was tomorrow night and there are French sentries in the offing.'

'Aye, aye, sir,' whispered the midshipman, followed by a gentle 'grappling-hook men, forward.'

The four men advanced until they stood beneath the lowered yard. They uncoiled their ropes and began to whirl the hooks in every larger circles. Russell had chosen his men with care. They were the largest and most powerful in his division. Evans's throw caught with ease, as did the next two, with only the final throw clattering back down onto the deck. The sailor who had missed looked around guiltily.

'Carry on as if this is the assault proper, Hibbert,' said Preston. 'What would you next do?' The big sailor gathered up the grappling-hook, whirled it around his head once more, and then threw it with more commitment. It flew over the yard this time, rattling into place as he drew the line back.

'Ladder men now,' murmured Russell. Eight smaller, lither sailors pattered forward. Each man was armed with a cutlass and a pistol, and between them they carried a bulky, rolled up rope ladder. One sailor hauled himself up the rope, hand over hand, while the second man stooped to tie the top of the ladder to the bottom of the jerking line. Once the first man sat astride the yard, he began to pull the ladder up behind him. When it reached him, he dropped the pair of long metal hooks fitted to the top of the ladder over the yard.

'Launch the attack,' breathed the midshipman, and the rest of the sailors swarmed up, one after another, until the yard was full of grinning faces.

'That is most impressive, Mr. Russell,' said Preston. 'I confess you have me taken all aback. I expected something less well-marshalled. Did you devise this process yourself?'

'I did, sir,' grinned the midshipman. 'The armourer fashioned the hooks for me for the ladders. It will be easier for the ladder men with a proper parapet to stand on, rather than the yard, and the ladder will sway a good deal less against a wall.'

'Doubtless it shall,' said Preston. He looked at Russell, and almost for the first time, noticed how he had grown. The seventeen year old was almost as tall as he himself, although still with a spare build. No longer the shy lad he had encountered when he first joined the *Titan*, he mused, but fast approaching manhood. 'I think your arrangements are singularly well contrived,' he said, 'and I shall bring the captain's attention to them. Let us have your men back on deck, and see what Mr. Butler has done with his division.'

'I be proper glad we got Rusty as our Snotty,' said Trevan to the others as they formed up behind Russell. 'That all went sound enough.'

'Sound is it?' snorted O'Malley. 'Only cause its fecking dumb show we're after doing. You wait for the real thing, in the dark, with a dozen Frogs a waitin' for us at the top of the wall.'

'Don't mind him, Adam,' said Evans. 'He's only sore 'cause you beat him to the bleeding top.'

'I'd have climbed the fecking rope swifter if you hadn't cast it so ill,' muttered the Irishman. A series of clatters rang out from falling grappling hooks striking the deck. Only one line from the second group had caught on the yard.

'No, no, Mr. Butler!' cried Preston. 'This will never do! You must allocate your men better, each to his most suitable task! The four most lusty are required for this part. Davis's throw was a good fathom short!' Midshipman Russell's division smiled at each other and exchanged fist-slaps at the discomfort of their colleagues. After a moment, Evans turned to the others.

'Why is it we has fathoms at sea, 'stead of yards, like folk ashore?' he asked.

'It ain't just at sea we has them, Sam lad,' said Trevan. 'The shafts of the tin mines back home be all in fathoms, but let me give you a proper embrace.' He enfolded the huge Londoner around the chest, and stretched up his face, his eyes closed and his lips puckered.

'Here! What you bleeding doing!' exclaimed Evans, trying to wriggle free. 'Don't you come on all fresh like!'

'Why, I be just showing you a fathom,' said the Cornish sailor. He released his victim, and stood with arms still wide apart. 'It be the old word for an embrace, 'cause it stretches from one hand to t'other.'

'Have you fitted any hooks to your rope ladders, Mr. Butler?' demanded Preston. The unfortunate midshipman's reply was an inaudible mumble. 'Perhaps Mr. Russell will be kind enough to lend you his division's, for now,' continued the lieutenant. 'But when we are finished here, kindly give Mr. Arkwright my compliments, and ask him to make you a set of similar hooks.'

Farther aft, on the quarterdeck, Lieutenant Macpherson was busy with his men. He had started by using the mizzen shrouds to practice the climbs that would be required of them, but they were under such extreme tension that they were as solid as if cast from iron. No practice on those would prepare his marines for the yielding softness of a rope ladder. He now had one slung down from the mizzen top, and held at the bottom by two privates.

'Quicker than that, Conway!' he ordered. 'Peace will be declared before you reach the top, at this rate.'

'Aye, aye, sir,' came the reply from the marine, who nevertheless continued to cling fiercely to the swaying ladder.

'See that Conway is one of the last to ascend tomorrow night, Edwards,' ordered Macpherson.

'Aye, probably for the best, sir,' replied the corporal.

At that moment, Sergeant Bristow came on deck, accompanied by his two colleagues. All three were finely turned out, as always, with polished boots and gleaming silver-topped canes. This only served to draw attention to the corpse-like pallor of their faces.

'Leeside of the deck, if you please, gentlemen,' said Jacob Armstrong, who was officer of the watch. The three men hesitated for a moment, and the sailing master pointed downwind. But once they had reached the rail, with barely a stumble, they showed no immediate sign of being sick. Indeed, the hint of green in Bristow's face faded a little, as the breeze brought on more colour. All three watched the marines at their training with interest. Armstrong wandered over to join Macpherson.

'I believe those three might volunteer to go with you, Tom,' said the American. 'If only to be spared the necessity of passing more time on board the ship.'

'They do have the look of men as might prove handy in a scrap, sir,' offered Corporal Evans. 'So long as they was prepared to get them regimentals a mite soiled. And I daresay they ain't wholly forgotten how to handle a musket.'

'Perhaps you could make a wee suggestion to them later, corporal,' said Macpherson. 'But for now, carry on with the training. I want every marine up that ladder within five minutes.' He drew out his pocket watch and flipped open the cover. 'Carry on, if you please.'

'Aye aye, sir,' said Edwards and then swivelled away to bawl at the line of marines.

'Did you speak with the captain yet?' asked Armstrong, once he had drawn the Scotsman to a quieter part of the deck.

'Aye, we spoke at some length, earlier,' confirmed Macpherson. 'He says he will ponder what I have said and decide what to do.'

'I guessed as much,' said Armstrong. 'He has not been seen on deck since then. Do you believe he will call off the attack?'

'I can't say,' said the marine officer. 'I feel like I am stumbling in the dark sometimes. I am certain there is a noose before us, and yet I cannot find where it is, or whether it has been set for us or the Royalists.' Armstrong reached out and touched Macpherson's arm.

'You have served with the captain as long as any of us,' he said. 'You know his worth. If there is a way through this, he will find it.'

*****

Beneath the two officer's feet, Clay was pacing across the length of his cabin. To and fro he walked, his head bent forward to avoid the deck above. To one side was the bright sea beyond the windows, the blue cut by the long, foaming wake of the frigate. On the other was the cabin, with its two doors, one to his sleeping quarters and the other to the world of his ship. From the bulkhead between them, the face of Lydia stared across at him, her expression serene and her blue eyes seeming to follow him as he walked.

'What am I to do, my dear?' he asked her, the rhythm of his feet on the deck imposing some order on his racing thoughts. He had always considered Macpherson as one of the steadiest officers he had served with -- he had even asked for him to lead his marines when he became captain of the *Titan*. Back then, she had been an unhappy ship, recovering from a brutal commander who had driven the crew to mutiny. Yet, the Macpherson he had met with this morning had been rattled. He had seen the fear in his eyes, heard the troubled way he had spoken. It was clear that he was convinced that the frigate was sailing into dangerous waters. He spun around and walked back the way he had come.

And yet, what had Macpherson really uncovered? That the sinister looking Major Fraser was a Jacobite sympathiser? Was that relevant? Surely the French Republic was just as hostile to royal families of any stripe, Stewart, Hanoverian or Bourbon? In which case, betrayal of his country to the French would not advance his cause at all. Very good; so he could ignore the man's Jacobite sympathies, at least. He turned about once more and set off back across his cabin.

Fraser was a trusted officer of the crown, assigned to him by the First Lord of the Admiralty himself. He had operated amongst the Royalist rebels on this coast for years now, risking his life every time he was landed on this hostile shore. Such a man was to be applauded for his bravery, was he not? He ran far greater risks than a simple captain of a Royal Navy frigate. If Clay fought and was captured, he would be treated honourably until a suitable cartel could be arranged.

Fraser wore his uniform to offer him some protection in case he, too, was captured, but the help it would give him was uncertain. Clay had heard of officers caught amongst French Royalists in the past. All had been tortured before they were hanged as spies. What right did he have, then, to question the major's sense of duty? He turned again, resolved to trust in Fraser once more.

But why had he lied to Macpherson about knowing D'Arzon? And what was he to make of these secret meetings in the woods? The count, the major, Royalists and treachery, how would he navigate his way through it all? He knew that Macpherson was trustworthy, but had his judgement become flawed? Had he spent too long in Fraser's world? Had all these months ashore, sharing the risk of capture, made him begin to see danger where none existed?'

'Shall I be bringing you a bite to eat, sir?' asked a voice. Clay marched on a few paces, before he realised that the words were not his own thoughts.

'What... what was that?' he said, turning around.

'You've been a-walking up and down for ages, sir,' said Harte. 'I doubt your shoes will bear much more tramping. I thought as how you might want your lunch. Got some cold pie left from yesterday and the Gloucester cheese is still nice, with a glass of wine, maybe?'

'Yes, yes, very well,' said Clay, waving away his steward as he tried to regain his thoughts, but the sailor merely planted his feet a little wider.

'Permission to speak, sir?' asked Harte.

'What is it now?' growled Clay. 'If you are proposing to discuss which pudding I would prefer, I shall stop your grog for a month!'

'No, it weren't that, sir,' said his steward, looking hurt. 'I was just worried as to what might be burdening you, like. I ain't seen you in such a state before.'

'Thank you for your concern, Harte,' said his captain. 'I

do have a lot on my mind at present.'

'I know it ain't my place to say, but I've known you for many a year now, sir, right back to the old *Agrius*, when you was only a lieutenant, and I was wardroom steward,' said the sailor.

'I suppose you have. What of it?'

'I been a thinking how in all that time we been in no end of scrapes, some very bleak indeed, sir,' Harte continued. 'I daresay, this attack as we is practicing for on deck is another of them. But you've always got us through, though sometimes I ain't got a clue how it were done.' Clay smiled a little at the memory.

'Any road, what I been trying to say is, how we all trust you, sir,' the steward continued. 'The crew, like. You just go and do what you reckon is best, and it'll turn out alright. It always has. Shall I go and get that food, now?'

'If you please, Harte,' said Clay. 'And thank you – I believe I will heed your counsel. I shall follow my instincts.'

Chapter 15
Tenth of August

Sometime later, Clay was entertaining guests in his cabin once more. Major Fraser and the Count D'Arzon sat at his table as the *Titan* sailed through the purple dark of a summer's night. They had been collected from a remote beach close to the start of the Quiberon peninsula, just as the sun dropped into the Atlantic. The frigate was now beating back along the coast, past the bulk of Fort de Penthievre, lost in the dark on its cliff. Ahead, a faint light on the horizon marked where the walled town of Quiberon lay, at the very end of the long finger of land.

Throughout the meal, Clay had watched the major, trying to decide what he should do. He had concluded that if Fraser was really about to betray his host and his country, he must be an actor of some brilliance. The conversation had flowed easily, with the Scotsman participating in his usual reserved way. He showed a little more tension than was normal and had a steelier look in his eye, but then, Clay reminded himself, this was hardly surprising. His guests were about to be landed on a hostile shore for the rendezvous with Quiberon's governor. One slip, Douglas Fraser, and I shall confront you, Clay told himself. But as the meal proceeded, no such error occurred.

'Are your soldiers ready, count?' asked Clay, when they had finished the last of the pudding. D'Arzon drained his wine glass and held it out to Harte before answering.

'Quite prepared, I thank you,' he confirmed. 'I have a few short of four thousand men, all concealed in the forest and ready for your signal that Penthievre is in our hands. There is a garrison of government troops in Carnac, which is close to our camp, but I have them under observation. Provided my men are not required to stay there too long, all will be fine. But if it is not impertinent, may I ask you the same question? Are your sailors quite ready, captain?'

'Mr. Preston and Mr. Macpherson have been toiling all day with the men, assaulting our masts time and again, as if they were cliff faces and fortifications,' said Clay. 'I shall be glad when tomorrow night comes, and we can make our attack in earnest, if only to restore some calm on board. My first lieutenant and the boatswain are growing vexed by all the minor damage inflicted on the rigging.'

'As for my part, all is in place, sir,' said Fraser. 'Once tonight's meeting is concluded to both parties' satisfaction, Quiberon will surrender the moment that the count and his men appear before the walls.'

'And do you have your arguments to hand?' asked Clay. The major patted his breast pocket.

'I have a treasury note of credit, to be drawn on one of Lower Canada's leading houses, and a letter of introduction to the Governor of Quebec, sir. But it is the count that he is truly coming to meet. He wishes to receive assurances as to the conduct of his men.'

'Have you gentlemen considered the possibility of treachery?' said Clay, ensuring his gaze was on Fraser when he said the word. 'I can get Lieutenant Macpherson to provide a file of marines to guard against that possibility.'

'I appreciate your concern, sir,' said the major. 'But the very essence of this meeting is trust. If the governor sees one soldier, it will be interpreted as a betrayal on our part. Both sides are to arrive alone, that is the agreement. Why, I have even persuaded the count here to come unarmed, much against his better judgement. Which reminds me, I must insist that the boat crew who take us in remain with their craft. Any intervention on their part would ruin matters.' Clay looked from one man to the next. The fingers of one hand drummed on the table top as he decided what to do. The sound was echoed from the cabin door, and Harte appeared with one of the frigate's smaller midshipman in tow.

'Mr. Taylor sends his compliments, sir,' squeaked the youngster, 'and Major Fraser's beach is just off the larboard quarter.' He paused, with his gaze resting on the beam above his captain's head, before the rest of the message returned to him. 'Ooh, and the frigate has backed topsails, and the red cutter is being swayed over the side, sir.'

'Thank you, Mr. Todd,' said Clay. 'Kindly give Mr. Taylor my compliments, and inform him that we shall be on deck directly.'

'How old is that boy?' asked D'Arzon, when the curly haired Todd had withdrawn.

'He turned thirteen last month,' said his host. 'The navy believes that much may be made of a boy, if he be caught young.' He drained his wine and dropped his napkin down beside his plate. 'I fear that our pleasant evening must come to an end at last, but I shall hold back the cheese and the rest of this claret against your return. Shall we go on deck?'

The three men rose from the table, and Clay indicated to the others that they should go first. He let D'Arzon leave the cabin and Fraser reach the door before calling out.

'Oh, Major Fraser?' The Scotsman turned back towards him.

'Was there something else, sir?' he asked.

'Yes,' said Clay, searching the other's face for any last trace of alarm. Then he extended out his hand. 'Good luck.'

'Thank you, sir.'

*****

The moon was a crescent of bright silver that hung behind the darkened frigate, as if caught in the net of its rigging. Its light gave shape to the oily swell as the cutter pulled away from the ship's side and towards the little bay. To Sedgwick, as he peered ahead, it was little more than a scoop, worn into the side of the peninsula. The land was faintly visible, backlit by stars and some light from Quiberon, behind the skyline. But, as the boat grew nearer, more detail appeared: the silhouette of some pines against the sky and the square block of a small building.

'I understand there is a stretch of beach, somewhere off to the right,' said Fraser from the other side of the tiller. He pointed in a vague way to a spot beneath the trees.

'Aye aye, sir,' said the coxswain. 'Beach off the starboard bow it is. Any reefs or rocks as should concern me?'

'I don't believe so,' replied the Scotsman. 'There is a fisherman who uses this beach, so I suppose not, but in truth, I have never been here before.'

'Fat lot of use that'll be when we are all fecking drowned,' muttered a voice from among the crew.

'Quiet in the boat!' ordered Sedgwick. 'Ship your oar in the bow there, and keep a look out.'

In silence the cutter carried on. Sedgwick compensated for the missing rower with little touches on the helm. The land loomed closer, turning from black to slate grey in the silver light. Something flashed on the water ahead and then vanished.

'Rock, dead ahoy, Cox,' reported the man in the bow. Sedgwick pushed the tiller over, and the cutter curved away from the danger. More detail of the cottage appeared as they entered the bay. It had a single, low storey crouched beneath a roof of thatch. The well of a door and a window looked black in contrast to the building's whitewashed walls.

'Are we truly to meet the governor in such a hovel?' queried D'Arzon, from his place in the stern sheets.

'Breakers ahoy!' reported the man in the bow. 'Beach is a point to larboard.' The noise of waves lapping on a shore sounded in the night, and the air was laced with the tang of seaweed. Sedgwick corrected his course once more and then rose into a low crouch to watch the boat's approach to the landing.

'Easy all!' he ordered, and the rowers halted their stroke together, oars held parallel to the water. The cutter swept on, a scrape, a bump, and then it came to a halt with a rattle of shingle. 'Over the side lads, and run us up.' Sedgwick sat back down and turned to his passengers. 'Now, is you certain you don't want a couple of the lads to sneak up and have a peek around, sir?' he asked.

'Absolutely not,' replied Fraser firmly. 'You are to wait for us here and not interfere. If things go ill, or we do not return within the hour, you must go back to the *Titan* and report to Captain Clay. Is that understood?'

'Aye aye, sir,' replied Sedgwick. He reached down into the boat, picked up a shuttered lantern by its brass ring, and handed it across. 'It's lit, with oil for a good while, sir. If you should change your mind, flash three times, and me and the lads will come a running.'

Fraser took the lantern, and set off up the beach. His boots slid and crunched through the stones, and after a moment of hesitation, the count followed him. The two men walked past an upturned boat, pulled high above the tide line, with a cluster of wicker lobster pots stacked beside it. On the far side, the shingle became more firm, gripped now by trailing plants and scrubby grass amongst the stones. Off to the left was the little croft, on a rise above the shore. Fraser slipped open the lantern and searched with its thin orange beam until he found a path.

'This way, Monsieur le Comte,' he said. His voice seemed

to hold the faintest tremble of excitement, and D'Arzon looked at him. But beneath his hat, his face was dark and unreadable. D'Arzon looked back down the beach, to where the cutter could be seen. The sound of conversation from the crew huddled around it was warm and reassuring in the night. Farther out he could just make out the black mass of the frigate, showing no light as it lay hove to, awaiting his return. All was as it should be, so he turned away, to follow the Scotsman up the narrow path.

*****

Inside the little cottage, Fraser had placed the shuttered lantern down on a bare table that stood in the middle of the floor. He pulled open the cover and bent forward to trim the wick. As the light grew, the interior resolved itself around the two men. They were in a single room with a dirt floor. In one corner a little stone chimney had been built, its empty fireplace gaping at them like a black mouth. Hanging from the low ceiling were a few smoke-blackened pots and some bundles of dried herbs. By the door was a white-washed dresser with turned wooden plates on it, while against the opposite wall was a bed. Beneath the table were two stools. D'Arzon pulled one out, examined it, and then took out his handkerchief. He spread it over the square wooden top before he sat down. Fraser settled opposite him on the other stool, and rummaged in the pocket of his coat. The count pulled out his watch, and angled it towards the lantern on the table.

'Was it at eleven o'clock that we were to meet with them?' he asked.

'That is correct,' said the Scot. He produced his battered silver flask, and put it on the table. 'Would you care for a drink?'

'Perhaps after we have met with the governor,' said

D'Arzon. 'Let us hope that he is punctual, and we are not required to spend more time than is necessary in this revolting place.'

'Oh, I think that we have plenty of time,' said the Scot, still busy in his pocket. He next produced a large pistol. Lamplight gleamed off the oiled surface of the barrel.

'I thought we have come for a parley?' said the Frenchman, his stomach suddenly knotting with fear.

'The pistol is not for the governor or his associates,' said Fraser. A loud click sounded as he pulled back the hammer and aimed it at his companion. 'For I regret to inform you that my discussions with him are a fiction I have created, to bring you here, alone, tonight. No, my friend, this gun is to keep you seated, until the gendarmes come for you.'

'But...but what are you doing?' spluttered the count. He pulled himself up off his stool. 'Gendarmes! Are you mad! What manner of treachery is this?'

'Sit down and be still!' barked the Scotsman. 'With your hands flat upon the table!' Once D'Arzon complied, Fraser continued in a more normal voice. 'Aye, I suppose it is treachery of a sort. Of course, you would recognise such things better than me, would you not, Lieutenant D'Arzon?' The count looked from the black 'O' of the pistol to the single eye of his companion.

'Why do you call me that?' he demanded.

'Because that is how I once knew you,' said Fraser. 'You truly cannot place me at all, can you?'

'Of course I can,' said the count. 'You are a British major, sent to help me. Why are you playing with me like this?'

'Do you know what day it is today?'

'What?' exclaimed D'Arzon.

'I asked you what day it is,' repeated Fraser. He leant forwards and pointed the gun at the Frenchman's heart.

'The twenty third day of Thermidor, by that ridiculous calendar Paris insists we use,' said D'Arzon, after a little thought. 'That would be, eh, the tenth of August in the old...' His voice trailed away, and he stared at Fraser. 'Who are you?'

'I am Vengeance,' smiled the Scotsman. 'But perhaps I should be more frank in the little time left to you. It would seem that I have changed much over the years or perhaps I was never worthy of your attention back then, not being of the same noble blood as you and your friends. Because to my eye, you are very little altered. Your character is still that of the arrogant young guard's officer who was at the Tuileries on the tenth day of August, eight years ago. The day that the mob came for the king.'

'You were there!' exclaimed D'Arzon.

'Aye, I was, together with a much loved older brother, Charles Fraser. We had the honour to serve His Majesty in his *Garde Écossaise*, just as our father had in his youth. A day of blood, was it not?' D'Arzon said nothing, still racking his brains to place the Scot, and after a pause, Fraser continued. His gaze was distant now, as if he addressed another person in the room, seated behind the shoulder of his prisoner.

'It was a hot summer's day, I recall, and the air was warm as milk,' he said. 'But we guards had been forewarned of what was to come, had we not? The rage of the Paris Commune at the king's defiance was well known, and they had made no secret of their intentions. Their damned firebrands had passed the night in whipping up the crowd.' He levered open the top of his flask with one hand and took a pull from the contents. 'Are you sure you will not take a dram? It may be the last occasion for you to have a drink.'

'Just get on and tell me what all this damned nonsense is about!' exclaimed the count.

'As you will,' shrugged Fraser. 'Now, where was I? Ah yes, the Tuileries. My countrymen and I were defending the side of the palace opposite the river. Your men faced the gardens, as I recall. But it mattered little, for soon the crowd had the palace encircled, like an ocean about a rock. Do you not recall the reckless fury of their attacks? Time after time they clambered up to the windows, only to be thrown back by our brave soldiers. I recall one great brute of a man armed with a sledge hammer, who almost got in before I ran him through. I can still see him now, tumbling backwards, to vanish like a stone in a pond, as the mob closed over his body. We held our own at first, as did the Swiss beside us, but then our powder began to run short, and our opponents became bolder. Charlie, who was my captain, despatched me with a dozen men to fetch more cartridges from the magazine.' Fraser returned his gaze onto D'Arzon.

'Do you recall where the magazine was, count? Down in that warren of cellars? Why, there must be tunnels that run all over that part of the city, where one palace gets built on the site of the last. But you must remember where our arms were stored? In the upper level, hard by that spiral stair that leads to the deeper parts, was it not?' The Scot leant forward, his pistol still pointing at D'Arzon's chest, his eye cold.

'I recall,' whispered the count.

'It is strange how sound can be conducted by such stairwells,' continued Fraser. 'Even over the noise that my men made in the magazine and the distant roar of the mob, I could still hear some manner of banging and hammering rising up from the cellar below. I went part of the way down the stairs to see what was afoot and I saw the glimmer of a light, not unlike that from this lantern.' He clinked the brass top with the barrel of his pistol. 'So, I advanced farther. And then I heard voices, one of which, I thought I recognised. "Wait a moment," it said, and then "I support the will of the *Commune*!" I heard the clang of a heavy door being thrown open. "Follow me", said the voice, and then came a rush of feet upon the stairs. Many feet.'

'It wasn't me, I swear!' pleaded the count. 'I never left my post!'

'Don't you give me the lie!' spat the major. 'To my damned face too! Where is your honour? If you had stayed at your post, you would have died like my brother. Yet here you are, unharmed, alive, a hero of the Revolution. I heard your voice, even as I ran back to gather my men at the top of the stairs. I well remember how those fiends of yours came up from the cellar, like demons released from the pit. Imagine my shock when I saw a damned Guard's officer waving them on. I saw your face, plain as I see it now. I may have been left for dead, but I still have that image burned into my soul. The mob left me at least one eye to see with.'

D'Arzon looked in horror at the Scotsman and then dropped his gaze. He put his head in his hands and his shoulders began to shake.

'Are you weeping?' said Fraser, incredulous. 'Who in damnation for! Not for my brother and all the others, murdered that day, I make no doubt. Is it for your own part?'

'I cry for shame!' sobbed the count. 'Haven't I lived with little else all these years!'

'For shame!' roared Fraser. 'Then why did you do such a contemptible thing, if you knew it was wrong?'

'I was afraid!' shouted the count. 'I was barely out of the schoolroom! I never wanted to join the Royal Guard and I certainly didn't want to end my life before it had even started! They told me that the king was receiving wicked advice, and that once he was in their hands, away from bad influences, the killing would stop.'

'And you believed them, these men of blood?' snorted Fraser. 'They tore poor Charlie's cadaver apart, even though he was long dead, and tossed it into the river. You sicken me! I had assumed that some principle, however misguided, might have driven you on. I had little notion that you were so unmanned that your only wish was to spare your miserable hide!'

'Yes, I was weak,' said D'Arzon, his tears glinting in the lamplight. 'And I have regretted it every day since. It haunts me! That is why I lead the *Choannerie*. To fight back against the Revolution, and by serving the new king, perhaps to earn the forgiveness of the old.'

'And how will that undo what happened to my brother?' said Fraser. The pistol trembled in his hand. 'Or to the others that perished? Or to me? I bear many wounds, beyond my eye, that trouble me every moment of every day.'

'I am truly sorry for what was done to you, major, but please think!' pleaded the count. 'What you do this night will never mend that! You only pile more woe upon what has already been done!'

'I can endure that,' said the Scotsman. 'The knowledge that my brother may lie still will comfort me.'

'And what will men say of your treachery, major?' said the count. 'Your friends on the frigate? The men whom I have led? How much blood must be spilt before your brother is revenged?' Fraser shrugged his shoulders, the movement magnified by the huge shadow he cast on the wall behind him.

'The rising is doomed,' he said. 'Paris will move to crush it soon, whether you lead it or no. As for Clay and the others, they can look after themselves. But you, you I shall crush completely.'

'Then why did you not just kill me sooner? Why all this deception?'

'Oh, it has not been easy, you know, staying my hand!' exclaimed Fraser. 'I did consider placing a ball in the back of your head when we were on the beach together, all those months ago, but that would have been too swift to repay all the years of hurt. Later, there have always been others about you who could have stopped me, your officers and servants, young Macpherson. But not tonight. No, this way is best. The men who are coming will question you with lingering ingenuity before they take you to the scaffold. And they will see that your estate, your family, your name are all quite erased. A much superior sort of revenge, I am sure you will agree.' The count opened his mouth to speak, but Fraser held up a hand as he heard sounds outside the little croft. 'I do declare, my new friends may have arrived.'

D'Arzon looked around him as he searched for a way out. A murmur of voices came from the far side of the door. A boot crunched just beyond the window, while from farther away, a horse snorted.

'Steady!' warned Fraser. 'Stay in your place!'

'Why should I not hazard your gun, and end matters now?' asked the count.

'Because I am quite skilled enough to merely wing you, and the crew of the cutter are ordered not to intervene, even if they hear a shot.'

There was a quiet knock on the door.

'Please come in, colonel!' called Fraser. The door swung open, and five figures in dark blue coats and high riding boots clattered in. The first four were troopers, all armed with carbines, and one carrying a lantern. The fifth man's coat was heavy with lace. Fraser pointed his pistol towards the ceiling, and un-cocked it. 'Colonel Vallaud, may I name Monsieur Le Comte Louis D'Arzon, Commander of the *Choannerie* here in the Morbihan. I believe you have been anxious to meet with him.'

The officer waved forward the trooper with the lantern. He handed his carbine to a colleague, left his lamp next to Fraser's on the table and pulled out a pair of light iron fetters from his coat pocket. He gestured for D'Arzon to hold out his hands, and after a moment of hesitation, the count did so. Once his wrists were secured, the gendarme hauled him to his feet and searched through his pockets, pulling out various items and scattering them onto the table. Then he turned his attention to his clothes, patting the lining here and running his fingers there. First, a small but sharp knife and then the little key from around his neck joined the other items. The colonel picked up the key and dangled it in front of his prisoner's nose.

'I wonder what secrets this key will reveal, my friend?' he asked. D'Arzon glared up at him in silence and the gendarme shrugged. 'No matter. I shall know by the end of the night, unless you are considerably tougher than you seem.'

Fraser pushed the stopper back into his silver flask and returned it, with the pistol, to his own coat. Then he rose from the table.

'Now that you have your man, colonel, I shall take my leave', he said.

'One moment, major,' said Vallaud. He stepped to the door and swung it closed with his boot. 'Where are all the traitors that this man commands?'

'That intelligence is not part of our agreement,' said Fraser.

'Perhaps not, but it would be of use to know if they are still gathered together in the forest above Carnac, or if some remain at the chateau,' said Vallaud, with a broad smile. The smile became a laugh as he watched the interplay between his prisoner and the Scotsman.

'What?' he scoffed. 'Did you think you could accept every peasant who arrives at your gate, count, and not have collected a few of my many spies amongst their number? Even as we speak, my friends in the army are surrounding your pathetic little force with a ring of iron. They may wait for your return, D'Arzon, but it will be altogether less welcome visitors who arrive with the dawn.'

'Murderers!' yelled D'Arzon, trying to pull free of the gendarme who had searched him. A second trooper drove the butt of his carbine into the count's stomach, and he crashed back onto his stool, gasping for air.

'Gag him,' ordered Vallaud, his tone quite calm, as if he

was commenting on the weather. Once the prisoner was silent, he returned his attention to Fraser. 'Now major, I am anxious to get this traitor back to Quiberon. Will I be inconvenienced by these sailors down by the shore?'

'Not if you follow my instructions,' said the Scot. 'In a moment I will rush from here, down the path, and report that we have been betrayed and that the count has been killed. A volley of shots from your men's carbines, fired into the air, would add colour to my story. Once back at the boat, we will make good our escape, and you shall have this little bay to yourself.'

'It is a good plan,' said Vallaud. 'But will the sailors not try and come to your aid when they hear firing?'

'Trust me to arrange matters better than that, colonel,' said Fraser. 'They have strict orders not to intervene, under any circumstances.'

'Do they, now?' said the gendarme. He stroked one arm of his moustache. 'That is well arranged.'

A moment later there was a flash of light that burst through the cottage window. It was gone almost before Fraser had registered it. Then the roar of a broadside swept in from the sea and rattled the door against its frame.

'What was that?' said Fraser, spinning towards the colonel. The officer met his gaze, his eyes flint.

'It sounds like a naval battle, somewhere in the bay,' he offered.

'But you gave me your word that the *Titan* would not be part of our arrangement!' exclaimed Fraser. 'What have you done?'

'I am not responsible for the navy, major,' said Vallaud. 'If they have learnt that one of your ships has been surveying our coastal fortifications it is, of course, their duty to oppose it.'

'But... you gave me your word!' repeated the Scot. 'Besides, once I return to the ship with word that D'Arzon is taken, there will be no attack on the fort!' Vallaud held the door open.

'I suggest you go and tell your friends all of that, major,' he said. 'While they yet live.' Fraser hesitated for a moment and then picked up the lantern from the table.

'Why do you need that?' asked the colonel.

'To signal to the boat crew,' said Fraser. 'To warn them that I am coming, so I am not killed in the dark.'

'Very well,' said Vallaud. 'Make your signal, and then leave. You shall have your volley.' When Fraser had left the croft, he gestured to his men.

'Go and shoot him dead,' he ordered. 'I will look after our friend here.' The four troopers clumped out, cocking their carbines as they went. Vallaud caught sight of his prisoner staring at him. 'I shall win great credit from your capture, my friend, but think!' he urged. 'How much more will I gain if I can also report the death of a dangerous British spy?'

*****

'So how fecking long are they after jawing up there?' asked O'Malley. He was seated on the beach with his back against the side of the cutter. 'It's been an age since all them folk on horses turned up!'

'Not sure as it be that long, Sean,' said Trevan, sitting cross legged beside him. 'The tide has only just turned. Mind, time do drag something else, when you've naught to do.'

'This don't seem right to me,' said Evans, who sat nearby. 'What's with all these sods on horses? I thought we was expecting some Frog bloke to show up with a brace of flunkies, not a bleeding cavalry regiment. Hard to tell in the dark, I grant you, but they ain't half making a racket.' As if in confirmation, a horse let out a whinny from somewhere farther up the slope. Evans shifted to get more comfortable on the stones, and the cutlass resting across his knees clattered to the ground.

'What was that!' said the voice of Sedgwick, anxious in the dark.

'Sorry, Able,' said the Londoner. He recovered the weapon and rose to his feet.

'Keep it quiet,' hissed the coxswain. He returned to his vigil, staring up towards the cottage at the top of the slanting path. He could see the square of light that spilt from the window, with the occasional shadow as someone moved across it. Then, for a flash of time, he saw the building clearly, bathed in yellow light, with several black figures like sentries in a ring around it. A moment later it was dark again, and a roar of noise came from out at sea.

'Sweet Jesus!' yelled O'Malley, as he too leapt to his feet. 'The fecking barky is in a scrap!' Sedgwick swung around, the image of the illuminated cottage still in his mind.

'Something's wrong!' he exclaimed. 'That cottage has soldiers all around it!'

'Forget the fecking shack!' said O'Malley. 'We have to get back to the ship.' Sedgwick stood for a moment, hesitating over what to do. He knew in his heart that all was not right with Fraser and the count, but then, what was happening with the ship? He turned towards the open sea. Where there had once been the single mass of the frigate, a second, much larger ship could be seen.

'That's a big bastard,' muttered the Londoner. 'What we bleeding well going to do, Able?'

'Evans, Trevan, O'Malley, follow me,' he ordered, drawing a pistol out from his belt. 'Rest of you turn around the cutter, and man the oars. Hold her in the shallows, ready to push off the moment we get back. Rodgers, you're in charge.' He turned and ran, slipping and sliding over the stones towards the path, with the others close behind. At the top of the beach he stopped.

'What you be a seeing?' asked Trevan as he arrived beside

him.

'That cottage door's just opened,' he explained, pointing with his pistol. A figure appeared in the light that shone from the opening and moments later there were three orange flashes. 'That's the major!' said Sedgwick. 'He's in trouble!'

'Holdfast a moment,' said Evans. 'He ain't the only bleeding one! What about us, with the barky in a mill, and this here cove full of bleeding soldiers?' Down the path towards them came the sound of someone running. Shots banged out from farther up the slope, yellow flashes in the dark, and a figure flew out of the night. He yelled with pain and then crashed to the ground a few yards from them. Another broadside, and the bay was lit in a flash of light once more, before night returned.

'It's Major Fraser!' exclaimed Sedgwick, and he dashed forward.

'Have a care,' warned Trevan. 'Them as shot him will be a coming.' The coxswain ignored him and knelt down beside the writhing body. He heaved him over into his arms. Warm blood flowed through his hands, soaking into his clothes and the Scotsman groaned. In the moonlight Sedgwick looked into the soldiers face. It was plastered with dirt and the patch had been ripped away to reveal a deep scar and empty eye socket. The other eye searched the coxswain's face.

'Oh... My God, w... what have I done...?' he gasped.

'What's bleeding happened!' urged Sedgwick. 'An' where's the count?'

'They have him! I... I gave him to them... but it was justice... f... for my brother.' O'Malley let fly with one of his pistols, and in the flash of the discharge, Sedgwick saw life leaking away from the soldier's face.

'Sir!' he urged. 'Speak plain! What brother? What is it you've gone and done?'

'We got to bleeding shift,' warned Evans, firing off his own gun. 'The bastards are coming.'

'The major's lips moved, and Sedgwick bent his head close to try and hear him.

'All my fault... b... betrayed... ship...,' stuttered Fraser, and then he seemed to smile in the moonlight. 'Charlie,' he whispered, and spoke no more.

CHAPTER 16

BATTLE

When Clay could wait no longer, he came up on deck and strode across to the group of men standing beside the ship's wheel.

'Good evening, Mr. Preston,' he said to the officer of the watch. 'Has anything been heard from the shore?'

'Nothing so far, sir,' said the young lieutenant. 'I can just make out a light in the window of that cottage with my spy glass, but otherwise, all is quiet.'

Clay crossed to the lee rail, and stared into the little bay with his telescope. He found the single orange square of light but could make out little else. He turned to look across his ship, hove to in the moonlight, and recognised the upright figure of Lieutenant Macpherson as he, too, watched the land.

'Good evening, Tom,' he said. 'Does the society of the wardroom not agree with you tonight? I am surprised not to find you hotly engaged at backgammon with Mr. Faulkner at this hour.'

'Good evening, sir,' the marine replied. 'That is our habit, but tonight I find that I have need of a little air.' The two men were silent for a moment, both looking towards the point of orange light in the warm dark.

'Tom, I do appreciate the concerns you brought to my attention,' said Clay. 'I have pondered them long and hard this day.'

'Thank you, sir,' said Macpherson. 'But did you not find them sufficiently convincing to act upon?'

'Not in the decisive way that you urged upon me,' said his captain. 'As I explained, the government has much riding on the success of this assault. If I am to disappoint them, I must have good cause.'

'And my arguments were not sufficient in that regard?'

'Not in my judgement,' said Clay. 'I had the opportunity of studying Major Fraser earlier this evening. I flatter myself that I am a sound judge of character. Unless my capabilities have quite deserted me, whatever he may have planned for this night, I cannot believe that he means us ill.'

'I wish I could share your confidence, sir,' said Macpherson. He idly tapped the toe of his boot against the slide of a carronade.

'You must trust me in this regard, Tom,' said his captain. 'I have made my decision, for good or ill.'

'Aye aye, sir,' said the Scot.

'Deck there!' yelled the lookout, followed by silence.

'Has the power of speech deserted you, Hobbs?' roared Preston. 'What in all creation is it you see?'

'Beg yer pardon, sir, only I ain't rightly sure. I thought I glimpsed the wake of a ship, away out to sea,' he replied, 'off the larboard beam.'

'A ship to larboard?' said Clay, striding across the deck. 'What the hell is it doing here?'

'Mr. Russell!' ordered Preston. 'Take a night glass and go aloft. See what you can make of her.' The midshipman ran for the main chains, and Preston went to join his captain as he stared out across the dark water.

'I can make out damn all!' Clay complained. 'What little moon there was has now gone behind a cloud.'

'Try with this, sir,' said Preston. He passed him a second night glass, and Clay focussed out to sea.

'Dark as pitch, sir,' commented Macpherson, who had

followed his captain across. 'And yet this ship will have us marked, against the lights of the shore. Tis a well sprung trap, if trap it is.'

'Trap? What trap, Mr. Macpherson?' said Taylor, who had come up on deck in response to the hail from the masthead.

'Come now, Tom, there is no call for talk like that just yet,' said Clay. 'I am still most uncertain if there is a ship there at all.'

'Who is the lookout, Mr. Preston?' asked Taylor.

'Hobbs, sir. He is very steady.' At that moment the cloud that had passed across the sickle moon thinned a little and allowed some milky light to break through. The black silhouette of a ship appeared, no more than a few miles off. Several voices spoke at once.

'There sir!' cried Preston. 'Ship under topsails!'

'Christ, she looks big!' added Macpherson. 'And has us caught against the coast.'

'Deck there!' came the voice of Russell from aloft. 'Warship, two miles off the larboard beam. Showing no lights. Looks to me like she may be a ship of the line.'

'Nine in ten that she is one of ours, this close to the fleet off Brest, gentlemen,' said Clay, as the moon disappeared once more, and the ship melted back into the night.

'Showing no lights, sir?' queried Macpherson.

'Nor are we, Tom,' said his captain. 'Perhaps they are on a secret mission, too. What is the current night recognition signal, Mr. Preston?'

'Two blue lights, displayed one above the other from the mizzen crosstree, sir.' he replied.

'Kindly make that, if you please,' replied Clay. He lifted his head towards the masthead. 'Mr. Russell!'

'Here, sir!' replied the midshipman.

'What can you make out on land? Any sign of the cutter returning?' There was a long pause, during which the quarterdeck was bathed in eerie blue light.

'Nothing, sir,' reported the midshipman.

'Keep an eye on the shore,' yelled Clay. 'I want to know the moment the cutter appears.'

'Signal sent sir,' reported Preston. 'No response observed.'

'Thank you, Mr. Preston. Kindly belay the blue lights,' said his captain, 'then beat to quarters and clear the ship for action. I shall return on deck presently.'

*****

Clay reached the bottom of the ladderway to see a small figure scampering across the deck towards him, with his hat awry and a drum bouncing wildly off his leg. The ship's young marine drummer looked up, just in time to avoid colliding with him, and skidded to a halt.

'Steady there, nipper!' urged the voice of Corporal Edwards, who was following him. 'There ain't no call for assaulting the captain, now, 'specially as that's an hanging matter. Frogs'll hold back until you have yourself in order, lad.'

'Sorry, sir,' said the little boy in a voice a touch above a whisper as he looked up at the tall figure of his captain.

'Carry on, then,' said Clay gravely. The drummer touched the side of his head with his drum sticks in salute and then marched to his place by the main mast. He crammed a few more blond curls under his hat, settled his instrument in front of him and held the sticks aloft. Then he glanced across at Corporal Edwards, who gave the briefest of nods, and the drum thundered out in a continuous roll. As he walked towards his cabin, the sound of the watch below jumping from their hammocks came up from beneath Clay's feet.

'Everything is in your sleeping quarters, sir,' said Yates, shepherding him that way. Clay exchanged glances with the portrait of Lydia on the bulkhead, but as he did so, her face swung round, as Harte lifted the picture off the wall.

'Box this up, Jake,' he said to one of the sailors who had run in after Clay. 'You others, get the desk.'

Yates shut the door of his sleeping cabin, dampening, but not extinguishing the sounds from outside.

'Let me take your coat, sir,' he said. He dressed Clay as if his captain was a child, and he, the eighteen year old servant, the parent. He coaxed his master's left arm, stiff from the old musket wound in the shoulder, into his full dress coat, buttoned it up and then passed him the gold Nile medal.

'Shall I fetch the king's sword, or your everyday hanger?' Clay looked at his face in the mirror above his washstand, his eyes troubled. His *Titan* against a ship of the line? This will be the fight of my professional life, he reflected. If the thing had to be done, it might as well be done properly.

'I think, the royal sword, if you please, Yates,' he said.

While his servant stooped to buckle the glittering weapon around his waist, Clay tried to thread the Nile medal into place at this throat, but found that his fingers were too clumsy for the task. Oh God, he thought, what have I done? How could I have I been so blind? Fraser had been talking to the French for weeks as he arranged this meeting. Even if Macpherson was wrong and he was loyal, the enemy will have known exactly where the *Titan* would be tonight, to the hour, caught in a place of their choosing. Or perhaps Macpherson was right, and that damned soldier has been playing me for a fool all along. Tom even told me that Fraser had met with a senior gendarme, and yet, I did nothing.

'Oh damn and blast it!' he exclaimed in frustration.

'Let me get that for you, sir,' said Yates, reaching for the medal. The edge of the burnished disc caught the light from the lantern, reminding Clay of the golden curls of the marine drummer boy.

'You look proper splendid, sir, if I may make so bold,' said Yates as he stepped back from him. 'Sedgwick would normally carry your pistols. Would you like to place them in your coat pockets, until he should return?'

'If you please,' said Clay. He took the two heavy weapons from his servant. Pistols, against a ship of the line, he thought, as he slipped one into each pocket. Then he turned to the door, collected his best hat from Yates, and stepped back into the cabin.

The space had been transformed. All his furniture had vanished, as had the lamps and pictures from the bulkheads. The interior walls themselves were coming down now, opening up the gun deck into one long uninterrupted space. Even the sleeping quarters he had just dressed in would shortly be taken below. The moment he was clear of the door, Harte led a press of sailors past him, to gather up the last of their captain's possessions. In what had been his day cabin, the crews had grouped around the two eighteen pounders that were normally concealed beneath drapes, rigging gun tackles and bringing up equipment.

'We'll give them feckers what for,' said an Irish sailor as he passed an eighteen pound ball from one hand to the other. Another member of the crew let out a snort.

'Hah! Ag'in a bleeding Frog ship of the line?' he scoffed. 'Them buggers carry thirty six pounders! I tell'ee lads, we've caught ourselves a tiger here, and no mistake.' The awkward looks of his shipmates caused the sailor to glance around. Just behind him was the captain, in all his glittering magnificence. 'Beggin' your pardon, sir.'

Clay pushed aside the cold despair he felt inside and moulded his features into a smile.

'Come now, Waite, this is not like you,' he said. 'We have been through fights as uncertain as this before, have we not?'

'Aye, that we have, sir,' agreed the sailor.

'But I am inclined to agree with you about the merits of O'Brien's eighteen pounder ball there,' said Clay, looking at the heavy sphere. 'They may not serve for hunting this tiger.

I shall see if I can find something better.' He turned to Yates, who was still behind him. 'Kindly go and find Mr. Rudgewick and ask him to join me on the quarterdeck, if you please.'

'Aye aye, sir,' said the servant, and he ran towards the aft hatchway.

'Carry on, here,' Clay said to the gun crews. 'Fire fast and true, and all will be well.' He strode down the gun deck, pretending a nonchalance he didn't feel, and ran back up the ladderway.

'See, Waite, you fecking arse,' said O'Brien, once he had disappeared. 'Your feller has a notion to fox them Frenchies, right enough. There be few Grunters deeper than our Pipe.'

'He better have some' it in mind,' muttered Waite, looking over the cannon. 'Hoy, Beaver, ain't you got that tackle rigged yet? Word not reached you that the Frogs are in the offing, an' coming for our arses?' The former mystic tried to fit the iron hook onto the side tackle ring again, but his hands were trembling too much. O'Brien stooped down to help him.

'You alright, Jack?' he asked. 'Don't you go a getting all shy now. Pipe will see us through.'

'Not this time,' muttered Beaver. 'See, I've been here before, in a dream, like.'

*****

'The ship is cleared for action, sir,' reported Taylor, as Clay joined him by the wheel. He looked around the quarterdeck, running his eye over the dark figures massed there, gauging their mood. The crews gathered about the big carronades, as they fussed over their weapons. The gentle clink of the marines' equipment as they manned the sides. The glow from the binnacle that showed the extra quartermasters by the wheel and the midshipmen poised to run messages. Just behind them stood Macpherson, his face impassive.

'Very good, Mr. Taylor,' said Clay. 'And what of the enemy?'

'Mr. Armstrong has them in view, sir,' he replied. He led the way across, to where the sailing master stood by the rail.

'What have you to report, Jacob?' said Clay. The American passed his night glass across.

'She's a ship of the line, for certain, sir. I saw her clearly when the moon was last out. Two gun decks, and all her cannon are run out. A seventy-four, I would guess.'

'More than three times our weight of shot then, sir,' added Taylor, 'with much thicker sides, to boot.'

'Thank you, Mr. Taylor,' said Clay, looking through the night glass. 'I believe I have her now, coming on very steady.'

'That's her, sir,' confirmed Armstrong. 'She's been slipping down toward us these last few minutes, while keeping herself between us and the open sea.' Clay could see the ship clearly now, her solid black hull dotted with a double row of orange squares, as light spilt from her open gun ports. Above the hull was the mass of her sails and rigging, hanging over her like a dark cloud and blotting out the stars. Around her bow was a faint glint of white, as she drove through the sea towards them.

'She will be in long cannon shot of our eighteen pounders soon,' said Clay.

'You cannot be meaning to fight her, sir,' protested Taylor in an urgent whisper.

'What would you have me do, George?' said his captain. 'Cut and run? Major Fraser and the count are still ashore, together with a dozen shipmates. We must at least wait for their return.'

'But surely, they are betrayed, sir?'

'Do you know that? For certain?' said Clay. 'The arrival of this French ship may be pure ill-fortune. Even now, the shore party may be on their way back to us, after a successful mission. We cannot just abandon them.'

'But a ship of the line, sir!' said Taylor.

'I mean to fight, at least until the cutter returns, but I have no intention of going toe-to-toe,' said Clay. 'We must endeavour to out-manoeuvre them and shoot away some spars, although, I daresay, we are still in for a mauling.'

A shape loomed up in the dark, and pulled off his hat.

'You passed word for me, sir,' said a broad Yorkshire accent.

'Yes, Mr. Rudgewick,' said Clay. 'Do we have any chain shot on board?'

'Chain shot, sir?' he queried, running a hand over his face. 'Aye, happen' we do an' all. I shouldn't think we have above four dozen rounds, mind, and that'll be proper rusty. Why, they've not seen light of day for many a long year.'

'No matter,' said Clay. 'Take what men you require, and have them issued to the larboard gun crews. Make haste now.'

'Aye aye, sir,' said Rudgewick. He placed his hat back on his head, and hurried away.

'Have you ever had occasion to use chain shot, George,' asked his captain.

'I can't say that I have, sir,' replied the first lieutenant. 'In all my time in the navy it has been a brisk fire of ball into an opponent's hull. Fancy munitions for wounding the rigging was more the enemy's game.'

'I fear the case has altered,' said Clay. 'I have the advantage of having seen it used once, but that was in the last war. I daresay, young Mr. Blake will never have witnessed it in action. Kindly pass the word for him to join us, if you please.'

While he waited for the lieutenant in charge of the guns to appear, he looked across at the enemy. The big ship had grown much larger now. The light from her open gun ports twinkled off the surface of the water; the huge black squares of her topsails seemed to spread across the sky.

'Not long now, sir,' said Armstrong. 'She is well within cannon shot.'

'She is holding her first broadside until she is certain that every ball will count, damn her!' exclaimed Clay.

'Did you want to see me, sir,' said Blake, as he hurried up.

'Mr. Rudgewick will be rousting out some chain shot for you presently, Mr. Blake.'

'Yes, sir, the first rounds have been brought to the main deck,' he said.

'Are you familiar with their use?' asked Clay.

'Only in theory, sir.'

'Then you had best attend now.' said Clay. 'Each round consists of two hemispheres, like the halves of an apple, joined by a fathom of chain. The men must marry the halves together to reform a sphere, and load that as if it were a normal ball, with the chain following it into the muzzle. When fired, the chain extends and the whole tumbles through the air. Is that clear?'

'Eh, I think I have it, sir.'

'Be sure that you have, Mr. Blake,' said Clay. 'I am relying on you. Once loaded, you can run out the guns at maximum elevation. I mean to try and cripple our opponent.'

'Aye aye, sir.'

'Chain shot can do wicked damage to rigging, but only at very short range,' explained Clay. 'It loses all momentum once it leaves the gun. We shall need to hold our fire until the enemy are devilish close.'

'You can rely on me, sir,' said the lieutenant.

'We have only a little over two rounds per gun, at best, Mr. Blake,' said Clay, 'See that they are not wasted. Carry on now, but wait for my order to fire.'

'Aye aye, sir,' said Blake. He touched his hat and hurried off, and Clay returned his attention to his opponent.

Closer and closer she came, growing all the time, as if to

intimidate with her massive presence. The frigate lay quietly downwind of her, with backed topsails.

'Masthead!' called Clay. 'Any sign of that cutter?'

'Nothing yet, sir,' replied the voice of Russell, from somewhere high above.

'Up ports!' ordered Blake, from the deck beneath him. Squares of orange light appeared along the length of the frigate.

'Mr. Taylor, once we fire, I shall want to get under way without delay,' said Clay. 'See that the men handle the sails promptly.'

'Aye aye, sir,' replied Taylor. Still the enemy ship held her fire.

'Run out, larboard side!' yelled Blake. There was a roar of noise, and the deck trembled under Clay's feet. The last gun banged into place, and quiet descended over the frigate once more. The enemy was so near now that Clay could hear the sound of her approach: the creak of her shrouds, the brush of wake along her side and the ripple and crack of her big, dark flag.

'Come on, fire, you bastard,' muttered one of the quarterdeck gun crew. As if in response, a faint shout came from over the water, and the enemy ship was lit with flame. For an instant Clay's mind registered that the black flag had become a French tricolour, and then the broadside smashed into the *Titan*. The rail next to one of the quarterdeck carronades exploded, sending a shower of splinters scything into the gun crew. Other balls howled overhead, slapping through the rigging and sending debris pattering down. Hammer blows sounded all along the side of the ship, and two columns of water spouted up near the bow. For a heartbeat there was silence, and then a cacophony of sound.

One of the wounded crew of the carronade was screaming; his cries echoed from a half dozen other places on the main deck.

'Afterguard! Get these wounded below to the surgeon!' ordered Taylor, from beside the wheel.

'Crowbars here!' roared Blake from the main deck. 'Get that man out from under there!'

'Aloft with you! I want them lines spliced!' came the deep base voice of Hutchinson from the forecastle, and then the voice of Taylor again.

'Mr. Macpherson! Two of your men to attend to Mr. Preston, please. He is down.' Clay turned and rushed across to where the lieutenant lay, at the centre of a group of dark figures.

'Where are you wounded, Edward?'

'Splinter... in my arm...,' he gasped. The jagged end of a piece of wood protruded from his upper arm. In the light of the binnacle, Clay could see it was slick with blood.

'Take him away,' ordered his captain. 'Handsomely, now.' He watched the two marines who had run up with Macpherson carry him gently towards the aft hatch. His eyes met those of the Scotsman, but it was Clay who looked away. Then he went back to the rail to re-join the sailing master.

'What have I brought upon my ship?' he muttered.

'How is Edward, sir?' asked Armstrong. Clay looked at the American and shook his head.

'If he survives the shock, he will lose his arm,' he said.

'They hit us hard, sir,' said the American. 'Good shooting, for Frogs.'

Clay leant far out over the rail and tried to see what damage had been done. In the faint moonlight he could make out a half dozen jagged holes punched in the side, and one of the eighteen pounders hung drunkenly out of its gun port. Then the flow of messages began to arrive.

'Mr. Blake's respects, sir, and one of the larboard guns has had its carriage smashed,' reported Butler.

'Mr. Hutchinson's compliments, and the forestay has parted,' said a breathless sailor. Then Taylor came over from beside the wheel.

'Carpenter reports two balls struck the bow between wind and water, sir,' he reported. 'He says that one of the frames has been smashed. He will do his utmost to stem the flooding, but it may take some time. I've ordered the pumps manned.'

'Thank you, Mr. Taylor,' said Clay, and he returned to watching the enemy. At first, all he could see was the image of Preston's arm with that cruel dagger of oak stuck in it, but he shook his head clear and forced himself to concentrate on the battle. The smoke of the broadside was drifting away, revealing the enemy ship again. She was closer now, still between the *Titan* and the Atlantic beyond. Across the water came the rumble of the first guns being run out.

'They have taken almost two minutes to reload, sir,' said Armstrong, returning his watch to his pocket. 'Typical slovenly Frenchmen. It is a darn shame we're not more closely matched.'

'Slow they may be, but they are still out of range of our chain shot,' said Clay. 'We will need to endure at least one more broadside, perhaps two.' The last few guns rumbled into place and then there was a moment of peace. Two beautiful ships, beneath the stars. Over the water came another shouted order, and the night vanished, as the French ship fired once more.

A gale of shot engulfed the *Titan*. She was struck so hard that the whole frigate heeled away from the impact. Balls crashed through the crowded gun deck, beneath Clay's feet. Debris tumbled down from above, clattering all around him. One large piece fell like a sandbag to thud onto the deck close by. It took Clay a moment to realise that it was the bloody remains of a marine sharpshooter. Another ball had ploughed through the men of the afterguard, slaughtering them as they stood in line. From the storm of shouts that followed the impact of the broadside, Clay knew his ship could not endure many more blows like that. He looked across at the enemy. She seemed to have quickened her approach, eager to finish off her unresisting opponent. Before the next flood of damage reports reached him, he was busy issuing his orders.

'Masthead! Any sign of that cutter?' he roared.

'Not yet, sir, but I can see some sort of commotion ashore,' reported Russell. 'Musket fire, from the look of it!'

'Mr. Taylor! I will have the topsails drawing if you please,' ordered Clay. 'Get us under way.'

'Aye aye, sir,' replied the first lieutenant.

Clay was on the move, now, crossing the quarterdeck towards the rail at the front. He had to work his way through the pairs of crewmen, either carrying the wounded below to the surgeon or dragging the dead to join the growing row of bodies that ran along the centre line of the ship. When he reached the quarterdeck rail, he looked down onto the gun deck. Beneath his feet, men were at work, turning the handles of the *Titan*'s twin pumps, and from over the side he heard the slosh of water as it left the frigate. More wounded were being carried away here, too, but the remaining larboard side guns were crewed and ready to fire. In the middle of the deck stood the figure of the ship's second lieutenant, directing what went on around him with calm instructions. His hat had vanished, and he had a trickle of blood staining the side of his head, but he looked up, alert enough, when Clay hailed him.

'Standby, Mr. Blake!' he ordered.

'Aye aye, sir,' replied the lieutenant. Clay returned his attention to the enemy. She was very close now, her hull high out of the water, a wall of open gun ports. He could see movement along her rail. Officers stared and pointed in the glow of battle lanterns as she slid down towards her opponent. Under his feet he felt the deck heel as the sails began to draw, and the *Titan* started to move through the water. Clay judged the distance between the ships with care. The French ship was very near, but not quite close enough.

'One point to larboard, helmsman,' called Clay over his shoulder.

'One to larboard, aye, sir,' he repeated, rolling the wheel through his hands. Taylor came across to join his captain at the rail.

'Boatswain says he can't replace the forestay while we are under way, and the upper foremast is badly wounded, sir,' he reported. 'It'll bear sail for now, but he won't answer for what will happen if the Frogs hit us again. Also, the carpenter says the last broadside holed us on the waterline astern. There is a foot of water in the well.'

'Thank you Mr. Taylor, but I shall require topgallants to be set shortly, even on the foremast.'

'Is that wise, sir?' asked the older man. Clay gestured to the huge ship alongside.

'We must draw clear of her guns, George,' he replied. 'We cannot endure many more such blows.' The first lieutenant nodded.

'I'll get the men aloft, sir.'

Clay returned to watching his opponent. Now the *Titan* had turned; the two ships were converging, with the swifter frigate head-reaching on the big seventy-four. Closer they came. The first of the Frenchman's canons began to appear in the moonlight, dotted across her twin gun decks as the quicker crews ran them out. It was now or never.

'Open fire, Mr. Butler,' he yelled.

At last, the frigate spoke in anger. Her remaining guns roared out. Moments later the air was full of piercing shrieks and howls as the chain shot whirled through the night. Just before a wall of smoke enveloped the *Titan*, he saw fluttering amongst the French ship's sails.

'Top gallants, Mr. Taylor!' he ordered. Aloft, fresh canvas bloomed in the moonlight to be rapidly sheeted home, and the frigate surged forward, accompanied by some ominous creaks from the foremast, but nothing seemed to have given way. As the *Titan* moved clear of her gun smoke, Clay scanned his opponent.

'God damn and blast them,' he roared, thumping the rail. He could see huge rents that had been torn in the French ship's sails, and some of her tattered rigging was waving like fronds of seaweed, but scan her mass of masts and yards as he might, he could find nothing vital missing. The frigate had forged ahead now, almost clear of their opponent's guns. Then the seventy-four came surging around, turning up into the wind and losing all her way, but bringing every gun to bear.

'For what we are about to receive...' muttered a marine standing nearby.

'Hit the hull and spare the masts, please God,' urged Clay, as the French ship disappeared in fire and smoke once more.

*****

Trevan was first into the boat, vaulting over the stern, and rushing to his place near the bow. The others splashed into the shallows and hauled themselves over the side, while Sedgwick came last, his head still full of Fraser's dying words.

'Row, you bastards!' he urged, the moment he had grabbed the tiller. The others were still making their unsteady way to their places when the cutter jerked forwards, sending Evans tumbling down. The boat rocked wildly and shipped water from over the side.

'Steady there,' said the coxswain. 'Take your places, lads.'

'Easy for you to bleeding say!' moaned the Londoner, as he gained his seat.

The crunch of boots on shingle came from astern, accompanied by cries in French. Sedgwick looked behind him. The boat was ten yards from the shore now and gathering speed. Where the path met the beach, he could see a ring of light from a lantern that was held aloft. Beneath it, a man in uniform prodded at the body of Fraser with the toe of his boot. Nearer at hand, he could see dark shapes on the shore. One came wading out towards the boat, a carbine held aloft.

'Rodgers, your pistol!' snapped Sedgwick, holding his hand out towards the nearest oarsman. He swung the weapon round, cocking and firing it in one smooth motion. A tongue of flame leaped out and there was a cry and splash from the shallows. Several shots banged out from the beach and one struck the surface of the water behind them. Sedgwick scanned the shore for the next threat, and then felt cold as he remembered the rock that they had passed on the way in.

'Bow!' he called. 'Quit rowing, and keep a lookout! Sharply, now!' He rose in his place to stare ahead, half expecting the smack of a musket ball in his back. Another bang and flash came from behind, but the boat must have been fast vanishing into the night, for he heard no passing shot.

'Reef showing to larboard, and that wicked rock is ahead, Cox,' reported the lookout. Sedgwick adjusted his line, and the boat swept onwards, across the dark water and out to sea. When he was certain they were clear of any rocks, he looked back towards the shore. What on earth has happened this night, he wondered to himself. All had seemed fine when the count and the major had headed up to the cottage. He thought about Fraser's last words. Could the major really have betrayed the count to the enemy? In which case, what else had he done? Almost the last thing he had mentioned was the ship. He stared ahead as he tried to make out what was happening in the bay.

Gun smoke drifted and turned in the faint light, tumbling

down towards him across the water. Ahead of that, he could make out two distinct masses, sailing alongside one another, at what looked to be very close range. Nearest to him was the frigate, the silver moonlight outlining the curve of her topsails and her delicate masts. He frowned to himself, wondering why the *Titan* wasn't firing. Behind her was the second, much bigger ship, her hull a mass of orange squares in the dark, her masts looming above those of the *Titan*.

'Christ, the barky's caught herself a proper tartar, lads,' said Sedgwick. 'Easy all! Rowing will not answer to overhaul her. We best get the mast stepped.' The cutter ran on in a curve as Sedgwick brought her head up into the wind. She rocked in the gentle swell as the crew set up the mast and boom and then hauled up the sails. While they worked, Sedgwick continued to watch the two ships moving across the sea, side by side, the gap between them narrowing all the time. Then the *Titan* fired, at last, sending clouds of smoke billowing up. The roar of her broadside arrived moments later, accompanied by an unearthly shrieking noise.

'What the bleeding hell was that?' exclaimed Evans as he twisted around.

'Oh, Sweet Mary, Mother of God, I know that sound!' said O'Malley. He let the halliard in his hand slip away, and the main sail slithered back down into the boat.

'What is it, Sean lad?' asked Trevan. 'What's making such a mournful din?' The Irishman dropped his head into his hands.

'T'is the keening of the Banchees,' wailed O'Malley. 'My Grandma warned me about them feckers!'

'So what's a bleeding Banchee, when it's at home?' asked Evans.

'Witches, as only shows at times of great slaughter,' whispered O'Malley. 'They wail in the night, coming to steal away the souls of the dead!' The crew of the cutter exchanged glances, their eyes white in the dark. Sedgwick looked back towards the main fight, trying to push back a rising sense of panic. It all seemed to be going wrong this night.

Ahead of him the frigate was now making more sail, forging ahead of her lumbering adversary. In response, the French ship turned up into the wind until she was stern-on to the cutter. Long tongues of fire leaped out from her side, lighting up the sea for miles around. The roar of her broadside boomed off the surface of the water. Sedgwick frowned, and then rounded on the others.

'Stow that nonsense, O'Malley!' he ordered. 'The Frogs just fired, and there weren't no wailing except from you. Look alive now! Trevan, get that jib drawing! Rogers, Evans, haul up the mainsail! I don't want no more talk of spooks and the like. I want to get back to the barky, and find out what the bloody hell's going on.'

Chapter 17
Low Water

When the French ship fired its broadside, Clay's whole attention was centred aloft, willing that his fragile masts would be spared. He barely felt the impact of the huge cannon balls as they smashed through the hull. He didn't register the fresh cries of the wounded, nor the tall columns of water, silver in the moonlight, that rose all around the ship. He watched the main topgallant yard snap into two spears of wood, each tumbling towards the deck until they were entangled in the rigging below. Fresh holes had been punched in several sails, but most of his precious spars had survived.

'My word, but that was poorly done, thank the Lord!' exclaimed Armstrong. 'Did you mark all the white water around us, sir? They must have poured much of their shot into the sea!' A little hope stirred in Clay's heart as he looked about him and realised his frigate still lived.

'Upon my soul, but I did fear the worst,' said Clay. 'How the devil did we survive?'

'Why, they let fly in haste, from a turning ship,' said the American. 'Add the dark, and that we were underway, and even some of our gun captains might have missed at that range.'

'Let us see if we can respond a little better,' said Clay. He called down onto the main deck. 'Mr. Blake! Are you ready to fire?'

'I am short two great guns, sir, but the balance are ready. Rigging again?'

'If you please. Make every shot count!'

The *Titan*'s guns roared out once more, filling the air with the howl of chain shot. The frigate's broadside had many fewer guns than her opponent, but she was sailing in a straight line; her target was almost stationary and her gun layers veterans, to a man. The smoke of the broadside rolled clear to reveal the huge foremast of the French ship leaning backwards, like a drunk against a wall. Somewhere aloft there was a series of sharp cracks as lines parted under the impossible strain, and the whole mass fell, gathering pace like an avalanche and thundering into the sea alongside. When the spray settled, a mound of sails and rigging hung across the bow of the two-decker. For the first time in the battle, a cheer rang out from the forecastle, and looking that way, Clay saw that Hutchinson was waving his hat in glee.

'By God, that's better!' yelled his captain. 'Lay us across their bow, Mr. Taylor, where every gun can bear, and then back the topsails.'

'Aye aye sir,' replied the first lieutenant.

'Ball now, Mr. Blake, into the hull,' Clay called down to the main deck. 'Serve them back in kind.'

There was another cheer from beneath his feet, as the gun crews set about their work. He looked down onto the main deck of his ship. The orange glow of the battle lanterns revealed a scene that was full, both of chaos and of purpose. Here they had taken the brunt of the enemy's fire. The second of the eighteen pounders to be put out of action lay on its side below him like the felled carcass of some beast, amongst the shattered remains of its carriage. Sailors were busy carrying away the wounded or dragging the dead clear, leaving lines of dark blood on the deck like oriental calligraphy. Fragments of wood and debris were strewn everywhere. Great furrows had been torn in the planking by cannon balls, and down the centreline of the deck was a long row of bodies. Clay counted them, pausing at those he could recognise, remembering their faces. Just beneath him was a thin figure with lank hair, huddled over like a sleeping child. When did Mystical Jack fall, he wondered, and did he see his end coming? Clay carried on along the line. He had reached thirty when his view was cut off by the break in the forecastle. With a shock, he realised that the last body he'd seen was that of Midshipman Butler.

But there was order to be seen, too. Ship's boys hurried to and fro, bringing fresh charges up from the magazine. Twin lines of men worked away, turning the long steel cranks of the ship's pumps. The surviving officers were an oasis of calm as they paced along behind their guns, encouraging here, redistributing men there. And the cannon themselves were being worked with urgent purpose amongst all the damage, as their crews flew through the stages of loading and firing. The roar of gun fire had become almost constant, as the better-manned pieces outpaced those that had lost the most crew members, and clouds of smoke billowed over the ship. Clay looked towards the enemy, and could see in the moonlight that his crew was hitting them hard, as ball after ball thudded into their towering bow. One of her two bow chasers, the only weapons she had which could point forwards, spat back at the frigate in defiance. Clay heard the crash of a ball striking home, while in the light of its muzzle flash, he saw the crowds of French sailors at work, cutting away the wreckage of her fallen mast.

'Deck there!' came a hail from above. 'Sail due astern and coming up fast! It looks like our red cutter.' Clay turned around.

'Cutter for certain, sir,' said Armstrong, who was leaning over the side and focusing his night glass towards the shore.

'Not before time,' said Clay. 'The moment we have the men back on board, we shall make our escape, before our enemy can cut herself free.'

*****

Once the crew of the cutter had scrambled up the frigate's disengaged side, and their boat had been swayed on board, the *Titan* got under way. A last few balls were hurled into the bow of the French ship and then the guns fell silent.

'By Jove, sir, I must confess that I had my doubts that we would escape from that battle!' said Armstrong. 'I give you joy of your victory, or do you suppose she will come after us, once she has cleared away her wreckage?' Clay watched their crippled opponent slip away behind them and shook his head.

'We were swifter than her, even when she had three masts,' he said. 'Besides, her captain will now be in fear of encountering one of our blockading ships sent to finish her off. No, she will head for the nearest port, as swiftly as she is able, rather than risk being caught at sea when dawn comes. But what I really want to understand is what the hell has been happening this night. Where are Major Fraser and the count?'

'Dead or taken, sir,' said the voice of Sedgwick from behind him. 'Leastways the major is dead for certain, and the Frogs have the count.'

'Taken! Killed!' exclaimed Clay. 'How is that possible?'

'We was bleeding ambushed, sir!' said the coxswain. Macpherson came over from his place beside his men to listen.

'Quickly now, what happened ashore?' said Clay, exchanging glances with the marine.

'We made the beach, right enough an' all seemed quiet, sir,' continued Sedgwick. 'The gentlemen went up together to the little house, and me an' the lads waited by the boat, like what we had been ordered to do. Then all these Frog soldiers turned up on horses. It were hard to tell how many in the dark, but a good dozen, I should say, maybe more. It seemed right enough at first, an' then all hell broke loose! That big ship showed up, I heard a deal of shouting, and the soldiers began firing. Major Fraser scarped back down to the boat, but the Frogs shot him. Then they was pressing us, so I thought it best to return to the ship and report, sir.' Sedgwick held Clay's gaze, his eyes full of meaning, then he glanced across at Macpherson.

'What more do you have to tell, Sedgwick?' asked his captain. 'You may speak openly.' The sailor stepped closer and dropped his voice.

'I was holding the major as he died, sir. He said as how he had given up the count to the Frogs.'

'No!' exclaimed Clay. 'What treachery is this? How could he have done such a thing?'

'I knew it,' said Macpherson. 'That bastard has been plotting something these last few months. Did he give you any idea as to why he did such a low thing?'

'He were in a bad way, sir, but he did say something about revenge for his brother...'

'Charles!' exclaimed Macpherson, slapping a hand against his forehead. 'The name on that flask of his – *a much loved brother*, he called him. He was his superior in the Royal Guard!'

'Aye, *Charlie* were the last word he spoke,' confirmed Sedgwick. 'I thought he had just got me muddled with another.'

'How could I have been such a fool?' said the marine. 'His brother perished during the Revolution, and he must have held D'Arzon responsible for what happened. No wonder he looked at the count with such hatred.' Clay held out his hand and touched Macpherson's arm.

'You did your best to warn me about him,' he said. 'You have nothing to reproach yourself for. If there is a fool here it is I, for disregarding your advice. Will you forgive me?'

'Of course sir, but it was I who had all the pieces...' said the Scot. 'Why could I not assemble them?'

'Did Major Fraser say anything else, Sedgwick?' asked Clay.

'Aye, sir, a little more, about betrayal and the barky, but you know all about that, it seems.' He waved towards the devastation around them and the officers waiting out of earshot to gain there captain's attention.

'Yes, we have had a hard pounding this night and there is much still to do,' said Clay. 'Thank you for your role in all this, and I am glad you are safe, Sedgwick. Kindly go and report to Mr. Taylor with your boat crew. There is plenty of work for them to attend to.'

'Aye aye, sir,' said the coxswain. He knuckled his forehead in salute, and was instantly replaced by the first of the officers.

'Yes, Mr. Hutchinson?' said Clay.

'I need all the sail taken in from the foremast, sir,' said the boatswain, twisting his hat between his huge hands. 'If not, I shan't be responsible for the consequences. No forestay, great wounds in the mast. How it's not come a-tumbling down already, I shall never fathom.' Clay looked back towards the French ship. It had almost vanished into the dark behind them.

'Make it so, but be swift with your repairs,' he said. 'I shall want to set sail again before the night is done, sooner if that damned Frenchman should come after us.'

'Aye aye, sir,' replied Hutchinson. He replaced his hat on his head, and hurried down the gangway, booming out orders as he went.

'What course should I set, sir?' asked the sailing master, who was next in line. The quarterdeck seemed to grow quiet for a moment.

'For Ushant and for home, if you please, Mr. Armstrong,'

said Clay. 'Let us return and report to the Channel Fleet. We can serve no useful purpose by remaining here.'

'Sir!' called Midshipman Todd, running up from the main deck. 'Mr. Taylor's compliments, and will you join him below. He says it's urgent.'

'Take command here, if you please, Mr. Armstrong,' said Clay, wondering when he would be able to rest a moment to gather his thoughts. He followed the little midshipman down the ladderway and out onto the main deck. Waiting for him there was Taylor, with an even more anxious face than normal. Beside him was the figure of Kennedy, the ship's Irish carpenter, who was dripping wet. The frigate's two chain pumps were nearby. One was turning while the other was silent. The men who should have been manning it stood to one side.

'What is going on here, Mr. Taylor?' he demanded. 'Why is the larboard pump not operating?'

'It is jammed solid, sir,' explained the first lieutenant. 'We think the gravel ballast has moved in the hold and got into the mechanism.'

'There be that much water washing about down there, sir, it's all starting to shift, so it is,' added the carpenter.

'The ship may be listing too, sir,' said Taylor. 'A touch to larboard?' Clay stepped back and concentrated for a moment. He felt for the natural heel of the deck with his feet, from the wind on the sails, and then he sensed more than saw the list, like an unnatural, dead grasp on the hull of his ship.

'Yes, I believe you are right,' he said. 'How much water is in the hold, Mr. Kennedy?'

'Three feet and rising sir,' said the carpenter.

'Three! Already!' exclaimed Clay.

'Them thirty-six pounder balls make fecking big holes, begging yer pardon, sir, and we've been struck by five, between wind and water,' said Kennedy.

'What has been done to stem the flow?'

'Sure, I have plugged them as best I can,' explained the carpenter. 'But that one at the bow as broke the frame is still leaking like a bastard, begging yer pardon again, and there's another hole near to the stern as I can barely come at, at all. I could maybe's cope if both pumps was working, but not with just the one.'

'And the deeper we settle, the more of these shot holes will be brought down to the waterline, sir,' said Taylor.

Clay pulled off his hat and rubbed at his aching forehead. Beneath his splitting headache he felt dread settling into his soul. Everything seemed to have gone wrong this night: betrayal on the shore, the French ship ambushing them out of the night, and now this. Just as he had got his beloved *Titan* clear of the enemy, battered and torn, she was sinking beneath his feet. If only he had listened to Macpherson! With difficulty, he pushed despair aside and returned to the present. Both Taylor and Kennedy were staring at him.

'Are you quite well, sir?' asked his first lieutenant.

'A little fatigued, perhaps, but that will not mend matters,' he said, forcing himself to sound brisk. 'We must try fothering an old sail against this hole in the stern. That may serve to stem the inflow. And get some volunteers to enter the hull and try to clear the second pump. They had best be tall men or swimmers, where possible.'

'Aye aye, sir,' said Taylor. 'I shall pass the word for the sail maker. Fothering will mean heaving the ship to, but that may help Mr. Hutchinson in his work aloft.'

'Mr. Kennedy, kindly resume your efforts in the hold, plugging and so forth,' said Clay. 'We shall try and have that pump back in action presently.'

*****

Dawn, silver and pink, had crept into the world, bringing

with it a little hope. The *Titan* was stationary, rocking gently in the swell. Clay could feel the unusual listlessness of the hull. Even when fully laden, the frigate normally moved with the lightness and grace of a thoroughbred. Now she was clumsy, shuddering as tons of seawater sloshed about, deep within her, moving in opposition to wave and wind. Under the light of the lanterns hung in the mizzen rigging, a party of men had worked through the night with needle and thread at making the fothering sail. They had passed a forest of short lengths of yarn through the canvas of an old storm jib, until it resembled a shaggy carpet. With the arrival of morning, the sail was ready, and Clay watched as Taylor went about his work, passing lines down over the stern and moving them back under the hull. Now he was hanging right out from the mizzen chains, so he could see the jagged hole torn in the *Titan*'s side, just beneath the waterline.

'Sternwards,' ordered Taylor, gesturing with an arm towards the working party on deck. The men with the fothering sail in their arms shuffled a few feet backwards. Taylor looked from them down to the gash in the hull. 'Another foot, if you please, Mr. Powell!' The scarred petty officer waved the line of men towards him.

'Easy there,' he growled.

'That will do,' said Taylor, with a final glance. He jumped down onto the planking, and looked across to the other side of the deck. Another party of men stood over there, holding onto to the lines that had been passed under the hull.

'Ready, Mr. Russell?' he called. The midshipman raised a hand in assent. 'Then heave away, handsomely now!' The men drew on the lines, and the square of sail began to snake out of the arms of those holding it and slide down over the outside of the battered hull, like some enormous hairy pelt.

'Steady now, Mr. Russell,' warned Taylor, as the canvas neared the waterline. 'Mr. Powell, have your men clapped on to their lines?'

'Aye, sir, we be ready,' said the petty officer, his party of sailors pulling back on lines attached to the top of the sail, to keep it taut.

'Haul again, Mr. Russell,' ordered the lieutenant. Clay leant out and watched as the sail passed over the hole and carried on under the ship.

'Easy all, and make fast,' said Taylor, when the sail was centred in place. He looked across to his captain.

'The inrush of the sea will have sucked it into the hole, sir,' he said. 'It should serve to reduce the inflow, so long as the weather stays kind.'

'Aye, reduce the inflow, but not stop it, Mr. Taylor,' said Clay. 'Get us back under way, if you please. Make as much progress as is consistent with keeping that sail in place. The sooner we can get up with the Channel Fleet off Ushant, the better. But what we truly need is that second pump. Carry on here, and I will see what is happening below.'

He walked forwards towards the ladderway that led down to the hold, and then paused to look over his frigate. Just beneath him, the men who served the one working pump were busy, sending a jet of water out into the dawn light. Above his head, the rigging was full of top men, splicing and repairing. The pieces of the broken top yard had been swayed down on deck now, while forward he could see Hutchinson as he supervised the setting up of the new forestay. He looked on with approval at all this progress with the rigging, and then he felt a heavy lurch beneath his feet, accompanied by a crash from somewhere in the hold. All the sail in the world would be useless if the *Titan* foundered.

He was about to go down the ladderway, when he saw the surgeon coming towards him in the grey light. He was a shocking sight. His leather apron was black with congealed blood, as were his arms and shoulders. His face was gaunt and drawn; the pale eyes behind his little round spectacles dark with fatigue. He passed the list he carried across to

Clay.

'How many, Mr. Corbett?' asked his captain.

'Thirty-five dead, sir, and another sixty-eight wounded,' he said. 'A bloody affair, I fear.'

'I am afraid so,' said Clay, glancing through the list. 'How is Mr. Preston?'

'He lives, for now, sir. I had to remove his arm at the shoulder. If he can endure the shock, and if no putrefaction sets in, he may yet recover.' Clay stared bleakly at the surgeon, thinking of the smiling young Yorkshireman he had witnessed develop from a teenage boy into manhood.

'Which arm?' he asked, struggling to remember, amidst all that had happened since the first broadside had ripped out of the dark.

'Eh, I believe the left, sir,' said Corbett, pulling off his glasses and rubbing at his eyes. 'Your pardon, but I have cut away so many limbs this night, it is hard...yes, the left for certain. To that extent, at least, he has been fortunate.'

'I will come and see the wounded when I am able, Mr. Corbett,' said Clay. 'For now, make them as comfortable as you can. Tell me of anything you require to ease their suffering.'

'Thank you, sir,' said the surgeon. He raised a weary hand in salute, and turned around. Clay slipped the list into his coat pocket and continued towards the hold.

Down on the orlop deck, the grating that covered the main hatch had been pulled aside to reveal a sea of water. The hull was at least half full now, the surface littered with debris that had washed free. A bundle of spare wads for the cannon, some pieces of timber and a half-filled sack bobbed past under his gaze and floated out of sight. Deeper in the hull he could hear larger items as they bumped and scraped together. A small group of sailors were gathered at the top of the steps that led down into the dark water. Some were peering into the gloom with lanterns while others held on to the ends of lines that trailed down into the hold.

'What is going on here?' asked Clay.

'Chips...eh, I mean Mr. Kennedy, begging your pardon, be in the hold, sir,' reported the petty officer in charge. 'He's got himself a party with shovels, a workin' at clearing that pump, but they keep getting clouted by stuff as is afloat, so we be holding fast on these here safety lines.'

'It's right tough down there, sir,' supplemented another. 'Some of the hogsheads have got loose, and them bastards are proper crushers.'

Clay went down a few steps and crouched low. In the gloom he could just make out the ring of men at work, plunging their shovels down into the water, and scraping the gravel ballast clear. He could pick out the huge figure of Evans, initially thigh deep, but then chest deep as the water surged past him. A smaller man beside him disappeared entirely, before he struggled back to his feet, coughing and spluttering, several yards away from where he had gone under.

'How is it proceeding, Mr. Kennedy?' he called, his voice echoing in the thin gap between the surface of the water and the deck above.

'Fecking ill, sir,' gasped the carpenter. 'The water is still rising, and there's a foot of shingle in the pump well if there's and inch, with more joining as quick as we can shift it. I'm not sure how much longer the men can endure it down here. Steady lads! Have a care!' As if to emphasis his point an empty barrel came spiralling past the group and bumped its way on towards the bow.

'What can I do to aid you?' asked Clay.

'Could you find a way to lighten the ship, at all?' said Kennedy. 'That would help matters.'

'Yes, perhaps I can,' said Clay. 'I could down two birds with the one shot, as it were. Carry on as long as you are able, and I shall see what can be achieved on that score.'

*****

'It is not the right way of proceeding, Mr. Hutchinson, but the ship must be lightened, and these shipmates can help us no further,' said Clay.

'Not right at all, sir,' agreed the boatswain. 'But needs must when the devil has the helm. I am sure they would understand.'

No, not the right way at all, thought Clay to himself, as he stood in the sun of early morning. The regulations stipulated that the ship should be as still as possible, but time was against them. They had to press on towards Ushant and the help they would get from the rest of the fleet. The crew should have been gathered in their divisions, dressed in their best clothes, not scattered around the ship, pausing for the briefest moment from their urgent tasks. Most of all, the fallen should have been neatly stitched into their hammocks, beneath a union flag, not wrapped in spare canvass with a few turns of line to hold it in place. There should be a black ensign flying overhead, too, he thought. That plume of dark smoke from the galley chimney would have to take its place, where the cooks were preparing a hot meal for the survivors, against the hard work that lay ahead. All unsatisfactory, but it would have to do.

'Carry on, Mr. Hutchinson, he ordered. The boatswain brought his call to his lips and blew a twittering blast. His mates picked up the call and their shouts echoed through the ship.

'All hands! All hands to witness burial!'

Across the deck, men stopped what they were doing, and turned towards him. Behind Clay, the one working chain pump fell silent.

'Off hats!' roared Hutchinson, removing his own black leather one, with the Royal Arms painted on the front. Clay was tempted to order the men at the pump to carry on working, but he decided against it. He could almost feel the sea gushing in beneath his feet, nonetheless, some things had to be done as well as circumstances allowed. He flipped open his service book to the page marked with the list that Corbett had given him earlier and mentally thanked the Admiralty for the brevity of the ceremony that was ordained for this moment. Then he looked at the body held on the shoulders of the six sailors. He had watched as they had bundled him up earlier. The uniform coat had been ripped to tatters by the spray of oak splinters that had torn into its owner, but one white colour patch had remained to show that its wearer had been a midshipman.

'For as much as it hath pleased Almighty God of His great mercy to take unto Himself the soul of our dear brother Peter Hector Butler here departed, we therefore commit his body to the deep. Amen.' The six sailors raised the in-board end of the mess table. The angle grew steeper until, with a rush, the body of the young man slid down it and off the end. A moment later, there was a splash from over the side and Clay and the party of seamen moved on to the next bundle.

*****

The frigate sailed across a blue sea beneath a cloudless sky. Away to one side was the coastline of France, green fields and grey cliffs, just visible in the haze. To a distant observer, all would have seemed fine aboard the pretty ship with her black and yellow hull and her big white sails, but closer to, the image changed. She sat deep in the water, listing to one side and dragging heavily, so that even the wash of her modest bow wave sometimes reached as high as the sill of her gun ports. There were jagged holes in her side that had yet to be patched and a sail was lashed across her quarter. Much of her rigging showed signs of having recently been spliced, and her sails spilt the wind through their torn fabric. She had no topgallant yard on her mainmast, and a constant, throbbing jet of water pulsed away to leeward. On her quarterdeck, a tired, anxious group of officers were gathered around their captain while the crew ate a hot meal.

'How long before we reach the fleet, Mr. Armstrong,' asked Clay.

'If the wind holds, we should raise the Inshore Squadron this time tomorrow, sir,' said the American.

'As long as that!' exclaimed Clay. 'Can we not proceed any swifter?'

'Not if we wish to keep that fothering sail in place, sir,' said Taylor. 'I am anxious about it, as it is.'

'And how much water is in the hold?' asked the captain.

'Five feet in the well, and still rising, sir,' said Taylor. 'The men did their best to clear that pump, but after the second broken arm, I had to pull them out. So much of our stores have worked loose now that no one can survive in there.'

'Five feet!' repeated Blake. 'I had not appreciated that matters were so grave. Should we not be following a course to close with the land, sir? In case the ship should founder?'

'The *Titan* will not founder,' said Clay, glaring at his second lieutenant. 'Not while I yet have breath in my body. Is that clear, gentlemen?'

'I understand, sir, but what shall we do to prevent it?' asked Blake.

'If we only have one pump, we must fashion another,' said Clay. 'Gather every bucket we have and form a party to take water from the hold to the side. Everyone is to take part: marines, officers, boys. Watch on and watch off. Mr. Blake, you can take command of that.'

'Aye aye, sir,' said the lieutenant.

'Then, there is much we can do to lighten the ship,' added Clay. He indicated the row of cannon balls beside the nearest of the quarterdeck carronades. 'Shot from the shot garlands can go by the board, to commence with. Busy those who are lightly wounded with pitching them into the sea, and let us see how that answers. I will give some consideration to what other measures we may take for our present relief.'

As soon as the crew had finished their meal, the work of saving the ship resumed. With so many casualties, it was a greatly reduced number of men whom Taylor had to allocate to the various tasks, and he did so with the reluctance of a miser handing out his gold. A minimal number were still required to sail and steer the ship. The men at the pump would need to be relieved at regular intervals. The rest, he split between reducing the frigate's weight and working with the buckets. The gratings on each of the decks above the main hatchway were removed to produce a deep, square opening that ran down through the middle of the frigate. On the main deck, the men were placed in a ring around the edge, peering straight down into the hold, like swimmers contemplating a dive. A heavy thud from somewhere made the surface of the water quiver for a moment.

Each man had a bucket with a line fastened to its handle. Dropped from that height, they plunged into the water of the hold, to be hauled back up and taken to the side for emptying.

'Take it steady, lads,' urged Blake, who was manning a bucket, too. 'We have four hours of this before we shall be relieved. Steady will answer best.'

'Four fecking hours,' moaned O'Malley, pulling up his first bucket. 'And there was I thinking how this would make a pleasant change from all that pumping.' He walked across to the nearest gun port, and waited while a marine rolled an eighteen pounder shot out of it. The water that he emptied seemed pitiful, compared with the huge amount in the hold.

'Is it dry, at all?' he asked, peering down on his return. 'Ah, well, perhaps one more pail will do it.' Trevan chuckled from beside him as he dropped his own bucket, and then nudged his friend.

'Good to see them idlers doing honest toil for a change,' he said.

'Aye, most of the Grunters are here too,' said Evans. 'Purser, cook, sailmaker, Mr. Macpherson over there, the cooper, even the bleeding Master at Arms.' He counted them off as he looked around the ring of men.

'I trust you shan't get the notion of serving that back to us as soup, Mr. Walker,' said Blake, indicating the cook's bucket, which was full of floating debris. The comment got a laugh from the sailors, and the bailing out of the hold carried on.

'And what are you after making of all the high and mighty joining the likes of us in our fecking labour, Big Sam?' asked O'Malley. The Londoner shrugged as he hauled up his bucket, arm over arm.

'They all wants to get the barky sorted, quick as quick,' he offered.

'Is that what you're thinking?' scoffed the Irishman. 'Coz I reckon that matters must have reached a pretty pass when even the wardroom's finest are after shitting themselves.'

'Your right there, Sean,' muttered Sedgwick, who was on the other side of Evans. 'This deck's heeling away to larboard like a bastard, and that ain't natural at all.'

'Hey lads!' hissed Trevan. 'Cast your eyes over there.' He jerked his thumb towards another part of the main deck. Hutchinson had just finished attaching a stout rope around one of the frigate's eighteen pounder cannon. The other end rose up to a heavy looking block and tackle suspended from the main yard.

'Haul away, Mr. Powell,' said the boatswain, to a row of men tailing on the end of a line. With a jerk and a heave, they leant back at a steep angle and the huge gun, carriage and all, eased up from the deck. As soon as it was clear of the planking, it began to twist in the air.

'Main braces!' ordered Hutchinson, when the cannon was high enough to clear the side. The yard swung in an arc, like the arm of a crane, until the gun was dangling over the sea. Hutchinson still held the end of his line, as if it were the halter of a horse. He peered over the side, checked that the cannon was clear, and then jerked hard on the rope. Down tumbled the eighteen pounder, throwing up a huge column of water, and the boatswain turned back towards his men. 'Bring up the next one, if you please, Mr. Powell,' he ordered.

'Why the bleeding hell is we ditching the guns?' asked Evans, as he poured his bucket of water over the side.

'Because we be in a world of fecking trouble, Big Sam,' said O'Malley. 'Best we gets back to bailing, unless you fancy swimming home.' He returned to the hatchway and dropped his bucket over the edge, but instead of a splash, a hollow thud echoed up from below. Looking down he could see that it was resting on a flat box that had drifted into view, bobbing on the water.

'That's an odd fecking crate,' he said, drawing up the bucket again. 'What you reckon it holds, at all?'

'It's the picture of Pipe's missus!' exclaimed Harte, from the far side of the hatchway. 'The one from his quarters!'

'Well, he can kiss adieu to her,' said Evans, as the box drifted on and began to disappear under the deck again. A shape flashed past the Londoner's shoulder and moments later there was a terrific splash.

'What in all creation... ?' exclaimed Blake. Sedgwick's head and shoulders reappeared in the filthy water and he struck out towards the case. He reached it just as it was vanishing under the deck, and hauled it towards the stair that emerged from the hold. As he climbed, dripping, onto the orlop deck, the box clasped in his arms, the sailors grouped around the hatchway gave him a cheer.

'See, it ain't all turning to dross,' grinned Trevan.

'Sedgwick, you're a damned fool,' said Blake, calling down

to the coxswain. 'There is no end of debris in that hold that might have broke your neck -- but bless you! I laboured long and hard on that portrait, and I know the captain will be pleased to have it returned to him.'

*****

The last of the frigate's eighteen pounders had gone by the board now, allowing Clay to look across a main deck that seemed wide and uncluttered for once. Much of the planking was filthy -- scarred by shot, blackened by powder or stained with blood -- but he had no spare manpower to clean it. Indeed, the emptiness of the deck only served to emphasise how few were the uninjured members of his crew. They barely filled the shaded area beneath the quarterdeck as they lay around in groups, resting or taking on some food and a cup of water.

'Vittles will be a problem presently, sir,' said Taylor from his side. 'Much of what is in the hold will be spoiled, even if we could come at it.'

'In truth, I have not thought much beyond reaching the fleet with our ship still afloat,' said Clay. 'I confess I would sooner have a few moments of sleep than a meal.'

'You could if you wished, sir,' said Taylor. 'I know your cabin furniture is still down in the hold, but I would be happy to loan you the use of my cot.'

'Thank you, George,' said Clay, 'That is kind, but I shall not be able to rest until I know that we are safe. Goodness, just look how the poor girl lists now!' The two officers stooped to sight across the deck, just as a pigtailed head appeared in the middle of it. The owner mounted the ladderway from below.

'Have you a sounding for us, Mr. Kennedy?' asked Clay, as the Irishman arrived to face him.

'A touch under six feet, sir,' he reported. 'And still

gaining, so it is. It's starting to wash over the orlop deck.'

'Six foot!' exclaimed Clay. 'Have we gained nothing from casting away the great guns?'

'There's that much adrift in the hold now, sir,' said the carpenter. 'You can hear it a banging and a clattering against the inside of the hull. Maybe a plank or two have been stoved in, or some of the caulking has started? The barky's set up to resist blows from without, not from within. That would be my guess.'

'Damnation!' muttered Clay. 'How long have the men been resting, Mr. Taylor?'

'Perhaps twenty minutes, sir,' answered the lieutenant.

'No more than another five, and then they must return to work,' he ordered. 'We have to lighten the ship further. The carronades may as well go by the board too, and cut free all the anchors, bar the best bower.'

'Aye aye, sir,' said the lieutenant. Clay turned away and began to pace the quarterdeck, his hands clasped behind his back, his chin low on his chest. Armstrong stood beside the wheel, his face grey with fatigue and his wig askew. He raised a hand in salute to his captain, and the torn sleeve of his coat flapped in the breeze.

Back and forth Clay walked, up and down the deck, trying to find a solution to his problems. What was it that Harte had said, last time he was pacing like this? Some nonsense about how the men trusted him to make the right decision? Go with your instincts, he had urged. He had certainly done that, and everything had gone wrong since that moment. Why had he not listened to Macpherson, instead of arrogantly overruling him? What sort of a captain was he? He had not even gone below to visit the wounded. Poor Preston could be dying, even now. One inner voice told him that he had been too busy saving his ship, but another whispered back that guilt was causing him to avoid the moment. All those mutilated men, their lives ruined because he was too stubborn to listen. He spun away from the gaze of his shipmates and stared over the rail. A white gull angled across the wind, followed by another, calling loudly, and the pair headed toward a group of islands. He tried to recall their name, but his mind was too choked with fatigue. He turned towards the sailing master in irritation.

'Mr. Armstrong,' he said. 'Pray what are those islands there? I am dull this morning, and the name quite escapes me.'

'They are the Glenan Iles, sir,' said the American, coming over. 'Where the *Moselle* hid from us back in the spring.'

'Quite so,' said Clay. 'Thank you. My, but that seems an age ago!'

'I had wondered if I should ever get the opportunity to complete my survey of them, sir,' said Armstrong. 'In the sailing directions for this coast they are very ill covered.' From under the quarterdeck came the squeal of a boatswain's pipe, followed by the rumble of the men standing back up.

'I fear we shall not have the occasion to dally there on this passage,' said Clay.

'Indeed not, sir,' smiled the American. 'What will become of the revolt in these parts, now?'

'If they have not been betrayed as we were, then it may stagger on, although without the count to lead it, I daresay it will fail,' said the captain.

'What is the hold up, here?' came the voice of Taylor from the main deck. 'Get that pump back in action directly!' Clay and Armstrong exchanged glances and then both men ran to the front of the quarterdeck. A line of seamen were trying to turn the handle of the only pump left in action, without success.

'Feckers... jammed... solid, sir,' said O'Malley, heaving on the bar.

'What is the matter, Mr. Taylor!' demanded Clay.

'The second chain pump has failed, too, sir,' said the first lieutenant.

'The fecking ballast must have shifted again, sir,' said Kennedy.

'Mr. Blake, add all these men to your bucket chain,' ordered Clay. 'Mr. Taylor, come up and report. You as well, Mr. Kennedy.' Clay forced himself to stand beside the sailing master, rocking on the soles of his shoes with his hands in a tight knot behind his back. The two men came running up the ladderway to join him.

'How long do we have without the pump?' he asked quietly.

'An hour at best, sir,' said the carpenter.

'And how long until we reach the Inshore Squadron?'

'Much longer than that, sir,' said Armstrong. 'The nearest ship will be the frigate stationed off Cape Penmac'h, but that is a good fifteen miles away.'

'The ship is doomed sir,' said Taylor. 'We should think about taking to the boats.'

'With almost seventy wounded?' exclaimed Clay. 'In open boats, so far from aid?'

'It was an ill chance that we ran in with that ship of the line, sir,' said the sailing master. 'You have done all that was possible to save the ship and the crew.'

'Not quite all, Mr. Armstrong,' said Clay. 'In your survey of those islands over there, did you note any beaches?'

Chapter 18

The Turn of the Tide

The air around the *Titan* was full of the cry of seabirds, outraged by the ship's intrusion amongst the islands. Armstrong conned the big frigate through the gap between a reef of weed-covered rocks and the cliffs of one of the larger Glenan Iles. The ship was so deep in the water now that the keel touched bottom, sending a jarring up through the hull as it dragged across a hidden obstruction and, for a moment, Clay thought they would ground. Then they were through, surrounded by rocky islands and sea cliffs. The wind was masked so that the *Titan* crept onwards, with just enough way for the rudder to bite.

'The beach is just around that headland, sir,' said Armstrong. 'It is fortunate that the tide is high, or we might not have made it this far.'

Clay looked over his battered ship as she crept on. Beneath him he could hear the hoarse, cracked voice of Blake as he encouraged his men to one final effort with their buckets. The task was a little easier now that the water had risen out of the hold to cover much of the orlop. The main deck had rows of the wounded on it, brought up above the flood water and lain out across the planking. The frigate sailed on through the warm sunshine, and as they drifted past the headland, the white sand of a beach appeared.

'Starboard your helm,' ordered Armstrong. 'Headsails!' The *Titan* laboured round and then headed towards the shore. Clay felt a rumble beneath him as the keel touched once more, broke free, and then the ship slid to a halt. She lay heeled over towards one side, hard aground in the shallows, a little way from where waves lapped against the sand.

'Belay those buckets, Mr. Blake,' ordered Clay. 'All hands aloft to take in sail, if you please, Mr. Hutchinson!' Clay watched the men as they made their way upwards, and wondered how many of them realised it would be for the last time. They were too tired to fly up the shrouds as top men should. He turned towards his remaining officers.

'Now gentlemen, it is my intention to abandon the ship, and transfer ourselves ashore,' he explained. 'Mr. Taylor, kindly have the boats launched. Mr. Macpherson, you and your surviving marines go first to secure the island. Then we shall need sails, spars and rope to make shelters – perhaps you can take charge of that, Mr. Blake?'

'Aye aye, sir,' replied the second lieutenant. 'I shall add your portrait of Mrs. Clay to the first load. Your coxswain recovered it from the hold.'

'Did he really?' smiled Clay. 'Why, that is welcome on such a sad day. I had thought it lost forever.' Then he became business-like once more. 'We shall need any provisions that can be salvaged, if you please, Mr. Faulkner. Mr. Corbett, you will supervise the transfer of the wounded. Mr. Armstrong, perhaps you would make sure that the ship's log books and the more valuable navigational instruments are brought with us. Is all that clear?'

'May I ask how long we shall be on this island, sir?' asked Corbett. 'I must inform you that many of the wounded are in a perilous state. It is a hospital that they require, and swiftly.'

'Trust me that the welfare of the wounded is at the forefront of my mind,' said Clay. 'I hope to be here only for as long as it takes for the Inshore Squadron to rescue us.'

'And how long might that be, sir,' persisted the surgeon.

'You thought the nearest frigate to be fifteen miles away, I believe, Mr. Armstrong?'

'I did, sir,' said the American.

'Then I expect them to come swiftly, once they note my signal, Mr. Corbett,' replied Clay.

'Signal, sir!' exclaimed Taylor. 'What signal can they possibly see at this range?'

'They will certainly see this one,' said Clay, his grey eyes bleak.

*****

It took two hours to ferry everything that could be saved the short distance to the beach. In that time the tide had turned, leaving most of the stranded frigate out of the water. Clay stood on the forecastle and looked over the rail at the figurehead. One of its arms had been knocked off, leaving a gash of unpainted wood, but his face still glared towards the island, apparently untroubled by the injury. Hanging down from the rail beside the carved titan was a rope ladder, which he recognised as one of those produced for the attack on Fort de Penthievre that would never take place. The foot of the ladder rested in the frigate's launch, where Sedgwick sat at the helm. Clay ran a hand along the rail, caressing the smooth wood and remembered the times he and his ship had endured. Mutiny and battle off this very coast. A chase the whole length of the Mediterranean. The fleet action of the age, in that sultry night at the mouth of the River Nile. A voyage of over a year to and from the Indian Ocean. The fierce wooden eyes beneath him had witnessed sea fights and storms beyond count, and now their voyage together had come to this. Below his feet he heard the bass voice of the boatswain as he led his men in their work. He heard a final few more splintering crashes, and then nothing.

'All done, sir,' reported Hutchinson from behind him. Clay looked around at the solemn faces of the work party.

Something in the tone of the boatswain's voice made him look more closely at him, and he saw that tears were rolling down his cheeks.

'I will do it,' said Clay, reaching out his hand for the lantern that swung from the older man's fist.

'Aye aye, sir,' said the boatswain, but he offered his other hand instead. After a moment's hesitation, Clay shook it.

'The ship is doomed, Mr. Hutchinson,' he said quietly. 'Only the French might be able to recover her from this isle. This way she can serve us one last time.' The veteran sailor nodded, not trusting himself to speak, and handed across the lantern. Clay touched his arm. 'Get your men into the launch. I shall join you presently.'

He headed across to the ladderway, and went down into the ship. When he reached the steeply sloping lower deck, the smell of lamp oil and tar was overpowering. Heaped around the base of the foremast was a pile of flammable material. Among the broken lumber, Clay could see mess tables, straw pulled from mattresses, wardroom chairs, the whole mass soaked with oil. He paused in front of the pyre and checked that all was as it should be.

'Alright Clay,' he told himself. 'Your error, you put it right.' He turned up the wick in the lantern until it flared and spluttered and then hurled it, over arm, deep into the mound of debris. With extraordinary speed, the fire took hold, roaring up to bathe the lower deck with orange light. Black smoke swirled around him, stinging his eyes, and hungry flames licked at the deck beams. He fled before the blaze and raced up the ladder.

As soon as he was settled in the stern sheets of the launch, Sedgwick pushed off and headed for the shore. It was only a matter of twenty yards now, and once the boat was pulled up on the sand, Clay looked back at his ship. The fore part of the frigate was ablaze, and flames were running up the rigging and out along the line of the bowsprit. Cracks and bangs could be heard from inside, and a heat haze trembled over the deck. From out of the open hatches, thick, black smoke poured, twisting and climbing in a huge column across the afternoon sky.

'Stone the crows, sir!' exclaimed one of the sailors. 'That will be seen for blooming miles!'

'Yes, I rather hope that it will, for fifteen at least,' said Clay to himself. Up and up the smoke rose, higher and higher. As he watched the flames consume his ship, Clay found that he, too, was in tears.

THE END

NOTE FROM THE AUTHOR

Historical fiction is a blend of the truth with the made up, and *The Turn of the Tide* is no exception. For readers who would like to understand where the boundary lies between the two, the *Titan* and the *Moselle* are fictitious, as are the characters that inhabit them. I have tried my best to make sure that my descriptions of those ships and the lives of their crews are as accurate as I am able to make them. Where I have failed to achieve this any errors are my own.

The historical background to *The Turn of the Tide* is accurate. History, with its metropolitan bias, tends to focus accounts of the French Revolution on events in Paris, but this is far from the whole truth. Almost a decade of armed resistance followed the Revolution in Brittany, Normandy, Maine and the Vendee. At its height, the *Chouannerie* were waging a virtual civil war, with up to fifty thousand armed followers. Much of their support came from Britain as portrayed in my novel.

The characters of Major Fraser, Count Louis D'Arzon and the various French officers who oppose them are fictitious, as are their various battles. Earl Spencer was First Lord of the Admiralty in 1800. During that summer a brigade of infantry under General Maitland, was sent to support rebels in Brittany, together with a Royal Navy squadron under the command of Sir Edward Pellew. They concluded that the rebellion was insufficient successful for them to risk a landing on the mainland, and instead they attempted to capture the French Island of Belle Isle, which is close to Quiberon.

1800 was also a time when the Abolitionist movement was at its most active as it campaigned for an end to the transatlantic trade in slaves. The Abolitionist meeting I portray, and the characters present are my own creation, but they are true to the spirit of the debate. The arguments I have used and the racial attitudes I show are faithful to contemporary views on the issue.

The places that I mention in the book are generally as geographically and historically accurate as I am able to make them, although they will naturally have changed greatly in two hundred years. The exception to this rule is Chateau D'Arzon, the cottages in the forest and near Quiberon, the various locations in Plymouth and the depot of the French 71st Infantry Regiment, all of which come purely from my imagination.

The *Garde Ecossaise* was a part of the French Royal Guard. Formed in 1418, they served the French crown until they were disbanded in 1791. The storming of the Tuileries Palace on the 10th August 1792 was one of the high points of the French Revolution, after which the monarchy fell. The foreign contingent of the Royal Guard was overwhelmingly Swiss. They refused to surrender to the mob and were massacred when they ran out of ammunition.

About The Author

Philip K Allan

Philip K. Allan comes from Watford in the United Kingdom. He still lives in Hertfordshire with his wife and his two teenage daughters. He has spent most of his working life to date as a senior manager in thc motor industry. It was only in the last few years that he has given that up to concentrate on his novels full time.

He has a good knowledge of the ships of the 18th century navy, having studied them as part of his history degree at London University, which awoke a lifelong passion for the period. He is a member of the Society for Nautical Research and a keen sailor. He believes the period has unrivalled potential for a writer, stretching from the age of piracy via the voyages of Cook to the battles and campaigns of Nelson.

From a creative point of view he finds it offers him a wonderful platform for his work. On the one hand there is the strange, claustrophobic wooden world of the period's ships; and on the other hand there is the boundless freedom to move those ships around the globe wherever the narrative takes them. All these possibilities are fully exploited in the Alexander Clay series of novels.

His inspiration for the series was to build on the works of novelists like C.S. Forester and in particular Patrick O'Brian. His prose is heavily influenced by O'Brian's immersive style. He, too, uses meticulously researched period language and authentic nautical detail to draw the reader into a different world. But the Alexander Clay books also bring something fresh to the genre, with a cast of fully formed lower deck characters with their own back histories and plot lines in addition to the officers. Think *Downton Abbey* on a ship, with the lower deck as the below stairs servants.

If You Enjoyed This Book Visit

PENMORE PRESS

www.penmorepress.com

The Captain's Nephew

by

Philip K.Allan

After a century of war, revolutions, and Imperial conquests, 1790s Europe is still embroiled in a battle for control of the sea and colonies. Tall ships navigate familiar and foreign waters, and ambitious young men without rank or status seek their futures in Naval commands. First Lieutenant Alexander Clay of HMS Agrius is self-made, clever, and ready for the new age. But the old world, dominated by patronage, retains a tight hold on advancement. Though Clay has proven himself many times over, Captain Percy Follett is determined to promote his own nephew.

Before Clay finds a way to receive due credit for his exploits, he'll first need to survive them. Ill-conceived expeditions ashore, hunts for privateers in treacherous fog, and a desperate chase across the Atlantic are only some of the challenges he faces. He must endeavor to bring his ship and crew through a series of adventures stretching from the bleak coast of Flanders to the warm waters of the Caribbean. Only then might high society recognize his achievements —and allow him to ask for the hand of Lydia Browning, the woman who loves him regardless of his station.

PENMORE PRESS
www.penmorepress.com

A Sloop of War

by

Philip K.Allan

This second novel in the series of Lieutenant Alexander Clay novels takes us to the island of Barbados, where the temperature of the politics, prejudices and amorous ambitions within society are only matched by the sweltering heat of the climate. After limping into the harbor of Barbados with his crippled frigate *Agrius* and accompanied by his French prize, Clay meets with Admiral Caldwell, the Commander in Chief of the island. The admiral is impressed enough by Clay's engagement with the French man of war to give him his own command.

The *Rush* is sent first to blockade the French island of St Lucia, then to support a landing by British troops in an attempt to take the island from the French garrison. The crew and officers of the *Rush* are repeatedly threatened along the way by a singular Spanish ship, in a contest that can only end with destruction or capture. And all this time, hanging over Clay is an accusation of murder leveled against him by the nephew of his previous captain.

Philip K Allan has all the ingredients here for a gripping tale of danger, heroism, greed, and sea battles, in a story that is well researched and full of excitement from beginning to end.

On the Lee Shore

by

Philip K.Allan

Newly promoted to Post Captain, Alexander Clay returns home from the Caribbean to recover from wounds sustained at the Battle of San Felipe. However, he is soon called upon by the Admiralty to take command of the frigate HMS Titan and join the blockade of the French coast. But the HMS Titan will be no easy command with its troubled crew that had launched a successful mutiny against its previous sadistic captain. Once aboard, Clay realizes he must confront the dangers of a fractious crew, rife with corrupt officers and disgruntled mutineers, if he is to have a united force capable of navigating the treacherous reefs of Brittany's notorious lee shore and successfully combating the French determined to break out of the blockade.

A Man of No Country

by

Philip K.Allan

In 1798, the Royal British Navy withdrew from the Mediterranean to combat the threat of invasion at home. In their absence, rumors abound of a French Army gathering in the south of France under General Napoleon Bonaparte, and of a large fleet gathering to transport them. Alexander Clay and his ship, Titan, are sent to the Mediterranean to investigate. Clay verifies the troubling rumors but is unable to learn where the French fleet and the army will be heading. When Admiral Lord Nelson arrives from Britain with reinforcements, Clay and Titan join Nelson's fleet heading for Southern France. But on their arrival, they discover Bonaparte's fleet is gone, and Nelson, aware of the dangers of an ambitious and ruthless general, orders an all-out hunt for Bonaparte's armies before it is too late.

As the Titan searches for Napoleon's forces, another threat has already gained passage on the ship. After engaging and destroying a Russian Privateer, the crew capture a mysterious stranger, claiming to be an English sailor who has been serving from childhood on Barbary ships. Shortly after he joins the ship, there begins a rash of thefts followed by the murder of another sailor. With the officers baffled as to who is behind this, it falls to Able Sedgwick, the Captain's coxswain and the lower deck to solve the crimes.

THE DISTANT OCEAN

BY

PHILIP K ALLAN

Newly returned from the Battle of the Nile, Alexander Clay and the crew of the Titan are soon in action again, just when he has the strongest reason to wish to abide in England. But a powerful French naval squadron is at large in the Indian Ocean, attacking Britain's vital East India trade. Together with his friend John Sutton, he is sent as part of the Royal Navy's response. On route the Titan runs to ground a privateer preying on slave ships on the coast of West Africa, stirring up memories of the past for Able Sedgwick, Clay's coxswain. They arrive in the Indian Ocean to find that danger lurks in the blue waters and on the palm-fringed islands. Old enemies with scores to settle mean that betrayal from amongst his own side may prove the hardest challenge Clay will face, and a dead man's hand may yet undo all he has fought to win. Will the curse of the captain's nephew never cease to bedevil Clay and his friends?

Printed in the USA
CPSIA information can be obtained
at www.ICGtesting.com
CBHW022044080924
14268CB00008BA/64